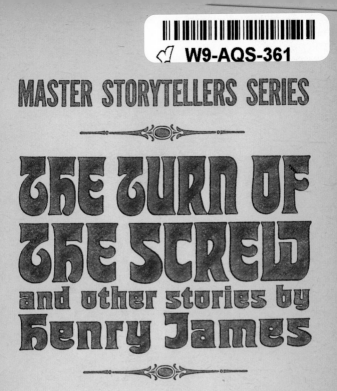

MASTER STORYTELLERS SERIES

THE TURN OF THE SCREW

and other stories by Henry James

Edited, with an afterword, a biographical sketch,
notes on the stories, and a selective bibliography by

John Felstiner
Assistant Professor of English
Stanford University

SBS SCHOLASTIC BOOK SERVICES
New York Toronto London Auckland Sydney

The stories in this book are reprinted with permission of Charles Scribner's Sons. Copyright 1908, 1909 Charles Scribner's Sons; renewal copyright 1936, 1937 Henry James.

4th printing . . . . January 1969

Printed in the U.S.A.

A SELECTIVE BIBLIOGRAPHY OF HENRY JAMES

Titles marked with an asterisk (*) are avaliable in paperback.

WORKS BY HENRY JAMES

* *The Ambassadors* (1903).

* *The American* (1877).

* *The Art of the Novel*, ed. R. P. Blackmur.
  A collection of James's prefaces to the revised editions of his works (1909), with a fine introduction by Blackmur.

* *Daisy Miller* (1878).

* *The Europeans* (1878).

* *The Ghostly Tales of Henry James*, ed. Leon Edel.

  Henry James and H. G. Wells, ed. Leon Edel and Gordon N. Ray.
  A record, mostly in letters, of their friendship, their debate on the art of fiction, and their quarrel.

* *The Portrait of a Lady* (1881).

* *The Notebooks of Henry James*, ed. F. O. Matthiessen and Kenneth B. Murdock.

* *The Portable Henry James*, ed. M. D. Zabel.
  Contains "The Beast in the Jungle," as well as selections from James's criticism, travel books, autobiography, and letters.

* *Stories of Writers and Artists*, ed. F. O. Matthiessen.

BIOGRAPHY AND CRITICISM

Blackmur, R. P., "Henry James," in Spiller, Thorp et al., *Literary History of the United States,* pp. 1039-1065. A superb introductory essay.

Dupee, F. W., *Henry James.* The most useful biography.

Dupee, F. W., ed., *The Question of Henry James: A Collection of Critical Essays.* Includes Edmund Wilson's study and Max Beerbohm's great parody of James.

Edel, Leon, ed., *Henry James: A Collection of Critical Essays.*

* Jefferson, D. W., *Henry James.*

Matthiessen, F. O., *Henry James: The Major Phase.*

Stewart, J. I. M., "Henry James," in *Eight Modern Writers.*

* Thurber, James, "Chanda Bell," in *Thurber Country.* A brilliant and funny parody of "The Figure in the Carpet."

Willen, Gerald, ed., *A Casebook on Henry James's "The Turn of the Screw."*

CONTENTS

The Turn of the Screw 1

The Pupil 156

The Tree of Knowledge 222

The Figure in the Carpet 244

To the Reader 298

Notes on the Stories 305

Henry James: A Biographical Sketch 310

A Selective Bibliography of Henry James 315

THE TURN
OF THE SCREW

THE STORY HAD HELD US, round the fire, sufficiently breathless, but except the obvious remark that it was gruesome, as on Christmas eve in an old house a strange tale should essentially be, I remember no comment uttered till somebody happened to note it as the only case he had met in which such a visitation had fallen on a child. The case, I may mention, was that of an apparition in just such an old house as had gathered us for the occasion — an appearance, of a dreadful kind, to a little boy sleeping in the room with his mother and waking her up in the terror of it; waking her not to dissipate his dread and soothe him to sleep again, but to encounter also herself, before she had succeeded in doing so, the same sight that had shocked him. It was this observation that drew from Douglas — not immediately, but later in the evening — a reply that had the interesting consequence to which I call attention. Some one else told a story not particularly effective, which I saw he was not following. This I took for a sign that he had himself something to produce and that we should only have to wait. We waited in fact till two nights later; but that same evening, before we scattered, he brought out what was in his mind.

"I quite agree — in regard to Griffin's ghost, or whatever it was — that its appearing first to the little boy, at so tender an age, adds a particular touch. But it's not the first occurrence of its charming kind that I know to have been concerned with a child. If the child gives the effect another turn of the screw, what do you say to two children — ?"

"We say, of course," somebody exclaimed, "that two children give two turns! Also that we want to hear about them."

I can see Douglas there before the fire, to which he had got up to present his back, looking down at this converser with his hands in his pockets. "Nobody but me, till now, has ever heard. It's quite too horrible." This was naturally declared by several voices to give the thing the utmost price, and our friend, with quiet art, prepared his triumph by turning his eyes over the rest of us and going on: "It's beyond everything. Nothing at all that I know touches it."

"For sheer terror?" I remember asking.

He seemed to say it wasn't so simple as that; to be really at a loss how to qualify it. He passed his hand over his eyes, made a little wincing grimace. "For dreadful — dreadfulness!"

"Oh how delicious!" cried one of the women.

He took no notice of her; he looked at me, but as if, instead of me, he saw what he spoke of. "For general uncanny ugliness and horror and pain."

"Well then," I said, "just sit right down and begin."

He turned round to the fire, gave a kick to a log, watched it an instant. Then as he faced us again: "I can't begin. I shall have to send to town." There was a unanimous groan at this, and much reproach; after which, in his preoccupied way, he explained. "The story's written. It's in a locked drawer — it has not been out for years. I could write to my man and enclose the key; he could send down the packet as he finds it." It was to me in particular that he appeared to propound this — appeared almost to appeal for aid not to hesitate. He had broken a thickness of ice, the formation of many a winter; had had his reasons for a long silence. The others resented postponement, but it was just his scruples that charmed me. I adjured him to write by the first post and to agree with us for an early hearing; then I asked him if the experience in question had been his own. To this his answer was prompt. "Oh thank God, no!"

"And is the record yours? You took the thing down?"

"Nothing but the impression. I took that *here*" — he tapped his heart. "I've never lost it."

"Then your manuscript — ?"

"Is in old faded ink and in the most beautiful hand." He hung fire again. "A woman's. She has been dead these twenty years. She sent me the pages in question before she died." They were all listening now, and of course there was somebody to be arch, or at any rate to draw the inference. But if he put the inference by without a smile it was also without irritation. "She was a most charming person, but she was ten years older than I. She was my sister's governess," he quietly said. "She was the most agreeable woman I've ever known in her position; she'd have been worthy of any whatever. It was long ago, and this episode was long before. I was at Trinity, and I found her at home on my coming down the second summer. I was much there that year — it was a beautiful one; and we had, in her off-hours, some strolls and talks in the garden — talks in which she struck me as awfully clever and nice. Oh yes; don't grin: I liked her extremely and am glad to this day to think she liked me too. If she hadn't she wouldn't have told me. She had never told anyone. It wasn't simply that she said so, but that I knew she hadn't. I was sure; I could see. You'll easily judge why when you hear."

"Because the thing had been such a scare?"

He continued to fix me. "You'll easily judge," he repeated: "*you* will."

I fixed him too. "I see. She was in love."

He laughed for the first time. "You are acute. Yes, she was in love. That is, she *had* been. That came out — she couldn't tell her story without its coming out. I saw it, and she saw I saw it; but neither of us spoke of it. I remember the time and the place — the corner of the lawn, the shade of the great beeches and the long hot summer afternoon. It wasn't a scene for a shudder; but oh — !" He quitted the fire and dropped back into his chair.

"You'll receive the packet Thursday morning?" I said.

"Probably not till the second post."

"Well then; after dinner — "

"You'll all meet me here?" He looked us round again. "Isn't anybody going?" It was almost the tone of hope.

"Everybody will stay!"

"*I* will — and *I* will!" cried the ladies whose departure had been fixed. Mrs. Griffin, however, expressed the need for a little more light. "Who was it she was in love with?"

"The story will tell," I took upon myself to reply.

"Oh I can't wait for the story!"

"The story *won't* tell," said Douglas; "not in any literal vulgar way."

"More's the pity then. That's the only way I ever understand."

"Won't *you* tell, Douglas?" somebody else enquired.

He sprang to his feet again. "Yes — tomorrow. Now I must go to bed. Good-night." And, quickly catching up a candlestick, he left us slightly bewildered. From our end of the great brown hall we heard his step on the stair; whereupon Mrs. Griffin spoke. "Well, if I don't know who she was in love with I know who *he* was."

"She was ten years older," said her husband.

"*Raison de plus* — at that age! But it's rather nice, his long reticence."

5

"Forty years!" Griffin put in.

"With this outbreak at last."

"The outbreak," I returned, "will make a tremendous occasion of Thursday night"; and everyone so agreed with me that in the light of it we lost all attention for everything else. The last story, however incomplete and like the mere opening of a serial, had been told; we handshook and "candlestuck," as somebody said, and went to bed.

I knew the next day that a letter containing the key had, by the first post, gone off to his London apartments; but in spite of — or perhaps just on account of — the eventual diffusion of this knowledge we quite let him alone till after dinner, till such an hour of the evening in fact as might best accord with the kind of emotion on which our hopes were fixed. Then he became as communicative as we could desire and indeed gave us his best reason for being so. We had it from him again before the fire in the hall, as we had had our mild wonders of the previous night. It appeared that the narrative he had promised to read us really required for a proper intelligence a few words of prologue. Let me say here distinctly, to have done with it, that this narrative, from an exact transcript of my own made much later, is what I shall presently give. Poor Douglas, before his death — when it was in sight — committed to me the manuscript that reached him on the third of these days and that, on the same spot, with immense effect, he began to read to our hushed little circle on the night of the fourth. The departing ladies who had said they would stay didn't, of course, thank heaven, stay: they departed, in consequence of arrangements made, in a rage of curiosity, as they professed, produced by the touches with which he had already worked us up. But that only made his little final auditory more compact and select, kept it, round the hearth, subject to a common thrill.

The first of these touches conveyed that the written statement took up the tale at a point after it had, in a manner, begun. The fact to be in possession of was therefore that his old friend, the youngest of several daughters of a poor country parson, had at the age of twenty, on taking service for the first time in the schoolroom, come up to London, in trepidation, to answer in person an advertisement that had already placed her in brief correspondence with the advertiser. This person proved, on her presenting herself for judgment at a house in Harley Street that impressed her as vast and imposing — this prospective patron proved a gentleman, a bachelor in the prime of life, such a figure as had never risen, save in a dream or an old novel, before a fluttered anxious girl out of a Hampshire vicarage. One could easily fix his type; it never, happily, dies out. He was handsome and bold and pleasant, off-hand and gay and kind. He struck her, inevitably, as gallant and splendid, but what took her most of all and gave her the courage she afterwards showed was that he put the whole thing to her as a favour, an obligation he should gratefully incur. She figured him as rich, but as fearfully extravagant — saw him all in a

7

glow of high fashion, of good looks, of expensive habits, of charming ways with women. He had for his town residence a big house filled with the spoils of travel and the trophies of the chase; but it was to his country home, an old family place in Essex, that he wished her immediately to proceed.

He had been left, by the death of his parents in India, guardian to a small nephew and a small niece, children of a younger, a military brother whom he had lost two years before. These children were, by the strangest of chances for a man in his position — a lone man without the right sort of experience or a grain of patience — very heavy on his hands. It had all been a great worry and, on his own part doubtless, a series of blunders, but he immensely pitied the poor chicks and had done all he could; had in particular sent them down to his other house, the proper place for them being of course the country, and kept them there from the first with the best people he could find to look after them, parting even with his own servants to wait on them and going down himself, whenever he might, to see how they were doing. The awkward thing was that they had practically no other relations and that his own affairs took up all his time. He had put them in possession of Bly, which was healthy and secure, and had placed at the head of their little establishment — but belowstairs only — an excellent woman, Mrs. Grose, whom he was sure his visitor would like and who had formerly been maid to his mother. She was now housekeeper and was also acting for the time as superintendent to the little girl, of whom, without children of her own, she was by good luck extremely fond. There were plenty of people to help, but of course the young lady who should go down as governess would be in supreme authority. She would also have, in holidays, to look after the small boy, who had been for a term at a school — young as he was to be sent, but what else could be done? — and who, as the holidays were about to begin, would be back from one day to the other. There had been for the two children at first a young lady whom they had had the misfortune to lose. She had done for them quite beautifully — she was a most respectable person — till her death, the great awkwardness of which had, precisely, left no alternative but the school for little Miles. Mrs. Grose, since then, in the way of manners and things, had done as she could for Flora; and there were, further, a cook, a housemaid, a dairywoman, an old pony, an old groom and an old gardener, all likewise thoroughly respectable.

So far had Douglas presented his picture when someone put a question. "And what did the former governess die of? — of so much respectability?"

Our friend's answer was prompt. "That will come out. I don't anticipate."

"Pardon me — I thought that was just what you *are* doing."

"In her successor's place," I suggested, "I should have wished to learn if the office brought with it — "

"Necessary danger to life?" Douglas completed my thought. "She did wish to learn, and she did learn. You shall hear tomorrow what she learnt. Meanwhile of course the prospect struck her as slightly grim. She was young, untried, nervous: it was a vision of serious duties and little company, of really great loneliness. She hesitated — took a couple of days to consult and consider. But the salary offered much exceeded her modest measure, and on a second interview she faced the music, she engaged." And Douglas, with this, made a pause that, for the benefit of the company, moved me to throw in —

"The moral of which was of course the seduction exercised by the splendid young man. She succumbed to it."

He got up and, as he had done the night before, went to the fire, gave a stir to a log with his foot, then stood a moment with his back to us. "She saw him only twice."

"Yes, but that's just the beauty of her passion."

A little to my surprise, on this, Douglas turned round to me. "It was the beauty of it. There were others," he went on, "who hadn't succumbed. He told her frankly all his difficulty — that for several applicants the conditions had been prohibitive. They were somehow simply afraid. It sounded dull — it sounded strange; and all the more so because of his main condition."

"Which was — ?"

"That she should never trouble him — but never, never: neither appeal nor complain nor write about anything; only meet all questions

10

herself, receive all moneys from his solicitor, take the whole thing over and let him alone. She promised to do this, and she mentioned to me that when, for a moment, disburdened, delighted, he held her hand, thanking her for the sacrifice, she already felt rewarded."

"But was that all her reward?" one of the ladies asked.

"She never saw him again."

"Oh!" said the lady; which, as our friend immediately again left us, was the only other word of importance contributed to the subject till, the next night, by the corner of the hearth, in the best chair, he opened the faded red cover of a thin old-fashioned gilt-edged album. The whole thing took indeed more nights than one, but on the first occasion the same lady put another question. "What's your title?"

"I haven't one."

"Oh *I* have!" I said. But Douglas, without heeding me, had begun to read with a fine clearness that was like a rendering to the ear of the beauty of his author's hand.

I

I REMEMBER the whole beginning as a succession of flights and drops, a little see-saw of the right throbs and the wrong. After rising, in town, to meet his appeal I had at all events a couple of very bad days — found all my doubts bristle again, felt indeed sure I had made a mistake. In this state of mind I spent the long hours of bumping swinging coach that carried me to the stopping-place at which I was to be met by a vehicle from the house. This convenience, I was told, had been ordered, and I found, towards the close of the June afternoon, a commodious fly in waiting for me. Driving at that hour, on a lovely day, through a country the summer sweetness of which served as a friendly welcome, my fortitude revived and, as we turned into the avenue, took a flight that was probably but a proof of the point to which it had sunk. I suppose I had expected, or had dreaded, something so dreary that what greeted me was a good surprise. I remember as a thoroughly pleasant impression the broad clear front, its open windows and fresh curtains and the pair of maids looking out; I remember the lawn and the bright flowers and the crunch of my wheels on the gravel and the clustered treetops over which the rooks circled and cawed in the golden sky. The scene had a greatness that made it a different affair from my own scant home, and there immediately appeared at the door, with a little girl in her hand, a civil person who dropped me as decent a curtsey as if I had been the mistress or a distinguished visitor. I had received in Harley Street a narrower notion of the place, and that, as I recalled it, made me think the proprietor still more of a gentleman, suggested that what I was to enjoy might be a matter beyond his promise.

I had no drop again till the next day, for I was carried triumphantly through the following hours by my introduction to the younger of my pupils. The little girl who accompanied Mrs.

Grose affected me on the spot as a creature too charming not to make it a great fortune to have to do with her. She was the most beautiful child I had ever seen, and I afterwards wondered why my employer hadn't made more of a point to me of this. I slept little that night — I was too much excited; and this astonished me too, I recollect, remained with me, adding to my sense of the liberality with which I was treated. The large, impressive room, one of the best in the house, the great state bed, as I almost felt it, the figured full draperies, the long glasses in which, for the first time, I could see myself from head to foot, all struck me — like the wonderful appeal of my small charge — as so many things thrown in. It was thrown in as well, from the first moment, that I should get on with Mrs. Grose in a relation over which, on my way, in the coach, I fear I had rather brooded. The one appearance indeed that in this early outlook might have made me shrink again was that of her being so inordinately glad to see me. I felt within half an hour that she was so glad — stout simple plain clean wholesome woman — as to be positively on her guard against showing it too much. I wondered even then a little why she should wish not to show it, and that, with reflexion, with suspicion, might of course have made me uneasy.

But it was a comfort that there could be no uneasiness in a connexion with anything so beatific as the radiant image of my little girl, the vision of whose angelic beauty had probably more than anything else to do with the restlessness that, before morning, made me several times rise and wander about my room to take in the whole picture and prospect; to watch from my open window the faint summer dawn, to look at such stretches of the rest of the house as I could catch, and to listen, while in the fading dusk the first birds began to twitter, for the possible recurrence of a sound or two, less natural and not without but within, that I had fancied I heard. There had been a moment when I believed I recognised, faint and far, the cry of a child; there had been another when I found myself just consciously starting as at the passage, before my door, of a light footstep. But these fancies were not marked enough not to be thrown off, and it is only in the light, or the gloom I should rather say, of other and subsequent matters that they now come back to me. To watch, teach, "form" little Flora would too evidently be the making of a happy and useful life. It had been agreed between us downstairs that after this first occasion I should have her as a matter of course at night, her small white bed being already arranged, to that end, in my room. What I had undertaken was the whole care of her, and she had remained just this last time with Mrs. Grose only as an effect of our consideration for my inevitable strangeness and her natural timidity. In spite of this timidity — which the child herself, in the oddest way in the world, had been perfectly frank and brave about, allowing it, without a sign of uncomfortable consciousness, with the deep sweet serenity indeed of one of Raphael's holy infants, to be discussed, to be imputed to her and to determine us — I felt quite sure she would presently like me. It was part of what I already liked Mrs. Grose herself for, the pleasure I could see her feel in my admiration and wonder as I sat at supper with four tall candles and with my pupil, in a high chair and a bib, brightly facing me between them over bread and milk. There were naturally things that in Flora's presence could pass between us only as prodigious and gratified looks, obscure and roundabout allusions.

"And the little boy — does he look like her? Is he too so very remarkable?"

One wouldn't, it was already conveyed between us, too grossly flatter a child. "Oh Miss, most remarkable. If you think well of this one!" — and she stood there with a plate in her hand, beaming at our companion, who looked from one of us to the other with placid heavenly eyes that contained nothing to check us.

"Yes; if I do — ?"

"You will be carried away by the little gentleman!"

"Well, that, I think, is what I came for — to be carried away. I'm afraid, however," I remember feeling the impulse to add, "I'm rather easily carried away. I was carried away in London!"

I can still see Mrs. Grose's broad face as she took this in. "In Harley Street?"

"In Harley Street."

"Well, Miss, you're not the first — and you won't be the last."

"Oh, I've no pretensions," I could laugh, "to being the only one. My other pupil, at any rate, as I understand, comes back tomorrow?"

"Not tomorrow — Friday, Miss. He arrives, as you did, by the coach, under care of the guard, and is to be met by the same carriage."

I forthwith wanted to know if the proper as well as the pleasant and friendly thing wouldn't therefore be that on the arrival of the public conveyance I should await him with his little sister; a proposition to which Mrs. Grose assented so heartily that I somehow took her manner as a kind of comforting pledge — never falsified, thank heaven! — that we should on every question be quite at one. Oh she was glad I was there!

What I felt the next day was, I suppose, nothing that could be fairly called a reaction from the cheer of my arrival; it was probably at the most only a slight oppression produced by a fuller measure of the scale, as I walked round them, gazed up at them, took them in, of my new circumstances. They had, as it were, an extent and mass for which I had not been prepared and in the presence of which I found myself, freshly, a little scared not less than a little proud. Regular lessons, in this agitation, certainly suffered some wrong; I reflected that my first duty was, by the gentlest arts I could contrive, to win the child into the sense of knowing me. I spent the day with her out of doors; I arranged with her, to her great satisfaction, that it should be she, she only, who might show me the place. She showed it step by step and room by room and secret by secret, with droll delightful childish talk about it and with the result, in half an hour, of our becoming tremendous friends. Young as she was I was struck, throughout our little tour, with her confidence and courage, with the way, in empty chambers and dull corridors, on crooked staircases that made me pause and even on the summit of an old machicolated square tower that made me dizzy, her morning music, her disposition to tell me so many more things than she asked, rang out and led me on. I have not seen Bly since the day I left it, and I dare say that to my present older and more informed eyes it would show a very reduced importance. But as my little conductress, with her hair of gold and her frock of blue, danced before me round corners and pattered down passages, I had the view of a castle of romance inhabited by a rosy sprite, such a place as would somehow, for diversion of the young idea, take all colour out of storybooks and fairy-tales. Wasn't it just a storybook over which I had fallen a-doze and a-dream? No; it was a big ugly antique but convenient house, embodying a few features of a building still older, half displaced and half utilised, in which I had the fancy of our being almost as lost as a handful of passengers in a great drifting ship. Well, I was strangely at the helm!

II

THIS CAME HOME TO ME when, two days later, I drove over with Flora to meet, as Mrs. Grose said, the little gentleman, and all the more for an incident that, presenting itself the second evening, had deeply disconcerted me. The first day had been, on the whole, as I have expressed, reassuring; but I was to see it wind up to a change of note. The postbag that evening — it came late — contained a letter for me which, however, in the hand of my employer, I found to be composed but of a few words enclosing another, addressed to himself, with a seal still unbroken. "This, I recognise, is from the headmaster, and the headmaster's an awful bore. Read him, please; deal with him; but mind you don't report. Not a word. I'm off!" I broke the seal with a great effort — so great a one that I was a long time coming to it; took the unopened missive at last up to my room and only attacked it just before going to bed. I had better have let it wait till morning, for it gave me a second sleepless night. With no counsel to take, the next day, I was full of distress; and it finally got so the better of me that I determined to open myself at least to Mrs. Grose.

"What does it mean? The child's dismissed his school."

She gave me a look that I remarked at the moment; then, visibly, with a quick blankness, seemed to try to take it back. "But aren't they all — ?"

"Sent home — yes. But only for the holidays. Miles may never go back at all."

Consciously, under my attention, she reddened. "They won't take him?"

"They absolutely decline."

At this she raised her eyes, which she had turned from me; I saw them fill with good tears. "What has he done?"

I cast about; then I judged best simply to hand

her my document — which, however, had the effect of making her, without taking it, simply put her hands behind her. She shook her head sadly. "Such things are not for me, Miss."

My counsellor couldn't read! I winced at my mistake, which I attenuated as I could, and opened the letter again to repeat it to her; then, faltering in the act and folding it up once more, I put it back in my pocket. "Is he really *bad?*"

The tears were still in her eyes. "Do the gentlemen say so?"

"They go into no particulars. They simply express their regret that it should be impossible to keep him. That can have only one meaning." Mrs. Grose listened with dumb emotion; she forbore to ask me what this meaning might be; so that, presently, to put the thing with some coherence and with the mere aid of her presence to my own mind, I went on: "That he's an injury to the others."

At this, with one of the quick turns of simple folk, she suddenly flamed up. "Master Miles! *him* an injury?"

There was such a flood of good faith in it that, though I had not yet seen the child, my very fears made me jump to the absurdity of the idea. I found myself, to meet my friend the better, offering it, on the spot, sarcastically. "To his poor little innocent mates!"

"It's too dreadful," cried Mrs. Grose, "to say such cruel things! Why, he's scarce ten years old."

"Yes, yes; it would be incredible."

She was evidently grateful for such a profession. "See him, Miss, first. *Then* believe it!" I felt forthwith a new impatience to see him; it was the beginning of a curiosity that, all the next hours, was to deepen almost to pain. Mrs. Grose was aware, I could judge, of what she had produced in me, and she followed it up with assurance. "You might as well believe it of the little lady. Bless her," she added the next moment — "*look* at her!"

I turned and saw that Flora, whom, ten minutes before, I had established in the schoolroom with a sheet of white paper, a pencil and a copy of nice "round O's," now presented herself to view at the open door. She expressed in her little way an extraordinary detachment from disagreeable duties, looking at me, however, with a great childish light that seemed to offer it as a mere result of the affection she had conceived for my person, which had rendered necessary that she should follow me. I needed nothing more than this to feel the full force of Mrs. Grose's comparison, and, catching my pupil in my arms, covered her with kisses in which there was a sob of atonement.

None the less, the rest of the day, I watched for further occasion to approach my colleague, especially as, towards evening, I began to fancy she rather sought to avoid me. I overtook her, I remember, on the staircase; we went down together and at the bottom I detained her, holding her there with a hand on her arm. "I take what you said to me at noon as a declaration that *you've* never known him to be bad."

She threw back her head; she had clearly, by this time, and very honestly, adopted an attitude.

"Oh never known him — I don't pretend *that!*"

I was upset again. "Then you *have* known him — ?"

"Yes indeed, Miss, thank God!"

On reflection I accepted this. "You mean that a boy who never is — ?"

"Is no boy for *me!*"

I held her tighter. "You like them with the spirit to be naughty?" Then, keeping pace with her answer, "So do I!" I eagerly brought out. "But not to the degree to contaminate — "

"To contaminate?" — my big word left her at a loss.

I explained it. "To corrupt."

She stared, taking my meaning in; but it produced in her an odd laugh. "Are you afraid he'll corrupt *you?*" She put the question with such a fine bold humor that with a laugh, a little silly doubtless, to match her own, I gave way for the time to the apprehension of ridicule.

But the next day, as the hour for my drive approached, I cropped up in another place. "What was the lady who was here before?"

"The last governess? She was also young and pretty — almost as young and almost as pretty, Miss, even as you."

"Ah then I hope her youth and her beauty helped her!" I recollect throwing off. "He seems to like us young and pretty!"

"Oh he *did*," Mrs. Grose assented: "it was the way he liked everyone!" She had no sooner spoken indeed than she caught herself up. "I mean that's *his* way — the master's."

I was struck. "But of whom did you speak first?"

She looked blank, but she coloured. "Why of *him*."

"Of the master?"

"Of who else?"

There was so obviously no one else that the next moment I had lost my impression of her having accidentally said more than she meant; and I merely asked what I wanted to know. "Did *she* see anything in the boy — ?"

"That wasn't right? She never told me."

I had a scruple, but I overcame it. "Was she careful — particular?"

Mrs. Grose appeared to try to be conscientious. "About some things — yes."

"But not about all?"

Again she considered. "Well, Miss — she's gone. I won't tell tales."

"I quite understand your feeling," I hastened to reply; but I thought it, after an instant not opposed to this concession to pursue: "Did she die here?"

"No — she went off."

I don't know what there was in this brevity of Mrs. Grose's that struck me as ambiguous. "Went off to die?" Mrs. Grose looked straight out of the window, but I felt that, hypothetically, I had a right to know what young persons engaged for Bly were expected to do. "She was taken ill, you mean, and went home?"

"She was not taken ill, so far as appeared, in this house. She left it, at the end of the year, to go home, as she said, for a short holiday, to which the time she had put in had certainly given her a right. We had then a young woman— a nurse-maid who had stayed on and who was a good girl and clever; and *she* took the children altogether for the interval. But our young lady never came back, and at the very moment I was expecting her I heard from the master that she was dead."

I turned this over. "But of what?"

"He never told me! But please, Miss," said Mrs. Grose, "I must get to my work."

III

HER THUS TURNING HER BACK ON ME was fortunately not, for my just preoccupations, a snub that could check the growth of our mutual esteem. We met, after I had brought home little Miles, more intimately than ever on the ground of my stupefaction, my general emotion: so monstrous was I then ready to pronounce it that such a child as had now been revealed to me should be under an interdict. I was a little late on the scene of his arrival and I felt, as he stood wistfully looking out for me before the door of the inn at which the coach had put him down, that I had seen him on the instant, without and within, in the great glow of freshness, the same positive fragrance of purity, in which I had from the first moment seen his little sister. He was incredibly beautiful, and Mrs. Grose had put her finger on it: everything but a sort of passion of tenderness for him was swept away by his presence. What I then and there took him to my heart for was something divine that I have never found

23

to the same degree in any child — his indescribable little air of knowing nothing in the world but love. It would have been impossible to carry a bad name with a greater sweetness of innocence, and by the time I had got back to Bly with him I remained merely bewildered — so far, this is, as I was not outraged — by the sense of the horrible letter locked up in one of the drawers of my room. As soon as I could compass a private word with Mrs. Grose I declared to her that it was grotesque.

She promptly understood me. "You mean the cruel charge — ?"

"It doesn't live an instant. My dear woman, *look* at him!"

She smiled at my pretension to have discovered his charm. "I assure you, Miss, I do nothing else! What will you say then?" she immediately added.

"In answer to the letter?" I had made up my mind. "Nothing at all."

"And to his uncle?"

I was incisive. "Nothing at all."

"And to the boy himself?"

I was wonderful. "Nothing at all."

She gave with her apron a great wipe to her mouth. "Then I'll stand by you. We'll see it out."

"We'll see it out!" I ardently echoed, giving her my hand to make it a vow.

She held me there a moment, then whisked up her apron again with her detached hand. "Would you mind, Miss, if I used the freedom — "

"To kiss me? No!" I took the good creature in my arms and after we had embraced like sisters felt still more fortified and indignant.

This at all events was for the time: a time so full that as I recall the way it went it reminds me of all the art I now need to make it a little distinct. What I look back at with amazement is the situation I accepted. I had undertaken, with my companion, to see it out, and I was under a charm apparently that could smooth away the extent and the far and difficult connexions of such an effort. I was lifted aloft on a great wave of infatuation and pity. I found it simple, in my ignorance, my confusion and perhaps my conceit, to assume that I could deal with a boy whose education for the world was all on the point of beginning. I am unable even to remember at this day what proposal I framed for the end of his holidays and the resumption of his studies. Lessons with me indeed, that charming summer, we all had a theory that he was to have; but I now feel that for weeks the lessons must have been rather my own. I learnt something — at first certainly — that had not been one of the teachings of my small smothered life; learnt to be amused, and even amusing, and not to think for the morrow. It was the first time, in a manner, that I had known space and air and freedom, all the music of summer and all the mystery of nature. And then there was consideration — and consideration was sweet. Oh it was a trap — not designed but deep — to my imagination, to my delicacy, perhaps to my vanity; to whatever in me was most excitable. The best way to picture it all is to say that I was off my guard. They gave me so little trouble — they were of a gentleness so extraordinary. I used to speculate — but even this was a dim disconnectedness — as to how the rough future (for all futures are rough!) would handle them and might bruise them. They had the bloom of health and happiness; and yet, as if I had been in charge of a pair of little grandees, of princes of the blood, for whom everything, to be right, would have to be fenced about and ordered and arranged, the only form that in my fancy the after-years could take for them was that of a romantic, a really royal extension of the garden and the park. It may be of course above all that what suddenly broke into this gives the previous time a charm of stillness — that hush in which something gathers or crouches. The change was actually like the spring of a beast.

In the first weeks the days were long; they often, at their finest, gave me what I used to call my own hour, the hour when, for my pupils, tea-time and bed-time having come and gone, I had before my final retirement a small interval alone. Much as I liked my companions this hour was the thing in the day I liked most; and I liked it best of all when, as the light faded — or rather, I should say, the day lingered and the last calls of the last birds sounded, in a flushed sky, from the old trees — I could take a turn into the grounds and enjoy, almost with a sense of property that amused and flattered me, the beauty and dignity of the place. It was a pleasure at these moments to feel myself tranquil and justified; doubtless perhaps also to reflect that by my discretion, my quiet good sense and general high propriety, I was giving pleasure — if he ever thought of it! — to the person to whose pressure

I had yielded. What I was doing was what he had earnestly hoped and directly asked of me, and that I *could,* after all, do it proved even a greater joy than I had expected. I dare say I fancied myself in short a remarkable young woman and took comfort in the faith that this would more publicly appear. Well, I needed to be remarkable to offer a front to the remarkable things that presently gave their first sign.

It was plump, one afternoon, in the middle of my very hour: the children were tucked away and I had come out for my stroll. One of the thoughts that, as I don't in the least shrink now from noting, used to be with me in these wanderings was that it would be as charming as a charming story suddenly to meet some one. Some one would appear there at the turn of a path and would stand before me and smile and approve. I didn't ask more than that — I only asked that he should *know;* and the only way to be sure he knew would be to see it, and the kind light of it, in his handsome face. That was exactly present to me — by which I mean the face was — when, on the first of these occasions, at the end of a long June day, I stopped short on emerging from one of the plantations and coming into view of the house. What arrested me on the spot — and with a shock much greater than any vision had allowed for — was the sense that my imagination had, in a flash, turned real. He did stand there! — but high up, beyond the lawn and at the very top of the tower to which, on that first morning, little Flora had conducted me. This tower was one of a pair — square incongruous crenellated structures — that were distinguished, for some reason, though I could see little difference, as the new and the old. They flanked opposite ends of the house and were probably architectural absurdities, redeemed in a measure indeed by not being wholly disengaged nor of a height too pretentious, dating, in their gingerbread antiquity, from a romantic revival that was already a respectable past. I admired them, had fancies about them, for we could all profit in a degree, especially when they loomed through the dusk, by the grandeur of their actual battlements; yet it was not at such an elevation that the figure I had so often invoked seemed most in place.

It produced in me, this figure, in the clear twilight, I remember, two distinct gasps of emotion, which were, sharply, the shock of my first and that of my second surprise. My second was a violent perception of the mistake of my first: the man who met my eyes was not the person I had precipitately supposed. There came to me thus a bewilderment of vision of which, after these years, there is no living view that I can hope to give. An unknown man in a lonely place is a permitted object of fear to a young woman privately bred; and the figure that faced me was — a few more seconds assured me — as little anyone else I knew as it was the image that had been in my mind. I had not seen it in Harley Street — I had not seen it anywhere. The place moreover, in the strangest way in the world, had on the instant and by the very fact of its appearance become a solitude. To me at least, making my statement here with a deliberation with which I have never made it, the whole feeling of the moment returns. It was as if, while I took in, what I did take in, all the rest of the scene had been stricken with death. I can hear again, as I write, the intense hush in which the sounds of evening dropped. The rooks stopped cawing in the golden sky and the friendly hour lost for the unspeakable minute all its voice. But there was no other change in nature, unless indeed it were a change that I saw with a stranger sharpness. The gold was still in the sky, the clearness in the air, and the man who looked at me over the battlements was as definite as a picture in a frame. That's how I thought, with extraordinary quickness, of each person he might have been and that he wasn't. We were confronted across our distance quite long enough for me to ask myself with intensity who then he was and to feel, as an effect of my inability to say, a wonder that in a few seconds more became intense.

The great question, or one of these, is afterwards, I know, with regard to certain matters, the question of how long they have lasted. Well, this matter of mine, think what you will of it, lasted while I caught at a dozen possibilities, none of which made a difference for the better, that I could see, in there having been in the house — and for how long, above all? — a person of whom I was in ignorance. It lasted while I just bridled a little with the sense of how my office seemed to inquire that there should be no such ignorance and no such person. It lasted while this visitant, at all events — and there was a touch of the strange freedom, as I remember,

in the sign of familiarity of his wearing no hat —
seemed to fix me, from his position, with just
the question, just the scrutiny through the fading
light, that his own presence provoked. We were
too far apart to call to each other, but there was
a moment at which, at shorter range, some challenge between us, breaking the hush, would have
been the right result of our straight mutual stare.
He was in one of the angles, the one away from
the house, very erect, as it struck me, and with
both hands on the ledge. So I saw him as I see the
letters I form on this page; then, exactly, after a
minute, as if to add to the spectacle, he slowly
changed his place — passed, looking at me hard
all the while, to the opposite corner of the plat-
form. Yes, it was intense to me that during this
transit he never took his eyes from me, and I
can see at this moment the way his hand, as he
went, moved from one of the crenellations to the
next. He stopped at the other corner, but less
long, and even as he turned away still markedly
fixed me. He turned away; that was all I knew.

IV

IT WAS NOT THAT I DIDN'T WAIT, on this occasion,
for more, since I was as deeply rooted as shaken.
Was there a "secret" at Bly — a mystery of
Udolpho or an insane, an unmentionable relative kept in unsuspected confinement? I can't say
how long I turned it over, or how long, in a confusion of curiosity and dread, I remained where
I had had my collision; I only recall that when I
re-entered the house darkness had quite closed

in. Agitation, in the interval, certainly had held me and driven me, for I must, in circling about the place, have walked three miles; but I was to be later on so much more overwhelmed that this mere dawn of alarm was a comparatively human chill. The most singular part of it in fact — singular as the rest had been — was the part I became, in the hall, aware of in meeting Mrs. Grose. This picture comes back to me in the general train — the impression, as I received it on my return, of the wide white panelled space, bright in the lamplight and with its portraits and red carpet, and of the good surprised look of my friend, which immediately told me she had missed me. It came to me straightway, under her contact, that, with plain heartiness, mere relieved anxiety at my appearance, she knew nothing whatever that could bear upon the incident I had there ready for her. I had not suspected in advance that her comfortable face would pull me up, and I somehow measured the importance of what I had seen by my thus finding myself hesitate to mention it. Scarce anything in the whole history seems to me so odd as this fact that my real beginning of fear was one, as I may say, with the instinct of sparing my companion. On the spot, accordingly, in the pleasant hall and with her eyes on me, I, for a reason that I couldn't then have phrased, achieved an inward revolution — offered a vague pretext for my lateness and, with the plea of the beauty of the night and of the heavy dew and wet feet, went as soon as possible to my room.

Here it was another affair; here, for many days

after, it was a queer affair enough. There were hours, from day to day — or at least there were moments, snatched even from clear duties — when I had to shut myself up to think. It was not so much yet that I was more nervous than I could bear to be as that I was remarkably afraid of becoming so; for the truth I had now to turn over was simply and clearly the truth that I could arrive at no account whatever of the visitor with whom I had been so inexplicably and yet, as it seemed to me, so intimately concerned. It took me little time to see that I might easily sound, without forms of inquiry and without exciting remark, any domestic complication. The shock I had suffered must have sharpened all my senses; I felt sure, at the end of three days and as the result of mere closer attention, that I had not been practised upon by the servants nor made the object of any "game." Of whatever it was that I knew nothing was known around me. There was but one sane inference: someone had taken a liberty rather monstrous. That was what, repeatedly, I dipped into my room and locked the door to say to myself. We had been, collectively, subject to an intrusion; some unscrupulous traveller, curious in old houses, had made his way in unobserved, enjoyed the prospect from the best point of view and then stolen out as he came. If he had given me such a bold hard stare, that was but a part of his indiscretion. The good thing, after all, was that we should surely see no more of him.

This was not so good a thing, I admit, as not to leave me to judge that what, essentially, made nothing else much signify was simply my charming work. My charming work was just my life with Miles and Flora, and through nothing could I so like it as through feeling that to throw myself into it was to throw myself out of my trouble. The attraction of my small charges was a constant joy, leading me to wonder afresh at the vanity of my original fears, the distaste I had begun by entertaining for the probable grey prose of my office. There was to be no grey prose, it appeared, and no long grind; so how could work not be charming that presented itself as daily beauty? It was all the romance of the nursery and the poetry of the schoolroom. I don't mean by this of course that we studied only fiction and verse; I mean I can express no otherwise the sort of interest my companions inspired. How can I describe that except by saying that instead of growing deadly used to them — and it's a marvel for a governess: I call the sisterhood to witness! — I made constant fresh discoveries. There was one direction, assuredly, in which these discoveries stopped: deep obscurity continued to cover the region of the boy's conduct at school. It had been promptly given me, I have noted, to face that mystery without a pang. Perhaps even it would be nearer the truth to say that — without a word — he himself had cleared it up. He had made the whole charge absurd. My conclusion bloomed there with the real rose-flush of his innocence: he was only too fine and fair for the little horrid unclean school-world, and he had paid a price for it. I reflected acutely that the sense of such individual differences, such superiorities of quality, always, on the part of the majority — which could include even stupid sordid headmasters — turns infallibly to the vindictive.

Both the children had a gentleness — it was their only fault, and it never made Miles a muff — that kept them (how shall I express it?) almost impersonal and certainly quite unpunishable. They were like those cherubs of the anecdote who had — morally at any rate — nothing to whack! I remember feeling with Miles in especial as if he had had, as it were, nothing to call even an infinitesimal history. We expect of a small child scant enough "antecedents," but there was in this beautiful little boy something extraordinarily sensitive, yet extraordinarily happy, that, more than in any creature of his age I have seen, struck me as beginning anew each day. He had never for a second suffered. I took this as a direct disproof of his having really been chastised. If he had been wicked he would have "caught" it, and I should have caught it by the rebound — I should have found the trace, should have felt the wound and the dishonour. I could reconstitute nothing at all, and he was therefore an angel. He never spoke of his school, never mentioned a comrade or a master; and I, for my part, was quite too much disgusted to allude to them. Of course I was under the spell, and the wonderful part is that, even at the time, I perfectly knew I was. But I gave myself up to it; it was an antidote to any pain, and I had more pains than one. I was in receipt in these days of disturbing letters from home, where things were not going well. But with this joy of my children what things in the world mattered? That was the question I used to put to my scrappy retirements. I was dazzled by their loveliness.

There was a Sunday — to get on — when it rained with such force and for so many hours that there could be no procession to church; in consequence of which, as the day declined, I had arranged with Mrs. Grose that, should the evening show improvement, we would attend together the late service. The rain happily stopped, and I prepared for our walk, which, through the park and by the good road to the village, would be a matter of twenty minutes. Coming downstairs to meet my colleague in the hall, I remembered a pair of gloves that had required three stitches and that had received them — with a publicity perhaps not edifying — while I sat with the children at their tea, served on Sundays, by exception, in that cold clean temple of mahogany and brass, the "grown-up" dining-room. The gloves had been dropped there, and I turned in to recover them. The day was grey enough, but the afternoon light still lingered, and it enabled me, on crossing the threshold, not only to recognise, on a chair near the wide window, then closed, the articles I wanted, but to become aware of a person on the other side of the window and looking straight in. One step into the room had sufficed; my vision was instantaneous; it was all there. The person looking straight in was the person who had already appeared to me. He appeared thus again with I won't say greater distinctness, for that was impossible, but with a nearness that represented a forward stride in our intercourse and made me, as I met him, catch my breath and turn cold. He was the same — he was the same, and seen, this time, as he had been seen before, from the waist up, the window, though the dining-room was on the ground floor, not going down to the terrace on which he stood. His face was close to the glass, yet the effect of this better view was, strangely, just to show me how intense the former had been. He remained but a few seconds — long enough to convince me he also saw and recognised; but it was as if I had been looking at him for years and had known him always. Something, however, happened this time that had not happened before; his stare into my face, through the glass and across the room, was as deep and hard as then, but it quitted me for a moment during which I could still watch it, see it fix successively several other things. On the spot there came to me the added shock of a certitude that it was not for me he had come. He had come for some one else.

The flash of this knowledge — for it was knowledge in the midst of dread — produced in me the most extraordinary effect, starting, as I stood there, a sudden vibration of duty and courage. I say courage because I was beyond all doubt already far gone. I bounded straight out of the door again, reached that of the house, got in an instant upon the drive, and, passing along the terrace as fast as I could rush, turned a corner and came full in sight. But it was in sight of nothing now — my visitor had vanished. I stopped, almost dropped, with the real relief of this; but I took in the whole scene — I gave him time to reappear. I call it time, but how long was it? I can't speak to the purpose today of the duration of these things. That kind of measure must have left me: they couldn't have lasted as they actually appeared to me to last. The terrace and the whole place, the lawn and the garden beyond it, all I could see of the park, were empty with a great emptiness. There were shrubberies and big trees, but I remember the clear assurance I felt that none of them concealed him. He was there or was not there: not there if I didn't see him. I got hold of this; then, instinctively, instead of returning as I had come, went to the window. It was confusedly present to me that I ought to place myself where he had stood. I did so; I applied my face to the pane and looked, as he had looked, into the room. As if, at this moment, to show me exactly what his range had been, Mrs. Grose, as I had done for himself just before, came in from the hall. With this I had the full image of a repetition of what had already occurred. She saw me as I had seen my own visitant; she pulled up short as I had done; I gave her something of the shock that I had received. She turned white, and this made me ask myself if I had blanched as much. She stared, in short, and retreated just on *my* lines, and I knew she had then passed out and come round to me and that I should presently meet her. I remained where I was, and while I waited I thought of more things than one. But there's only one I take space to mention. I wondered why *she* should be scared.

V

OH SHE LET ME KNOW as soon as, round the corner of the house, she loomed again into view. "What in the name of goodness is the matter? — " She was now flushed and out of breath.

I said nothing till she came quite near. "With me?" I must have made a wonderful face. "Do I show it?"

"You're as white as a sheet. You look awful."

I considered; I could meet on this, without scruple, any degree of innocence. My need to respect the bloom of Mrs. Grose's had dropped, without a rustle, from my shoulders, and if I wavered for the instant it was not with what I kept back. I put out my hand to her and she took it; I held her hard a little, liking to feel her close to me. There was a kind of support in the shy heave of her surprise. "You came for me for church, of course, but I can't go."

"Has anything happened?"

"Yes. You must know now. Did I look very queer?"

"Through this window? Dreadful!"

"Well," I said, "I've been frightened." Mrs. Grose's eyes expressed plainly that *she* had no wish to be, yet also that she knew too well her place not to be ready to share with me any marked inconvenience. Oh it was quite settled that she *must* share! "Just what you saw from the dining-room a minute ago was the effect of that. What *I* saw — just before — was much worse."

Her hand tightened. "What was it?"

"An extraordinary man. Looking in."

"What extraordinary man?"

"I haven't the least idea."

Mrs. Grose gazed round us in vain. "Then where is he gone?"

"I know still less."

"Have you seen him before?"

"Yes — once. On the old tower."

She could only look at me harder. "Do you mean he's a stranger?"

"Oh very much!"

"Yet you didn't tell me?"

"No — for reasons. But now that you've guessed — "

Mrs. Grose's round eyes encountered this charge. "Ah I haven't guessed!" she said very simply. "How can I if *you* don't imagine?"

"I don't in the very least."

"You've seen him nowhere but on the tower?"

"And on this spot just now."

Mrs. Grose looked round again. "What was he doing on the tower?"

"Only standing there and looking down at me."

She thought a minute. "Was he a gentleman?"

I found I had no need to think. "No." She gazed in deeper wonder. "No."

"Then nobody about the place? Nobody from the village?"

"Nobody — nobody. I didn't tell you, but I made sure."

She breathed a vague relief: this was, oddly, so much to the good. It only went indeed a little way. "But if he isn't a gentleman — "

"What *is* he? He's a horror."

"A horror?"

"He's — God help me if I know *what* he is!"

Mrs. Grose looked round once more; she fixed her eyes on the duskier distance and then, pulling herself together, turned to me with full inconsequence. "It's time we should be at church."

"Oh, I'm not fit for church!"

"Won't it do you good?"

"It won't do *them* — !" I nodded at the house.

"The children?"

"I can't leave them now."

"You're afraid — ?"

I spoke boldly. "I'm afraid of *him*."

Mrs. Grose's large face showed me, at this, for the first time, the far-away faint glimmer of a consciousness more acute: I somehow made out in it the delayed dawn of an idea I myself had not given her and that was as yet quite obscure to me. It comes back to me that I thought instantly of this as something I could get from her; and I felt it to be connected with the desire she presently showed to know more. "When was it — on the tower?"

"About the middle of the month. At this same hour."

"Almost at dark," said Mrs. Grose.

"Oh no, not nearly. I saw him as I see you."

"Then how did he get in?"

"And how did he get out?" I laughed. "I had no opportunity to ask him! This evening, you see," I pursued, "he has not been able to get in."

"He only peeps?"

"I hope it will be confined to that!" She had

now let go my hand; she turned away a little. I waited an instant; then I brought out: "Go to church. Good-bye. I must watch."

Slowly she faced me again. "Do you fear for them?"

We met in another long look. "Don't *you?*" Instead of answering she came nearer to the window and, for a minute, applied her face to the glass. "You see how he could see," I meanwhile went on.

She didn't move. "How long was he here?"

"Till I came out. I came to meet him."

Mrs. Grose at last turned round, and there was still more in her face. "*I* couldn't have come out."

"Neither could I!" I laughed again. "But I did come. I've my duty."

"So have I mine," she replied; after which she added: "What's he like?"

"I've been dying to tell you. But he's like nobody."

"Nobody?" she echoed.

"He has no hat." Then seeing in her face that she already, in this, with a deeper dismay, found a touch of picture, I quickly added stroke to stroke. "He has red hair, very red, close-curling, and a pale face, long in shape, with straight good features and little rather queer whiskers that are as red as his hair. His eyebrows are somehow darker; they look particularly arched and as if they might move a good deal. His eyes are sharp, strange — awfully; but I only know clearly that they're rather small and very fixed. His mouth's wide, and his lips are thin, and except for his little whiskers he's quite clean-shaven. He gives me a sort of sense of looking like an actor."

"An actor!" It was impossible to resemble one less, at least, than Mrs. Grose at that moment.

"I've never seen one, but so I suppose them. He's tall, active, erect," I continued, "but never — no, never! — a gentleman."

My companion's face had blanched as I went on; her round eyes started and her mild mouth gaped. "A gentleman?" she gasped, confounded, stupefied: "a gentleman, *he?*"

"You know him then?"

She visibly tried to hold herself. "But he *is* handsome?"

I saw the way to help her. "Remarkably!"

"And dressed — ?"

"In somebody's clothes. They're smart, but they're not his own."

She broke into a breathless affirmative groan. "They're the master's!"

I caught it up. "You *do* know him?"

She faltered but a second. "Quint!" she cried.

"Quint?"

"Peter Quint — his own man, his valet, when he was here!"

"When the master was?"

Gaping still, but meeting me, she pieced it all together. "He never wore his hat, but he did wear — well, there were waistcoats missed! They were both here — last year. Then the master went, and Quint was alone."

I followed, but halting a little. "Alone?"

"Alone with *us*." Then, as from a deeper depth, "In charge," she added.

"And what became of him?"

She hung fire so long that I was still more mystified. "He went too," she brought out at last.

"Went where?"

Her expression, at this, became extraordinary. "God knows where! He died."

"Died?" I almost shrieked.

She seemed fairly to square herself, plant herself more firmly to express the wonder of it. "Yes. Mr. Quint's dead."

VI

IT TOOK OF COURSE more than that particular passage to place us together in presence of what we had now to live with as we could, my dreadful liability to impressions of the order so vividly exemplified, and my companion's knowledge henceforth — a knowledge half consternation and half compassion — of that liability. There had been this evening, after the revelation that left me for an hour so prostrate — there had been for either of us no attendance on any service but a little service of tears and vows, of prayers and promises, a climax to the series of mutual challenges and pledges that had straightway ensued on our retreating together to the schoolroom and shutting ourselves up there to have everything out. The result of our having everything out was simply to reduce our situation to the last rigour of its elements. She herself had seen nothing, not the shadow of a shadow, and nobody in the house but the governess was in the governess's plight; yet she accepted without directly impugning my sanity the truth as I gave it to her, and ended by showing me on this ground an awestricken tenderness, a deference to my more than questionable privilege, of which the very breath has remained with me as that of the sweetest of human charities.

What was settled between us accordingly that night was that we thought we might bear things together; and I was not even sure that in spite of her exemption it was she who had the best of the burden. I knew at this hour, I think, as well as I knew later, what I was capable of meeting to shelter my pupils; but it took me some time to be wholly sure of what my honest comrade was prepared for to keep terms with so stiff an agreement. I was queer company enough — quite as queer as the company I received; but as I trace over what we went through I see how much common ground we must have found in the one idea that, by good fortune, *could* steady us. It was the idea, the second movement, that led me straight out, as I may say, of the inner chamber of my dread. I could take the air in the court, at least, and there Mrs. Grose could join me. Perfectly can I recall now the particular way strength came to me before we separated for the night. We had gone over and over every feature of what I had seen.

"He was looking for someone else, you say — someone who was not you?"

"He was looking for little Miles." A portentous clearness now possessed me. "*That's* whom he was looking for."

"But how do you know?"

"I know, I know, I know!" my exaltation grew. "And *you* know, my dear!"

She didn't deny this, but I required, I felt, not even so much telling as that. She took it up again in a moment. "What if he should see him?"

"Little Miles? That's what he wants!"

She looked immensely scared again. "The child?"

"Heaven forbid! The man. He wants to appear *to them*." That he might was an awful conception, and yet somehow I could keep it at bay; which moreover, as we lingered there, was what I succeeded in practically proving. I had an absolute certainty that I should see again what I had already seen, but something within me said that by offering myself bravely as the sole subject of such experience, by accepting, by inviting, by surmounting it all, I should serve as an expiatory victim and guard the tranquillity of the rest of the household. The children in especial I should thus fence about and absolutely save. I recall one of the last things I said that night to Mrs. Grose.

"It does strike me that my pupils have never mentioned —"

She looked at me hard as I musingly pulled up. "His having been here and the time they were with him?"

"The time they were with him, and his name, his presence, his history, in any way. They've never alluded to it."

"Oh the little lady doesn't remember. She never heard or knew."

"The circumstances of his death?" I thought

with some intensity. "Perhaps not. But Miles would remember — Miles would know."

"Ah don't try him!" broke from Mrs. Grose.

I returned her the look she had given me. "Don't be afraid." I continued to think. "It *is* rather odd."

"That he has never spoken of him?"

"Never by the least reference. And you tell me they were 'great friends'?"

"Oh it wasn't *him!*" Mrs. Grose with emphasis declared. "It was Quint's own fancy. To play with him, I mean — to spoil him." She paused a moment; then she added: "Quint was much too free."

This gave me, straight from my vision of his face — such a face! — a sudden sickness of disgust. "Too free with *my* boy?"

"Too free with everyone!"

I forbore for the moment to analyse this description further than by the reflexion that a part of it applied to several of the members of the household, of the half-dozen maids and men who were still of our small colony. But there was everything, for our apprehension, in the lucky fact that no discomfortable legend, no perturbation of scullions, had ever, within any one's memory, attached to the kind old place. It had neither bad name nor ill fame, and Mrs. Grose, most apparently, only desired to cling to me and to quake in silence. I even put her, the very last thing of all, to the test. It was when, at midnight, she had her hand on the schoolroom door to take leave. "I have it from you then — for it's of great importance — that he was definitely and admittedly bad?"

"Oh not admittedly. *I* knew it — but the master didn't."

"And you never told him?"

"Well, he didn't like tale-bearing — he hated complaints. He was terribly short with anything of that kind, and if people were all right to *him* — "

"He wouldn't be bothered with more?" This squared well enough with my impression of him: he was not a trouble-loving gentleman, nor so very particular perhaps about some of the company he himself kept. All the same, I pressed my informant. "I promise you *I* would have told!"

She felt my discrimination. "I dare say I was wrong. But really I was afraid."

"Afraid of what?"

"Of things that man could do. Quint was so clever — he was so deep."

I took this in still more than I probably showed. "You weren't afraid of anything else? Not of his effect — ?"

"His effect?" she repeated with a face of anguish and waiting while I faltered.

"On innocent little precious lives. They were in your charge."

"No, they weren't in mine!" she roundly and distressfully returned. "The master believed in him and placed him here because he was supposed not to be quite in health and the country air so good for him. So he had everything to say. Yes" — she let me have it — "even about *them*."

"Them — that creature?" I had to smother a kind of howl. "And you could bear it!"

"No. I couldn't — and I can't now!" And the poor woman burst into tears.

A rigid control, from the next day, was as I have said, to follow them; yet how often and how passionately, for a week, we came back together to the subject! Much as we had discussed it that Sunday night, I was, in the immediate later hours in especial — for it may be imagined whether I slept — still haunted with the shadow of something she had not told me. I myself had kept back nothing, but there was a word Mrs. Grose had kept back. I was sure moreover by morning that this was not from a failure of frankness, but because on every side there were fears. It seems to me indeed, in raking it all over, that by the time the morrow's sun was high I had restlessly read into the facts before us almost all the meaning they were to receive from subsequent and more cruel occurrences. What they gave me above all was just the sinister figure of the living man — the dead one would keep awhile! — and of the months he had continuously passed at Bly, which, added up, made a formidable stretch. The limit of this evil time had arrived only when, on the dawn of a winter's morning, Peter Quint was found, by a labourer going to early work, stone dead on the road from the village: a catastrophe explained — superficially at least — by a visible wound to his head; such a wound as might have been produced (and as, on the final evidence, *had* been) by a fatal slip, in the dark and after leaving the public house, on the steepish icy slope, a wrong path altogether, at the bottom of which he lay. The icy slope, the turn mistaken at night and in liquor, accounted for much — practically, in the end and after the inquest and boundless chatter, for everything; but there had

48

been matters in his life, strange passages and perils, secret disorders, vices more than suspected, that would have accounted for a good deal more.

I scarce know how to put my story into words that shall be a credible picture of my state of mind; but I was in these days literally able to find a joy in the extraordinary flight of heroism the occasion demanded of me. I now saw that I had been asked for a service admirable and difficult; and there would be a greatness in letting it be seen — oh in the right quarter! — that I could succeed where many another girl might have failed. It was an immense help to me — I confess I rather applaud myself as I look back! — that I saw my response so strongly and so simply. I was there to protect and defend the little creatures in the world the most bereaved and the most loveable, the appeal of whose helplessness had suddenly become only too explicit, a deep constant ache of one's own engaged affection. We were cut off, really, together; we were united in our danger. They had nothing but me, and I — well, I had *them*. It was in short a magnificent chance. This chance presented itself to me in an image richly material. I was a screen — I was to stand before them. The more I saw the less they would. I began to watch them in a stifled suspense, a disguised tension that might well, had it continued too long, have turned to something like madness. What saved me, as I now see, was that it turned to another matter altogether. It didn't last as suspense — it was superseded by horrible proofs. Proofs, I say, yes — from the moment I really took hold.

This moment dated from an afternoon hour

that I happened to spend in the grounds with the younger of my pupils alone. We had left Miles indoors, on the red cushion of a deep window-seat; he had wished to finish a book, and I had been glad to encourage a purpose so laudable in a young man whose only defect was a certain ingenuity of restlessness. His sister, on the contrary, had been alert to come out, and I strolled with her half an hour, seeking the shade, for the sun was still high and the day exceptionally warm. I was aware afresh with her, as we went, of how, like her brother, she contrived — it was the charming thing in both children — to let me alone without appearing to drop me and to accompany me without appearing to oppress. They were never importunate and yet never listless. My attention to them all really went to seeing them amuse themselves immensely without me: this was a spectacle they seemed actively to prepare and that employed me as an active admirer. I walked in a world of their invention — they had no occasion whatever to draw upon mine; so that my time was taken only with being for them some remarkable person or thing that the game of the moment required and that was merely, thanks to my superior, my exalted stamp, a happy and highly distinguished sinecure. I forget what I was on the present occasion; I only remember that I was something very important and very quiet and that Flora was playing very hard. We were on the edge of the lake, and, as we had lately begun geography, the lake was the Sea of Azof.

Suddenly, amid these elements, I became

aware that on the other side of the Sea of Azof
we had an interested spectator. The way this
knowledge gathered in me was the strangest
thing in the world — the strangest, that is, except
the very much stranger in which it quickly
merged itself. I had sat down with a piece of
work — for I was something or other that could
sit — on the old stone bench which overlooked
the pond; and in this position I began to take in
with certitude and yet without direct vision the
presence, a good way off, of a third person. The
old trees, the thick shrubbery, made a great and
pleasant shade, but it was all suffused with the
brightness of the hot still hour. There was no
ambiguity in anything; none whatever at least in
the conviction I from one moment to another
found myself forming as to what I should see
straight before me and across the lake as a consequence of raising my eyes. They were attached
at this juncture to the stitching in which I was
engaged, and I can feel once more the spasm of
my effort not to move them till I should so have
steadied myself as to be able to make up my
mind what to do. There was an alien object in
view — a figure whose right of presence I instantly and passionately questioned. I recollect
counting over perfectly the possibilities, reminding myself that nothing was more natural for instance than the appearance of one of the men
about the place, or even of a messenger, a post-
man or a tradesman's boy, from the village. That
reminder had as little effect on my practical certitude as I was conscious — still even without
looking — of its having upon the character and

attitude of our visitor. Nothing was more natural than that these things should be the other things they absolutely were not.

Of the positive identity of the apparition I would assure myself as soon as the small clock of my courage should have ticked out the right second; meanwhile, with an effort that was already sharp enough, I transferred my eyes straight to little Flora, who, at the moment, was about ten yards away. My heart had stood still for an instant with the wonder and terror of the question whether she too would see; and I held my breath while I waited for what a cry from her, what some sudden innocent sign either of interest or of alarm, would tell me. I waited, but nothing came; then in the first place — and there is something more dire in this, I feel, than in anything I have to relate — I was determined by a sense that within a minute all spontaneous sounds from her had dropped; and in the second by the circumstance that also within the minute she had, in her play, turned her back to the water. This was her attitude when I at last looked at her — looked with the confirmed conviction that we were still, together, under direct personal notice. She had picked up a small flat piece of wood which happened to have in it a little hole that had evidently suggested to her the idea of sticking in another fragment that might figure as a mast and make the thing a boat. This second morsel, as I watched her, she was very markedly and intently attempting to tighten in its place. My apprehension of what she was doing sustained me so that after some seconds I felt I was

ready for more. Then I again shifted my eyes —
I faced what I had to face.

VII

I GOT HOLD OF MRS. GROSE as soon after this as I
could; and I can give no intelligible account
of how I fought out the interval. Yet I still hear
myself cry as I fairly threw myself into her arms:
"They *know* — it's too monstrous: they know,
they know!"

"And what on earth — ?" I felt her incredulity
as she held me.

"Why all that *we* know — and heaven knows
what more besides!" Then as she released me I
made it out to her, made it out perhaps only now
with full coherency even to myself. "Two hours
ago, in the garden" — I could scarce articulate
— "Flora *saw!*"

Mrs. Grose took it as she might have taken a
blow in the stomach. "She has told you?" she
panted.

"Not a word — that's the horror. She kept it
to herself! The child of eight, *that* child!" Unutterable still for me was the stupefaction of it.

Mrs. Grose of course could only gape the
wider. "Then how do you know?"

"I was there — I saw with my eyes: saw she
was perfectly aware."

"Do you mean aware of *him?*"

"No — of *her.*" I was conscious as I spoke that
I looked prodigious things, for I got the slow reflexion of them in my companion's face. "Another person — this time; but a figure of quite as

unmistakable horror and evil: a woman in black, pale and dreadful — with such an air also, and such a face! — on the other side of the lake. I was there with the child — quiet for the hour; and in the midst of it she came."

"Came how — from where?"

"From where they come from! She just appeared and stood there — but not so near."

"And without coming nearer?"

"Oh for the effect and the feeling she might have been as close as you!"

My friend, with an odd impulse, fell back a step. "Was she someone you've never seen?"

"Never. But someone the child has. Someone *you* have." Then to show how I had thought it all out: "My predecessor — the one who died."

"Miss Jessel?"

"Miss Jessel. You don't believe me?" I pressed.

She turned right and left in her distress. "How can you be sure?"

This drew from me, in the state of my nerves, a flash of impatience. "Then ask Flora — *she's* sure!" But I had no sooner spoken than I caught myself up. "No, for God's sake *don't!* She'll say she isn't — she'll lie!"

Mrs. Grose was not too bewildered instinctively to protest. "Ah how *can* you?"

"Because I'm clear. Flora doesn't want me to know."

"It's only then to spare you."

"No, no — there are depths, depths! The more I go over it the more I see in it, and the more I see in it the more I fear. I don't know what I *don't* see, what I *don't* fear!"

Mrs. Grose tried to keep up with me. "You mean you're afraid of seeing her again?"

"Oh no; that's nothing — now!" Then I explained. "It's of *not* seeing her."

But my companion only looked wan. "I don't understand."

"Why, it's that the child may keep it up — and that the child assuredly *will* — without my knowing it."

At the image of this possibility Mrs. Grose for a moment collapsed, yet presently to pull herself together again as from the positive force of the sense of what, should we yield an inch, there would really be to give way to. "Dear, dear — we must keep our heads! And after all, if she doesn't mind it — !" She even tried a grim joke. "Perhaps she likes it!"

"Likes *such* things — a scrap of an infant!"

"Isn't it just a proof of her blest innocence?" my friend bravely inquired.

She brought me, for the instant, almost round. "Oh we must clutch at *that* — we must cling to it! If it isn't a proof of what you say, it's a proof of — God knows what! For the woman's a horror of horrors."

Mrs. Grose, at this, fixed her eyes a minute on the ground; then at last raising them, "Tell me how you know," she said.

"Then you admit it's what she was?" I cried.

"Tell me how you know," my friend simply repeated.

"Know? By seeing her! By the way she looked."

"At you, do you mean — so wickedly?"

"Dear me, no — I could have borne that. She gave me never a glance. She only fixed the child."

Mrs. Grose tried to see it. "Fixed her?"

"Ah with such awful eyes!"

She stared at mine as if they might really have resembled them. "Do you mean of dislike?"

"God help us, no. Of something much worse."

"Worse than dislike?" — this left her indeed at a loss.

"With a determination — indescribable. With a kind of fury of intention."

I made her turn pale. "Intention?"

"To get hold of her." Mrs. Grose — her eyes just lingering on mine — gave a shudder and walked to the window; and while she stood there looking out I completed my statement. "*That's* what Flora knows."

After a little she turned round. "The person was in black, you say?"

"In mourning — rather poor, almost shabby. But — yes — with extraordinary beauty." I now recognised to what I had at last, stroke by stroke, brought the victim of my confidence, for she quite visibly weighed this. "Oh handsome — very, very," I insisted; "wonderfully handsome. But infamous."

She slowly came back to me. "Miss Jessel — *was* infamous."

She once more took my hand in both her own, holding it as tight as if to fortify me against the increase of alarm I might draw from this disclosure. "They were both infamous," she finally said.

So for a little we faced it once more together;

and I found absolutely a degree of help in seeing it now so straight. "I appreciate," I said, "the great decency of your not having hitherto spoken; but the time has certainly come to give me the whole thing." She appeared to assent to this, but still only in silence; seeing which I went on: "I must have it now. Of what did she die? Come, there was something between them."

"There was everything."

"In spite of the difference — ?"

"Oh of their rank, their condition" — she brought it woefully out. "She was a lady."

I turned it over; I again saw. "Yes — she was a lady."

"And he so dreadfully below," said Mrs. Grose.

I felt that I doubtless needn't press too hard, in such company, on the place of a servant in the scale; but there was nothing to prevent an acceptance of my companion's own measure of my predecessor's abasement. There was a way to deal with that, and I dealt; the more readily for my full vision — on the evidence — of our employer's late clever good-looking "own" man; impudent, assured, spoiled, depraved. "The fellow was a hound."

Mrs. Grose considered as if it were perhaps a little a case for a sense of shades. "I've never seen one like him. He did what he wished."

"With *her?*"

"With them all."

It was as if now in my friend's own eyes Miss Jessel had again appeared. I seemed at any rate for an instant to trace their evocation of her as distinctly as I had seen her by the pond; and I brought out with decision: "It must have been also what *she* wished!"

Mrs. Grose's face signified that it had been indeed, but she said at the same time: "Poor woman — she paid for it!"

"Then you do know what she died of?" I asked.

"No — I know nothing. I wanted not to know; I was glad enough I didn't; and I thanked heaven she was well out of this!"

"Yet you had then your idea — "

"Of her real reason for leaving? Oh yes — as to that. She couldn't have stayed. Fancy it here — for a governess! And afterwards I imagined — and I still imagine. And what I imagine is dreadful."

"Not so dreadful as what *I* do," I replied; on which I must have shown her — as I was indeed but too conscious — a front of miserable defeat. It brought out again all her compassion for me, and at the renewed touch of her kindness my power to resist broke down. I burst, as I had the other time made her burst, into tears; she took me to her motherly breast, where my lamentation overflowed. "I don't do it!" I sobbed in despair; "I don't save or shield them! It's far worse than I dreamed. They're lost!"

VIII

WHAT I HAD SAID TO MRS. GROSE was true enough: there were in the matter I had put before her depths and possibilities that I lacked resolution to sound; so that when we met once more in the wonder of it we were of a common mind about the duty of resistance to extravagant fancies. We were to keep our heads if we should keep nothing else — difficult indeed as that might be in the face of all that, in our prodigious experience, seemed least to be questioned. Late that night, while the house slept, we had another talk in my room; when she went all the way with me as to its being beyond doubt that I had seen exactly what I had seen. I found that to keep her thoroughly in the grip of this I had only to ask her how, if I had "made it up," I came to be able to give, of each of the persons appearing to me, a picture disclosing, to the last detail, their special marks — a portrait on the exhibition of which she had instantly recognised and named them. She wished, of course — a small blame to her! — to sink the whole subject; and I was quick to assure her that my own interest in it had now violently taken the form of a search for the way to escape from it. I closed with her cordially on the article of the likelihood that with recurrence — for recurrence we took for granted — I should get used to my danger; distinctly professing that my personal exposure had suddenly become the least of my discomforts. It was my new suspicion that was intolerable; and yet even to this complication the later hours of the day had brought a little ease.

On leaving her, after my first outbreak, I had of course returned to my pupils, associating the right remedy for my dismay with that sense of their charm which I had already recognised as a resource I could positively cultivate and which had never failed me yet. I had simply, in other words, plunged afresh into Flora's special society and there become aware — it was almost a luxury! — that she could put her little conscious hand straight upon the spot that ached. She had looked at me in sweet speculation and then had accused me to my face of having "cried." I had supposed the ugly signs of it brushed away; but I could literally — for the time at all events — rejoice, under this fathomless charity, that they had not entirely disappeared. To gaze into the depths of blue of the child's eyes and pronounce their loveliness a trick of premature cunning was to be guilty of a cynicism in preference to which I naturally preferred to abjure my judgment and, so far as might be, my agitation. I couldn't abjure for merely wanting to, but I could repeat to Mrs. Grose — as I did there, over and over, in the small hours — that with our small friends' voices in the air, their pressure on one's heart and their fragrant faces against one's cheek, everything fell to the ground but their incapacity and their beauty. It was a pity that, somehow, to settle this once for all, I had equally to re-enumerate the signs of subtlety that, in the afternoon, by the lake, had made a miracle of my show of self-possession. It was a pity to be obliged to re-investigate the certitude of the moment itself and repeat how it had come to me as a revelation that the inconceivable communion I then surprised must have been for both parties a matter of habit. It was a pity I should have had to quaver out again the reasons for my not having, in my delusion, so much as questioned that the little girl saw our visitant even as I actually saw Mrs. Grose herself, and that she wanted, by just so much as she did thus see, to make me suppose she didn't, and at the same time, without showing anything, arrive at a guess as to whether I myself did! It was a pity I needed to recapitulate the portentous little activities by which she sought to divert my attention — the perceptible increase of movement, the greater intensity of play, the singing, the gabbling of nonsense and the invitation to romp.

Yet if I had not indulged, to prove there was nothing in it, in this review, I should have missed the two or three dim elements of comfort that still remained to me. I shouldn't for instance have been able to asseverate to my friend that I was certain — which was so much to the good — that *I* at least had not betrayed myself. I shouldn't have been prompted, by stress of need, by desperation of mind — I scarce know what to call it — to invoke such further aid to intelligence as might spring from pushing my colleague fairly to the wall. She had told me, bit by bit, under pressure, a great deal; but a small shifty spot on the wrong side of it all still sometimes brushed my brow like the wing of a bat; and I remember how on this occasion — for the sleeping house and the concentration alike of our danger and our watch seemed to help — I felt the importance of giving the last jerk to the curtain. "I don't believe anything so horrible," I recollect saying; "no, let us put it definitely, my dear, that I don't. But if I did, you know, there's a thing I should require now, just without sparing you the least bit more — oh not a scrap, come! — to get out of you. What was it you had in mind when, in our distress, before Miles came back, over the letter from his school, you said, under my insistence, that you didn't pretend for him he had not literally *ever* been 'bad?' He has *not* truly 'ever,' in these weeks that I myself have lived with him and so closely watched him; he has been an imperturbable little prodigy of delightful loveable goodness. Therefore you might perfectly have made the claim for him if you had not, as it happened, seen an exception to take. What was your exception, and to what passage in your personal observation of him did you refer?"

It was a straight question enough but levity was not our note, and in any case I had before the grey dawn admonished us to separate got my answer. What my friend had had in mind proved immensely to the purpose. It was neither more nor less than the particular fact that for a period of several months Quint and the boy had been perpetually together. It was indeed the very appropriate item of evidence of her having ventured to criticise the propriety, to hint at the incongruity, of so close an alliance, and even to go so far on the subject as a frank overture to Miss Jessel would take her. Miss Jessel had, with a very high manner about it, requested her to mind her business, and the good woman had on this directly approached little Miles. What she had said to him, since I pressed, was that she liked to see young gentlemen not forget their station.

I pressed again, of course, the closer for that. "You reminded him that Quint was only a base menial?"

"As you might say! And it was his answer, for one thing, that was bad."

"And for another thing?" I waited. "He repeated your words to Quint?"

"No, not that. It's just what he *wouldn't!*" she could still impress on me. "I was sure, at any rate," she added, "that he didn't. But he denied certain occasions."

"What occasions?"

"When they had been about together quite as if Quint were his tutor — and a very grand one — and Miss Jessel only for the little lady. When he had gone off with the fellow, I mean, and spent hours with him."

"He then prevaricated about it — he said he hadn't?" Her assent was clear enough to cause me to add in a moment: "I see. He lied."

"Oh!" Mrs. Grose mumbled. This was a suggestion that it didn't matter; which indeed she backed up by a further remark. "You see, after all, Miss Jessel didn't mind. She didn't forbid him."

I considered. "Did he put that to you as a justification?"

At this she dropped again. "No, he never spoke of it."

"Never mentioned her in connection with Quint?"

She saw, visibly flushing, where I was coming out. "Well, he didn't show anything. He denied," she repeated; "he denied."

Lord, how I pressed her now! "So that you could see he knew what was between the two wretches?"

"I don't know — I don't know!" the poor woman wailed.

"You do know, you dear thing," I replied; "only you haven't my dreadful boldness of mind, and you keep back, out of timidity and modesty and delicacy, even the impression that in the past, when you had, without my aid, to flounder about in silence, most of all made you miserable. But I shall get it out of you yet! There was something in the boy that suggested to you," I continued, "his covering and concealing their relation."

"Oh he couldn't prevent —"

"Your learning the truth? I dare say! But, heavens," I fell, with vehemence, a-thinking, "what it shows that they must, to that extent, have succeeded in making of him!"

"Ah nothing that's not nice *now!*" Mrs. Grose lugubriously pleaded.

"I don't wonder you looked queer," I persisted, "when I mentioned to you the letter from his school!"

"I doubt if I looked as queer as you!" she retorted with homely force. "And if he was so bad then as that comes to, how is he such an angel now?"

"Yes indeed — and if he was a fiend at school! How, how, how? Well," I said in my torment, "you must put it to me again, though I shall not be able to tell you for some days. Only put it to me again!" I cried in a way that made my friend stare. "There are directions in which I mustn't for the present let myself go." Meanwhile I returned to her first example — the one to which she had just previously referred — of the boy's happy capacity for an occasional slip. "If Quint — on your remonstrance at the time you speak of — was a base menial, one of the things Miles said to you, I find myself guessing, was that you were another." Again her admission was so adequate that I continued: "And you forgave him *that?*"

"Wouldn't you?"

"Oh yes!" And we exchanged there, in the stillness, a sound of the oddest amusement. Then I went on: "At all events, while he was with the man — "

"Miss Flora was with the woman. It suited them all!"

It suited me too, I felt, only too well; by which I mean that it suited exactly the particular deadly view I was in the very act of forbidding myself to entertain. But I so far succeeded in checking the expression of this view that I will throw, just here, no further light on it than may be offered by the mention of my final observation to Mrs. Grose. "His having lied and been impudent are, I confess, less engaging specimens than I had hoped to have from you of the outbreak in him of the little natural man. Still," I mused, "they must do, for they make me feel more than ever that I must watch."

It made me blush, the next minute, to see in my friend's face how much more unreservedly she had forgiven him than her anecdote struck me as pointing out to my own tenderness any way to do. This was marked when, at the schoolroom door, she quitted me. "Surely you don't accuse *him* — "

"Of carrying on an intercourse that he conceals from me? Ah remember that, until further evidence, I now accuse nobody." Then before shutting her out to go by another passage to her own place, "I must just wait," I wound up.

IX

I WAITED AND WAITED, and the days took as they elapsed something from my consternation. A very few of them, in fact, passing, in constant sight of my pupils, without a fresh incident, sufficed to give to grievous fancies and even to odious memories a kind of brush of the sponge. I have spoken of the surrender to their extraordinary childish grace as a thing I could actively promote in myself, and it may be imagined if I neglected now to apply at this source for whatever balm it would yield. Stranger than I can express, certainly, was the effort to struggle against my new lights. It would doubtless have been a greater tension still, however, had it not been so frequently successful. I used to wonder how my little charges could help guessing that I thought strange things about them; and the circumstance that these things only made them more interesting was not by itself a direct aid to keeping them in the dark. I trembled lest they should see that they *were* so immensely more interesting. Putting things at the worst, at all events, as in meditation I so often did, any clouding of their innocence could only be — blameless and foredoomed as they were — a reason the more for taking risks. There were moments when I knew myself to catch them up by an irresistible impulse and press them to my heart. As soon as I had done so I used to wonder: "What will they think of that? Doesn't it betray too much?" It would have been easy to get into a sad wild tangle about how much I might betray; but the real account, I feel, of the hours of peace I could still enjoy was that the immediate charm of my companions was a beguilement still effective even under the shadow of the possibility that it was studied. For if it occurred to me that I might occasionally excite suspicion by the little outbreaks of my sharper passion for them, so too I remember asking if I mightn't see a queerness in the traceable increase of their own demonstrations.

They were at this period extravagantly and preternaturally fond of me; which, after all, I could reflect, was no more than a graceful response in children perpetually bowed down over and hugged. The homage of which they were so lavish succeeded in truth for my nerves quite as well as if I never appeared to myself, as I may say, literally to catch them at a purpose in it. They had never, I think, wanted to do so many things for their poor protectress; I mean — though they got their lessons better and better, which was naturally what would please her most — in the way of diverting, entertaining, surprising her; reading her passages, telling her stories, acting her charades, pouncing out at her, in disguises, as animals and historical characters, and above all astonishing her by the "pieces" they had secretly got by heart and could interminably recite. I should never get to the bottom — were I to let myself go even now — of the prodigious private commentary, all under still more private correction, with which I in these days over-scored their full hours. They had shown me from the first a facility for everything, a general faculty which, taking a fresh start, achieved remarkable flights. They got their little tasks as if they loved them; they indulged, from the mere exuberance of the gift, in the most unimposed little miracles of memory. They not only popped out at me as tigers and as Romans, but as Shakespeareans, astronomers and navigators. This was so singularly the case that it had presumably much to do with the fact as to which, at the present day, I am at a loss for a different explanation: I allude to my unnatural composure on the subject of another school for Miles. What I remember is that I was content for the time not to open the question, and that contentment must have sprung from the sense of his perpetually striking show of cleverness. He was too clever for a bad governess, for a parson's daughter, to spoil; and the strangest if not the brightest thread in the pensive embroidery I just spoke of was the impression I might have got, if I had dared to work it out, that he was under some influence operating in his small intellectual life as a tremendous incitement.

If it was easy to reflect, however, that such a boy could postpone school, it was at least as marked that for such a boy to have been "kicked out" by a schoolmaster was a mystification without end. Let me add that in their company now — and I was careful almost never to be out of it — I could follow no scent very far. We lived in a cloud of music and affection and success and private theatricals. The musical sense in each of the children was of the quickest, but the elder in especial had a marvellous knack of catching and repeating. The schoolroom piano broke into all gruesome fancies; and when that failed there were confabulations in corners, with a sequel of one of them going out in the highest spirits in order to "come in" as something new. I had had brothers myself, and it was no revelation to me that little girls could be slavish idolaters of little boys. What surpassed everything was that there was a little boy in the world who could have for the inferior age, sex and intelligence so fine a consideration. They were extraordinarily at one, and to say that they never either quarrelled or complained is to make the note of praise coarse for their quality of sweetness. Sometimes perhaps indeed (when I dropped into coarseness) I come across traces of little understandings between them by which one of them should keep me occupied while the other slipped away. There is a naïf side, I suppose, in all diplomacy; but if my pupils practiced upon me it was surely with the minimum of grossness. It was all in the other quarter that, after a lull, the grossness broke out.

I find that I really hang back; but I must take my horrid plunge. In going on with the record of what was hideous at Bly I not only challenge the most liberal faith — for which I little care; but (and this is another matter) I renew what I myself suffered, I again push my dreadful way through it to the end. There came suddenly an hour after which, as I look back, the business seems to me to have been all pure suffering; but I have at least reached the heart of it, and the straightest road out is doubtless to advance. One evening — with nothing to lead up or prepare it — I felt the cold touch of the impression that had breathed on me the night of my arrival and which, much lighter then as I have mentioned, I should probably have made little of in memory had my subsequent sojourn been less agitated. I had not gone to bed; I sat reading by a couple of candles. There was a roomful of old books at Bly — last-century fiction some of it, which, to the extent of a distinctly deprecated renown, but never to so much as that of a stray specimen, had reached the sequestered home and appealed to the unavowed curiosity of my youth. I remember that the book I had in my hand was Fielding's *Amelia*; also that I was wholly awake. I recall further both a general conviction that it was horribly late and a particular objection to looking at my watch. I figure, finally, that the white curtain draping, in the fashion of those days, the head of Flora's little bed, shrouded, as I had assured myself long before, the perfection of childish rest. I recollect in short that though I was deeply interested in my author I found myself, at the turn of a page and with his spell all scattered, looking straight up from him and hard at the door of my room. There was a moment during which I listened, reminded of the faint sense I had had, the first night, of there being something undefinably astir in the house, and noted the soft breath of the open casement just move the half-drawn blind. Then, with all the marks of a deliberation that must have seemed magnificent had there been anyone to admire it, I laid down my book, rose to my feet and, taking a candle, went straight out of the room and, from the passage, on which my light made little impression, noiselessly closed and locked the door.

I can say now neither what determined nor what guided me, but I went straight along the lobby, holding my candle high, till I came within sight of the tall window that presided over the great turn of the staircase. At this point I precipitately found myself aware of three things. They were practically simultaneous, yet they had flashes of succession. My candle, under a bold flourish, went out, and I perceived, by the uncovered window, that the yielding dusk of earliest morning rendered it unnecessary. Without it, the next instant, I knew that there was a figure on the stair. I speak of sequences, but I required no lapse of seconds to stiffen myself for a third encounter with Quint. The apparition had reached the landing halfway up and was therefore on the spot nearest the window, where, at sight of me, it stopped short and fixed me exactly as it had fixed me from the tower and from the garden. He knew me as well as I knew him; and so, in the cold faint twilight, with a glimmer in the high glass and another on the polish of the oak stair below, we faced each other in our common intensity. He was absolutely, on this occasion, a living detestable dangerous presence. But that was not the wonder of wonders; I reserve this distinction for quite another circumstance: the circumstance that dread had unmistakably quitted me and that there was nothing in me unable to meet and measure him.

I had plenty of anguish after that extraordinary moment, but I had, thank God, no terror. And he knew I hadn't — I found myself at the end of an instant magnificently aware of this. I felt, in a fierce rigour of confidence, that if I stood my ground a minute I should cease — for the time at least — to have him to reckon with; and during the minute, accordingly, the thing was as human and hideous as a real interview: hideous just because it *was* human, as human as to have met alone, in the small hours, in a sleeping house, some enemy, some adventurer, some criminal. It was the dead silence of our long gaze at such close quarters that gave the whole horror, huge as it was, its only note of the unnatural. If I had met a murderer in such a place and at such an hour we still at least would have spoken. Something would have passed, in life, between us; if nothing had passed one of us would have moved. The moment was so prolonged that it would have taken but little more to make me doubt if even *I* were in life. I can't express what followed it save by saying that the silence itself — which was indeed in a manner an attestation of my strength — became the element into which I saw the figure disappear; in which

I definitely saw it turn, as I might have seen the low wretch to which it had once belonged turn on receipt of an order, and pass, with my eyes on the villainous back that no hunch could have more disfigured, straight down the staircase and into the darkness in which the next bend was lost.

X

I REMAINED AWHILE at the top of the stair, but with the effect presently of understanding that when my visitor had gone, he had gone; then I returned to my room. The foremost thing I saw there by the light of the candle I had left burning was that Flora's little bed was empty; and on this I caught my breath with all the terror that, five minutes before, I had been able to resist. I dashed at the place in which I had left her lying and over which — for the small silk counterpane and the sheets were disarranged — the white curtains had been deceivingly pulled forward; then my step, to my unutterable relief, produced an answering sound: I noticed an agitation of the window-blind, and the child, ducking down, emerged rosily from the other side of it. She stood there in so much of her candour and so little of her nightgown, with her pink bare feet and the golden glow of her curls. She looked intensely grave, and I had never had such a sense of losing an advantage acquired (the thrill of which had just been so prodigious) as on my consciousness that she addressed me with a reproach. "You naughty: where *have* you been?" Instead of challenging her own irregularity I found myself arraigned and explaining. She herself explained, for that matter, with the loveliest eagerest simplicity. She had known suddenly, as she lay there, that I was out of the room, and had jumped up to see what had become of me. I had dropped, with the joy of her reappearance, back into my chair — feeling then, and then only, a little faint; and she had pattered straight over to me, thrown herself upon my knee, given herself to be held with the flame of the candle full in the wonderful little face that was still flushed with sleep. I remember closing my eyes an instant, yielding, consciously, as before the excess of something beautiful that shone out of the blue of her own. "You were looking for me out of the window?" I said. "You thought I might be walking in the grounds?"

"Well, you know, I thought someone was" — she never blanched as she smiled out that at me.

Oh how I looked at her now! "And did you see anyone?"

"Ah *no!*" she returned almost (with the full privilege of childish inconsequence) resentfully, though with a long sweetness in her little drawl of the negative.

At that moment, in the state of my nerves, I absolutely believed she lied; and if I once more closed my eyes it was before the dazzle of the three or four possible ways in which I might take this up. One of these for a moment tempted me with such singular force that, to resist it, I must have gripped my little girl with a spasm that, wonderfully, she submitted to without a cry or a sign of fright. Why not break out at her on the spot and have it all over? — give it to her straight in her lovely little lighted face? "You see, you see, you *know* that you do and that you already quite suspect I believe it; therefore why not frankly confess it to me, so that we may at least live with it together and learn perhaps, in the strangeness of our fate, where we are and what it means?" This solicitation dropped, alas, as it came: if I could immediately have succumbed to it I might have spared myself — well, you'll see what. Instead of succumbing I sprang again to my feet, looked at her bed and took a helpless middle way. "Why did you pull the curtain over the place to make me think you were still there?"

Flora luminously considered; after which, with her little divine smile: "Because I don't like to frighten you!"

"But if I had, by your idea, gone out — ?"

She absolutely declined to be puzzled; she turned her eyes to the flame of the candle as if the question were as irrelevant, or at any rate as impersonal, as Mrs. Marcet or nine-times-nine. "Oh but you know," she quite adequately answered, "that you might come back, you dear, and that you *have!*" And after a little, when she had got into bed, I had, a long time, by almost sitting on her for the retention of her hand, to show how I recognized the pertinence of my return.

You may imagine the general complexion, from that moment, of my nights. I repeatedly sat up till I didn't know when; I selected moments when my room-mate unmistakably slept, and, stealing out, took noiseless turns in the passage. I even pushed so far as to where I had last met Quint. But I never met him there again, and I may as well say at once that I on no other occasion saw him in the house. I just missed, on the staircase, nevertheless, a different adventure. Looking down it from the top I once recognised the presence of a woman seated on one of the lower steps with her back presented to me, her body half-bowed and her head, in an attitude of woe, in her hands. I had been there but an instant, however, when she vanished without looking round at me. I knew, for all that, exactly what dreadful face she had to show; and I wondered whether, if instead of being above I had been below, I should have had the same nerve for going up that I had lately shown Quint. Well, there continued to be plenty of call for nerve. On the eleventh night after my latest encounter with that gentleman — they were all numbered now — I had an alarm that perilously skirted it and that indeed, from the particular quality of its unexpectedness, proved quite my sharpest shock. It was precisely the first night during this series that, weary with vigils, I had conceived I might again without laxity lay myself down at my old hour. I slept immediately and, as I afterwards knew, till about one o'clock; but when I woke it was to sit straight up, as completely roused as if a hand had shaken me. I had left a light burning, but it was now out, and I felt an instant certainty that Flora had extinguished it. This brought me to my feet and straight, in the darkness, to her bed, which I found she had left. A glance at the window enlightened me further, and the striking of a match completed the picture.

The child had again got up — this time blowing out the taper, and had again, for some purpose of observation or response, squeezed in behind the blind and was peering out into the night. That she now saw — as she had not, I had satisfied myself, the previous time — was proved to me by the fact that she was disturbed neither by my re-illumination nor by the haste I made to get into slippers and into a wrap. Hidden, protected, absorbed, she evidently rested on the sill — the casement opened forward — and gave herself up. There was a great still moon to help her, and this fact had counted in my quick decision. She was face to face with the apparition we had met at the lake, and could now communicate with it as she had not then been able to do. What I, on my side, had to care for was, without disturbing her, to reach, from the corridor, some other window turned to the same quarter. I got to the door without her hearing me; I got out of it, closed it and listened, from the other side, for some sound from her. While I stood in the passage I had my eyes on her brother's door, which was but ten steps off and which, indescribably, produced in me a renewal of the strange impulse that I lately spoke of as my temptation. What if I should go straight in and march to *his* window? — what if, by risking to his boyish bewilderment a revelation of my motive, I should throw across the rest of the mystery the long halter of my boldness?

This thought held me sufficiently to make me

cross to his threshold and pause again. I preternaturally listened; I figured to myself what
might portentously be; I wondered if his bed
were also empty and he also secretly at watch. It
was a deep soundless minute, at the end of which
my impulse failed. He was quiet; he might be
innocent; the risk was hideous; I turned away.
There was a figure in the grounds — a figure
prowling for a sight, the visitor with whom
Flora was engaged; but it wasn't the visitor most
concerned with my boy. I hesitated afresh, but
on other grounds and only a few seconds; then
I had made my choice. There were empty rooms
enough at Bly, and it was only a question of
choosing the right one. The right one suddenly
presented itself to me as the lower one —
though high above the gardens — in the solid
corner of the house that I have spoken of as the
old tower. This was a large square chamber, arranged with some state as a bedroom, the extravagant size of which made it so inconvenient
that it had not for years, though kept by Mrs.
Grose in exemplary order, been occupied. I had
often admired it and I knew my way about in it;
I had only, after just faltering at the first chill
gloom of its disuse, to pass across it and unbolt
in all quietness one of the shutters. Achieving
this transit I uncovered the glass without a
sound and, applying my face to the pane, was
able, the darkness without being much less than
within, to see that I commanded the right direction. Then I saw something more. The moon
made the night extraordinarily penetrable and
showed me on the lawn a person, diminished by

distance, who stood there motionless and as if fascinated, looking up to where I had appeared — looking, that is, not so much straight at me as at something that was apparently above me. There was clearly another person above me — there was a person on the tower; but the presence on the lawn was not in the least what I had conceived and had confidently hurried to meet. The presence on the lawn — I felt sick as I made it out — was poor little Miles himself.

XI

It was not till late next day that I spoke to Mrs. Grose; the rigour with which I kept my pupils in sight making it often difficult to meet her privately: the more as we each felt the importance of not provoking — on the part of the servants quite as much as on that of the children — any suspicion of a secret flurry or of a discussion of mysteries. I drew a great security in this particular from her mere smooth aspect. There was nothing in her fresh face to pass on to others the least of my horrible confidences. She believed me, I was sure, absolutely: if she hadn't I don't know what would have become of me, for I couldn't have borne the strain alone. But she was a magnificent monument to the blessing of a want of imagination, and if she could see in our little charges nothing but their beauty and amiability, their happiness and cleverness, she had no direct communication with the sources of my trouble. If they had been at all visibly blighted or battered she would doubtless have grown, on tracing it back haggard enough to match them; as matters stood, however, I could feel her, when she surveyed them with her large white arms folded and the habit of serenity in all her look, thank the Lord's mercy that if they were ruined the pieces would still serve. Flights of fancy gave place, in her mind, to a steady fireside glow, and I had already begun to perceive how, with the development of the conviction that — as time went on without a public accident — our young things could, after all, look out for themselves, she addressed her greatest solicitude to the sad case presented by their deputy-guardian. That, for myself, was a sound simplification: I could engage that, to the world, my face should tell no tales, but it would have been, in the conditions, an immense added worry to find myself anxious about hers.

At the hour I now speak of she had joined me, under pressure, on the terrace, where, with the lapse of the season, the afternoon sun was now agreeable; and we sat there together while, before us and at a distance, yet within call if we wished, the children strolled to and fro in one of their most manageable moods. They moved slowly, in unison, below us, over the lawn, the boy, as they went, reading aloud from a story-book and passing his arm round his sister to keep her quite in touch. Mrs. Grose watched them with positive placidity; then I caught the suppressed intellectual creak with which she conscientiously turned to take from me a view of the back of the tapestry. I had made her a receptacle of lurid things, but there was an odd recognition of my superiority — my accomplishments and my function — in her patience under my pain. She offered her mind to my disclosures as, had I wished to mix a witch's broth and proposed it with assurance, she would have held out a large clean saucepan. This had become thoroughly her attitude by the time that, in my recital of the events of the night, I reached the point of what Miles had said to me when, after seeing him, at such a monstrous hour, almost on the very spot where he happened now to be, I had gone down to bring him in; choosing then, at the window, with a concentrated need of not alarming the house, rather that method than any noisier process. I had left her meanwhile in little doubt of my small hope of representing with success even to her actual sympathy my sense of the real splendour of the little inspiration with which, after I had got him into the house, the boy met my final articulate challenge. As soon as I appeared in the moonlight on the terrace he had come to me as straight as possible; on which I had taken his hand without a word and led him, through the dark spaces, up the staircase where Quint had so hungrily hovered for him, along the lobby where I had listened and trembled, and so to his forsaken room.

Not a sound, on the way, had passed between us, and I had wondered — oh *how* I had wondered! — if he were groping about in his dreadful little mind for something plausible and not too grotesque. It would tax his invention certainly, and I felt, this time, over his real embarrassment, a curious thrill of triumph. It was a sharp trap for any game hitherto successful. He could play no longer at perfect propriety, nor could he pretend to it; so how the deuce would he get out of the scrape? There beat in me indeed, with the passionate throb of this question, an equal dumb appeal as to how the deuce *I* should. I was confronted at last, as never yet, with all the risk attached even now to sounding my own horrid note. I remember in fact that as we pushed into his little chamber, where the bed had not been slept in at all and the window, uncovered to the moonlight, made the place so clear that there was no need of striking a match — I remember how I suddenly dropped, sank upon the edge of the bed from the force of the idea that he must know how he really, as they say, "had" me. He could do what he liked, with all his cleverness to help him, so long as I should continue to defer to the old tradition of the criminality of those caretakers of the young who minister to superstitions and fears. He "had" me indeed, and in a cleft stick; for who would ever absolve me, who would consent that I should go unhung, if, by the faintest tremor of an overture, I were the first to introduce into our perfect intercourse an element so dire? No, no: it was useless to attempt to to convey to Mrs. Grose, just as it is scarcely less so to attempt to suggest here, how, during our short stiff brush there in the dark, he fairly shook me with admiration. I was of course, thoroughly kind and merciful; never never yet had I placed on his small shoulders hands of such tenderness as those with which, while I rested against the bed, I held him there well under fire. I had no alternative but, in form at least, to put it to him.

"You must tell me now — and all the truth. What did you go out for? What were you doing there?"

I can still see his wonderful smile, the whites of his beautiful eyes and the uncovering of his clear teeth shine to me in the dusk. "If I tell you why, will you understand?" My heart, at this, leaped into my mouth. *Would* he tell me why? I found no sound on my lips to press it, and I was aware of answering only with a vague repeated grimacing nod. He was gentleness itself, and while I wagged my head at him he stood there more than ever a little fairy prince. It was his brightness indeed that gave me a respite. Would it be so great if he were really going to tell me? "Well," he said at last, "just exactly in order that you should do this."

"Do what?"

"Think me — for a change — *bad!*" I shall never forget the sweetness and gaiety with which he brought out the word, nor how, on top of it, he bent forward and kissed me. It was practically the end of everything. I met his kiss and I had to make, while I folded him for a minute in my arms, the most stupendous effort not to cry. He had given exactly the account of himself that permitted least my going behind it, and it was only with the effect of confirming my acceptance of it that, as I presently glanced about the room, I could say —

"Then you didn't undress at all?"

He fairly glittered in the gloom. "Not at all. I sat up and read."

"And when did you go down?"

"At midnight. When I'm bad I *am* bad!"

"I see, I see — it's charming. But how could you be sure I should know it?"

"Oh I arranged that with Flora." His answers rang out with a readiness! "She was to get up and look out."

"Which is what she did do." It was I who fell into the trap!

"So she disturbed you, and, to see what she was looking at, you also looked — you saw."

"While you," I concurred, "caught your death in the night air!"

He literally bloomed so from this exploit that he could afford radiantly to assent. "How otherwise should I have been bad enough?" he asked. Then, after another embrace, the incident and our interview closed on my recognition of all the reserves of goodness that, for his joke, he had been able to draw upon.

XII

THE PARTICULAR IMPRESSION I had received proved in the morning light, I repeat, not quite successfully presentable to Mrs. Grose, though I reinforced it with the mention of still another remark that he had made before we separated. "It all lies in half-a-dozen words," I said to her, "words that really settle the matter. 'Think, you know, what I *might* do!' He threw that off to show me how good he is. He knows down to the ground what he 'might' do. That's what he gave them a taste of at school."

"Lord, you do change!" cried my friend.

"I don't change — I simply make it out. The four, depend upon it, perpetually meet. If on either of these last nights you had been with either child, you'd clearly have understood. The more I've watched and waited the more I've felt that if there were nothing else to make it sure it would be made so by the systematic silence of each. *Never,* by a slip of the tongue, have they so much as alluded to either of their old friends, any more than Miles has alluded to his expulsion. Oh yes, we may sit here and look at them, and they may show off to us there to their fill; but even while they pretend to be lost in their fairy-tale they're steeped in their vision of the dead restored to them. He's not reading to her," I declared; "they're talking of *them* — they're talking horrors! I go on, I know, as if I were crazy; and it's a wonder I'm not. What I've seen would have made *you* so; but it has only made me more lucid, made me get hold of still other things."

My lucidity must have seemed awful, but the charming creatures who were victims of it, passing and repassing in their interlocked sweetness, gave my colleague something to hold on by; and I felt how tight she held as, without stirring in the breath of my passion, she covered them still with her eyes. "Of what other things have you got hold?"

"Why, of the very things that have delighted,

fascinated, and yet, at bottom, as I now so strangely see, mystified and troubled me. Their more than earthly beauty, their absolutely unnatural goodness. It's a game," I went on; "it's a policy and a fraud!"

"On the part of little darlings — ?"

"As yet mere lovely babies? Yes, mad as that seems!" The very act of bringing it out really helped me to trace it — follow it all up and piece it all together. "They haven't been good — they've only been absent. It has been easy to live with them because they're simply leading a life of their own. They're not mine — they're not ours. They're his and they're hers!"

"Quint's and that woman's?"

"Quint's and that woman's. They want to get to them."

Oh how, at this, poor Mrs. Grose appeared to study them! "But for what?"

"For the love of all the evil that, in those dreadful days, the pair put into them. And to ply them with that evil still, to keep up the work of demons, is what brings the others back."

"Laws!" said my friend under her breath. The exclamation was homely, but it revealed a real acceptance of my further proof of what in the bad time — for there had been a worse even than this! — must have occurred. There could have been no such justification for me as the plain assent of her experience to whatever depth of depravity I found credible in our brace of scoundrels. It was in obvious submission of memory that she brought out after a moment: "They were rascals! But what can they now do?" she pursued.

"Do?" I echoed so loud that Miles and Flora, as they passed at their distance, paused an instant in their walk and looked at us. "Don't they do enough?" I demanded in a lower tone, while the children, having smiled and nodded and kissed hands to us, resumed their exhibition. We were held by it a minute; then I answered: "They can destroy them!" At this my companion did turn, but the appeal she launched was a silent one, the effect of which was to make me more explicit. "They don't know as yet quite how—but they're trying hard. They're seen only across, as it were, and beyond—in strange places and on high places, the top of towers, the roof of houses, the outside of windows, the further edge of pools; but there's a deep design, on either side, to shorten the distance and overcome the obstacle: so the success of the tempters is only a question of time. They've only to keep to their suggestions of danger."

"For the children to come?"

"And perish in the attempt!" Mrs. Grose slowly got up, and I scrupulously added: "Unless, of course, we can prevent!"

Standing there before me while I kept my seat, she visibly turned things over. "Their uncle must do the preventing. He must take them away."

"And who's to make him?"

She had been scanning the distance, but she now dropped on me a foolish face. "You, Miss."

"By writing to him that his house is poisoned and his little nephew and niece mad?"

"But if they are, Miss?"

"And if I am myself, you mean? That's

87

charming news to be sent him by a person enjoying his confidence and whose prime undertaking was to give him no worry."

Mrs. Grose considered, following the children again. "Yes, he do hate worry. That was the great reason — "

"Why those fiends took him in so long? No doubt, though his indifference must have been awful. As I'm not a fiend, at any rate, I shouldn't take him in."

My companion, after an instant and for all answer, sat down again and grasped my arm. "Make him at any rate come to you."

I stared. "To me?" I had a sudden fear of what she might do. " 'Him'?"

"He ought to *be* here — he ought to help."

I quickly rose and I think I must have shown her a queerer face than ever yet. "You see me asking him for a visit?" No, with her eyes on my face she evidently couldn't. Instead of it even — as a woman reads another — she could see what I myself saw: his derision, his amusement, his contempt for the breakdown of my resignation at being left alone and for the fine machinery I had set in motion to attract his attention to my slighted charms. She didn't know — no one knew — how proud I had been to serve him and to stick to our terms; yet she none the less took the measure, I think, of the warning I now gave her. "If you should so lose your head to appeal to him for me — "

She was really frightened. "Yes, Miss?"

"I would leave, on the spot, both him and you."

XIII

IT WAS ALL VERY WELL to join them, but speaking to them proved quite as much as ever an effort beyond my strength — offered, in close quarters, difficulties as insurmountable as before. This situation continued a month, and with new aggravations and particular notes, the note above all, sharper and sharper, of the small ironic consciousness on the part of my pupils. It was not, I am as sure today as I was sure then, my mere infernal imagination: it was absolutely traceable that they were aware of my predicament and that this strange relation made, in a manner, for a long time, the air in which we moved. I don't mean that they had their tongues in their cheeks or did anything vulgar, for that was not one of their dangers: I do mean, on the other hand, that the element of the unnamed and untouched became, between us, greater than any other, and that so much avoidance couldn't have been made successful without a great deal of tacit arrangement. It was as if, at moments, we were perpetually coming into sight of subjects before which we must stop short, turning suddenly out of alleys that we perceived to be blind, closing with a little bang that made us look at each other — for, like all bangs, it was something louder than we had intended — the doors we had indiscreetly opened. All roads lead to Rome, and there were times when it might have struck us that almost every branch of study or subject of conversation skirted forbidden ground. Forbidden ground was the question of the return of the dead in general and of whatever, in especial, might survive, for memory, of the friends little children had lost. There were days when I could have sworn that one of them had, with a small invisible nudge, said to the other: "She thinks she'll do it this time — but she *won't!*" To "do it" would have been to indulge for instance — and for once in a way — in some direct reference to the lady who had prepared them for my discipline. They had a delightful endless appetite for passages in my own history to which I had again and again treated them; they were in possession of everything that had ever happened to me, had had, with every circumstance, the story of my smallest adventures and of those of my brothers and sisters and of the cat and the dog at home, as well as many particulars of the whimsical bent of my father, of the furniture and arrangement of our house, and of the conversation of the old women of our village. There were things enough, taking one with another, to chatter about, if one went very fast and knew by instinct when to go round. They pulled with an art of their own the strings of my invention and my memory; and nothing else perhaps, when I thought of such occasions afterwards, gave me so the suspicion of being watched from under cover. It was in any case over *my* life, *my* past and *my* friends alone that we could take anything like our ease; a state of affairs that led them sometimes without the least pertinence to break out into sociable reminders. I was invited — with no visible connexion — to repeat afresh Goody Goslin's celebrated *mot* or to confirm the details already supplied as to the cleverness of the vicarage pony.

It was partly at such junctures as these and partly at quite different ones, that, with the turn my matters had now taken, my predicament, as I have called it, grew most sensible. The fact that the days passed for me without another encounter ought, it would have appeared, to have done something towards soothing my nerves. Since the light brush, that second night on the upper landing, of the presence of a woman at the foot of the stair, I had seen nothing, whether in or out of the house, that one had better not have seen. There was many a corner round which I expected to come upon Quint, and many a situation that, in a merely sinister way, would have favoured the appearance of Miss Jessel. The summer had turned, the summer had gone; the autumn had dropped upon Bly and had blown out half our lights. The place, with its grey sky and withered garlands, its bared spaces and scattered dead leaves, was like a theatre after the performance — all strewn with crumpled playbills. There were exactly states of the air, conditions of sound and of stillness, unspeakable impressions of the kind of ministering moment, that brought back to me, long enough to catch it, the feeling of the medium in which, that June evening out of doors, I had had my first sight of Quint, and in which too, at those other instants, I had, after seeing him through the window, looked for him in vain in the circle of shrubbery. I recognised the signs, the portents — I recognised the moment, the spot. But they remained unaccompanied and empty, and I continued unmolested; if unmolested one could call a young woman whose sensibility had, in the most extraordinary fashion, not declined but deepened. I had said in my talk with Mrs. Grose on that horrid scene of Flora's by the lake — and had perplexed her by so saying — that it would from that moment distress me much more to lose my power than to keep it. I had then expressed what was vividly in my mind: the truth that, whether the children really saw or not — since, that is, it was not yet definitely proved — I greatly preferred, as a safeguard, the fullness of my own exposure. I was ready to know the very worst that was to be known. What I had then had an ugly glimpse of was that my eyes might be sealed, it appeared, at present — a consummation for which it seemed blasphemous not to thank God. There was, alas, a difficulty about that: I would have thanked him with all my soul had I not had in a proportionate measure this conviction of the secret of my pupils.

How can I retrace today the strange steps of my obsession? There were times of our being together when I would have been ready to swear that, literally, in my presence, but with my direct sense of it closed, they had visitors who were known and were welcome. Then it was that, had I not been deterred by the very chance that such an injury might prove greater than the injury to be averted, my exaltation would have broken out. "They're here, they're here, you little wretches," I would have cried, "and you can't deny it now!" The little wretches denied it with all the added volume of their sociability and their tenderness, just in the crystal depths of which — like the flash of a fish in a stream — the mockery of their advantage peeped up. The shock in truth had sunk into me still deeper than I knew on the night when, looking out either for Quint or Miss Jessel under the stars, I had seen there the boy over whose rest I watched and who had immediately brought in with him — had straightway there turned on me — the lovely upward look with which, from the battlements above us, the hideous apparition of Quint had played. If it was a question of a scare my discovery on this occasion had scared me more than any other, and it was essentially in the scared state that I drew my actual conclusions. They harassed me so that sometimes, at odd moments, I shut myself up audibly to rehearse — it was at once a fantastic relief and a renewed despair — the manner in which I might come to the point. I approached it from one side and the other while, in my room, I flung myself about, but I always broke down in the monstrous utterance of names. As they died away on my lips I said to myself that I should indeed help them to represent something infamous if by pronouncing them I should violate as rare a little case of instinctive delicacy as any schoolroom probably had ever known. When I said to myself: "They have the manners to be silent, and you, trusted as you are, the baseness to speak!" I felt myself crimson and covered my face with my hands.

After these secret scenes I chattered more than ever, going on volubly enough till one of our prodigious palpable hushes occurred — I can call them nothing else — the strange dizzy lift or swim (I try for terms!) into a stillness, a pause of all life, that had nothing to do with the more or less noise we at the moment might be engaged in making and that I could hear through any intensified mirth or quickened recitation or louder strum of the piano. Then it was that the others, the outsiders, were there. Though they were not angels they "passed," as the French say, causing me, while they stayed, to tremble with the fear of their addressing to their younger victims some yet more infernal message or more vivid image than they had thought good enough for myself.

What it was least possible to get rid of was the cruel idea that, whatever I had seen, Miles and Flora saw *more* — things terrible and unguessable and that sprang from dreadful passages of intercourse in the past. Such things naturally left on the surface, for the time, a chill that we vociferously denied we felt; and we had all three, with repetition, got into such splendid training that we went, each time, to mark the close of the incident, almost automatically through the very same movements. It was striking of the children at all events to kiss me inveterately with a wild irrelevance and never to fail — one or the other — of the precious question that had helped us through many a peril. "When do you think he *will* come? Don't you think we *ought* to write?" — there was nothing

94

like that inquiry, we found by experience, for carrying off an awkwardness. "He" of course was their uncle in Harley Street; and we lived in much profusion of theory that he might at any moment arrive to mingle in our circle. It was impossible to have given less encouragement than he had administered to such a doctrine, but if we had not had the doctrine to fall back upon we should have deprived each other of some of our finest exhibitions. He never wrote to them — that may have been selfish, but it was a part of the flattery of his trust of myself; for the way in which a man pays his highest tribute to a woman is apt to be but by the more festal celebration of one of the sacred laws of his comfort. So I held that I carried out the spirit of the pledge given not to appeal to him when I let our young friends undertstand that their own letters were but charming literary exercises. They were too beautiful to be posted; I kept them myself; I have them all to this hour. This was a rule indeed which only added to the satiric effect of my being plied with the supposition that he might at any moment be among us. It was exactly as if our young friends knew how almost more awkward than anything else that might be for me. There appears to me moreover as I look back no note in all this more extraordinary than the mere fact that, in spite of my tension and of their triumph, I never lost patience with them. Adorable they must in truth have been, I now feel, since I didn't in these days hate them! Would exasperation, however, if relief had longer been postponed, finally have betrayed me? It little matters, for relief arrived. I call it relief though it was only the relief that a snap brings to a strain or the burst of a thunderstorm to a day of suffocation. It was at least change, and it came with a rush.

XIV

WALKING TO CHURCH a certain Sunday morning, I had little Miles at my side and his sister, in advance of us and at Mrs. Grose's, well in sight. It was a crisp clear day, the first of its order for some time; the night had brought a touch of frost and the autumn air, bright and sharp, made the church-bells almost gay. It was an odd accident of thought that I should have happened at such a moment to be particularly and very gratefully struck with the obedience of my little charges. Why did they never resent my inexorable, my perpetual society? Something or other had brought nearer home to me that I had all but pinned the boy to my shawl, and that in the way our companions were marshalled before me I might have appeared to provide against some danger of rebellion. I was like a gaoler with an eye to possible surprises and escapes. But all this belonged — I mean their magnificent little surrender — just to the special array of the facts that were most abysmal. Turned out for Sunday by his uncle's tailor, who had had a free hand and a notion of pretty waistcoats and of his grand little air, Miles's whole title to independence, the rights of his sex and situation, were so stamped upon him that if he had suddenly struck for freedom I should have had nothing to say. I was by the strangest of chances wondering how I should meet him when the revolution unmistakably occurred. I call it a revolution because I now see how, with the word he spoke, the curtain rose on the last act of my dreadful drama and the catastrophe was precipitated. "Look here, my dear, you know," he charmingly said, "when in the world, please, am I going back to school?"

Transcribed here the speech sounds harmless enough, particularly as uttered in the sweet, high, casual pipe with which, at all interlocutors, but above all at his eternal governess, he threw off intonations as if he were tossing roses. There was something in them that always made one "catch," and I caught at any rate now so effectually that I stopped as short as if one of the trees of the park had fallen across the road. There was something new, on the spot, between us, and he was perfectly aware I recognised it, though to enable me to do so he had no need to look a whit less candid and charming than usual. I could feel in him how he already, from my at first finding nothing to reply, perceived the advantage he had gained. I was so slow to find anything that he had plenty of time, after a minute, to continue with his suggestive but inconclusive smile: "You know, my dear, that for a fellow to be with a lady always — !" His "my dear" was constantly on his lips for me, and nothing could have expressed more the exact shade of the sentiment with which I desired to inspire my pupils than its fond familiarity. It was so respectfully easy.

But oh how I felt that at present I must pick

my own phrases! I remember that, to gain time. I tried to laugh, and I seemed to see in the beautiful face with which he watched me how ugly and queer I looked. "And always with the same lady?" I returned.

He neither blenched nor winked. The whole thing was virtually out between us. "Ah of course she's a jolly 'perfect' lady; but after all I'm a fellow, don't you see? who's — well, getting on."

I lingered there with him an instant ever so kindly. "Yes, you're getting on." Oh but I felt helpless!

I have kept to this day the heartbreaking little idea of how he seemed to know that and to play with it. "And you can't say I've not been awfully good, can you?"

I laid my hand on his shoulder, for though I felt how much better it would have been to walk on I was not yet quite able. "No, I can't say that, Miles."

"Except just that one night, you know — !"

"That one night?" I couldn't look as straight as he.

"Why when I went down — went out of the house."

"Oh yes. But I forget what you did it for."

"You forget?" — he spoke with the sweet extravagance of childish reproach. "Why — it was to show you I could!"

"Oh yes — you could."

"And I can again."

I felt I might perhaps after all succeed in keeping my wits about me. "Certainly. But you won't."

"No, not *that* again. It was nothing."

"It was nothing," I said. "But we must go on."

He resumed our walk with me, passing his hand into my arm. "Then when am I going back?"

I wore, in turning it over, my most responsible air. "Were you very happy at school?"

He just considered. "Oh I'm happy enough anywhere!"

"Well then," I quavered, "if you're just as happy here — !"

"Ah, but that isn't everything! Of course *you* know a lot — "

"But you hint that you know almost as much?" I risked as he paused.

"Not half I want to!" Miles honestly professed. "But it isn't so much that."

"What is it then?"

"Well — I want to see more life."

"I see; I see." We had arrived within sight of the church and of various persons, including several of the household of Bly, on their way to it and clustered about the door to see us go in. I quickened our step. I wanted to get there before the question between us opened up much further; I reflected hungrily that he would have for more than an hour to be silent; and I thought with envy of the comparative dusk of the pew and of the almost spiritual help of the hassock on which I might bend my knees. I seemed literally to be running a race with some confusion to which he was about to reduce me, but I felt he had got in first when, before we had even entered the churchyard, he threw out —

"I want my own sort!"

It literally made me bound forward. "There aren't many of your own sort, Miles!" I laughed. "Unless perhaps dear little Flora!"

"You really compare me to a baby girl?"

This found me singularly weak. "Don't you then love our sweet Flora?"

"If I didn't — and you too; if I didn't — !" he repeated as if retreating for a jump, yet leaving his thought so unfinished that, after we had come into the gate, another stop, which he imposed on me by the pressure of his arm, had become inevitable. Mrs. Grose and Flora had passed into the church, the other worshippers had followed and we were, for the minute, alone among the old thick graves. We had paused, on the path from the gate, by a low oblong table-like tomb.

"Yes, if you didn't — ?"

He looked, while I waited, about at the graves. "Well, you know what!" But he didn't move, and he presently produced something that made me drop straight down on the stone slap as if suddenly to rest. "Does my uncle think what *you* think?" I markedly rested. "How do you know what I think?"

"Ah well, of course I don't; for it strikes me you never tell me. But I mean does he know?"

"Know what, Miles?"

"Why the way I'm going on."

I recognized quickly enough that I could make, to this inquiry, no answer that wouldn't involve something of a sacrifice of my employer Yet it struck me that we were all, at Bly, sufficiently sacrificed to make that venial. "I don't think your uncle much cares."

Miles, on this, stood looking at me. "Then don't you think he can be made to?"

"In what way?"

"Why by his coming down."

"But who'll get him to come down?"

"I will!" the boy said with extraordinary brightness and emphasis. He gave me another look charged with that expression and then marched off alone into church.

XV

THE BUSINESS WAS PRACTICALLY SETTLED from the moment I never followed him. It was a pitiful surrender to agitation, but my being aware of this had somehow no power to restore me. I only sat there on my tomb and read into what our young friend had said to me the fullness of its meaning; by the time I had grasped the whole of which I had also embraced, for absence, the pretext that I was ashamed to offer my pupils and the rest of the congregation such an example of delay. What I said to myself above all was that Miles had got something out of me and that the gage of it for him would be just this awkward collapse. He had got out of me that there was something I was much afraid of, and that he should probably be able to make use of my fear to gain, for his own purpose, more freedom. My fear was of having to deal with the intolerable question of the grounds of his dismisssal from school, since that was really but the question of the horrors gathered behind. That his uncle should arrive to treat with me of these things was a solution that, strictly speaking, I ought now to have desired to bring on; but I could so little face the ugliness and the pain of it that I simply procrastinated and lived from hand to mouth. The boy, to my deep discomposure, was immensely in the right, was in a position to say to me: "Either you clear up with my guardian the mystery of this interruption of my studies, or you cease to expect me to lead with you a life that's so unnatural for a boy." What was so unnatural for the particular boy I was concerned with was this sudden revelation of a consciousness and a plan.

That was what really overcame me, what prevented my going in. I walked round the church, hesitating, hovering; I reflected that I had already, with him, hurt myself beyond repair. Therefore I could patch up nothing and it was too extreme an effort to squeeze beside him into the pew: he would be so much more sure than ever to pass his arm into mine and make me sit there for an hour in close mute contact with his commentary on our talk. For the first minute since his arrival I wanted to get away from him. As I paused beneath the high east window and listened to the sounds of worship I was taken with an impulse that might master me, I felt, and completely, should I give it the least encouragement. I might easily put an end to my ordeal by getting away altogether. Here was my chance; there was no one to stop me; I could give the whole thing up — turn my back and bolt. It was only a question of hurrying again, for a few preparations, to the house which the attendance at church of so many of the servants would practically have left unoccupied. No one, in short, could blame me if I should just drive desperately off. What was it to get away if I should get away only till dinner? That would be in a couple of hours, at the end of which — I had the acute prevision — my little pupils would play at innocent wonder about my non-appearance in their train.

"What *did* you do, you naughty, bad thing? Why in the world, to worry us so — and take our thoughts off too, don't you know? — did you desert us at the very door?" I couldn't meet such questions nor, as they asked them, their false little lovely eyes; yet it was all so exactly what I should have to meet that, as the prospect grew sharp to me, I at last let myself go.

I got, so far as the immediate moment was concerned, away; I came straight out of the churchyard and, thinking hard, retraced my steps through the park. It seemed to me that by the time I reached the house I had made up my mind to cynical flight. The Sunday stillness both of the approaches and of the interior, in which I met no one, fairly stirred me with a sense of opportunity. Were I to get off quickly this way I should get off without a scene, without a word. My quickness would have to be remarkable, however, and the question of a conveyance was the great one to settle. Tormented, in the hall, with difficulties and obstacles, I remember sinking down at the foot of the staircase — suddenly collapsing there on the lowest step and then, with a revulsion, recalling that it was exactly where, more than a month before, in the darkness of night and just so bowed with evil things, I had seen the spectre of the most horrible of women. At this I was able to straighten myself; I went the rest of the way up; I made, in my turmoil, for the schoolroom, where there were objects belonging to me that I should have to take. But I opened the door to find again, in a flash, my eyes unsealed. In the presence of what I saw I reeled straight back upon my resistance.

Seated at my own table in the clear noonday light I saw a person whom, without my previous experience, I should have taken at the first blush for some housemaid who might have stayed at home to look after the place and who, availing herself of rare relief from observation and of the schoolroom table and my pens, ink and paper, had applied herself to the considerable effort of a letter to her sweetheart. There was an effort in the way that, while her arms rested on the table, her hands, with evident weariness, supported her head; but at the moment I took this in I had already become aware that, in spite of my entrance, her attitude strangely persisted. Then it was — with the very act of its announcing itself — that her identity flared up in a change of posture. She rose, not as if she had heard me, but with an indescribable grand melancholy of indifference and detachment, and, within a dozen feet of me, stood there as my vile predecessor. Dishonoured and tragic, she was all before me; but even as I fixed and, for memory, secured it, the awful image passed away. Dark as midnight in her black dress, her haggard beauty and her unutterable woe, she had looked at me long enough to appear to say that her right to sit at my table was as good as mine to sit at hers. While these instants lasted indeed I had the extraordinary chill of a feeling that it was I who was the intruder. It was as a wild protest against it that, actually addressing her — "You terrible miserable woman!" — I heard myself break into a sound that, by the open door, rang through the long passage and the empty house. She looked at me as if she heard me, but I had recovered myself and cleared the air. There was nothing in the room the next minute but the sunshine and a sense that I must stay.

XVI

I HAD SO PERFECTLY EXPECTED the return of the others to be marked by a demonstration that I was freshly upset at having to find them merely dumb and discreet about my desertion. Instead of gaily denouncing and caressing me they made no allusion to my having failed them, and I was left, for the time, on perceiving that she too said nothing, to study Mrs. Grose's odd face. I did this to such purpose that I made sure they had in some way bribed her to silence; a silence that, however, I would engage to break down on the first private opportunity. This opportunity came before tea: I secured five minutes with her in the housekeeper's room, where, in the twilight, amid a smell of lately-baked bread, but with the place all swept and garnished, I found her sitting in pained placidity before the fire. So I see her still, so I see her best: facing the flame from her straight chair in the dusky shin-

ing room, a large clean picture of the "put away"
— of drawers closed and locked and rest without
a remedy.

"Oh yes, they asked me to say nothing; and to
please them — so long as they were there — of
course I promised. But what had happened to
you?"

"I only went with you for the walk," I said. "I
had then to come back to meet a friend."

She showed her surprise. "A friend — *you*?"

"Oh yes, I've a couple!" I laughed. "But did
the children give you a reason?"

"For not alluding to your leaving us? Yes; they
said you'd like it better. *Do* you like it better?"

My face had made her rueful. "No, I like it
worse!" But after an instant I added: "Did they
say why I should like it better?"

"No; Master Miles only said, 'We must do
nothing but what she likes!' "

"I wish indeed he would! And what did Flora
say?"

"Miss Flora was too sweet. She said 'Oh of
course, of course!' — and I said the same."

I thought a moment. "You were too sweet too
— I can hear you all. But none the less, between
Miles and me, it's now all out."

"All out?" My companion stared. "But what,
Miss?"

"Everything. It doesn't matter. I've made up
my mind. I came home, my dear," I went on, "for
a talk with Miss Jessel."

I had by this time formed the habit of having
Mrs. Grose literally well in hand in advance of
my sounding that note; so that even now, as she
bravely blinked under the signal of my word, I

could keep her comparatively firm. "A talk! Do you mean she spoke?"

"It came to that. I found her, on my return, in the schoolroom."

"And what did she say?" I can hear the good woman still, and the candour of her stupefaction.

"That she suffers the torments — !"

It was this, of a truth, that made her, as she filled out my picture, gape. "Do you mean," she faltered, " — of the lost?"

"Of the lost. Of the damned. And that's why, to share them — " I faltered myself with the horror of it.

But my companion, with less imagination, kept me up. "To share them — ?"

"She wants Flora." Mrs. Grose might, as I gave it to her, fairly have fallen away from me had I not been prepared. I still held her there, to show I was. "As I've told you, however, it doesn't matter."

"Because you've made up your mind? But to what?"

"To everything."

"And what do you call 'everything?' "

"Why to sending for their uncle."

"Oh Miss, in pity do," my friend broke out.

"Ah but I will, I *will!* I see it's the only way. What's 'out,' as I told you, with Miles is that if he thinks I'm afraid to — and has ideas of what he gains by that — he shall see he's mistaken. Yes, yes; his uncle shall have it here from me on the spot (and before the boy himself if necessary) that if I'm to be reproached with having done nothing again about more school — "

"Yes, Miss — " my companion pressed me.

"Well, there's that awful reason."

There were now clearly so many of these for my poor colleague that she was excusable for being vague. "But — a — which?"

"Why the letter from his old place."

"You'll show it to the master?"

"I ought to have done so on the instant."

"Oh no!" said Mrs. Grose with decision.

"I'll put it before him," I went on inexorably, "that I can't undertake to work the question on behalf of a child who has been expelled — "

"For we've never in the least known what!" Mrs. Grose declared.

"For wickedness. For what else — when he's so clever and beautiful and perfect? Is he stupid? Is he untidy? Is he infirm? Is he ill-natured? He's exquisite — so it can be only *that;* and that would open up the whole thing. After all," I said, "it's their uncle's fault. If he left here such people — !"

"He didn't really in the least know them. The fault's mine." She had turned quite pale.

"Well, you shan't suffer," I answered.

"The children shan't!" she emphatically returned.

I was silent awhile; we looked at each other. "Then what am I to tell him?"

"You needn't tell him anything. *I'll* tell him."

I measured this. "Do you mean you'll write — ?" Remembering she couldn't, I caught myself up. "How do you communicate?"

"I tell the bailiff. *He* writes."

"And should you like him to write our story?"

My question had a sarcastic force that I had

not fully intended, and it made her after a moment inconsequently break down. The tears were again in her eyes. "Ah Miss, *you* write!"

"Well — to-night," I at last returned; and on this we separated.

XVII

I WENT SO FAR, in the evening as to make a beginning. The weather had changed back, a great wind was abroad, and beneath the lamp, in my room, with Flora at peace beside me, I sat for a long time before a blank sheet of paper and listened to the lash of the rain and the batter of the gusts. Finally I went out, taking a candle; I crossed the passage and listened a minute at Miles's door. What, under my endless obsession, I had been impelled to listen for was some betrayal of his not being at rest, and I presently caught one, but not in the form I had expected. His voice tinkled out. "I say, you there — come in." It was a gaiety in the gloom!

I went in with my light and found him in bed, very wide awake but very much at his ease. "Well, what are *you* up to?" he asked with a grace of sociability in which it occurred to me that Mrs. Grose, had she been present, might have looked in vain for proof that anything was "out."

I stood over him with my candle. "How did you know I was there?"

"Why of course I heard you. Did you fancy you made no noise? You're like a troop of cavalry!" he beautifully laughed.

"Then you weren't asleep?"

"Not much! I lie awake and think."

I had put my candle, designedly, a short way off, and then, as he held out his friendly old hand to me, had sat down on the edge of his bed. "What is it," I asked, "that you think of?"

"What in the world, my dear, but *you?*"

"Ah the pride I take in your appreciation doesn't insist on that! I had so far rather you slept."

"Well, I think also, you know, of this queer business of ours."

I marked the coolness of his firm little hand. "Of what queer business, Miles?"

"Why the way you bring me up. And all the rest!"

I fairly held my breath for a minute, and even from my glimmering taper there was light enough to show how he smiled up at me from his pillow. "What do you mean by all the rest?"

"Oh you know, you know!"

I could say nothing for a minute, though I felt as I held his hand and our eyes continued to meet that my silence had all the air of admitting his charge and that nothing in the whole world of reality was perhaps at that moment so fabulous as our actual relation. "Certainly you shall go back to school," I said, "if it be that that troubles you. But not to the old place — we must find another, a better. How could I know it did trouble you, this question, when you never told me so, never spoke of it at all?" His clear listening face, framed in its smooth whiteness, made him for the minute as appealing as some wistful patient in a children's hospital; and I would have given, as the resemblance came to me, all I possessed on earth really to be the nurse or the sister of charity who might have helped to cure him. Well, even as it was I perhaps might help! "Do you know you've never said a word to me about your school — I mean the old one; never mentioned it in any way?"

He seemed to wonder; he smiled with the same loveliness. But he clearly gained time; he waited, he called for guidance. "Haven't I?" It wasn't for *me* to help him — it was for the thing I had met!

Something in his tone and the expression of his face, as I got this from him, set my heart aching with such a pang as it had never yet known; so unutterably touching was it to see his little brain puzzled and his little resources taxed to play, under the spell laid on him, a part of innocence and consistency. "No, never — from the hour you came back. You've never mentioned to me one of your masters, one of your comrades, nor the least little thing that ever happened to you at school. Never, little Miles — no never — have you given me an inkling of anything that *may* have happened there. Therefore you can fancy how much I'm in the dark. Until you came out, that way, this morning, you had since the first hour I saw you scarce even made a reference to anything in your previous life. You seemed so perfectly to accept the present." It was extraordinary how my absolute conviction of his secret precocity — or whatever I might call the poison of an influence that I dared but half-phrase —

made him, in spite of the faint breath of his inward trouble, appear as accessible as an older person, forced me to treat him as an intelligent equal. "I thought you wanted to go on as you are."

It struck me that at this he just faintly coloured. He gave, at any rate, like a convalescent slightly fatigued, a languid shake of his head. "I don't — I don't. I want to get away."

"You're tired of Bly?"

"Oh no, I like Bly."

"Well then — ?"

"Oh *you* know what a boy wants!"

I felt I didn't know so well as Miles, and I took temporary refuge. "You want to go to your uncle?"

Again, at this, with his sweet ironic face, he made a movement on the pillow. "Ah you can't get off with that!"

I was silent a little, and it was I now, I think, who changed colour. "My dear, I don't want to get off!"

"You can't even if you do. You can't, you can't!" — he lay beautifully staring. "My uncle must come down, and you must completely settle things."

"If we do," I returned with some spirit, "you may be sure it will be to take you quite away."

"Well, don't you understand that that's exactly what I'm working for? You'll have to tell him — about the way you've let it all drop: you'll have to tell him a tremendous lot!"

The exultation with which he uttered this helped me somehow for the instant to meet him rather more. "And how much will *you,* Miles, have to tell him? There are things he'll ask you!"

He turned it over. "Very likely. But what things?"

"The things you've never told me. To make up his mind what to do with you. He can't send you back — "

"I don't want to go back!" he broke in. "I want a new field."

He said it with admirable serenity, with positive unimpeachable gaiety; and doubtless it was that very note that most evoked for me the poignancy, the unnatural childish tragedy, of his probable reappearance at the end of three months with all this bravado and still more dishonour. It overwhelmed me now that I should never be able to bear that, and it made me let myself go. I threw myself upon him and in the tenderness of my pity I embraced him. "Dear little Miles, dear little Miles — !"

My face was close to his, and he let me kiss him, simply taking it with indulgent good humour. "Well, old lady?"

"Is there nothing — nothing at all that you want to tell me?"

He turned off a little, facing round towards the wall and holding up his hand to look at as one had seen sick children look. "I've told you — I told you this morning."

Oh I was sorry for him! "That you just want me not to worry you?"

He looked round at me now as if in recognition of my understanding him; then ever so gently, "To let me alone," he replied.

There was even a strange little dignity in it, something that made me release him, yet, when I had slowly risen, linger beside him. God knows *I* never wished to harass him, but I felt that merely, at this, to turn my back on him was to abandon or, to put it more truly, lose him. "I've just begun a letter to your uncle," I said.

"Well then, finish it!"

I waited a minute. "What happened before?"

He gazed up at me again. "Before what?"

"Before you came back. And before you went away."

For some time he was silent, but he continued to meet my eyes. "What happened?"

It made me, the sound of the words, in which it seemed to me I caught for the very first time a small faint quaver of consenting consciousness —it made me drop on my knees beside the bed and seize once more the chance of possessing him. "Dear little Miles, dear little Miles, if you *knew* how I want to help you! It's only that, it's nothing but that, and I'd rather die than give you a pain or do you a wrong—I'd rather die than hurt a hair of you. Dear little Miles"—oh I brought it out now even if I *should* go too far —"I just want you to help me to save you!" But I knew in a moment after this that I had gone too far. The answer to my appeal was instantaneous but it came in the form of an extraordinary blast and chill, a gust of frozen air and a shake of the room as great as if, in the wild wind, the casement had crashed in. The boy gave a loud high shriek, which, lost in the rest of the shock of sound, might have seemed, indistinctly, though I was so close to him, a note either of jubilation or of terror. I jumped to my feet again and was conscious of darkness. So for a moment we remained, while I stared about me and saw the drawn curtains unstirred and the window still tight. "Why, the candle's out!"

"It was I who blew it, dear!" said Miles.

XVIII

THE NEXT DAY, after lessons, Mrs. Grose found a moment to say to me quietly: "Have you written, Miss?"

"Yes — I've written." But I didn't add — for the hour — that my letter, sealed and directed, was still in my pocket. There would be time enough to send it before the messenger should go to the village. Meanwhile there had been on the part of my pupils no more brilliant, more exemplary morning. It was exactly as if they had both had at heart to gloss over any recent little friction. They performed the dizziest feats of arithmetic, soaring quite out of *my* feeble range, and perpetrated, in higher spirits than ever, geographical and historical jokes. It was conspicuous of course in Miles in particular that he appeared to wish to show how easily he could let me down. This child, to my memory, really lives in a setting of beauty and misery that no words can translate; there was a distinction all his own in every impulse he revealed; never was a small natural creature, to the uninformed eye all frankness and freedom, a more ingenious, a more extraordinary little gentleman. I had perpetually to guard against the wonder of contemplation into which my initiated view betrayed me; to check the irrelevant gaze and discouraged sigh in which I constantly both attacked and renounced the enigma of what such a little gentleman could have done that deserved a penalty. Say that, by the dark prodigy I knew, the imagination of all evil *had* opened up to him: all the justice within me ached for the proof that it could ever have flowered into an act.

He had never at any rate, been such a little gentleman as when, after our early dinner on this dreadful day, he came round to me and asked if I shouldn't like him for half an hour to play to me. David playing to Saul could never have shown a finer sense of the occasion. It was literally a charming exhibition of tact, of magnanimity, and quite tantamount to his saying outright: "The true knights we love to read about never push an advantage too far. I know what you mean now: you mean that — to be let alone yourself and not followed up — you'll cease to worry and spy upon me, won't keep me so close to you, will let me go and come. Well, I 'come,' you see — but I don't go! There'll be plenty of time for that. I do really delight in your society and I only want to show you that I contended for a principle." It may be imagined whether I resisted this appeal or failed to accompany him again, hand in hand, to the schoolroom. He sat down at the old piano and played as he had never played; and if there are those who think he had better have been kicking a football I can only say that I wholly agree with

116

them. For at the end of a time that under his in-fluence I had quite ceased to measure I started up with a strange sense of having literally slept at my post. It was after luncheon, and by the schoolroom fire, and yet I hadn't really in the least slept; I had only done something much worse — I had forgotten. Where all this time was Flora? When I put the question to Miles he played on a minute before answering, and then could only say: "Why, my dear, how do *I* know?" — breaking moreover into a happy laugh which immediately after, as if it were a vocal accompa-niment, he prolonged into incoherent extrava-gant song.

I went straight to my room, but his sister was not there; then, before going downstairs, I looked into several others. As she was nowhere about she would surely be with Mrs. Grose, whom in the comfort of that theory I accordingly proceeded in quest of. I found her where I had found her the evening before, but she met my quick challenge with blank scared ignorance. She had only supposed that, after the repast, I had carried off both the children; as to which she was quite in her right, for it was the very first time I had allowed the little girl out of my sight without some special provision. Of course now indeed she might be with the maids, so that the immediate thing was to look for her without an air of alarm. This we promptly arranged between us; but when, ten minutes later and in pursu-ance of our arrangement, we met in the hall, it was only to report on either side that after guarded enquiries we had altogether failed to trace her. For a minute there, apart from observation, we exchanged mute alarms, and I could feel with what high interest my friend returned me all those I had from the first given her.

"She'll be above," she presently said — "in one of the rooms you haven't searched."

"No; she's at a distance." I had made up my mind. "She has gone out."

Mrs. Grose stared. "Without a hat?"

I naturally also looked volumes. "Isn't that woman always without one?"

"She's with *her*?"

"She's with *her*!" I declared. "We must find them."

My hand was on my friend's arm, but she failed for the moment, confronted with such an account of the matter, to respond to my pressure. She communed, on the contrary, where she stood, with her uneasiness. "And where's Master Miles?"

"Oh *he's* with Quint. They'll be in the schoolroom."

"Lord, Miss!" My view, I was myself aware — and therefore I suppose my tone — had never yet reached so calm an assurance.

"The trick's played," I went on; "They've successfully worked their plan. He found the most divine little way to keep me quiet while she went off."

" 'Divine?' " Mrs. Grose bewilderedly echoed.

"Infernal then!" I almost cheerfully rejoined. "He has provided for himself as well. But come!"

She had helplessly gloomed at the upper regions. "You leave him — ?"

118

"So long with Quint? Yes — I don't mind that now."

She always ended at these moments by getting possession of my hand, and in this manner she could at present still stay me. But after gasping an instant at my sudden resignation, "Because of your letter?" she eagerly brought out.

I quickly, by way of answer, felt for my letter, drew it forth, held it up, and then, freeing myself, went and laid it on the great hall-table. "Luke will take it," I said as I came back. I reached the house-door and opened it; I was already on the steps.

My companion still demurred: the storm of the night and the early morning had dropped, but the afternoon was damp and grey. I came down to the drive while she stood in the doorway. "You go with nothing on?"

"What do I care when the child has nothing? I can't wait to dress," I cried, "and if you must do so I leave you. Try meanwhile yourself upstairs."

"With *them?*" Oh on this the poor woman promptly joined me!

XIX

WE WENT STRAIGHT TO THE LAKE, as it was called at Bly, and I dare say rightly called, though it may have been a sheet of water less remarkable than my untravelled eyes supposed it. My acquaintance with sheets of water was small, and the pool of Bly, at all events on the few occasions of my consenting, under the protection of my pupils, to affront its surface in the old flat-bottomed boat moored there for our use, had impressed me both with its extent and its agitation. The usual place of embarkation was half a mile from the house, but I had an intimate conviction that, wherever Flora might be, she was not near home. She had not given me the slip for any small adventure, and, since the day of the very great one that I had shared with her by the pond, I had been aware, in our walks, of the quarter to which she most inclined. This was why I had now given to Mrs. Grose's steps so marked a direction — a direction making her, when she perceived it, oppose a resistance that showed me she was freshly mystified. "You're going to the water, Miss? — you think she's in — ?"

"She may be, though the depth is, I believe, nowhere very great. But what I judge most likely is that she's on the spot from which, the other day, we saw together what I told you."

"When she pretended not to see — ?"

"With that astounding self-possession! I've always been sure she wanted to go back alone. And now her brother has managed it for her."

Mrs. Grose still stood where she had stopped. "You suppose they really talk of them?"

I could meet this with an assurance! "They say things that, if we heard them, would simply appal us."

"And if she *is* there — ?"

"Yes?"

"Then Miss Jessel is?"

"Beyond a doubt. You shall see."

"Oh thank you!" my friend cried, planted so

firm that, taking it in, I went straight on without her. By the time I reached the pool, however, she was close behind me, and I knew that, whatever, to her apprehension, might befall me, the exposure of sticking to me struck her as her least danger. She exhaled a moan of relief as we at last came in sight of the greater part of the water without a sight of the child. There was no trace of Flora on that nearer side of the bank where my observation of her had been most startling, and none on the opposite edge, where, save for a margin of some twenty yards, a thick copse came down to the pond. This expanse, oblong in shape, was so narrow compared to its length that, with its ends out of view, it might have been taken for a scant river. We looked at the empty stretch, and then I felt the suggestion in my friend's eyes. I knew what she meant and I replied with a negative headshake.

"No, no; wait! She has taken the boat."

My companion stared at the vacant mooring-place and then again across the lake. "Then where is it?"

"Our not seeing it is the strongest of proofs. She has used it to go over and then has managed to hide it."

"All alone — that child?"

"She's not alone, and at such times she's not a child: she's an old, old woman." I scanned all the visible shore while Mrs. Grose took again, into the queer element I offered her, one of her plunges of submission; then I pointed out that the boat might perfectly be in a small refuge formed by one of the recesses of the pool, an indentation masked, for the hither side, by a projection of the bank and by a clump of trees growing close to the water.

"But if the boat's there, where on earth's *she?*" my colleague anxiously asked.

"That's exactly what we must learn." And I started to walk further.

"By going all the way round?"

"Certainly, far as it is. It will take us but ten minutes, yet it's far enough to have made the child prefer not to walk. She went straight over."

"Laws!" cried my friend again: the chain of my logic was ever too strong for her. It dragged her at my heels even now, and when we had got halfway round — a devious tiresome process, on ground much broken and by a path choked with overgrowth — I paused to give her breath. I sustained her with a grateful arm, assuring her that she might hugely help me; and this started us afresh so that in the course of but few minutes more we reached a point from which we found the boat to be where I had supposed it. It had been intentionally left as much as possible out of sight and was tied to one of the stakes of a fence that came, just there, down to the brink and that had been an assistance to disembarking. I recognised, as I looked at the pair of short thick oars, quite safely drawn up, the prodigious character of the feat for a little girl; but I had by this time lived too long among wonders and had panted to too many livelier measures. There was a gate in the fence, through which we passed, and that brought us after a trifling interval more into the open. Then "There she is!" we both exclaimed at once.

Flora, a short way off, stood before us on the

grass and smiled as if her performance had now become complete. The next thing she did, however, was to stoop straight down and pluck — quite as if it were all she was there for — a big ugly spray of withered fern. I at once felt sure she had just come out of the copse. She waited for us, not herself taking a step, and I was conscious of the rare solemnity with which we presently approached her. She smiled and smiled, and we met; but it was all done in a silence by this time flagrantly ominous. Mrs. Grose was the first to break the spell: she threw herself on her knees and, drawing the child to her breast, clasped in a long embrace the little tender yielding body. While this dumb convulsion lasted I could only watch it — which I did the more intently when I saw Flora's face peep at me over our companion's shoulder. It was serious now — the flicker had left it; but it strengthened the pang with which I at that moment envied Mrs. Grose the simplicity of *her* relation. Still, all this while nothing more passed between us save that Flora had let her foolish fern again drop to the ground. What she and I had virtually said to each other was that pretexts were useless now. When Mrs. Grose finally got up she kept the child's hand, so that the two were still before me; and the singular reticence of our communion was even more marked in the frank look she addressed me. "I'll be hanged," it said, "if *I'll* speak!"

It was Flora who, gazing all over me in candid wonder, was the first. She was struck with our bareheaded aspect. "Why where are your things?"

"Where yours are, my dear!" I promptly returned.

She had already got back her gaiety and appeared to take this as an answer quite sufficient. "And where's Miles?" she went on.

There was something in the small valour of it that quite finished me: these three words from her were in a flash like the glitter of a drawn blade, the jostle of the cup that my hand, for weeks and weeks, had held high and full to the brim and that now, even before speaking, I felt overflow in a deluge. "I'll tell you if you'll tell me — " I heard myself say, then heard the tremor in which it broke.

"Well, what?"

Mrs. Grose's suspense blazed at me, but it was too late now, and I brought the thing out handsomely. "Where, my pet, is Miss Jessel?"

XX

JUST AS IN THE CHURCHYARD WITH MILES, the whole thing was upon us. Much as I had made of the fact that this name had never once, between us, been sounded, the quick smitten glare with which the child's face now received it fairly likened my breach of the silence to the smash of a pane of glass. It added to the interposing cry, as if to stay the blow, that Mrs. Grose at the same instant uttered over my violence — the shriek of a creature scared, or rather wounded, which, in turn, within a few seconds, was completed by a gasp of my own. I seized my colleague's arm. "She's there, she's there!"

Miss Jessel stood before us on the opposite bank exactly as she had stood the other time, and I remember, strangely, as the first feeling now produced in me, my thrill of joy at having brought on a proof. She was there, so I was justified; she was there, so I was neither cruel nor mad. She was there for poor scared Mrs. Grose, but she was there most for Flora; and no moment of my monstrous time was perhaps so extraordinary as that in which I consciously threw out to her — with the sense that, pale and ravenous demon as she was, she would catch and understand it — an inarticulate message of gratitude. She rose erect on the spot my friend and I had lately quitted, and there wasn't in all the long reach of her desire an inch of her evil that fell short. This first vividness of vision and emotion were things of a few seconds, during which Mrs. Grose's dazed blink across to where I pointed struck me as showing that she too at last saw, just as it carried my own eyes precipitately to the child. The revelation then of the manner in which Flora was affected startled me in truth far more than it would have done to find her also merely agitated, for direct dismay was of course not what I had expected. Prepared and on her guard as our pursuit had actually made her, she would repress every betrayal; and I was therefore at once shaken by my first glimpse of the particular one for which I had not allowed. To see her, without a convulsion of her small pink face, not even feign to glance in the direction of the prodigy I announced, but only, instead of that, turn at me an expression of hard still gravity, an expression absolutely new and unprecedented and that appeared to read and accuse and judge me — this was a stroke that somehow converted the little girl herself into a figure portentous. I gaped at her coolness even though my certitude of her thoroughly seeing was never greater than at that instant, and then, in the immediate need to defend myself, I called her passionately to witness. "She's there, you little unhappy thing — there, there, *there*, and you know it as well as you know me!" I had said shortly before to Mrs. Grose that she was not at these times a child, but an old, old woman, and my description of her couldn't have been more strikingly confirmed than in the way in which, for all notice of this, she simply showed me, without an expressional concession, or admission, a countenance of deeper and deeper, of indeed suddenly quite fixed reprobation. I was by this time — if I can put the whole thing at all together — more appalled at what I may properly call her manner than at anything else, though it was quite simultaneously with this that I became aware of having Mrs. Grose also, and very formidably, to reckon with. My elder companion, the next moment, at any rate, blotted out everything but her own flushed face and her loud shocked protest, a burst of high disapproval. "What a dreadful turn, to be sure, Miss! Where on earth do you see anything?"

I could only grasp her more quickly yet, for even while she spoke the hideous plain presence stood undimmed and undaunted. It had already lasted a minute, and it lasted while I continued, seizing my colleague, quite thrusting her at it and presenting her to it, to insist with my pointing hand. "You don't see her exactly as we see? — you mean to say you don't now — *now*? She's as big as a blazing fire! Only look, dearest woman, *look* — !" She looked, just as I did, and gave me, with her deep groan of negation, repulsion, compassion — the mixture with her pity of her relief at her exemption — a sense, touching to me even then, that she would have backed me up if she had been able. I might well have needed that, for with this hard blow of the proof that her eyes were hopelessly sealed I felt my own situation horribly crumble, I felt — I *saw* — my livid predecessor press, from her position, on my defeat, and I took the measure, more than all, of what I should have from this instant to deal with in the astounding little attitude of Flora. Into this attitude Mrs. Grose immediately and violently entered, breaking, even while there pierced through my sense of ruin a prodigious private triumph, into breathless reassurance.

"She isn't there, little lady, and nobody's there — and you never see nothing, my sweet! How can poor Miss Jessel? — when poor Miss Jessel's dead and buried? We know, don't we, love?" — and she appealed, blundering in, to the child. "It's all a mere mistake and a worry and a joke — and we'll go home as fast as we can!"

Our companion, on this, had responded with a strange, quick primness of propriety, and they were again, with Mrs. Grose on her feet, united, as it were, in shocked opposition to me. Flora continued to fix me with her small mask of disaffection, and even at that minute I prayed God to forgive me for seeming to see that, as she stood there holding tight to our friend's dress, her incomparable childish beauty had suddenly failed, had quite vanished. I've said it already — she was literally, she was hideously hard; she had turned common and almost ugly. "I don't know what you mean. I see nobody. I see nothing. I never *have*. I think you're cruel. I don't like you!" Then, after this deliverance, which might have been that of a vulgarly pert little girl in the street, she hugged Mrs. Grose more closely and buried in her skirts the dreadful little face. In this position she launched an almost furious wail. "Take me away, take me away — oh take me away from her!"

"From *me*?" I panted.

"From you — from you!" she cried.

Even Mrs. Grose looked across at me dismayed; while I had nothing to do but communicate again with the figure that, on the opposite bank, without a movement, as rigidly still as if catching, beyond the interval, our voices, was as vividly there for my disaster as it was not there for my service. The wretched child had spoken exactly as if she had got from some outside source each of her stabbing little words, and I could therefore, in the full despair of all I had to accept, but sadly shake my head at her. "If I had ever doubted all my doubt would at present have gone. I've been living with the miserable truth, and now it has only too much closed round me. Of course I've lost you: I've interfered, and you've seen under *her* dictation" — with which

I faced, over the pool again, our infernal witness — "the easy and perfect way to meet it. I've done my best, but I've lost you. Good-bye." For Mrs. Grose I had an imperative, an almost frantic "Go, go!" before which, in infinite distress, but mutely possessed of the little girl and clearly convinced, in spite of her blindness, that something awful had occurred and some collapse engulfed us, she retreated, by the way we had come, as fast as she could move.

Of what first happened when I was left alone I had no subsequent memory. I only knew that at the end of, I suppose, a quarter of an hour, an odorous dampness and roughness, chilling and piercing my trouble, had made me understand that I must have thrown myself, on my face, to the ground and given way to a wildness of grief. I must have lain there long and cried and wailed, for when I raised my head the day was almost done. I got up and looked a moment, through the twilight, at the grey pool and its blank haunted edge, and then I took, back to the house, my dreary and difficult course. When I reached the gate in the fence the boat, to my surprise, was gone, so that I had a fresh reflexion to make on Flora's extraordinary command of the situation. She passed that night, by the most tacit and, I should add, were not the word so grotesque a false note, the happiest of arrangements, with Mrs. Grose. I saw neither of them on my return, but, on the other hand I saw, as by an ambiguous compensation, a great deal of Miles. I saw — I can use no other phrase — so much of him that it fairly measured more than it had ever measured. No evening I had passed at Bly was to have had the portentous quality of this one; in spite of which — and in spite also of the deeper depths of consternation that had opened beneath my feet — there was literally, in the ebbing actual, an extraordinary sweet sadness. On reaching the house I had never so much as looked for the boy; I had simply gone straight to my room to change what I was wearing and to take in, at a glance, much material testimony to Flora's rupture. Her little belongings had all been removed. When later, by the schoolroom fire, I was served with tea by the usual maid, I indulged, on the article of my other pupil, in no enquiry whatever. He had his freedom now — he might have it to the end! Well, he did have it; and it consisted — in part at least — of his coming in at about eight o'clock and sitting down with me in silence. On the removal of the tea-things I had blown out the candles and drawn my chair closer: I was conscious of a mortal coldness and felt as if I should never again be warm. So when he appeared I was sitting in the glow with my thoughts. He paused a moment by the door as if to look at me; then — as if to share them — came to the other side of the hearth and sank into a chair. We sat there in absolute stillness; yet he wanted, I felt, to be with me.

XXI

BEFORE A NEW DAY, in my room, had fully broken, my eyes opened to Mrs. Grose, who had come to my bedside with worse news. Flora was so markedly feverish that an illness was perhaps at hand; she had passed a night of extreme unrest, a night agitated above all by fears that had for their subject not in the least her former but wholly her present governess. It was not against the possible re-entrance of Miss Jessel on the scene that she protested — it was conspicuously and passionately against mine. I was at once on my feet, and with an immense deal to ask; the more that my friend had discernibly now girded her loins to meet me afresh. This I felt as soon as I had put to her the question of her sense of the child's sincerity as against my own. "She persists in denying to you that she saw, or has ever seen, anything?"

My visitor's trouble truly was great. "Ah Miss, it isn't a matter on which I can push her! Yet it isn't either, I must say, as if I much needed to. It has made her, every inch of her, quite old."

"Oh I see her perfectly from here. She resents, for all the world like some high little personage, the imputation on her truthfulness and, as it were, her respectability. 'Miss Jessel indeed — she!' Ah she's 'respectable,' the chit! The impression she gave me there yesterday was, I assure you, the very strangest of all: it was quite beyond any of the others. I *did* put my foot in it! She'll never speak to me again."

Hideous and obscure as it all was, it held Mrs. Grose briefly silent; then she granted my point with a frankness which, I made sure, had more behind it. "I think indeed, Miss, she never will. She do have a grand manner about it!"

"And that manner" — I summed it up — "is practically what's the matter with her now."

Oh that manner, I could see in my visitor's face, and not a little else besides! "She asks me every three minutes if I think you're coming in."

"I see — I see." I too, on my side, had so much more than worked it out. "Has she said to you since yesterday — except to repudiate her familiarity with anything so dreadful — a single other word about Miss Jessel?"

"Not one, Miss. And of course, you know," my friend added, "I took it from her by the lake that just then and there at least there *was* nobody."

"Rather! And naturally you take it from her still."

"I don't contradict her. What else can I do?"

"Nothing in the world! You've the cleverest little person to deal with. They've made them — their two friends, I mean — still cleverer even than nature did; for it was wondrous material to play on! Flora has now her grievance, and she'll work it to the end."

"Yes, Miss; but to *what* end?"

"Why that of dealing with me to her uncle. She'll make me out to him the lowest creature — !"

I winced at the fair show of the scene in Mrs. Grose's face; she looked for a minute as if she sharply saw them together. "And him who thinks so well of you!"

"He has an odd way — it comes over me now," I laughed, " — of proving it! But that doesn't matter. What Flora wants of course is to get rid of me."

My companion bravely concurred. "Never again to so much as look at you."

132

"So that what you've come to me now for," I asked, "is to speed me on my way?" Before she had time to reply, however, I had her in check. "I've a better idea — the result of my reflections. My going *would* seem the right thing, and on Sunday I was terribly near it. Yet that won't do. It's *you* who must go. You must take Flora."

My visitor, at this, did speculate. "But where in the world — ?"

"Away from here. Away from *them*. Away, even most of all, now, from me. Straight to her uncle."

"Only to tell on you — ?"

"No, not 'only'! To leave me, in addition, with my remedy."

She was still vague. "And what *is* your remedy?"

"Your loyalty, to begin with. And then Miles's."

She looked at me hard. "Do you think he — ?"

"Won't, if he has the chance, turn on me? Yes, I venture still to think it. At all events I want to try. Get off with his sister as soon as possible and leave me with him alone." I was amazed, myself, at the spirit I had still in reserve, and therefore perhaps a trifle the more disconcerted at the way in which, in spite of this fine example of it, she hesitated. "There's one thing, of course," I went on: "they mustn't, before she goes, see each other for three seconds." Then it came over me that, in spite of Flora's presumable sequestration from the instant of her return from the pool, it might already be too late. "Do you mean," I anxiously asked, "that they *have* met?"

At this she quite flushed. "Ah Miss, I'm not such a fool as that! If I've been obliged to leave her three or four times, it has been each time with one of the maids, and at present, though she's alone, she's locked in safe. And yet — and yet!" There were too many things.

"And yet what?"

"Well, are you so sure of the little gentleman?"

"I'm not sure of anything but *you*. But I have, since last evening a new hope. I think he wants to give me an opening. I do believe that — poor little exquisite wretch! — he wants to speak. Last evening, in the firelight and the silence, he sat with me for two hours as if it were just coming."

Mrs. Grose looked hard through the window at the grey gathering day. "And did it come?"

"No, though I waited and waited I confess it didn't, and it was without a breach of the silence, or so much as a faint allusion to his sister's condition and absence, that we at last kissed for good-night. All the same," I continued, "I can't, if her uncle sees her, consent to his seeing her brother without my having given the boy — and most of all because things have got so bad — a little more time."

My friend appeared on this ground more reluctant than I could quite understand. "What do you mean by more time?"

"Well, a day or two — really to bring it out. He'll then be on *my* side — of which you see the importance. If nothing comes I shall only fail, and you at the worst have helped me by doing on your arrival in town whatever you may have found possible." So I put it before her, but she

134

continued for a little so lost in other reasons that I came again to her aid. "Unless indeed," I wound up, "you really want *not* to go."

I could see it, in her face, at last clear itself: she put out her hand to me as a pledge. "I'll go — I'll go. I'll go this morning."

I wanted to be very just. "If you *should* wish still to wait I'd engage she shouldn't see me."

"No, no: it's the place itself. She must leave it." She held me a moment with heavy eyes, then brought out the rest. "Your idea's the right one. I myself, Miss — "

"Well?"

"I can't stay."

The look she gave me with it made me jump at possibilities. "You mean that, since yesterday, you *have* seen — ?"

She shook her head with dignity. *"I've heard — !"*

"Heard?"

"From that child — horrors! There!" she sighed with tragic relief. "On my honour, Miss, she says things — !" But at this evocation she broke down; she dropped with a sudden cry upon my sofa and, as I had seen her do before, gave way to all the anguish of it.

It was quite in another manner that I for my part let myself go. "Oh thank God!"

She sprang up again at this, drying her eyes with a groan. " 'Thank God?' "

"It so justifies me!"

"It does that, Miss!"

I couldn't have desired more emphasis, but I just waited. "She's so horrible?"

I saw my colleague scarce knew how to put it. "Really shocking."

"And about me?"

"About you, Miss — since you must have it. It's beyond everything, for a young lady; and I can't think wherever she must have picked up — "

"The appalling language she applies to me? I can then!" I broke in with a laugh that was doubtless significant enough.

It only in truth left my friend still more grave. "Well, perhaps I ought to also — since I've heard some of it before! Yet I can't bear it," the poor woman went on while with the same movement she glanced, on my dressing-table, at the face of my watch. "But I must go back."

I kept her, however. "Ah if you can't bear it — "

"How can I stop with her, you mean? Why just *for* that: to get her away. Far from this," she pursued, "far from *them* — "

"She may be different? she may be free?" I seized her almost with joy. "Then in spite of yesterday you *believe* — "

"In such doings?" Her simple description of them required, in the light of her expression, to be carried no further, and she gave me the whole thing as she had never done. "I believe."

Yes, it was a joy, and we were still shoulder to shoulder: if I might continue sure of that I should care but little what else happened. My support in the presence of disaster would be the same as it had been in my early need of confidence, and if my friend would answer for my honesty I would answer for all the rest.

On the point of taking leave of her, none the less, I was to some extent embarrassed. "There's one thing of course — it occurs to me — to remember. My letter giving the alarm will have reached town before you."

I now felt still more how she had been beating about the bush and how weary at last it had made her. "Your letter won't have got there. Your letter never went."

"What then became of it?"

"Goodness knows! Master Miles — "

"Do you mean *he* took it?" I gasped.

She hung fire, but she overcame her reluctance. "I mean that I saw yesterday, when I came back with Miss Flora, that it wasn't where you had put it. Later in the evening I had the chance to question Luke, and he declared that he had neither noticed nor touched it." We could only exchange, on this, one of our deeper mutual soundings, and it was Mrs. Grose who first brought up the plumb with an almost elate "You see!"

"Yes, I see that if Miles took it instead he probably will have read it and destroyed it."

"And don't you see anything else?"

I faced her a moment with a sad smile. "It strikes me that by this time your eyes are open even wider than mine."

They proved to be so indeed, but she could still almost blush to show it. "I make out now what he must have done at school." And she gave, in her simple sharpness, an almost droll disillusioned nod. "He stole!"

I turned it over — I tried to be more judicial. "Well — perhaps."

She looked as if she found me unexpectedly calm. "He stole *letters!*"

She couldn't know my reasons for a calmness after all pretty shallow; so I showed them off as I might. "I hope then it was to more purpose than in this case! The note, at all events, that I put on the table yesterday," I pursued, "will have given him so scant an advantage — for it contained only the bare demand for an interview — that he's already much ashamed of having gone so far for so little, and that what he had on his mind last evening was precisely the need of confession." I seemed to myself for the instant to have mastered it, to see it all. "Leave us, leave us" — I was already, at the door, hurrying her off. "I'll get it out of him. He'll meet me. He'll confess. If he confesses, he's saved. And if he's saved — "

"Then *you* are?" The dear woman kissed me on this, and I took her farewell. "I'll save you without him!" she cried as she went.

XXII

YET IT WAS WHEN SHE HAD GOT OFF — and I missed her on the spot — that the great pinch really came. If I had counted on what it would give me to find myself alone with Miles I quickly recognised that it would give me at least a measure. No hour of my stay in fact was so assailed with apprehensions as that of my coming down to learn that the carriage containing Mrs. Grose and my younger pupil had already rolled out of the gates. Now I *was*, I said to myself, face

to face with the elements, and for much of the
rest of the day, while I fought my weakness, I
could consider that I had been supremely rash.
It was a tighter place still than I had yet turned
round in; all the more that, for the first time, I
could see in the aspect of others a confused reflexion of the crisis. What had happened naturally caused them all to stare; there was too little of the explained, throw out whatever we
might, in the suddenness of my colleague's act.
The maids and the men looked blank; the effect
of which on my nerves was an aggravation until
I saw the necessity of making it a positive aid. It
was in short by just clutching the helm that I
avoided total wreck; and I dare say that, to bear
up at all, I became that morning very grand and
very dry. I welcomed the consciousness that I was
charged with much to do, and I caused it to be
known as well that, left thus to myself, I was
quite remarkably firm. I wandered with that
manner, for the next hour or two, all over the
place and looked, I have no doubt, as if I were
ready for any onset. So, for the benefit of whom
it might concern, I paraded with a sick heart.

The person it appeared least to concern
proved to be, till dinner, little Miles himself. My
perambulations had given me meanwhile no
glimpse of him, but they had tended to make
more public the change taking place in our relation as a consequence of his having at the piano,
the day before, kept me, in Flora's interest, so beguiled and befooled. The stamp of publicity had
of course been fully given by her confinement
and departure, and the change itself was now

ushered in by our non-observance of the regular custom of the schoolroom. He had already disappeared when, on my way down, I pushed open his door, and I learned below that he had breakfasted — in the presence of a couple of the maids — with Mrs. Grose and his sister. He had then gone out, as he said, for a stroll; than which nothing, I reflected, could better have expressed his frank view of the abrupt transformation of my office. What he would now permit this office to consist of was yet to be settled: there was at the least a queer relief — I mean for myself in especial — in the renouncement of one pretension. If so much had sprung to the surface I scarce put it too strongly in saying that what had perhaps sprung highest was the absurdity of our prolonging the fiction that I had anything more to teach him. It sufficiently stuck out that, by tacit little tricks in which even more than myself he carried out the care for my dignity, I had had to appeal to him to let me off straining to meet him on the ground of his true capacity. He had at any rate his freedom now; I was never to touch it again: as I had amply shown, moreover, when, on his joining me in the schoolroom the previous night, I uttered, in reference to the interval just concluded, neither challenge nor hint. I had too much, from this moment, my other ideas. Yet when he at last arrived the difficulty of applying them, the accumulations of my problem, were brought straight home to me by the beautiful little presence on which what had occurred had as yet, for the eye, dropped neither stain nor shadow.

To mark, for the house, the high state I cultivated I decreed that my meals with the boy should be served, as we called it, downstairs; so that I had been awaiting him in the ponderous pomp of the room outside the window of which I had had from Mrs. Grose, that first scared Sunday, my flash of something it would scarce have done to call light. Here at present I felt afresh — for I had felt it again and again — how my equilibrium depended on the success of my rigid will, the will to shut my eyes as tight as possible to the truth that what I had to deal with was, revoltingly, against nature. I could only get on at all by taking "nature" into my confidence and my account, by treating my monstrous ordeal as a push in a direction unusual, of course, and unpleasant, but demanding, after all, for a fair front, only another turn of the screw of ordinary human virtue. No attempt, none the less, could well require more tact than just this attempt to supply, one's self, *all* the nature. How could I put even a little of that article into a suppression of reference to what had occurred? How on the other hand could I make a reference without a new plunge into the hideous obscure? Well, a sort of answer, after a time, had come to me, and it was so far confirmed as that I was met, incontestably, by the quickened vision of what was rare in my little companion. It was indeed as if he had found even now — as he had so often found at lessons — still some other delicate way to ease me off. Wasn't there light in the fact which, as we shared our solitude, broke out with a specious glitter it had never yet quite worn? —

the fact that (opportunity aiding, precious opportunity which had now come) it would be preposterous, with a child so endowed, to forgo the help one might wrest from absolute intelligence? What had his intelligence been given him for but to save him? Mightn't one, to reach his mind, risk the stretch of a stiff arm across his character? It was as if, when we were face to face in the dining-room, he had literally shown me the way. The roast mutton was on the table and I had dispensed with attendance. Miles, before he sat down, stood a moment with his hands in his pockets and looked at the joint, on which he seemed on the point of passing some humorous judgment. But what he presently produced was: "I say, my dear, is she really very awfully ill?"

"Little Flora? Not so bad but that she'll presently be better. London will set her up. Bly had ceased to agree with her. Come here and take your mutton."

He alertly obeyed me, carried the plate carefully to his seat and, when he was established, went on. "Did Bly disagree with her so terribly all at once?"

"Not so suddenly as you might think. One had seen it coming on."

"Then why didn't you get her off before?"

"Before what?"

"Before she became too ill to travel."

I found myself prompt. "She's *not* too ill to travel; she only might have become so if she had stayed. This was just the moment to seize. The journey will dissipate the influence" — oh I was grand! — "and carry it off."

"I see, I see" — Miles, for that matter, was grand too. He settled to his repast with the charming little "table manner" that, from the day of his arrival, had relieved me of all grossness of admonition. Whatever he had been expelled from school for, it wasn't for ugly feeding. He was irreproachable, as always, today; but was unmistakably more conscious. He was discernibly trying to take for granted more things than he found, without assistance, quite easy; and he dropped into peaceful silence while he felt his situation. Our meal was of the briefest — mine a vain pretense, and I had the things immediately removed. While this was done Miles stood again with his hands in his little pockets and his back to me — stood and looked out of the wide window through which, that other day, I had seen what pulled me up. We continued silent while the maid was with us — as silent, it whimsically occurred to me, as some young couple who, on their wedding-journey, at the inn, feel shy in the presence of the waiter. He turned round only when the waiter had left us. "Well — so we're alone!"

XXIII

"OH, MORE OR LESS." I imagine my smile was pale. "Not absolutely. We shouldn't like that!" I went on.

"No — I suppose we shouldn't. Of course we've the others."

"We've the others — we've indeed the others," I concurred.

"Yet even though we have them," he returned, still with his hands in his pockets and planted there in front of me, "they don't much count, do they?"

I made the best of it, but I felt wan. "It depends on what you call 'much.' "

"Yes" — with all accommodation — "everything depends!" On this, however, he faced to the window again and presently reached it with his vague restless cogitating step. He remained there awhile with his forehead against the glass, in contemplation of the stupid shrubs I knew and the dull things of November. I had always my hypocrisy of "work," behind which I now gained the sofa. Steadying myself with it there as I had repeatedly done at those moments of torment that I have described as the moments of my knowing the children to be given to something from which I was barred, I sufficiently obeyed my habit of being prepared for the worst. But an extraordinary impression dropped on me as I extracted a meaning from the boy's embarrassed back — none other than the impression that I was not barred now. This inference grew in a few minutes to sharp intensity and seemed bound up with the direct perception that it was positively *he* who was. The frames and squares of the great window were a kind of image, for him, of a kind of failure. I felt that I saw him, in any case, shut in or shut out. He was admirable but not comfortable: I took it in with a throb of hope. Wasn't he looking through the haunted pane for something he couldn't see? — and wasn't it the first time in the whole business that he had known such a lapse? The first, the very first: I found it a splendid portent. It made him anxious, though he watched himself; he had been anxious all day and, even while in his usual sweet little manner he sat at table, had needed all his small strange genius to give it a gloss. When he at last turned round to meet me it was almost as if this genius had succumbed. "Well, I think I'm glad Bly agrees with *me!*"

"You'd certainly seem to have seen, these twenty-four hours, a good deal more of it than for some time before. I hope," I went on bravely, "that you've been enjoying yourself."

"Oh yes, I've been ever so far; all round about — miles and miles away. I've never been so free."

He had really a manner of his own, and I could only try to keep up with him. "Well, do you like it?"

He stood there smiling; then at last he put into two words — "Do *you?*" — more discrimination than I had ever heard two words contain. Before I had time to deal with that, however, he continued as if with the sense that this was an impertinence to be softened. "Nothing could be more charming than the way you take it, for of course if we're alone together now it's you that are alone most. But I hope," he threw in, "you don't particularly mind!"

"Having to do with you?" I asked. "My dear child, how can I help minding? Though I've renounced all claim to your company — you're so beyond me — I at least greatly enjoy it. What else should I stay on for?"

He looked at me more directly, and the expression of his face, graver now, struck me as the most beautiful I had ever found in it. "You stay on just for *that?*"

"Certainly. I stay on as your friend and from the tremendous interest I take in you till something can be done for you that may be more worth your while. That needn't surprise you." My voice trembled so that I felt it impossible to suppress the shake. "Don't you remember how I told you, when I came and sat on your bed the night of the storm, that there was nothing in the world I wouldn't do for you?"

"Yes, yes!" He, on his side, more and more visibly nervous, had a tone to master; but he was so much more successful than I that, laughing out through his gravity, he could pretend we were pleasantly jesting. "Only that, I think, was to get me to do something for *you!*"

"It was partly to get you to do something," I conceded. "But, you know, you didn't do it."

"Oh yes," he said with the brightest superficial eagerness, "you wanted me to tell you something."

"That's it. Out, straight out. What you have on your mind, you know."

"Ah then, is *that* what you've stayed over for?"

He spoke with a gaiety through which I could still catch the finest little quiver of resentful passion; but I can't begin to express the effect upon me of an implication of surrender even so faint. It was as if what I had yearned for had come at last only to astonish me. "Well, yes — I may as well make a clean breast of it. It was precisely for that."

He waited so long that I supposed it for the purpose of repudiating the assumption on which my action had been founded; but what he finally said was: "Do you mean now — here?"

"There couldn't be a better place or time." He looked round him uneasily, and I had the rare — oh the queer! — impression of the very first symptom I had seen in him of the approach of immediate fear. It was as if he were suddenly afraid of me — which struck me indeed as perhaps the best thing to make him. Yet in the very pang of the effort I felt it vain to try sternness, and I heard myself the next instant so gentle as to be almost grotesque. "You want so to go out again?"

"Awfully!" He smiled at me heroically, and the touching little bravery of it was enhanced by his actual flushing with pain. He had picked up his hat, which he had brought in, and stood twirling it in a way that gave me, even as I was just nearly reaching port, a perverse horror of what I was doing. To do it in *any* way was an act of violence, for what did it consist of but the obtrusion of the idea of grossness and guilt on a small helpless creature who had been for me a revelation of the possibilities of beautiful intercourse? Wasn't it base to create for a being so exquisite a mere alien awkwardness? I suppose I now read into our situation a clearness it couldn't have had at the time, for I seem to see our poor eyes already lighted with some spark of a prevision of the anguish that was to come. So we circled about with terrors and scruples, fighters not daring to close. But it was for each other we feared! That kept us a little longer suspended and unbruised. "I'll tell you everything," Miles said — "I mean I'll tell you anything you like. You'll stay on with me, and we shall both be all right and I *will* tell you — I *will*. But not now."

"Why not now?"

My insistence turned him from me and kept him once more at his window in a silence during which, between us, you might have heard a pin drop. Then he was before me again with the air of a person for whom, outside, someone who had frankly to be reckoned with was waiting. "I have to see Luke."

I had not yet reduced him to quite so vulgar a lie, and I felt proportionately ashamed. But, horrible as it was, his lies made up my truth. I achieved thoughtfully a few loops of my knitting. "Well then go to Luke, and I'll wait for what you promise. Only, in return for that satisfy, before you leave me, one very much smaller request."

He looked as if he felt he had succeeded enough to be able still a little to bargain. "Very much smaller — ?"

"Yes, a mere fraction of the whole. Tell me" — oh my work preoccupied me, and I was off-hand! — "if, yesterday afternoon, from the table in the hall, you took, you know, my letter."

XXIV

MY GRASP OF HOW HE RECEIVED THIS suffered for a minute from something that I can describe only as a fierce split of my attention — a stroke that at first, as I sprang straight up, reduced me to the mere blind movement of getting hold of him, drawing him close and, while I just fell for support against the nearest piece of furniture, instinctively keeping him with his back to the window. The appearance was full upon us that I had already had to deal with here: Peter Quint had come into view like a sentinel before a prison. The next thing I saw was that, from outside, he had reached the window, and then I knew that, close to the glass and glaring in through it, he offered once more to the room his white face of damnation. It represents but grossly what took place within me at the sight to say that on the second my decision was made; yet I believe that no woman so overwhelmed ever in so short a time recovered her command of the *act*. It came to me in the very horror of the immediate presence that the act would be, seeing and facing what I saw and faced, to keep the boy himself unaware. The inspiration — I can call it by no other name — was that I felt how voluntarily, how transcendently, I *might*. It was like fighting with a demon for a human soul, and when I had fairly so appraised it I saw how the human soul — held out, in the tremor of my hands, at arm's length — had a perfect dew of sweat on a lovely childish forehead. The face that was close to mine was as white as the face against the glass, and out of it presently came a sound, not low nor weak, but as if from much further away, that I drank like a waft of fragrance.

"Yes — I took it."

At this, with a moan of joy, I enfolded, I drew him close; and while I held him to my breast, where I could feel in the sudden fever of his little body the tremendous pulse of his little heart, I kept my eyes on the thing at the window and saw it move and shift its posture. I have likened it to a sentinel, but its slow wheel, for a moment, was rather the prowl of a baffled beast. My present quickened courage, however, was such that, not too much to let it through, I had to shade, as it were, my flame. Meanwhile the glare of the face was again at the window, the scoundrel fixed as if to watch and wait. It was the very confidence that I might now defy him, as well as the positive certitude, by this time, of the child's unconsciousness, that made me go on. "What did you take it for?"

"To see what you said about me."

"You opened the letter?"

"I opened it."

My eyes were now, as I held him off a little again, on Miles's face, in which the collapse of mockery showed me how complete was the ravage of uneasiness. What was prodigious was that at last, by my success, his sense was sealed and his communication stopped: he knew that he was in presence, but knew not of what, and knew still less that I also was and that I did know. And what did this strain of trouble matter when my eyes went back to the window only to see that the air was clear again and — by my personal triumph — the influence quenched? There was nothing there. I felt that the cause was mine and that I should surely get *all*. "And you found nothing!" — I let my elation out.

He gave the most mournful, thoughtful little headshake. "Nothing."

"Nothing, nothing!" I almost shouted in my joy.

"Nothing, nothing," he sadly repeated.

I kissed his forehead; it was drenched. "So what have you done with it?"

"I've burnt it."

"Burnt it?" It was now or never. "Is that what you did at school?"

Oh what this brought up! "At school?"

"Did you take letters? — or other things?"

"Other things?" he appeared now to be thinking of something far off and that reached him only through the pressure of his anxiety. Yet it did reach him. "Did I *steal?*"

I felt myself redden to the roots of my hair as well as wonder if it were more strange to put to a gentleman such a question or to see him take it with allowances that gave the very distance of his fall in the world. "Was it for that you mightn't go back?"

The only thing he felt was rather a dreary little surprise. "Did you know I mightn't go back?"

"I know everything."

He gave me at this the longest and strangest look. "Everything?"

"Everything. Therefore *did* you — ?" But I couldn't say it again.

Miles could, very simply. "No. I didn't steal."

My face must have shown him I believed him utterly; yet my hands — but it was for pure tenderness — shook him as if to ask him why, if it was all for nothing, he had condemned me to months of torment. "What then did you do?"

He looked in vague pain all round the top of the room and drew his breath, two or three times over, as if with difficulty. He might have been standing at the bottom of the sea and raising his eyes to some faint green twilight. "Well — I said things."

"Only that?"

"They thought it was enough!"

"To turn you out for?"

Never, truly, had a person "turned out" shown so little to explain it as this little person! He appeared to weigh my question, but in a manner quite detached and almost helpless. "Well, I suppose I oughtn't."

"But to whom did you say them?"

He evidently tried to remember, but it dropped — he had lost it. "I don't know!"

He almost smiled at me in the desolation of his surrender, which was indeed practically, by this time, so complete that I ought to have left it there. But I was infatuated — I was blind with victory, though even then the very effect that was to have brought him so much nearer was already that of added separation. "Was it to everyone?" I asked.

"No; it was only to — " But he gave a sick little headshake. "I don't remember their names."

"Were they then so many?"

"No — only a few. Those I liked."

Those he liked? I seemed to float not into clearness, but into a darker obscure, and within a minute there had come to me out of my very pity the appalling alarm of his being perhaps innocent. It was for the instant confounding and bottomless, for if he *were* innocent, what then on earth was I? Paralysed, while it lasted, by the mere brush of the question, I let him go a little, so that, with a deep-drawn sigh, he turned away from me again; which, as he faced towards the clear window, I suffered, feeling that I had nothing now there to keep him from. "And did they repeat what you said?" I went on after a moment.

He was soon at some distance from me, still breathing hard and again with the air, though now without anger for it, of being confined against his will. Once more, as he had done before, he looked up at the dim day as if, of what had hitherto sustained him, nothing was left but an unspeakable anxiety. "Oh yes," he nevertheless replied — "they must have repeated them. To those *they* liked," he added.

There was somehow less of it than I had expected; but I turned it over. "And these things came round — ?"

"To the masters? Oh yes!" he answered very simply. "But I didn't know they'd tell."

"The masters? They didn't — they've never told. That's why I ask you."

He turned to me again his little beautiful fevered face. "Yes, it was too bad."

"Too bad?"

"What I suppose I sometimes said. To write home."

I can't name the exquisite pathos of the contradiction give to such a speech by such a speaker; I only know that the next instant I heard myself throw off with homely force: "Stuff and nonsense!" But the next after that I must have sounded stern enough. "What *were* these things?"

My sternness was all for his judge, his executioner; yet it made him avert himself again, and that movement made *me*, with a single bound and an irrepressible cry, spring straight upon him. For there again, against the glass, as if to blight his confession and stay his answer, was the hideous author of our woe — the white face of damnation. I felt a sick swim at the drop of my victory and all the return of my battle, so that the wildness of my veritable leap only served as a great betrayal. I saw him, from the midst of my act, meet it with a divination, and on the perception that even now he only guessed, and that the window was still to his own eyes free, I let the impulse flame up to convert the climax of his dismay into the very proof of his liberation. "No more, no more, no more!" I shrieked to my visitant as I tried to press him against me.

"Is she *here*?" Miles panted as he caught with his sealed eyes the direction of my words. Then as his strange "she" staggered me and, with a gasp, I echoed it, "Miss Jessel, Miss Jessel!" he with a sudden fury gave me back.

I seized, stupefied, his supposition — some sequel to what we had done to Flora, but this made me only want to show him that it was better still than that. "It's not Miss Jessel! But it's at the window — straight before us. It's *there* — the coward horror, there for the last time!"

At this, after a second in which his head made the movement of a baffled dog's on a scent and then gave a frantic little shake for air and light, he was at me in a white rage, bewildered, glaring vainly over the place and missing wholly, though

154

it now, to my sense, filled the room like the taste of poison, the wide, overwhelming presence. "It's *he?*"

I was so determined to have all my proof that I flashed into ice to challenge him. "Whom do you mean by 'he'?"

"Peter Quint — you devil!" His face gave again, round the room, its convulsed supplication. *"Where?"*

They are in my ears still, his supreme surrender of the name and his tribute to my devotion. "What does he matter now, my own? — what will he *ever* matter? *I* have you," I launched at the beast, "but he has lost you for ever!" Then for the demonstration of my work, "There, *there!*" I said to Miles.

But he had already jerked straight round, stared, glared again, and seen but the quiet day. With the stroke of the loss I was so proud of he uttered the cry of a creature hurled over an abyss, and the grasp with which I recovered him might have been that of catching him in his fall. I caught him, yes, I held him — it may be imagined with what a passion; but at the end of a minute I began to feel what it truly was that I held. We were alone with the quiet day, and his little heart, dispossessed, had stopped.

✦ THE PUPIL

THE POOR YOUNG MAN HESITATED and procrastinated: it cost him such an effort to broach the subject of terms, to speak of money to a person who spoke only of feelings and, as it were, of the aristocracy. Yet he was unwilling to take leave, treating his engagement as settled, without some more conventional glance in that direction than he could find an opening for in the manner of the large affable lady who sat there drawing a pair of soiled *gants de Suède* through a fat jewelled hand and, at once pressing and gliding, repeated over and over everything but the thing he would have liked to hear. He would have liked to hear the figure of his salary; but just as he was nervously about to sound that note the little boy came back — the little boy Mrs. Moreen had sent out of the room to fetch her fan. He came back without the fan, only with the casual observation that he couldn't find

As he dropped this cynical confession he

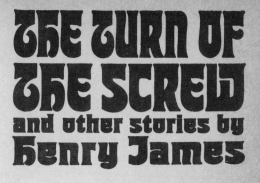

THE TURN OF THE SCREW

and other stories by

Henry James

Teaching Guide

By Kenneth McElheny

The Phillips Exeter Academy, Arlington School

Part I
A Guide to Approaching Henry James

The language and rhetoric of Henry James will seem very demanding to most students; the average student will need much guidance as he goes through the stories in this collection. Before beginning to read at all, however, the student might be strengthened for the task through writing experimentation of his own. Some suggested writing assignments follow.

Naturally, there are many ways these four stories may be used in the classroom, many ways they may fit into various writing programs. The suggestions in this guide will reflect one way I deal with James.

The following writing assignments are designed (1) to lead to a better understanding of "point of view" and (2) to provide notes for, or fragments of, complete themes. According to the teacher's judgment, according to the writing already in progress, they might be 50 to about 500 words.

Sequence A

1. ......nt of a moment in which you struck ......ou hit a tennis ball; you were struck ......pit).

......nts (only a few of endless possibili-......ence: Write an account of (a) a ......other person disagreed; (b) an ......hile you were moving (slowly) ......a vehicle) (on foot); (c) an incident which involves two characters and a projectile (a baseball, a sling-stone).

2. Transform this account into the third person, as if you were the main character in a story.

3. Tell about the same incident, in either first or third person, but from the point of view of another participant.

Sequence B

1. Write for 5 to 15 minutes whatever comes into your mind, without stopping to think or organize. (These papers need not — probably should not — be read by anyone else.)

2. Underline in the above stream-of-consciousness material any hint of your relationship to another person. If you really find none, choose any one-to-one relationship you can think of now.

3. Record for 5 or 10 minutes everything which comes into your mind about this relationship.

4. At least a day later, repeat No. 3.

5. Using both 3 and 4, compose a brief sketch of your relationship, told from your own point of view.

6. Revise 5, making it a story told by an author. Reveal only what you as the main character would have observed and understood.

7. Still in the third person, revise 6, making the other party to the relationship the main character; tell the story through his (her) eyes.

In addition to the notes and questions which follow, certain standard questions based on the student's understanding of the above writing experiences can be applied to the four stories in the collection, as they are read.

1. Is the story in first or third person?

2. How much does a first-person narrator really *know* about what he is observing? How do you go about understanding anything he doesn't seem to tell you?

How many eyes does the author, in third person, see

through? How many minds does he go into? Does he let the reader know what is happening mainly (a) by letting the reader simply see what the character(s) sees; or (b) by telling the reader directly what is going on? What combination of these two techniques is used?

3. Do the characters in "The Pupil" and "The Tree of Knowledge" seem to understand as much as you do?

Do the first-person narrators of "The Figure in the Carpet" and "The Turn of the Screw" seem to understand as much as you do about what they are relating to you?

4. The tutor in "The Pupil" and the governess in "The Turn of the Screw" appear to be "good" parents who try to offset the influence of "bad" parents. Are they equally well-meaning?

5. James, the author, chooses to tell the story of "The Pupil" in the third person, while the governess is given the task of telling her own story. Why? Why does James provide such an elaborate introduction, also in the first person, to the governess's manuscript?

6. Peter Brench, the viewpoint figure in "The Tree of Knowledge," and the narrator of "The Figure in the Carpet" are both involved in the pursuit of knowledge.

Peter only gradually realizes the extent of his ignorance. James tells his story, like the tutor's, in the third person. When the third person is used, the reader cannot always be sure just how much the main character understands.

The "searcher" in "The Figure in the Carpet" knows nearly the full extent of his ignorance. He, like the governess, is entrusted with the narration of his own story; his manuscript is given no elaborate introduction. Generally the first person tells the reader all he knows; one can judge directly how much he seems to understand.

Why might James wish to give the reader closer access to the "searcher's" mind than to Brench's? Why, similarly, closer access to the governess's mind than to Pemberton's?

"Peter had turned red . . . There was now . . . in his young friend a strange, an adopted insistence . . . 'She [Lance's mother, Mrs. Mallow] cares only for my father,' said Lance the Parisian." This quotation from the ending of "The Tree of Knowledge" provides a good example of James's mode of storytelling, of his handling of knowledge in all four of the stories in this collection.

In "The Tree of Knowledge" James sets the literary camera on the shoulder, and at times in the mind, of Peter, the older of the two characters above. Occasionally —and quite noticeably at the end of the story—the author picks up the camera and aims it at Peter himself. In the sentence, " 'She cares only for my father,' said Lance the Parisian," knowledge is conveyed to Peter and to the reader through a slight shift in point of view. Although, for much of the story, the camera has been placed behind Peter's eyes or at least at the end of his nose, it has just been turned on him sharply, when we see his "red" face.

For most of the story Peter has been a sharp observer of all the feelings and doings of the three Mallows: father, son, and mother; he has been aware of all their limitations, and of his own too. Now the tables are turned on him; there is something he has missed, and Lance has found it: Mrs. Mallow, too, knows that Mr. Mallow's work is worthless. But having allowed Lance to take Peter down a peg, James restores the balance of the story, casting a gentle beam of irony on Lance too. In the phrase, "Lance the Parisian" all of Lance's own self-delusion, exemplified by his pompous search for himself in Paris, is brought out.

It is through just such combinations of point of view and word choice that "the tree of knowledge" bears fruit for characters and readers in all four of these stories.

Tempting as it might seem to start with "The Turn of the Screw," a mystery, it would probably be a good idea to begin with the relatively short uncomplicated "The Tree of Knowledge," to have students simply read it through without much introduction, then begin the discussion of it with them, guided by the questions on the story in Part II. Possibly you might send some of those questions home with them to look at as they read the story. Once the story has been read, and with the help of some probing, what has happened in it been established, the real discussion of the story might begin with the phrase, "Lance the Parisian":

In what sense is Lance (not) a Parisian?

Has it been good, even if painful, for him to become one?

Why has it been important for Peter to believe that Mrs. Mallow has been taken in by her husband's work?

Looking back at the story, is Peter right at the end; is it true that he tried to keep Lance from finding out *anything* in order to keep himself from finding out anything *more*?

Now that "The Tree of Knowledge" has been read and taken in (though not exhausted), the irony suggested in the phrase "Lance the Parisian" can be taken up again at the start of "The Pupil." This can be done in class, reading over the first page or so in class, before the students are asked to read it. One can begin with the first line: "The *poor* young man hesitated . . ." Here again is a combination of word choice and point of view. Already the third-person approach has been established — the reader is plunged right into an employment interview at the elbow of "poor" Pemberton. In the use of the single word "poor," James has set the tone of the story; he has hinted at the attitude the reader may take toward Pemberton; Pemberton is "poor," a viewpoint figure to be taken with a grain of salt. The inadequacy of Pemberton to deal, singlehanded, with life is confirmed throughout the story and most forcefully at the end, when it turns out that he is completely unequal to the challenge of looking after Morgan Moreen.

To emphasize this point, look back with the students at the opening paragraph of "The Tree of Knowledge": Peter's success in keeping to himself his true opinion of Mallow's sculpture is "a triumph," * one "which had its honour even for a man of other triumphs." Peter is someone the reader can, and should, rely on, judge favorably. His new "knowledge" should break upon the reader as it breaks on Peter. But from the very beginning of "The Pupil," James serves warning, the reader must be on his guard as he looks through the eyes of Pemberton. The reader must not be taken in as much as Pemberton is.

Once this introductory discussion has taken place, the students should go on to read the story, "The Pupil," again perhaps accompanied by some of the questions on the story in Part II. Once read, the story is ready for the discussion given the previous one, again focused on particular phrases at the end:

Is Mr. Moreen right in saying that Morgan had not really wanted to go with Pemberton?

Mrs. Moreen thought Morgan *wanted* to go to" Pemberton; has Morgan's death really proved her wrong?

Morgan has implied throughout the story, and said so at times, that he cares more for Pemberton than his family. Mrs. Moreen, too, speaks of this. Has Morgan really felt that way all along?

Even while wanting to "escape" from his parents, as any child may at times, no child will want his parents to agree to the idea easily. Does Morgan die because his parents seem to force "escape" upon him?

As he dies, Morgan seems to be joining the rest of his family in taking from another (Pemberton), giving nothing in return. Do you see Pemberton or Morgan as the greater victim of circumstances?

Just what *are* Pemberton's motives in being so self-sacrificing? Does James give us enough clues?

---

* Even if such a "triumph," like "remaining unmarried," is at most an empty victory.

At the end of the story, who now appears to be "The Pupil"?

Now that certain aspects of point of view have been dealt with, in the two less demanding stories, the students are ready to deal with the shift from third to first person. As most of us are aware, a large proportion of fiction — short fiction in particular — is told in the third person and through the eyes, ears, and other senses of a single character. Much of the time, in order not to "break the spell," not to destroy the reader's identification with tne single character, the author will not exercise his option to break into that single character's consciousness. Although the reader of "The Pupil" is on his own most of the time, words like "poor" in the first line are used to place the reader on his guard; although Peter Brench in "The Tree of Knowledge" is allowed to seek the respect of the reader by himself most of the time, James intervenes at crucial moments: when Peter is off balance, James gently reminds us that Lance is a partly foolish "Parisian."

In moving to the first-person narratives to follow, the student must begin to think about how he will judge the two viewpoint figures — neither of them named — who will tell the stories themselves. James, the all-powerful author, will now be in the background; he will not be able to intervene so easily as to label the governess "poor" or the literary critic "Parisian." James must control the reader's response to his narrators by controlling what *they* observe and experience, and what *they* say about it. In reading first "The Figure in the Carpet" the student will sharpen his ability to evaluate the reliability of a narrator without the direct help of the author.

Once again, beginnings and endings would be worth discussing in advance. As the students approach reading "The Figure in the Carpet" one might discuss both stories' beginnings with them, without spoiling suspense in "The Turn of the Screw" in any way. When the literary critic narrator begins, "I had done a few things and earned a few pence," one might suspect false pride. When he reveals his feeling that his colleague Corvick has done more and earned more pence "though there were chances for cleverness I thought he sometimes missed," he also reveals a jealous tendency — something for the reader to watch out for. But when he generously concedes that Corvick also never misses a chance "for kindness," he has fairly well established himself as a level-headed, reliable narrator. One simply does not know yet how clever or perceptive he is.

In taking a preliminary look at the governess-narrator, the reader might be inclined to think pretty well of her, too. The governess sounds pretty well-balanced, at the beginning, and even throughout the tale; she is judicious, thoughtful: She remembers her decision as "a little seesaw of the right throbs and the wrong" — she does not rush to conclusions. "I suppose I had expected, or had dreaded, something so dreary that what had greeted me was a good surprise." She is well-meaning, ready to correct herself. Throughout the story, the reader will want to sympathize with her. The "right" estimate of her is still very much disputed by the critics. Consciously or unconsciously, James must have intended this. He simply does not make it unequivocally clear how much to believe (in) the governess. Some critics argue that James's family's interest in and experience with psychology must have made him familiar with Freud; they argue that one must view the governess's problem as one of hysteria: she sees apparitions which reflect her own personal conflicts and problems. Other critics point out that James more than once spoke of this story as hack work, "a pot-boiler," a ghost story to be enjoyed but not fought over. Leon Edel, perhaps the critic of critics of James, in a preface to Volume X of *The Collected Tales of Henry James,* suggests a middle course: the young lady does see *something;* read for yourself.

In any case, it is probably clear where the author stands on the first three stories in the volume; the opinion one forms at the beginning of each of the viewpoint-figures can probably be counted on; the governess's constant appearance of reasonableness, of hesitation to believe in the outlandish, is harder to evaluate. Having simply glanced at the opening page or two of the governess's manuscript, one might set aside the question of Douglas's long preface to her story until students have read and discussed "The Figure in the Carpet."

Do you share the critic's pleasure in his "revenge"?

Do he and Deane both really believe there *is* a figure in the carpet?

Is it possible that Mrs. Corvick/Deane did not know, and pretended to out of animosity or dislike for the critic?

Is it possible that Vereker meant critics finally to know that "the figure in the carpet" could not be described in fewer words than there were in all of his work?

Now that the first three stories have been "downed," and the question of what has really "happened" to the governess been touched upon, "The Turn of the Screw" might now be approached in two stages. First, ask the students to read only the introduction about Douglas's manuscript.

On the basis of the introduction alone, how reliable do you expect the governess's narrative to be?

Douglas read "with a fine clearness" which seemed to recapture the beauty of the governess's own telling, "the beauty of his [Douglas's] author's hand." With this statement the narrator of the introduction leaves you. Does he leave you expecting to sympathize with the governess? What other references to the governess in the introduction might predispose you to sympathize with her?

At the end of the introduction, are you inclined to *trust,* to rely on, the governess as a reporter of events?

Will she be reliable as an evaluator, a judge, of the events she reports?

Having analyzed in some detail the influences in the introduction the reader does not usually stop to recognize, the student is ready to go on to read the governess's manuscript itself. The discussion of it after reading might return to her opening remarks; the students might remind themselves of how they felt on first reading them, and ask whether they would view them any differently now.

Does the governess seem, at the start, to be the woman Douglas, who had held the manuscript so long, admired?

Does Douglas's view of her lend credit to her reporting?

Once this has been explored, move to the end of the story.

The governess says she "was so determined to have all my proof that I flashed into ice . . ." Was the governess determined to have the truth? What does she mean by "my proof"?

What *has* Miles seen? He had stared — at what?

When he glared again, he had seen only "the quiet day." Why, if Quint had been visible to the governess, had Quint disappeared so quickly?

Just as the governess points out Quint to Miles, saying "There, there!" Quint has evidently disappeared: He has gone in a "stroke"; the governess is proud of this loss. This stroke leads to Miles's death.

Did the governess cause Miles's death?

Did Quint cause it by disappearing?

Who really administered this final turn of the screw?

If Quint's disappearance has triggered the death itself, but the governess has triggered the disappearance, is she still responsible for Miles's death?

Would the screw have turned so far if the governess had not insisted on defeating the Jessel-Quint influence? Was her interference worth the death of Miles, or was her victory too costly?

Does the governess reveal any clues which back up her version of the mystery? Is there any evidence other than what she provides that Flora or Miles, or anyone else, has seen the apparitions of Quint and Jessel?

Are the apparitions the governess sees real?

If they are not, what is the story about?

If they are real, is the story more about them, or more about the governess's reactions to them?

Part II
Notes and Questions About the Four Stories

The following questions might be handed out, or played out like rope, to the students, either just before class discussion or for reference at home while reading. The teacher might wish to withhold the further questions in Part I about beginnings and endings for oral presentation. Or the teacher might, if individual students or student panels are to lead discussion, give those questions only to those students.

Notes and Questions, "The Tree of Knowledge"

1. **Page 222, lines 11-16.** Is it also a triumph to reach fifty, to escape marriage? Is it admirable to have lived within your means, to have loved another man's wife for years and kept quiet about it? What do you think of a man who has judged himself once and for all?

2. **Page 225, lines 31-34.** Morgan Mallow looked like a flattering self-portrait in the Uffizi gallery which is given over to such self-portraits.

3. **Page 226, lines 8, 9.** The Mallows' pleasures and pains seem to appear in "delicate morsels." Does James expect the reader to sympathize?

4. **Page 226, line 34; page 227, line 1.** Mrs. Mallow says Peter knows nothing of artistic passion. Has she forgotten his writing, or is she dismissing it? Having learned

more of Mrs. Mallow at the end of the story, return to this question.

5. Lines 1, 2. Mrs. Mallow has asserted that her husband's artistic passion has not burned out. Can there have been any to burn? What is Peter thinking as he keeps up a sound "between a smothered whistle and a subdued hum"? Line 5. What does Peter mean when he asks whether Lance will be another master?

6. Lines 8, 9. Mrs. Mallow is quick to interpret what Peter means. Is she right?

7. Lines 20, 21. Mrs. Mallow says Lance will share his father's satisfaction. Just what does she mean, "He'll *know*"? (What?)

8. Lines 24, 25. Can Mrs. Mallow be right? Is she impatient because Peter will not see the truth, or is she doubtful herself?

9. Lines 22, 23. How strongly does Peter hint here at his true feelings? Is it possible that Mrs. Mallow realizes Peter is hinting at a lack of respect for Mallow's work? Return to this question at the end of the story.

10. **Page 228.** Is there a difference (line 14) between what Lance means by "to know" and what his mother meant on page 227?

11. Line 21. *Does* Peter think Lance has no talent? Is there any evidence that Peter knows any of Lance's work? Peter does not answer Lance's question. Why not?

12. Line 28. How *does* Peter know? James tells us that Peter's way of answering is his "queer" trick of kindness. What does the word "kind" imply about Peter's attitude?

13. Lines 29, 30. *Is* it Peter's own ignorance he is defending? Return to this question at the end of the story.

14. **Page 229,** line 13. Why does Peter parry Lance's question?

15. **Page 230,** lines 4, 5. Do you agree with Lance's (and the Master's?) definition of success?

16. Lines 17, 18. Why did Lance's innocence "perversely" give Peter a chill?

17. Line 18. Did Lance believe in "cabals and things,"

the cliques which refused to recognize the Master's work?

18. **Page 232,** lines 33-35. How would success have spoiled the Mallows' innocence? How would a small, constant, commercial success have affected Mallow's self-esteem? Might it have led to "the worst" (p. 230)?

19. **Page 233,** lines 4-5. Had the Mallows escaped vulgarity simply by avoiding — or not achieving — success?

20. Line 27. What does Mrs. Mallow mean, *Lance* must sell?

21. Lines 31, 32. Is Mallow confident that Lance will learn to sell?

22. Lines 33, 34; page 234, lines 1, 2. What would Peter not hear of?

23. Lines 19-21. What is Mrs. Mallow afraid of?

24. **Page 235,** line 29. Why is Peter relieved?

25. Line 27. What does Peter refuse to tell?

26. **Page 240,** lines 6-10. Why had the Mallows ceased to confide in Peter?

27. Line 20. What sort of success had Lance's father been?

28. **Page 241,** line 12. Should Lance be hypocritical?

Notes and Questions, "The Pupil"

1. **Page 156,** line 1. Does the word "poor" make you sympathize with, or look down upon, the "young man"?

2. "The Tree of Knowledge" begins with almost five pages of information about the characters and their situation. Why do you suppose James plunges the reader into the story of "The Pupil" without such preparation? Do the introductory pages of "Tree" help the reader to judge Peter Brench's intelligence, or understanding? Why might James prefer to leave you on your own to judge Pemberton's intelligence?

3. Lines 2-5. Why does Pemberton care about what Mrs. Moreen would think of his mentioning money?

4. Line 10. Putting the phrase "suede gloves" in French suggests a habit of the circle in which the Moreens

probably move, just as James means to tell a good deal about the Mallows by naming their home "Carrara Lodge." What does the word "soiled," contrasting so sharply with the elegant French, suggest about Mrs. Moreen? Return to this question at the end of the story.

5. In this first paragraph, do we see everything through the eyes of Pemberton? Does the author seem to impose his view in any way? Is the phrase "gants de suede" the author's comment on Mrs. Moreen, or is it Pemberton's?

6. **Page 160,** line 3. What is Mrs. Moreen warning Pemberton to expect?

7. Line 5. What does Morgan mean, "The less you expect the better!" Return to this question at end of story.

8. **Page 161,** lines 11, 12. What might Mrs. Moreen be afraid Morgan might say?

9. **Page 163,** lines 27-34; **page 164,** lines 1, 2. Why does James make such a point of reminding us that much time has passed between the happening and telling of the tale? Why does he want the reader to know now that Pemberton's connection with the Moreens has been over for a long time?

10. Line 5. How are the Moreens so obviously equipped for failure?

11. Line 12. What "gypsy" trick have the Moreens played on Pemberton?

12. Line 17. What are the "reversed conventions" of the Moreens?

13. Lines 13, 14. Why did their antics at his expense amuse him? Did he realize the extent of his expense?

14. **Page 167,** lines 11, 12. Why should the Moreens give up somebody's "day" for Morgan's sake?

15. Lines 25-27. What would Morgan find out? Is there anything to know about the Moreens that Morgan does not appear already to know?

16. **Page 169,** lines 1-3. Is Pemberton right in thinking school would not have been good for Morgan?

17. Line 22. In what ways is Morgan still a child? What toys does he smash?

18. **Page 170,** line 18. Does Pemberton really expect Morgan to believe him?

19. Line 23. Why does Pemberton change color?

20. Line 25. Why does Morgan, too, turn red? Does this scene remind you in any way of the one in which Peter Brench turns red in conversation with Lance Mallow?

21. **Page 171,** lines 3-5. What moment is Pemberton recalling? What understanding has now broadened? Who has understood so much, Morgan or Pemberton? Why has it taken him so long?

22. **Page 172,** lines 1-3. What is Pemberton fighting against realizing? Does James expect us to be aware of it now, ahead of Pemberton?

23. Line 11. Does James mean here by "knowledge" what he mean by it in "Tree"?

24. **Page 173,** lines 21, 22. Why does James make a point of saying, at this point, that Pemberton's Paris memories have subsequently blurred?

25. Line 27. Why does Pemberton still remember so vividly the holes in Morgan's stockings, if he cannot separate, in his memory, whole spans of time?

26. **Page 174,** lines 1-3. James has pointed out earlier how unusual Morgan's understanding is. Why should he now point out that Morgan is capable of joking about being in such places as the elegant Louvre art museum with holes in his stockings?

27. **Page 176,** line 23. What is Mr. Moreen's idea of being a man of the world?

28. **Page 179,** line 5. Why does the fact that the Moreens try to ingratiate themselves with people above make them adventurers? Do you agree with this idea of Pemberton's?

29. Line 10. How has Morgan prepared Pemberton to see his family as toadies and snobs?

30. Lines 11-13. What information about the Moreens can there be yet to reveal? Why has James emphasized the extent of Pemberton's ignorance at this point?

31. Page 180, line 24. Why does Morgan press Pemberton to leave?

32. Page 182, line 7. What does Morgan mean by "the stern reality"?

33. Line 24. Why does Morgan cry?

34. Page 183, line 8. Why might the Moreens want Morgan to know that they don't pay Pemberton?

35. Page 185, line 19. How much difference is there, really, between paid and free services, as far as Pemberton is concerned?

36. Page 186, line 1. Does Mrs. Moreen really not know what Pemberton means?

37. Line 31. Is Mrs. Moreen aware of the irony of speaking of earning to a "servant" she doesn't pay?

38. Page 187, lines 9, 10. Pemberton is bending over backward to be so polite; why does he go so far out of his way?

39. Line 18. Is Mrs. Moreen fair in accusing Pemberton, in turn, of "blackmail"?

40. Page 188, line 4. Does Pemberton guess right about what goes on in Mrs. Moreen's mind? What was her "stronger" impulse?

41. Page 190, lines 9-12. Why should it be a punishment to find yourself the only gentleman in your family?

42. Lines 16-19. Naturally Pemberton is "drawn on" by curiosity; but what "scruple" slows him in investigating the deeper waters of Morgan's nature?

43. Lines 20-24. Is this a reference to any childhood, or just Morgan's? Is Morgan's childhood like "morning twilight . . . never fixed . . . already flushing faintly into" daylight?

44. Line 24. What does James mean here by "knowledge"?

45. Lines 26-28. Is it true that Pemberton really does

not know enough to be able to repair Morgan's situation?

46. **Page 194,** lines 7, 8. Why does it sicken people when they are allowed to treat you badly?

47. Line 30. Is Pemberton admitting that Morgan is partly right, that Pemberton is staying on without pay to "finish" Morgan off for his own satisfaction?

48. **Page 195,** line 10. In what way *is* Morgan Pemberton's tutor?

49. Line 28. Is Pemberton admitting that Morgan is right, that Pemberton does not expect Morgan's heart condition to allow him to live?

50. **Page 201,** lines 25-28. Why is Morgan so unrealistic about college plans when he is so realistic about his parents?

51. **Page 204,** lines 5-7. Why does Pemberton sympathize with Mrs. Moreen?

52. **Page 205,** line 21. Why does Morgan reject Pemberton's attempt to speak kindly of his family?

53. **Page 207,** lines 25-29. What is there, probably, in Morgan's letters which Pemberton is afraid would not be properly respected if he showed them to his present pupil?

54. **Page 209,** lines 11-14. What had Pemberton done earlier to suggest he might put up with Mrs. Moreen's deceitfulness now?

55. Lines 29, 30. Does Morgan really hope Pemberton will take him away?

56. **Page 210,** line 7. Does Mrs. Moreen really feel Morgan is an idol? How might it be an advantage to her to believe that Morgan is extraordinary?

57. **Page 211,** lines 8, 9. Would Morgan's life with Pemberton be any more "hand-to-mouth" than it is?

58. Lines 19, 20. "Don't you agree, dear?" says Mrs. Pemberton; does she really expect Morgan to agree? What emotion, in line 22, does her "surging" around the room suggest?

59. **Page 212,** lines 3-10. Pemberton is sadly amused, Morgan seems so ill, that Morgan should claim not to

need him. Does Pemberton take this view in order to rationalize staying with Morgan?

60. **Page 213**, line 31. Why does James emphasize, "as Pemberton was to see," that Pemberton again has failed to judge the Moreens' situation?

61. **Page 221**, line 4. Why does Mrs. Moreen's showing love for Morgan show lack of respect for "the idol"?

62. Line 19. Lance had to leave home "to know." Morgan expires at the prospect of leaving home; is he afraid that *he* will come "to know"?

63. Line 25. Does James mean here by "man of the world" what he meant on page 207? Why does the story end on such a cold note?

64. Has Pemberton become Morgan's pupil in the same way Peter became Lance's?

65. Why do foreign phrases appear frequently in "The Pupil," fairly often in "The Figure in the Carpet," but hardly at all in "The Turn of the Screw"? The Mallows and Brench in "The Tree of Knowledge" are perhaps cosmopolitan. Why don't more elegant foreign phrases turn up in their story?

Notes and Questions, "The Figure in the Carpet"

1. **Page 245**, lines 20, 21. Why does the critic emphasize the distance in time between when the story happened and the time he is now writing?

2. Line 33. Is this remark offensive?

3. **Page 246**, line 30. Why not compare Vereker's work to others'?

4. **Page 247**, lines 7-10. How does the critic manage to show that Vereker's work is not the best?

5. Lines 18, 19. If the critic had written that Vereker was not "the best," why is he afraid that Vereker will feel that he laid his compliments on "too thick"?

6. Lines 21-23. Is the critic cold-blooded about Mrs. Erme?

7. **Page 245**, line 22; page 248, lines 25-30. Why does

the critic take such pains to confess how innocent, stupid, he had been? What effect does the narrator expect these confessions to have on the reader?

8. **Page 248, lines 16, 17.** Does Vereker mean he doesn't care what people think of his work?

9. **Lines 25, 26.** Is Vereker's success as independent of popularity as Mallow's? Does the critic's favorable notice in *The Middle* correspond to "popular" success?

10. **Line 29.** If the critics really have "caught up" with Vereker, if he really has lost his "mystery," what are Corvick and the critic still looking for?

11. **Page 252, line 3.** "My acute little study." Is the critic still indignant, or is he now smiling at himself as he narrates?

12. **Lines 34, 35.** Why is the critic so quick to dismiss his own work?

13. **Page 253, line 10.** The critic again emphasizes that time has passed in saying "as I afterwards knew." Watch for evidence supporting this statement.

14. **Page 254, lines 12-14.** Why does Vereker particularly regret the failure of a young critic to understand him?

15. **Lines 22, 23.** Why does the critic let the reader know *now,* so soon, that his search for the truth about Vereker's work will not succeed, at least not entirely?

16. **Line 26.** Is Vereker himself at fault if his work is incompletely understood?

17. **Page 257, lines 2-5.** If keeping his secret is as important to him as his work, can Vereker really have left it out for all to see?

18. **Line 12.** Why need not Vereker worry?

19. **Page 258, lines 12, 13, 33-35.** Is Vereker implying that his scheme will be less great if unraveled? James's story touches on the usefulness of critics: If a literary scheme can be condensed and explained at all, why should it be written out in fiction at any greater length?

20. **Page 259, lines 29, 30.** Does Vereker think his "buried treasure" really cannot be described by a critic?

Or does he feel this particular critic is unequal to the chase?

21. Lines 31, 32. Is Vereker's advice designed simply to save the critic's peace of mind or to imply the secret cannot be found?

22. **Page 260**, lines 30-32. Is Vereker's scheme a joke? If so, does he know it?

23. **Page 262**, line 34; **page 263**, line 1. If Vereker has been so certain the riddle will not be solved by a critic, why does he want to conceal his interview with the critic?

24. **Page 264**, lines 12. 13. Is Vereker really "indifferent" or just trying to seem so?

25. Lines 31-34. Although he agrees that his secret is like a complicated design in an oriental rug, Vereker also says it's something very simple, like a string for pearls. Is he contradicting himself?

26. **Page 265**, lines 6, 7. Is there any particular significance in the fact that the critic was never—he makes a point of telling us—to see Vereker again? If he is never to see Vereker again, will he be able to verify any discovery by mail?

27. Lines 8, 9. Is it likely that a writer would calculate his effects as precisely as a critic would describe them?

28. **Page 267**, lines 20, 21. How did critics (Mr. Snooks-Joe Doakes) know there *was* a mystery to solve? Lines 21-23. The critic refers to the critics who have found hidden "figures" or hidden patterns in Shakespeare's work even without Shakespeare's saying there were any; the critic wonders whether Vereker's *saying* there is one in his work is convincing.

29. Lines 33, 34. Does the critic really think Vereker is a fake?

30. **Page 272**, line 7. Is the critic right? Lines 18, 19. Is Corvick only trying to pretend he has given up the chase?

31. Line 21. What does the critic mean here by "knowledge" in the first two stories?

32. **Page 273**, lines 31, 32. Is it true that when you see "the real thing" you know it?

33. **Page 274**, lines 24, 25. Was the difference of thought or surroundings which showed Corvick the light the same difference of thought which showed Lance the light in Paris?

34. **Page 275**, lines 7-9. Do you share the critic's suspicion, or is he just jealous?

35. **Page 278**, line 32. Why is Gwendolyn astonished that the critic does not know of her engagement?

36. **Page 279**, line 20. Does Gwendolyn seem to want to marry Corvick more for his own sake or for the secret's sake?

37. **Page 279**, Section VIII. Henry James simply was less concerned about too many coincidences than with unraveling points of view.

38. **Page 281**, lines 6-8. Did Corvick really mean to "soothe" the critic? Why does the critic once again so strongly emphasize the difference between his feelings "then and now" — and so strongly emphasize that subsequent events did not fill in the facts that Corvick did not provide in the letter?

39. **Page 282**, lines 14-19. Why, once again, does James rudely shatter suspense, refuse to allow the reader to enjoy wondering "how it all came out"?

40. **Page 283**. Why does James have Gwendolyn so conveniently escape unhurt? Often an author will try to foster the illusion that he is recounting "the way it happened." James, in this story particularly, seems to keep saying "This is the way I invented it." Why?

41. Line 34. Why does the critic compare Vereker's secret, Corvick's discovery, to an "idol"? Does the comparison compliment Vereker's scheme?

42. **Page 284**, line 2. Once again James emphasizes knowledge. Does he mean here "understanding" or simply the possession of facts?

43. Lines 26-30. Does Mrs. Corvick's possession of the secret compensate for her husband's death?

44. **Page 285,** line 5. Is the critic hinting here that as he writes he knows the secret?

45. Lines 14, 15. Is the critic just too eager?

46. Lines 15-20. Do you share the critic's attitude toward Mrs. Corvick? Has he, or the author, made it possible for you to think better of her than the critic does?

47. Line 25. In speaking of his "luckless" idea, has the critic revealed without doubt that as he writes he does not know the secret?

48. **Page 286,** lines 9, 10. Was the secret only for the married?

49. Line 35. What is Mrs. Corvick's life — fidelity to her husband's memory, or selfish clinging to a secret?

50. **Page 287,** line 19. Why should Mrs. Corvick be so sensitive?

51. Line 28. Whose peeping face might there be?

52. Lines 32, 33. How does the critic know the figure in Mrs. Corvick's book is not the one he is looking for?

53. **Page 289,** lines 21, 22. Will it be an advantage to Mrs. Corvick to have Vereker dead?

54. Lines 22-30. Vereker told Corvick he had "got it" (the secret). But can even the author be sure?

55. **Page 290,** line 7. By admitting he has compared Mrs. Corvick unfavorably to himself, does the critic seem to regain some of his impartiality?

56. Lines 12-14. Is it really just "delicacy" that kept the critic from going to Vereker? Why would it have been so hard for him to admit defeat to Vereker?

57. Lines 21, 22. Was the critic just in saying "he couldn't read" Vereker?

58. **Page 292,** lines 6-8. Why doesn't Deane take up Vereker? Is James just prolonging the suspense?

59. **Page 293,** lines 30, 31. Must the author himself approve the truth in so many words?

60. **Page 294,** line 35. Does the phrase "mouth of the cave" give any further hint about the truth? Why the last-minute shift to such a different comparison?

61. **Page 297,** lines 18, 19. Is Deane in the same condition as the critic? How far can one trust the critic's version of the outcome?

Notes and Questions, "The Turn of the Screw"

1. **Page 16,** line 26. What does the governess mean by "a sense of 'knowing' me"? Is James using the word "know" in the same sense he has before?

2. **Page 17,** lines 7-11. Again we have the narrator strongly stressing the long interval between the happening and the telling of the tale. Why? The entire introduction serves to provide this stress too. Why? The introduction mentions that the governess conceded that her manuscript would show she was in love with her employer. Does that admission, in addition to this admission that her vision of the tower was distorted, suggest that she is a reliable narrator?

3. **Lines 24, 25.** The governess felt at the time as if she were the helm of a great, drifting ship. Does she imply here that she was wrong to see things that way?

4. **Page 18,** lines 15-17. Why does the governess not reveal to the reader what was in the letter?

5. **Lines 21, 22.** What effect is created by withholding the information until it is told to Mrs. Grose?

6. **Lines 23-25.** Is Mrs. Grose surprised?

7. **Line 26.** Why doesn't Mrs. Grose finish her question? Has the governess interrupted her?

8. **Page 20,** lines 17-19. Is the reader, too, convinced that Flora had followed the governess out of affection?

9. **Page 21,** line 7. The governess has picked up the habit of leaving sentences in the air. Why?

10. **Page 21,** line 33. Mrs. Grose had caught herself up. Does she mean the master?

11. **Page 23,** lines 21-31; page 24, lines 1-5. How would you compare Miles to Morgan Moreen?

12. **Page 26,** lines 18, 19. Is it true that the governess only wishes approval?

13. Lines 15, 16, 30. Why did the governess jump to the conclusion that the figure on the tower was her employer?

14. **Page 35,** lines 30, 31. Having been mistaken once before, should the governess be sure of what she sees? Describing the figure the way she does, is there any chance that she is having a hallucination?

15. **Page 36,** lines 22, 23. What does the governess mean by "knowledge" here?

16. **Page 37,** line 32. Why should Mrs. Grose have been so scared?

17. **Page 38,** lines 10, 11. Why has the governess stopped needing to treat Mrs. Grose with kid gloves?

18. **Page 42,** line 22. Mrs. Grose recognizes the governess's description. Is there evidence Mrs. Grose has seen any ghosts too?

19. **Page 43,** lines 13-17. Does Mrs. Grose believe that the governess has seen an apparition of Quint?

20. **Page 45,** line 1. How does the governess know? Line 3. Mrs. Grose does not "deny" that she knows, does she? What attitude does she take toward the governess?

21. **Page 46,** lines 19-23. Why does the governess avoid going into the question of what "too free" meant? Does James prefer that we supply our own details?

22. Lines 25-27. Why should it matter that the estate has had no previous scandals or mysteries?

23. **Page 47,** line 13. Why does the governess criticize Mrs. Grose for not going to the master when she knows she herself is not supposed to?

24. Line 26. Later in the story Mrs. Grose will insist that she did have some responsibility for the children. Return to this note when she does. Ask yourself why she contradicts herself.

25. **Page 48,** lines 9, 10. What is it, the governess thinks, that Mrs. Grose has not told her?

26. Lines 12-17. The governess tells the reader that within a day she had already come to "know" — to read into the facts before her — all that she would in the

subsequent three quarters of her narrative. Why, then, does it go on so long?

27. **Page 50,** lines 17-27. Is the governess at all disturbed that she seems to have been more the children's audience than their governess?

28. **Page 51,** lines 2-4. To have an "interested spectator," as the governess says, is a strange enough "knowledge." Why is "the way this knowledge gathered" almost equally strange? Does James here mean by "knowledge" what he meant in "The Tree of Knowledge"?

29. **Page 52,** lines 4, 5. How will the governess assure herself of the positive identity of the apparition? Has she seen it or the actual person represented by it before?

30. **Page 53,** line 2. Does Flora see anything? What *did* the governess have to face? Are you convinced she did face it? Why does she drop the subject?

31. Lines 7, 8. How does the governess know that the children also know about the apparitions? How did little Flora hint at knowing?

32. Line 20. How does the governess know Flora saw if she did not utter a word?

33. Lines 25, 26. Mrs. Grose, too, wonders how the governess knew. Does the governess give a satisfactory answer?

34. **Page 54,** line 18. Why is the governess so sure the apparition was Miss Jessel?

35. **Page 55,** lines 7-9. What evidence has the governess that Flora will "keep it up"?

36. Line 19. What does Mrs. Grose mean? How can Flora's consorting with a demon be proof of her innocence?

37. Line 30. Mrs. Grose still does not openly agree with the governess.

38. **Page 56,** lines 13-15. Does Mrs. Grose appear to believe the governess?

39. Line 29. In taking the governess's hand, does Mrs. Grose believe at last?

40. **Page 57,** lines 2-4, 9. What has Mrs. Grose not

yet spoken of? Have you, as well as the governess, suspected it? Why hasn't the governess mentioned the possibility before? Is this the word (**page 48,** lines 9, 10) Mrs. Grose has withheld?

41. **Page 58,** line 8. Why does Mrs. Grose not want to know what Miss Jessel died of?

42. Lines 29-31. On page 48 the governess had said that she would essentially come to know within a day all she was to know by the end of the story. Here she affirms that there were "depths and possibilities" she had not had courage to investigate. Is the day not up yet, or is the governess's recollection, years later, faulty?

43. **Page 59,** lines 12-14. The governess tells us that Mrs. Grose has become convinced that the governess is telling the truth. Does this assurance remove all doubts? Why does the governess only mention this conversation with Mrs. Grose when she has described previous ones in such detail?

44. Lines 15-20. How else than seeing their ghosts could the governess have known what the apparitions looked like? Does the fact that her testimony fits Mrs. Grose's knowledge prove the governess right once and for all? How do we know that the two descriptions match?

45. Lines 30, 31. What is the governess's new suspicion?

46. Line 32. Is "the day" here referred to the one within which, on page 48, the governess says she learned all there was to learn?

47. **Page 60,** lines 25-32. Has the governess made clear what signs showed that Flora's and Miss Jessel's relationship was habitual?

48. Line 34. What delusion is the governess talking about?

49. **Page 61.** Do any of Flora's actions in lines 8-11 really seem unusual?

50. Line 18. How can the governess be so sure that she has not given herself away to Flora?

51. Lines 24, 25. What might Mrs. Grose be concealing?

52. **Page 63,** lines 10, 11. Miles has lied about spending much time with Quint. Why?

53. **Page 65,** line 21. What deadly view is the governess trying not to take?

54. **Page 68,** lines 18, 19. The governess brings in a reference, once more, to the present day, to the fact that everything has "blown over." Why?

55. **Page 69,** line 23. Are the children unbelievably sweet?

56. Lines 26, 27. Does their trick of one keeping the governess occupied to allow the other to slip away seem at all unlike most children's behavior?

57. **Page 70,** lines 4-6. Why does the governess remind the reader she has survived?

58. Line 7. What is "the heart of it"?

59. Lines 10, 11. What was the impression that had "breathed" on the governess the night of her arrival?

60. **Page 71,** line 4. Does James use the word "breath" here to echo the breath of the first night's impression referred to on page 70?

61. Line 26. What were the governess's first two encounters with Quint?

62. Lines 26, 27. The governess tells us of another apparition. How would James have treated this moment in the third person? Would the author have had to make it clear whether or not he himself believed in the apparition?

63. Line 31. Does Quint's recognition of the governess add to, or affect, the believability of what she testifies here?

64. **Page 72,** line 1. What interest might the governess and Quint have in common to produce a "common" or similar intensity?

65. Lines 1-3. Does the governess say this with any greater or lesser authority than James would? Could the author have described this "dangerous presence" without

taking a stand on the question of whether it was real or not? What would be the effect of "It seemed to the governess that . . ." or "The apparition appeared to the governess . . ." or "There was, on the stair, an apparition"?

66. Line 6. Why had the governess's fear left her?

67. Line 17. Could the governess have imagined all this?

68. Line 23. Is the governess right? Is the silence unnatural? Line 25. Would a real intruder have spoken? Does her report of this episode lend credibility to her narrative?

69. **Page 73,** line 5. In what sense is Quint's back disfigured?

70. **Pages 71-73.** Why had the apparition come at this point? Might Quint have worried about overconfidence on the governess's part? Why?

71. **Page 73,** lines 14, 15. Why has the governess's terror returned?

72. **Page 75,** line 21. Was Flora being caught in a lie?

73. **Page 76,** lines 5, 6. Does the governess intentionally imply that she might have seen Quint outside the house?

74. Line 9. Does the governess say "a woman" because she really is unsure who it is?

75. Line 15. How is the governess so sure "what face" the woman would present?

76. **Page 77,** lines 14, 15, 17, 18. How does the governess know that Flora saw the apparition encountered at the lake?

77. **Page 79,** line 10. Do we know whether Miles can see "the person"?

78. **Page 81,** lines 23, 24. Why doesn't the governess press Miles to explain?

79. **Page 83,** line 12. Does the governess still doubt her own senses? Why not speak to Miles?

80. Line 23. Does Miles's explanation sound sensible?

Why might he wish to be considered "bad" by the governess?

81. **Page 84,** line 31. What is Miles hinting at?

82. **Page 87,** line 35. Does Mrs. Grose mean the governess, too, is mad?

83. **Page 88,** lines 33, 34. Why is the governess so unwilling to call the master into the situation? Does she possibly think he might be right to accuse her of being mad? Is she simply afraid of losing her job?

84. **Page 91,** line 11. Does the governess imply that her nerves have not been soothed?

85. **Page 92,** lines 25, 26. In another moment of detachment the governess refers to "today." Why does she refer to her constant problem as an obsession?

86. **Page 95,** lines 24-27. Why should it be so awkward for the governess to have her employer arrive?

87. Lines 33, 34; **page 96,** line 1. How would frustration have betrayed the governess?

88. **Page 98,** line 22. Why has Miles brought up the night he was "bad"?

89. **Page 99,** line 20. Does the governess "see"?

90. Line 35. Is Miles's plea normal?

91. **Page 100,** line 20. Does the governess know what? Do you? Is this a hint about Quint?

92. **Page 101,** lines 27-29. Why is the question of Miles's dismissal so intolerable?

93. **Page 102,** lines 9-12. Is Miles's consciousness, his plan, unnatural?

94. Line 16. How has the governess "hurt herself" with Miles beyond repair?

95. **Page 104,** lines 6, 7. Are the governess's eyes unsealed? To what? Hasn't she seen this apparition before?

96. **Page 106,** lines 8, 9. Does the governess give an accurate report to Mrs. Grose?

97. **Page 107,** line 16. Has this information come from the recent confrontation with Miss Jessel?

98. **Page 108,** lines 21, 22. Here Mrs. Grose contra-

dicts her earlier statement that she was not responsible. Why?

99. **Page 109,** line 3. Why had Mrs. Grose briefly tried to take over the sending of the message, then changed her mind?

100. **Page 110,** lines 15, 16. What does Miles mean by "all the rest"?

101. **Page 115,** line 7. Has Miles blown out the candle to keep from discussing the situation?

102. **Page 124,** line 18. Why does the governess drop the narrative here before Flora answers?

103. **Page 125,** line 7. Does Mrs. Grose see too?

104. Line 20. Why doesn't the governess let Mrs. Grose speak for herself? How do we know what Mrs. Grose really saw?

105. **Page 135,** line 31. Does what Flora has talked about justify the governess? Might her bad speech refer to bad teaching on Miss Jessel's part? Does Mrs. Grose ever recount precisely what Flora said? Has James made Mrs. Grose squeamish up to now in order to make it realistic that she will not repeat Flora's speech?

106. **Page 136,** line 28. *Does* Mrs. Grose believe? Should she?

107. **Page 138,** line 31; **page 139,** line 1. What elements is the governess "face to face" with? How has she been rash?

108. **Page 143,** line 1. What does little Miles see?

109. **Page 149,** line 5. The governess says "us." Is there any evidence that Miles, too, has seen Quint?

110. **Page 150,** line 16. Is this a reasonable explanation of Miles's taking the letter?

111. Line 35. What had Miles expected to find?

112. **Page 151,** lines 13, 14. Is Miles really surprised?

113. Line 23. What is meant by "everything"?

114. **Page 152,** line 17. What has Miles surrendered?

115. Lines 33, 34. What *was* the governess if Miles was innocent? Here is the governess again, ready to correct herself, reasonable, perhaps unprejudiced.

116. **Page 153**, lines 33, 34. Why *is* Miles so reticent?

117. **Page 154**, line 8. What victory has dropped?

118. Line 11. What may Miles have divined?

119. Line 19. If Miles really *did* say *she,* is his saying it proof of his knowledge? Or has he overheard Mrs. Grose and the governess?

120. Line 33. What causes Miles's rage?

121. **Page 155**, line 7. Does Miles mean the Quint he has seen or the Quint he knows the governess is hysterical about?

122. Why does the manuscript end with the death? Could not "the master" and further speculation by the governess clear up the matter?

123. The governess's tale, and Pemberton's, begin at midstream and end with the deaths of their pupils. Why?

124. Brench's and the critic's tales begin with considerable background information. Why?

125. Brench's situation has been resolved by James, but the three other stories end "up in the air." Why?

126. James develops the governess's tale far more extensively than the other three. Why?

127. Of the four viewpoint figures, who is most (least) convincing? Why?

looked straight and hard at the candidate for the honour of taking his education in hand. This personage reflected somewhat grimly that the first thing he should have to teach his little charge would be to appear to address himself to his mother when he spoke to her — especially not to make her such an improper answer as that.

When Mrs. Moreen bethought herself of this pretext for getting rid of their companion Pemberton supposed it was precisely to approach the delicate subject of his remuneration. But it had been only to say some things about her son that it was better a boy of eleven shouldn't catch. They were extravagantly to his advantage save when she lowered her voice to sigh, tapping her left side familiarly, "And all overclouded by *this,* you know; all at the mercy of a weakness — !" Pemberton gathered that the weakness was in the region of the heart. He had known the poor child was not robust: this was the basis on which he had been invited to treat, through an English lady, an Oxford acquaintance, then at Nice, who happened to know both his needs and those of the amiable American family looking out for something really superior in the way of a resident tutor.

The young man's impression of his prospective pupil who had come into the room as if to see for himself the moment Pemberton was admitted, was not quite the soft solicitation the visitor had taken for granted. Morgan Moreen was somehow sickly without being "delicate," and that he looked intelligent — it is true Pemberton wouldn't have enjoyed his being stupid — only added to the suggestion that, as with his big mouth and big ears he really couldn't be called pretty, he might too utterly fail to please. Pemberton was modest, was even timid; and the chance that his small scholar would prove cleverer than himself had quite figured, to his anxiety, among the dangers of an untried experiment. He reflected, however, that these risks one had to run when one accepted a position, as it was called, in a private family; when as yet one's university honours had, pecuniarily speaking, remained barren. At any rate when Mrs. Moreen got up as to intimate that, since it was understood he would enter upon his duties within the week she would let him off now, he succeeded, in spite of the presence of the child, in squeezing out a phrase about the rate of payment. It was not the fault of the conscious smile which seemed a reference to the lady's expensive identity, it was not the fault of this demonstration, which had, in a sort, both vagueness and point, if the allusion didn't sound rather vulgar. This was exactly because she became still more gracious to reply: "Oh I can assure you that all that will be quite regular."

Pemberton only wondered, while he took up his hat, what "all that" was to amount to — people had such different ideas. Mrs. Moreen's words, however, seemed to commit the family to a pledge definite enough to elicit from the child a strange little comment in the shape of the mocking foreign ejaculation, "Oh la-la!"

Pemberton, in some confusion, glanced at him as he walked slowly to the window with his back turned, his hands in his pockets and the air in

his elderly shoulders of a boy who didn't play.
The young man wondered if he should be able
to teach him to play, though his mother had said
it would never do and that this was why school
was impossible. Mrs. Moreen exhibited no discomfiture; she only continued blandly: "Mr.
Moreen will be delighted to meet your wishes.
As I told you, he has been called to London for
a week. As soon as he comes back you shall have
it out with him."

This was so frank and friendly that the young
man could only reply, laughing as his hostess
laughed: "Oh I don't imagine we shall have
much of a battle."

"They'll give you anything you like," the boy
remarked unexpectedly, returning from the window. "We don't mind what anything costs — we
live awfully well."

"My darling, you're too quaint!" his mother
exclaimed, putting out to caress him a practised
but ineffectual hand. He slipped out of it, but
looked with intelligent innocent eyes at Pemberton, who had already had time to notice
that from one moment to the other his small
satiric face seemed to change its time of life. At
this moment it was infantine, yet it appeared also
to be under the influence of curious intuitions
and knowledges. Pemberton rather disliked precocity and was disappointed to find gleams of it
in a disciple not yet in his teens. Nevertheless
he divined on the spot that Morgan wouldn't
prove a bore. He would prove on the contrary a
source of agitation. This idea held the young
man, in spite of a certain repulsion.

"You pompous little person! We're not extravagant!" Mrs. Moreen gaily protested, making another unsuccessful attempt to draw the boy to her side. "You must know what to expect," she went on to Pemberton.

"The less you expect the better!" her companion interposed. "But we *are* people of fashion."

"Only so far as *you* make us so!" Mrs. Moreen tenderly mocked. "Well then, on Friday — don't tell me you're superstitious — and mind you don't fail us. Then you'll see us all. I'm so sorry the girls are out. I guess you'll like the girls. And, you know, I've another son, quite different from this one."

"He tries to imitate me," Morgan said to their friend.

"He tries? Why he's twenty years old!" cried Mrs. Moreen.

"You're very witty," Pemberton remarked to the child — a proposition his mother echoed with enthusiasm, declaring Morgan's sallies to be the delight of the house.

The boy paid no heed to this; he only enquired abruptly of the visitor, who was surprised afterwards that he hadn't struck him as offensively forward: "Do you *want* very much to come?"

"Can you doubt it after such a description of what I shall hear?" Pemberton replied. Yet he didn't want to come at all; he was coming because he had to go somewhere, thanks to the collapse of his fortune at the end of a year abroad spent on the system of putting his scant patrimony into a single full wave of experience. He had his full wave but couldn't pay the score at his inn. Moreover he had caught in the boy's eyes the glimpse of a far-off appeal.

"Well, I'll do the best I can for you," said Morgan; with which he turned away again. He passed out of one of the long windows; Pemberton saw him go and lean on the parapet of the terrace. He remained there while the young man took leave of his mother, who, on Pemberton's looking as if he expected a farewell from him, interposed with: "Leave him, leave him; he's so strange!" Pemberton supposed her to fear something he might say. "He's a genius — you'll love him," she added. "He's much the most interesting person in the family." And before he could invent some civility to oppose to this she would up with: "But we're all good, you know!"

"He's a genius — you'll love him!" were words that recurred to our aspirant before the Friday, suggesting among many things that geniuses were not invariably loveable. However, it was all the better if there was an element that would make tutorship absorbing: he had perhaps taken too much for granted it would only disgust him. As he left the villa after his interview he looked up at the balcony and saw the child leaning over it. "We shall have great larks!" he called up.

Morgan hung fire a moment and then gaily returned: "By the time you come back I shall have thought of something witty!"

This made Pemberton say to himself "After all he's rather nice."

II

ON THE FRIDAY he saw them all, as Mrs. Moreen had promised, for her husband had come back and the girls and the other son were at home. Mr. Moreen had a white moustache, a confiding manner and, in his buttonhole, the ribbon of a foreign order — bestowed, as Pemberton eventually learned, for services. For what services he never clearly ascertained: this was a point — one of a larger number — that Mr. Moreen's manner never confided. What it emphatically did confide was that he was even more a man of the world than you might first make out. Ulick, the firstborn, was in visible training for the same profession — under the disadvantage as yet, however, of a buttonhole but feebly floral and a moustache with no pretensions to type. The girls had hair and figures and manners and small fat feet, but had never been out alone. As for Mrs. Moreen, Pemberton saw on a nearer view that her elegance was intermittent and her parts didn't always match. Her husband, as she had promised, met with enthusiasm Pemberton's ideas in regard to a salary. The young man had endeavoured to keep these stammerings modest, and Mr. Moreen made it no secret that *he* found them wanting in "style." He further mentioned that he aspired to be intimate with his children, to be their best friend, and that he was always looking out for them. That was what he went off for, to London and other places — to look out; and this vigilance was the theory of life, as well as the real occupation, of the whole family. They all looked out, for they were very frank on the subject of its being necessary. They desired it to be understood that they were earnest people, and also that their fortune, though quite adequate for earnest people, required the most careful administration. Mr. Moreen, as the parent bird, sought sustenance for the nest. Ulick invoked support mainly at the club, where Pemberton guessed that it was usually served on green cloth. The girls used to do up their hair and their frocks themselves, and our young man felt appealed to to be glad, in regard to Morgan's education, that, though it must naturally be of the best, it didn't cost too much. After a little he *was* glad, forgetting at times his own needs in the interest inspired by the child's character and culture and the pleasure of making easy terms for him.

During the first weeks of their acquaintance Morgan had been as puzzling as a page in an unknown language — altogether different from the obvious little Anglo-Saxons who had misrepresented childhood to Pemberton. Indeed the whole mystic volume in which the boy had been amateurishly bound demanded some practice in translation. Today after a considerable interval, there is something phantasmagoric, like a prismatic reflexion or a serial novel, in Pemberton's memory of the queerness of the Moreens. If it were not for a few tangible tokens — a lock of Morgan's hair cut by his own hand, and the half-dozen letters received from him when they were disjoined — the whole episode and the figures

163

peopling it would seem too inconsequent for anything but dreamland. Their supreme quaintness was their success — as it appeared to him for a while at the time; since he had never seen a family so brilliantly equipped for failure. Wasn't it success to have kept him so hatefully long? Wasn't it success to have drawn him in that first morning at *déjeuner,* the Friday he came — it was enough to *make* one superstitious — so that he utterly committed himself, and this not by calculation or on a signal, but from a happy instinct which made them, like a band of gipsies, work so neatly together? They amused him as much as if they had really been a band of gipsies. He was still young and had not seen much of the world — his English years had been properly arid; therefore the reversed conventions of the Moreens — for they had *their* desperate properties — struck him as topsy-turvy. He had encountered nothing like them at Oxford; still less had any such note been struck to his younger American ear during the four years at Yale in which he had richly supposed himself to be reacting against a Puritan strain. The reaction of the Moreens, at any rate, went ever so much further. He had thought himself very sharp that first day in hitting them all off in his mind with the "cosmopolite" label. Later it seemed feeble and colourless — confessedly helplessly provisional.

He yet when he first applied it felt a glow of joy — for an instructor he was still empirical — rise from the apprehension that living with them would really be to see life. Their sociable

strangeness was an imitation of that — their
chatter of tongues, their gaiety and good humour, their infinite dawdling (they were always
getting themselves up, but it took for ever, and
Pemberton had once found Mr. Moreen shaving
in the drawing-room), their French, their Italian
and, cropping up in the foreign fluencies, their
cold tough slices of American. They lived on
macaroni and coffee — they had these articles
prepared in perfection — but they knew recipes
for a hundred other dishes. They overflowed
with music and song, were always humming
and catching each other up, and had a sort
of professional acquaintance with Continental
cities. They talked of "good places" as if they had
been pickpockets or strolling players. They had
at Nice a villa, a carriage, a piano and a banjo,
and they went to official parties. They were
a perfect calendar of the "days" of their friends,
which Pemberton knew them, when they were
indisposed, to get out of bed to go to, and which
made the week larger than life when Mrs.
Moreen talked of them with Paula and Amy.
Their initiations gave their new inmate at first
an almost dazzling sense of culture. Mrs. Moreen
had translated something at some former period
— an author whom it made Pemberton feel
borné never to have heard of. They could
imitate Venetian and sing Neapolitan, and
when they wanted to say something very particular communicated with each other in an ingenious dialect of their own, an elastic spoken cipher
which Pemberton at first took for some *patois* of
one of their countries, but which he "caught on

165

to" as he would not have grasped provincial development of Spanish or German.

"It's the family language — Ultramoreen," Morgan explained to him drolly enough; but the boy rarely condescended to use it himself, though he dealt in colloquial Latin as if he had been a little prelate.

Among all the "days" with which Mrs. Moreen's memory was taxed she managed to squeeze in one of her own, which her friends sometimes forgot. But the house drew a frequented air from the number of fine people who were freely named there and from several mysterious men with foreign titles and English clothes whom Morgan called the Princes and who, on sofas with the girls, talked French very loud — though sometimes with some oddity of accent — as if to show they were saying nothing improper. Pemberton wondered how the Princes could ever propose in that tone and so publicly: he took for granted cynically that this was what was desired of them. Then he recognised that even for the chance of such an advantage Mrs. Moreen would never allow Paula and Amy to receive alone. These young ladies were not at all timid, but it was just the safeguards that made them so candidly free. It was a houseful of Bohemians who wanted tremendously to be Philistines.

In one respect, however, certainly, they achieved no rigour — they were wonderfully amiable and ecstatic about Morgan. It was a genuine tenderness, an artless admiration, equally strong in each. They even praised his beauty, which was small, and were as afraid of him as if they felt him of finer clay. They spoke of him as a little angel and a prodigy — they touched on his want of health with long, vague faces. Pemberton feared at first an extravagance that might make him hate the boy, but before this happened he had become extravagant himself. Later, when he had grown rather to hate the others, it was a bribe to patience for him that they were at any rate nice about Morgan, going on tiptoe if they fancied he was showing symptoms, and even giving up somebody's "day" to procure him a pleasure. Mixed with this too was the oddest wish to make him independent, as if they had felt themselves not good enough for him. They passed him over to the new members of their circle very much as if wishing to force some charity of adoption on so free an agent and get rid of their own charge. They were delighted when they saw Morgan take so to his kind play-fellow, and could think of no higher praise for the young man. It was strange how they contrived to reconcile the appearance, and indeed the essential fact, of adoring the child with their eagerness to wash their hands of him. Did they want to get rid of him before he should find them out? Pemberton was finding them out month by month. The boy's fond family, however this might be, turned their backs with exaggerated delicacy, as if to avoid the reproach of interfering. Seeing in time how little he had in common with them — it was by *them* he first observed it; they proclaimed it with complete humility — his companion was moved to speculate on the mysteries of transmission, the far jumps of heredity. Where his detachment from most of the things they represented had come from was more than an observer could say — it certainly had burrowed under two or three generations.

As for Pemberton's own estimate of his pupil, it was a good while before he got the point of view, so little had he been prepared for it by the smug young barbarians to whom the tradition of tutorship, as hitherto revealed to him, had been adjusted. Morgan was scrappy and surprising, deficient in many properties supposed common to the *genus* and abounding in others that were the portion only of the supernaturally clever. One day his friend made a great stride; it cleared up the question to perceive that Morgan *was* supernaturally clever and that, though the formula was temporarily meagre, this would be the only assumption on which one could successfully deal with him. He had the general quality of a child for whom life had not been simplified by school, a kind of homebred sensibility which might have been bad for himself but was charming for others, and a whole range of refinement and perception — little musical vibrations as taking as picked-up airs — begotten by wandering about Europe at the tail of his migratory tribe. This might not have been an education to recommend in advance, but its results with so special a subject were as appreciable as the marks on a piece of fine porcelain. There was at the same time in him a small strain of stoicism, doubtless the fruit of having had to begin early to bear pain, which counted for pluck and made it of less consequence that he might have been thought at school rather a polyglot little beast. Pemberton indeed quickly found himself rejoicing that school was out of the question: in any million of boys it was probably good for all but one, and Morgan was that millionth. It would have made him comparative and superior — it might have made him really require kicking. Pemberton would try to be school himself — a bigger seminary than five hundred grazing donkeys, so that, winning no prizes, the boy would remain unconscious and irresponsible and amusing — amusing, because, though life was already intense in his childish nature, freshness still made there a strong draught for jokes. It turned out that even in the still air of Morgan's various disabilities jokes flourished greatly. He was a pale lean acute undeveloped little cosmopolite, who liked intellectual gymnastics and who also, as regards the behaviour of mankind, had noticed more things than you might suppose, but who nevertheless had his proper playroom of superstitions, where he smashed a dozen toys a day.

III

At Nice once, toward evening, as the pair rested in the open air after a walk, and looked over the sea at the pink western lights, he said suddenly to his comrade: "Do you like it, you know — being with us all in this intimate way?"

"My dear fellow, why should I stay if I didn't?"

"How do I know you'll stay? I'm almost sure you won't, very long."

"I hope you don't mean to dismiss me," said Pemberton.

Morgan debated, looking at the sunset. "I think if I did right I ought to."

"Well, I know I'm supposed to instruct you in virtue; but in that case don't do right."

"You're very young — fortunately," Morgan went on, turning to him again.

"Oh yes, compared with you!"

"Therefore it won't matter so much if you do lose a lot of time."

"That's the way to look at it," said Pemberton accommodatingly.

They were silent a minute; after which the boy asked: "Do you like my father and my mother very much?"

"Dear me, yes. Charming people."

Morgan received this with another silence; then unexpectedly, familiarly, but at the same time affectionately, he remarked: "You're a jolly old humbug!"

For a particular reason the words made our young man change colour. The boy noticed in an instant that he had turned red, whereupon he turned red himself and pupil and master exchanged a longish glance in which there was a consciousness of many more things than are usually touched upon, even tacitly, in such a relation. It produced for Pemberton an embarrassment; it raised in a shadowy form a question — this was the first glimpse of it — destined to play a singular and, as he imagined, owing to the altogether peculiar conditions, an unprecedented part in his intercourse with his little companion.

Later, when he found himself talking with the youngster in a way in which few youngsters could ever have been talked with, he thought of that clumsy moment on the bench at Nice as the dawn of understanding that had broadened. What had added to the clumsiness then was that he thought it his duty to declare to Morgan that he might abuse him, Pemberton, as much as he liked, but must never abuse his parents. To this Morgan had the easy retort that he hadn't dreamed of abusing them; which appeared to be true: it put Pemberton in the wrong.

"Then why am I a humbug for saying I think them charming?" the young man asked, conscious of a certain rashness.

"Well — they're not your parents."

"They love you better than anything in the world — never forget that," said Pemberton.

"Is that why you like them so much?"

"They're very kind to me," Pemberton replied evasively.

"You *are* a humbug!" laughed Morgan, passing an arm into his tutor's. He leaned against him looking off at the sea again and swinging his long thin legs.

"Don't kick my shins," said Pemberton while he reflected "Hang it, I can't complain of them to the child!"

"There's another reason too," Morgan went on, keeping his legs still.

"Another reason for what?"

"Besides their not being your parents."

"I don't understand you," said Pemberton.

"Well, you will before long. All right!"

He did understand fully before long, but he made a fight even with himself before he confessed it. He thought it the oddest thing to have a struggle with the child about. He wondered he didn't hate the hope of the Moreens for bringing the struggle on. But by the time it began any such sentiment for that scion was closed to him. Morgan was a special case, and to know him was to accept him on his own odd terms. Pemberton had spent his aversion to special cases before arriving at knowledge. When at last he did arrive his quandary was great. Against every interest he had attached himself. They would have to meet things together. Before they went home that evening at Nice the boy had said, clinging to his arm:

"Well, at any rate you'll hang on to the last."

"To the last?"

"Till you're fairly beaten."

"*You* ought to be fairly beaten!" cried the young man, drawing him closer.

IV

A YEAR AFTER he had come to live with them Mr. and Mrs. Moreen suddenly gave up the villa at Nice. Pemberton had got used to suddenness, having seen it practised on a considerable scale during two jerky little tours — one in Switzerland the first summer, and the other late in the winter, when they all ran down to Florence and then, at the end of ten days, liking it much less than they had intended, straggled back in mysterious depression. They had returned to

Nice "for ever," as they said; but this didn't prevent their squeezing, one rainy muggy May night, into a second-class railway-carriage — you could never tell by which class they would travel — where Pemberton helped them to stow away a wonderful collection of bundles and bags. The explanation of this manoeuvre was that they had determined to spend the summer "in some bracing place"; but in Paris they dropped into a small furnished apartment — a fourth floor in a third-rate avenue, where there was a smell on the staircase and the *portier* was hateful — and passed the next four months in blank indigence.

The better part of this baffled sojourn was for the preceptor and his pupil, who, visiting the Invalides and Notre Dame, the Conciergerie and all the museums, took a hundred remunerative rambles. They learned to know their Paris, which was useful for they came back another year for a longer stay, the general character of which in Pemberton's memory today mixes pitiably and confusedly with that of the first. He sees Morgan's shabby knickerbockers — the everlasting pair that didn't match his blouse and that as he grew longer could only grow faded. He remembers the particular holes in his three or four pair of coloured stockings.

Morgan was dear to his mother, but he never was better dressed than was absolutely necessary — partly, no doubt, by his own fault, for he was as indifferent to his appearance as a German philosopher. "My dear fellow, you *are* coming to pieces," Pemberton would say to him in sceptical remonstrance; to which the child would reply, looking at him serenely up and down: "My dear fellow, so are you! I don't want to cast you in the shade." Pemberton could have no rejoinder for this — the assertion so closely represented the fact. If however the deficiencies of his own wardrobe were a chapter by themselves he didn't like his little charge to look too poor. Later he used to say "Well, if we're poor, why, after all, shouldn't we look it?" and he consoled himself with thinking there was something rather elderly and gentlemanly in Morgan's disrepair — it differed from the untidiness of the urchin who plays and spoils his things. He could trace perfectly the degrees by which, in proportion as her little son confined himself to his tutor for society, Mrs. Moreen shrewdly forbore to renew his garments. She did nothing that didn't show, neglected him because he escaped notice, and then, as he illustrated this clever policy, discouraged at home his public appearances. Her position was logical enough — those members of her family who did show had to be showy.

During this period and several others Pemberton was quite aware of how he and his comrade might strike people wandering languidly through the Jardin des Plantes as if they had nowhere to go, sitting on the winter days in the galleries of the Louvre, so splendidly ironical to the homeless, as if for the advantage of the *calorifère*. They joked about it sometimes: it was the sort of joke that was perfectly within the boy's compass. They figured themselves as part of the vast vague hand-to-mouth multitude of the enormous city and pretended they were

174

proud of their position in it — it showed them "such a lot of life" and made them conscious of a democratic brotherhood. If Pemberton couldn't feel a sympathy in destitution with his small companion — for after all Morgan's fond parents would never have let him really suffer — the boy would at least feel it with him, so it came to the same thing. He used sometimes to wonder what people would think they were — to fancy they were looked askance at, as if it might be a suspected case of kidnapping. Morgan wouldn't be taken for a young patrician with a preceptor — he wasn't smart enough; though he might pass for his companion's sickly little brother. Now and then he had a five-franc piece, and except once, when they bought a couple of lovely neckties, one of which he made Pemberton accept, they laid it out scientifically in old books. This was sure to be a great day, always spent on the quays, in a rummage of the dusty boxes that garnish the parapets. Such occasions helped them to live, for their books ran low very soon after the beginning of their acquaintance. Pemberton had a good many in England, but he was obliged to write to a friend and ask him kindly to get some fellow to give him something for them.

If they had to relinquish that summer the advantage of the bracing climate the young man couldn't but suspect this failure of the cup when at their very lips to have been the effect of a rude jostle of his own. This had represented his first blow-out, as he called it, with his patrons; his first successful attempt — though there was little other success about it — to bring

175

them to a consideration of his impossible position. As the ostensible eve of a costly journey the moment had struck him as favourable to an earnest protest, the presentation of an ultimatum. Ridiculous as it sounded, he had never yet been able to compass an uninterrupted private interview with the elder pair or with either of them singly. They were always flanked by their elder children, and poor Pemberton usually had his own little charge at his side. He was conscious of its being a house in which the surface of one's delicacy got rather smudged; nevertheless he had preserved the bloom of his scruple against announcing to Mr. and Mrs. Moreen with publicity that he shouldn't be able to go on longer without a little money. He was still simple enough to suppose Ulick and Paula and Amy might not know that since his arrival he had only had a hundred and forty francs; and he was magnanimous enough to wish not to compromise their parents in their eyes. Mr. Moreen now listened to him, as he listened to every one and to every thing, like a man of the world, and seemed to appeal to him — though not of course too grossly — to try and be a little more of one himself. Pemberton recognized in fact the importance of the character — from the advantage it gave Mr. Moreen. He was not even confused or embarrassed, whereas the young man in his service was more so than there was any reason for. Neither was he surprised — at least any more than a gentleman had to be who freely confessed himself a little shocked — though not perhaps strictly at Pemberton.

176

"We must go into this, mustn't we, dear?" he said to his wife.

He assured his young friend that the matter should have his very best attention; and he melted into space as elusively as if, at the door, he were taking an inevitable but deprecatory precedence. When, the next moment, Pemberton found himself alone with Mrs. Moreen it was to hear her say "I see, I see" — stroking the roundness of her chin and looking as if she were only hesitating between a dozen easy remedies. If they didn't make their push Mr. Moreen could at least disappear for several days. During his absence his wife took up the subject again spontaneously, but her contribution to it was merely that she had thought all the while they were getting on so beautifully. Pemberton's reply to this revelation was that unless they immediately put down something on account he would leave them on the spot and for ever. He knew she would wonder how he would get away, and for a moment expected her to enquire. She didn't for which he was almost grateful to her, so little was he in a position to tell.

"You won't, you *know* you won't — you're too interested," she said. "You *are* interested, you know you are, you dear kind man!" She laughed with almost condemnatory archness, as if it were a reproach — though she wouldn't insist; and flirted a soiled pocket-handkerchief at him.

Pemberton's mind was fully made up to take his step the following week. This would give him time to get an answer to a letter he had dispatched to England. If he did in the event nothing of the sort — that is if he stayed another year and then went away only for three months — it was not merely because before the answer to his letter came (most unsatisfactory when it did arrive) Mr. Moreen generously counted out to him, and again with the sacrifice to "form" of a marked man of the world, three hundred francs in elegant ringing gold. He was irritated to find that Mrs. Moreen was right, that he couldn't at the pinch bear to leave the child. This stood out clearer for the very reason that, the night of his desperate appeal to his patrons, he had seen fully for the time where he was. Wasn't it another proof of the success with which those patrons practised their arts that they had managed to avert for so long the illuminating flash? It descended on our friend with a breadth of effect which perhaps would have struck a spectator as comical, after he had returned to his little servile room, which looked into a close court where a bare dirty opposite wall took, with the sound of shrill clatter, the reflexion of lighted back windows. He had simply given himself away to a band of adventurers. The idea, the word itself, wore a romantic horror for him — he had always lived on such safe lines. Later it assumed a more interesting, almost a soothing, sense: it pointed a moral, and Pemberton could enjoy a moral. The Moreens were adventurers not merely because they didn't pay their debts, because they lived on society, but because their whole view of life, dim and confused and instinctive, like that of clever colour-blind animals, was speculative and rapacious and mean. Oh they

178

were "respectable," and that only made them more *immondes!* The young man's analysis, while he brooded, put it at last very simply — they were adventurers because they were toadies and snobs. That was the completest account of them — it was the law of their being. Even when this truth became vivid to their ingenious inmate he remained unconscious of how much his mind had been prepared for it by the extraordinary little boy who had now become such a complication in his life. Much less could he then calculate on the information he was still to owe the extraordinary little boy.

V

BUT IT WAS DURING THE ENSUING TIME that the real problem came up — the problem of how far it was excusable to discuss the turpitude of parents with a child of twelve, of thirteen, of fourteen. Absolutely inexcusable and quite impossible it of course at first appeared; and indeed the question didn't press for some time after Pemberton had received his three hundred francs. They produced a temporary lull, a relief from the sharpest pressure. The young man frugally amended his wardrobe and even had a few francs in his pocket. He thought the Moreens looked at him as if he were almost too smart, as if they ought to take care not to spoil him. If Mr. Moreen hadn't been such a man of the world he would perhaps have spoken of the freedom of such neckties on the part of a subordinate. But Mr. Moreen was always enough a man of the world to let things pass — he had certainly shown that. It was singular how Pemberton guessed that Morgan, though saying nothing about it, knew something had happened. But three hundred francs, especially when one owed money, couldn't last for ever; and when the treasure was gone — the boy knew when it had failed — Morgan did break ground. The party had returned to Nice at the beginning of the winter, but not to the charming villa. They went to an hotel, where they stayed three months, and then moved to another establishment, explaining that they had left the first because, after waiting and waiting, they couldn't get the rooms they wanted. These apartments, the rooms they wanted, were generally very splendid; but fortunately they never could get them — fortunately, I mean, for Pemberton, who reflected always that if they had got them there would have been a still scanter educational fund. What Morgan said at last was said suddenly, irrelevantly, when the moment came, in the middle of a lesson, and consisted of the apparently unfeeling words: "You ought to *filer*, you know — you really ought."

Pemberton stared. He had learnt enough French slang from Morgan to know that to *filer* meant to cut sticks. "Ah, my dear fellow, don't turn me off!"

Morgan pulled a Greek Lexicon toward him — he used a Greek-German — to look out a word, instead of asking it of Pemberton. "You can't go on like this, you know."

"Like what, my boy?"

"You know they don't pay you up," said Morgan, blushing and turning his leaves.

"Don't pay me?" Pemberton stared again and feigned amazement. "What on earth put that into your head?"

"It has been there a long time," the boy replied rummaging his book.

Pemberton was silent, then he went on: "I say, what are you hunting for? They pay me beautifully."

"I'm hunting for the Greek for awful whopper," Morgan dropped.

"Find that rather for gross impertinence and disabuse your mind. What do I want of money?"

"Oh that's another quesion!"

Pemberton wavered — he was drawn in different ways. The severely correct thing would have been to tell the boy that such a matter was none of his business and bid him go on with his lines. But they were really too intimate for that; it was not the way he was in the habit of treating him; there had been no reason it should be. On the other hand Morgan had quite lighted on the truth — he really shouldn't be able to keep it up much longer; therefore why not let him know one's real motive for forsaking him? At the same time it wasn't decent to abuse to one's pupil the family of one's pupil; it was better to misrepresent than to do that. So in reply to his comrade's last exclamation he just declared, to dismiss the subject, that he had received several payments.

"I say — I say!" the boy ejaculated, laughing.

"That's all right," Pemberton insisted. "Give me your written rendering."

Morgan pushed a copy book across the table, and he began to read the page, but with something running in his head that made it no sense. Looking up after a minute or two he found the child's eyes fixed on him and felt in them something strange. Then Morgan said: "I'm not afraid of the stern reality."

"I haven't yet seen the thing you *are* afraid of — I'll do you that justice!"

This came out with a jump — it was perfectly true — and evidently gave Morgan pleasure. "I've thought of it a long time," he presently resumed.

"Well, don't think of it any more."

The boy appeared to comply, and they had a comfortable and even an amusing hour. They had a theory that they were very thorough, and yet they seemed to be in the amusing part of lessons, the intervals between the dull dark tunnels, where there were waysides and jolly views. Yet the morning was brought to a violent end by Morgan's suddenly leaning his arms on the table, burying his head in them and bursting into tears: at which Pemberton was the more startled that, as it then came over him, it was the first time he had ever seen the boy cry and that the impression was consequently quite awful.

The next day, after much thought, he took a decision, and, believing it to be just, immediately acted on it. He cornered Mr. and Mrs. Moreen again and let them know that if on the spot they didn't pay him all they owed him he wouldn't only leave their house but would tell Morgan exactly what had brought him to it.

"Oh, you *haven't* told him?" cried Mrs.

Moreen with a pacifying hand on her well-dressed bosom.

"Without warning you? For what do you take me?" the young man returned.

Mr. and Mrs. Moreen looked at each other; he could see that they appreciated, as tending to their security, his superstition of delicacy, and yet there was a certain alarm in their relief. "My dear fellow," Mr. Moreen demanded, "what use *can* you have, leading the quiet life we all do, for such a lot of money?" — a question to which Pemberton made no answer, occupied as he was in noting that what passed in the mind of his patrons was something like: "Oh then, if we've felt that the child, dear little angel, has judged us and how he regards us, and we haven't been betrayed, he must have guessed — and in short it's *general!*" an inference that rather stirred up Mr. and Mrs. Moreen, as Pemberton had desired it should. At the same time, if he had supposed his threat would do something towards bringing them round, he was disappointed to find them taking for granted — how vulgar their perception *had* been! — that he had already given them away. There was a mystic uneasiness in their parental breasts, and that had been the inferior sense of it. None the less, however, his threat did touch them; for if they had escaped it was only to meet a new danger. Mr. Moreen appealed to him, on every precedent, as a man of the world; but his wife had recourse, for the first time since his domestication with them, to a fine *hauteur*, reminding him that a devoted mother, with her child, had arts that protected her against gross misrepresentation.

"I should misrepresent you grossly if I accused you of common honesty!" our friend replied; but as he closed the door behind him sharply, thinking he had not done himself much good, while Mr. Moreen lighted another cigarette, he heard his hostess shout after him more touchingly:

"Oh you do, you *do,* put the knife to one's throat!"

The next morning, very early, she came to his room. He recognised her knock, but had no hope she brought him money; as to which he was wrong, for she had fifty francs in her hand. She squeezed forward in her dressing-gown, and he received her in his own, between his bath-tub and his bed. He had been tolerably schooled by this time to the "foreign ways" of his hosts. Mrs. Moreen was ardent, and when she was ardent she didn't care what she did; so she now sat down on his bed, his clothes being on the chairs, and, in her preoccupation, forgot, as she glanced round, to be ashamed of giving him such a horrid room. What Mrs. Moreen's ardour now bore upon was the design of persuading him that in the first place she was very good-natured to bring him fifty francs, and that in the second, if he would only see it, he was really too absurd to expect to be *paid*. Wasn't he paid enough without perpetual money — wasn't he paid by the comfortable luxurious home he enjoyed with them all, without a care, an anxiety, a solitary want? Wasn't he sure of his position, and wasn't that everything to a young man like him, quite unknown, with singularly little to show, the ground of whose exorbitant pretensions it had never been easy to discover? Wasn't he paid above all by the sweet relation he had established with Morgan — quite ideal as from master to pupil — and by the simple privilege of knowing and living with so amazingly gifted a child; than whom really (and she meant literally what she said) there was no better company in Europe? Mrs. Moreen herself took to appealing to him as a man of the world; she said "Voyons, mon cher," and "My dear man, look here now"; and urged him to be reasonable, he would prove himself worthy to be her son's tutor and of the extraordinary confidence they had placed in him.

After all, Pemberton reflected, it was only a difference of theory and the theory didn't matter much. They had hitherto gone on that of remunerated, as now they would go on that of gratuitous, service; but why should they have so many words about it? Mrs. Moreen at all events continued to be convincing; sitting there with her fifty francs she talked and reiterated as women reiterate, and bored and irritated him, while he leaned against the wall with his hands in the pockets of his wrapper, drawing it together round his legs and looking over the head of his visitor at the grey negations of his window. She wound up with saying: "You see I bring you a definite proposal."

"A definite proposal?"

"To make our relations regular, as it were — to put them on a comfortable footing."

"I see — it's a system," said Pemberton. "A kind of organised blackmail."

Mrs. Moreen bounded up, which was exactly

185

what he wanted. "What do you mean by that?"

"You practise on one's fears — one's fears about the child if one should go away."

"And pray what would happen to him in that event?" she demanded with majesty.

"Why he'd be alone with *you*."

"And pray with whom *should* a child be but with those whom he loves most?"

"If you think that, why don't you dismiss me?"

"Do you pretend he loves you more than he loves *us?*" cried Mrs. Moreen.

"I think he ought to. I make sacrifices for him. Though I've heard of those *you* make I don't see them."

Mrs. Moreen stared a moment; then with emotion she grasped her inmate's hand. "*Will* you make it — the sacrifice?"

He burst out laughing. "I'll see. I'll do what I can. I'll stay a little longer. Your calculation's just — I *do* hate intensely to give him up; I'm fond of him and he thoroughly interests me, in spite of the inconvenience I suffer. You know my situation perfectly. I haven't a penny in the world and, occupied as you see with Morgan, am unable to earn money."

Mrs. Moreen tapped her undressed arm with her folded bank-note. "Can't you write articles? Can't you translate as *I* do?"

"I don't know about translating; it's wretchedly paid."

"I'm glad to earn what I can," said Mrs. Moreen with prodigious virtue.

"You ought to tell me who you do it for." Pemberton paused a moment, and she said nothing; so he added: "I've tried to turn off some little sketches, but the magazines won't have them — they're declined with thanks."

"You see then you're not such a phoenix," his visitor pointedly smiled — "to pretend to abilities you're sacrificing for our sake."

"I haven't time to do things properly," he ruefully went on. Then as it came over him that he was almost abjectly good-natured to give these explanations he added: "If I stay on longer it must be on one condition — that Morgan shall know distinctly on what footing I am."

Mrs. Moreen demurred. "Surely you don't want to show off to a child?"

"To show *you* off, do you mean?"

Again she cast about, but this time it was to produce a still finer flower. "And *you* talk of blackmail!"

"You can easily prevent it," said Pemberton.

"And *you* talk of practising on fears!" she bravely pushed on.

"Yes, there's no doubt I'm a great scoundrel."

His patroness met his eyes — it was clear she was in straits. Then she thrust out her money at him. "Mr. Moreen desired me to give you this on account."

"I'm much obliged to Mr. Moreen, but we *have* no account."

"You won't take it?"

"That leaves me more free," said Pemberton.

"To poison my darling's mind?" groaned Mrs. Moreen.

"Oh your darling's mind — !" the young man laughed.

She fixed him a moment, and he thought she was going to break out tormentedly, pleadingly: "For God's sake, tell me what *is* in it!" But she checked this impulse — another was stronger. She pocketed the money — the crudity of the alternative was comical — and swept out of the room with the desperate concession: "You may tell him any horror you like!"

VI

A COUPLE OF DAYS AFTER THIS, during which he had failed to profit by so free a permission, he had been for a quarter of an hour walking with his charge in silence when the boy became sociable again with the remark: "I'll tell you how I know it; I know it through Zénobie."

"Zénobie? Who in the world is *she?*"

"A nurse I used to have — ever so many years ago. A charming woman. I liked her awfully, and she liked me."

"There's no accounting for tastes. What is it you know through her?"

"Why what their idea is. She went away because they didn't fork out. She did like me awfully, and she stayed two years. She told me all about it — that at last she could never get her wages. As soon as they saw how much she liked me they stopped giving her anything. They thought she'd stay for nothing — just *because,* don't you know?" And Morgan had a queer little conscious lucid look. "She did stay ever so long — as long as she could. She was only a poor girl. She used to send money to her mother. At last she couldn't afford it any longer, and went away in a fearful rage one night — I mean of course in a rage against *them*. She cried over me tremendously, she hugged me nearly to death. She told me all about it," the boy repeated. "She told me it was their idea. So I guessed, ever so long ago, that they have had the same idea with you."

"Zénobie was very sharp," said Pemberton. "And she made you so."

"Oh, that wasn't Zénobie; that was nature. And experience!" Morgan laughed.

"Well, Zénobie was a part of your experience."

"Certainly I was a part of hers, poor dear!" the boy wisely sighed. "And I'm part of yours."

"A very important part. But I don't see how you know I've been treated like Zénobie."

"Do you take me for the biggest dunce you've known?" Morgan asked. "Haven't I been conscious of what we've been through together?"

"What we've been through?"

"Our privations — our dark days."

"Oh our days have been bright enough."

Morgan went on in silence for a moment. Then he said: "My dear chap, you're a hero!"

"Well, you're another!" Pemberton retorted.

"No I'm not, but I ain't a baby. I won't stand it any longer. You must get some occupation that pays. I'm ashamed, I'm ashamed!" quavered the boy with a ring of passion, like some high silver note from a small cathedral chorister, that deeply touched his friend.

"We ought to go off and live somewhere together," the young man said.

"I'll go like a shot if you'll take me."

"I'd get some work that would keep us both afloat," Pemberton continued.

"So would I. Why shouldn't *I* work? I ain't such a beastly little muff as *that* comes to."

"The difficulty is that your parents wouldn't hear of it. They'd never part with you; they worship the ground you tread on. Don't you see the proof of it?" Pemberton developed. "They don't dislike me: they wish me no harm: they're very amiable people; but they're perfectly ready to expose me to any awkwardness in life for your sake."

The silence in which Morgan received his fond sophistry struck Pemberton somehow as expressive. After a moment the child repeated: "You *are* a hero!" Then he added: "They leave me with you altogether. You've all the responsibility. They put me off on you from morning till night. Why then should they object to my taking up with you completely? I'd help you."

"They're not particularly keen about my being helped, and they delight in thinking of you as *theirs*. They're tremendously proud of you."

"I'm not proud of *them*. But you know that," Morgan returned.

"Except for the little matter we speak of they're charming people," said Pemberton, not taking up the point made for his intelligence, but wondering greatly at the boy's own, and especially at this fresh reminder of something he had been conscious of from the first — the strangest thing in his friend's large little composition, a temper, a sensibility, even a private ideal, which

made him as privately disown the stuff his people
were made of. Morgan had in secret a small lofti-
ness which made him acute about betrayed mean-
ness; as well as a critical sense for the manners
immediately surrounding him that was quite
without precedent in a juvenile nature, especially when one noted that it had not made this
nature "old-fashioned," as the word is of children — quaint or wizened or offensive. It was as
if he had been a little gentleman and had paid
the penalty by discovering that he was the only
such person in his family. This comparison
didn't make him vain, but it could make him
melancholy and a trifle austere. While Pemberton guessed at these dim young things, shadows
of shadows, he was partly drawn on and partly
checked, as for a scruple, by the charm of attempting to sound the little cool shallows that were so
quickly growing deeper. When he tried to figure
to himself the morning twilight of childhood, so
as to deal with it safely, he saw it was never fixed,
never arrested, that ignorance, at the instant he
touched it, was already flushing faintly into
knowledge, that there was nothing that at a
given moment you could say an intelligent child
didn't know. It seemed to him that he himself
knew too much to imagine Morgan's simplicity
and too little to disembroil his tangle.

The boy paid no heed to his last remark; he
only went on: "I'd have spoken to them about
their idea, as I call it, long ago, if I hadn't been
sure what they'd say."

"And what would they say?"

"Just what they said about what poor Zénobie
191

told me — that it was a horrid dreadful story, that they had paid her every penny they owed her."

"Well, perhaps they had," said Pemberton.

"Perhaps they've paid you!"

"Let us pretend they have, and *n'en parlons plus*."

"They accused her of lying and cheating" — Morgan stuck to historic truth. "That's why I don't want to speak to them."

"Lest they should accuse me too?" To this Morgan made no answer, and his companion, looking down at him — the boy turned away his eyes, which had filled — saw that he couldn't have trusted himself to utter. "You're right. Don't worry them," Pemberton pursued. "Except for that, they *are* charming people."

"Except for *their* lying and *their* cheating?"

"I say — I say!" cried Pemberton, imitating a little tone of the lad's which was itself an imitation.

"We must be frank, at the last; we *must* come to an understanding," said Morgan with the importance of the small boy who lets himself think he is arranging great affairs — almost playing at shipwreck or at Indians. "I know all about everything."

"I dare say your father has his reasons," Pemberton replied, but too vaguely, as he was aware.

"For lying and cheating?"

"For saving and managing and turning his means to the best account. He has plenty to do with his money. You're an expensive family."

"Yes, I'm very expensive," Morgan concurred

in a manner that made his preceptor burst out laughing.

"He's saving for *you*," said Pemberton. "They think of you in everything they do."

"He might, while he's about it, save a little — " The boy paused, and his friend waited to hear what. Then Morgan brought out oddly: "A little reputation."

"Oh, there's plenty of that. That's all right!"

"Enough of it for the people they know, no doubt. The people they know are awful."

"Do you mean the princes? We mustn't abuse the princes."

"Why not? They haven't married Paula — they haven't married Amy. They only clean out Ulick."

"You *do* know everything!" Pemberton declared.

"No I don't after all. I don't know what they live on, or how they live, or *why* they live! What have they got and how did they get it? Are they rich, are they poor, or have they a *modeste aisance*? Why are they always chiveying me about — living one year like ambassadors and the next like paupers? Who are they, anyway, and what are they? I've thought of all that — I've thought of a lot of things. They're so beastly worldly. That's what I hate most — oh I've *seen* it! All they care about is to make an appearance and to pass for something or other. What the dickens do they want to pass for? What *do* they, Mr. Pemberton?"

"You pause for a reply," said Pemberton, treating the question as a joke, yet wondering too and greatly struck with his mate's intense if imperfect vision. "I haven't the least idea."

"And what good does it do? Haven't I seen the way people treat them — the 'nice' people, the ones they want to know? They'll take anything from them — they'll lie down and be trampled on. The nice ones hate that — they just sicken them. You're the only really nice person we know."

"Are you sure? They don't lie down for me!"

"Well, you shan't lie down for them. You've got to go — that's what you've got to do," said Morgan.

"And what will become of you?"

"Oh, I'm growing up. I shall get off before long. I'll see you later."

"You had better let me finish you," Pemberton urged, lending himself to the child's strange superiority.

Morgan stopped in their walk, looking up at him. He had to look up much less than a couple of years before — he had grown, in his loose leanness, so long and high. "Finish me?" he echoed.

"There are such a lot of jolly things we can do together yet. I want to turn you out — I want you to do me credit."

Morgan continued to look at him. "To give you credit — do you mean?"

"My dear fellow, you're too clever to live."

"That's just what I'm afraid you think. No, no; it isn't fair — I can't endure it. We'll separate next week. The sooner it's over the sooner to sleep."

194

"If I hear of anything — any other chance —
I promise to go," Pemberton said.

Morgan consented to consider this. "But you'll
be honest," he demanded; "you won't pretend
you haven't heard?"

"I'm much more likely to pretend I have."

"But what can you hear of, this way, stuck in
a hole with us? You ought to be on the spot, to
go to America."

"One would think you were *my* tutor!" said
Pemberton.

Morgan walked on and after a little had begun again: "Well, now that you know I know
and that we look at the facts and keep nothing
back — it's much more comfortable, isn't it?"

"My dear boy, it's so amusing, so interesting,
that it will surely be quite impossible for me to
forego such hours as these."

This made Morgan stop once more. "You do
keep something back. Oh you're not straight —
I am!"

"How am I not straight?"

"Oh you've got your ideal"

"My idea?"

"Why that I probably shan't make old — make
older — bones, and that you can stick it out till
I'm removed."

"You are too clever to live!" Pemberton repeated.

"I call it a mean idea," Morgan pursued. "But
I shall punish you by the way I hang on."

"Look out or I'll poison you!" Pemberton
laughed.

"I'm stronger and better every year. Haven't
195

you noticed that there hasn't been a doctor near me since you came?"

"I'm your doctor," said the young man, taking his arm and drawing him tenderly on again.

Morgan proceeded and after a few steps gave a sigh of mingled weariness and relief. "Ah now that we look at the facts it's all right!"

VII

THEY LOOKED AT THE FACTS a good deal after this; and one of the first consequences of their doing so was that Pemberton stuck it out, in his friend's parlance, for the purpose. Morgan made the facts so vivid and so droll, and at the same time so bald and so ugly, that there was fascination in talking them over with him, just as there would have been heartlessness in leaving him alone with them. Now that the pair had such perceptions in common it was useless for them to pretend they didn't judge such people; but the very judgment and the exchange of perceptions created another tie. Morgan had never been so interesting as now that he himself was made plainer by the sidelight of these confidences. What came out in it most was the small fine passion of his pride. He had plenty of that, Pemberton felt — so much that one might perhaps wisely wish for it some early bruises. He would have liked his people to have a spirit and had waked up to the sense of their perpetually eating humble-pie. His mother would consume any amount, and his father would consume even more than his mother. He had a theory that
196

Ulick had wriggled out of an "affair" at Nice: there had once been a flurry at home, a regular panic, after which they all went to bed and took medicine, not to be accounted for on any other supposition. Morgan had a romantic imagination, fed by poetry and history, and he would have liked those who "bore his name" — as he used to say to Pemberton with the humour that made his queer delicacies manly — to carry themselves with an air. But their one idea was to get in with people who didn't want them and to take snubs as if they were honourable scars. Why people didn't want them more he didn't know — that was people's own affair; after all they weren't superficially repulsive, they were a hundred times cleverer than most of the dreary grandees, the "poor swells" they rushed about Europe to catch up with. "After all they *are* amusing — they are!" he used to pronounce with the wisdom of the ages. To which Pemberton always replied: "Amusing — the great Moreen troupe? Why they're altogether delightful; and if it weren't for the hitch that you and I (feeble performers!) make in the ensemble they'd carry everything before them."

What the boy couldn't get over was the fact that this particular blight seemed, in a tradition of self-respect, so undeserved and so arbitrary. No doubt people had a right to take the line they liked; but why should *his* people have liked the line of pushing and toadying and lying and cheating? What had their forefathers — all decent folk, so far as he knew — done to them, or what had *he* done to them? Who had poisoned their blood with the fifth-rate social ideal, the fixed idea of making smart acquaintances and getting into the *monde chic*, especially when it was foredoomed to failure and exposure? They showed so what they were after; that was what made the people they wanted not want *them*. And never a wince for dignity, never a throb of shame at looking each other in the face, never any independence or resentment or disgust. If his father or his brother would only knock some one down once or twice a year! Clever as they were they never guessed the impression they made. Morgan had dim memories of an old grandfather, the maternal, in New York, whom he had been taken across the ocean at the age of five to see: a gentleman with a high neckcloth and a good deal of pronunciation, who wore a dress-coat in the morning, which made one wonder what he wore in the evening, and had, or was supposed to have, "property" and something to do with the Bible Society. It couldn't have been but that *he* was a good type. Pemberton himself remembered Mrs. Clancy, a widowed sister of Mr. Moreen's, who was as irritating as a moral tale and had paid a fortnight's visit to the family at Nice shortly after he came to live with them. She was "pure and refined," as Amy said over the banjo, and had the air of not knowing what they meant when they talked, and of keeping something rather important back. Pemberton judged that what she kept back was an approval of many of their ways; therefore it was to be supposed that she too was of a good type, and that Mr. and Mrs. Moreen and Ulick and

Paula and Amy might easily have been of a better one if they would.

But that they wouldn't was more and more perceptible from day to day. They continued to "chivey," as Morgan called it, and in due time became aware of a variety of reasons for proceeding to Venice. They mentioned a great many of them — they were always strikingly frank and had the brightest friendly chatter, at the late foreign breakfast in especial, before the ladies had made up their faces, when they leaned their arms on the table, had something to follow the *demitasse,* and, in the heat of familiar discussion as to what they "really ought" to do, fell inevitably into the languages in which they could *tutoyer.* Even Pemberton liked them then; he could endure even Ulick when he heard him give his little flat voice for the "sweet sea-city." That was what made him have a sneaking kindness for them — that they were so out of the workaday world and kept him so out of it. The summer had waned when, with cries of ecstasy, they all passed out on the balcony that overhung the Grand Canal. The sunsets then were splendid and the Dorringtons had arrived. The Dorringtons were the only reason they hadn't talked of at breakfast; but the reasons they didn't talk of at breakfast always came out in the end. The Dorringtons on the other hand came out very little; or else when they did they stayed — as was natural — for hours, during which periods Mrs. Moreen and the girls sometimes called at their hotel (to see if they had returned) as many as three times running. The gondola was for the ladies, as in Venice too there were "days," which Mrs. Moreen knew in their order an hour after she arrived. She immediately took one herself, to which the Dorringtons never came, though on a certain occasion when Pemberton and his pupil were together at Saint Mark's — where, taking the best walks they had ever had and haunting a hundred churches, they spent a great deal of time — they saw the old lord turn up with Mr. Moreen and Ulick, who showed him the dim basilica as if it belonged to them. Pemberton noted how much less, among its curiosities, Lord Dorrington carried himself as a man of the world; wondering too whether, for such services, his companions took a fee from him. The autumn at any rate waned, the Dorringtons departed, and Lord Verschoyle, the eldest son, had proposed neither for Amy nor for Paula.

One sad November day, while the wind roared round the old palace and the rain lashed the lagoon, Pemberton, for exercise and even somewhat for warmth — the Moreens were horribly frugal about fires; it was a cause of suffering to their inmate — walked up and down the big bare *sala* with his pupil. The scagliola floor was cold, the high battered casements shook in the storm, and the stately decay of the place was unrelieved by a particle of furniture. Pemberton's spirits were low, and it came over him that the fortune of the Moreens was now even lower. A blast of desolation, a portent of disgrace and disaster, seemed to draw through the comfortless hall. Mr. Moreen and Ulick were in the Piazza, looking out for something, strolling drearily, in mackintoshes, under the arcades; but still, in spite of mackintoshes, unmistakable men of the world. Paula and Amy were in bed — it might have been thought they were staying there to keep warm. Pemberton looked askance at the boy at his side, to see to what extent he was conscious of these dark omens. But Morgan, luckily for him, was now mainly conscious of growing taller and stronger and indeed of being in his fifteenth year. This fact was intensely interesting to him and the basis of a private theory — which, however, he had imparted to his tutor — that in a little while he should stand on his own feet. He considered that the situation would change — that in short he should be "finished," grown up, producible in the world of affairs and ready to prove himself of sterling ability. Sharply as he was capable at times of analysing, as he called it, his life, there were happy hours when he remained, as he also called it — and as the name, really, of their real ideal — "jolly" superficial; the proof of which was his fundamental assumption that he should presently go to Oxford, to Pemberton's college, and aided and abetted by Pemberton, do the most wonderful things. It depressed the young man to see how little in such a project he took account of ways and means; in other connexions he mostly kept to the measure. Pemberton tried to imagine the Moreens at Oxford and fortunately failed; yet unless they were to adopt it as a residence there would be no *modus vivendi* for Morgan. How could he live without an allowance, and where was the allowance to come from? He, Pemberton, might live on Morgan;

but how could Morgan live on *him?* What was to become of him anyhow? Somehow the fact that he was a big boy now, with better prospects of health, made the question of his future more difficult. So long as he was markedly frail the great consideration he inspired seemed enough of an answer to it. But at the bottom of Pemberton's heart was the recognition of his probably being strong enough to live and not yet strong enough to struggle or to thrive. Morgan himself at any rate was in the first flush of the rosiest consciousness of adolescence, so that the beating of the tempest seemed to him after all but the voice of life and the challenge of fate. He had on his shabby little overcoat, with the collar up, but was enjoying his walk.

It was interrupted at last by the appearance of his mother at the end of the *sala*. She beckoned him to come to her, and while Pemberton saw him, complaisant, pass down the long vista and over the damp false marble, he wondered what was in the air. Mrs. Moreen said a word to the boy and made him go into the room she had quitted. Then, having closed the door after him, she directed her steps swiftly to Pemberton. There *was* something in the air, but his wildest flight of fancy wouldn't have suggested what it proved to be. She signified that she had made a pretext to get Morgan out of the way, and then she enquired — without hesitation — if the young man could favour her with the loan of three louis. While, before bursting into a laugh, he stared at her with surprise, she declared that she was awfully pressed for the money; she was desperate for it — it would save her life.

"Dear lady, *c'est trop fort!*" Pemberton laughed in the manner and with the borrowed grace of idiom that marked the best colloquial, the best anecdotic, moments of his friends themselves. "Where in the world do you suppose I should get three louis, *du train dont vous allez?*"

"I thought you worked — wrote things. Don't they pay you?"

"Not a penny."

"Are you such a fool as to work for nothing?"

"You ought surely to know that."

Mrs. Moreen stared, then she coloured a little. Pemberton saw she had quite forgotten the terms — if "terms" they could be called — that he had ended by accepting from herself; they had burdened her memory as little as her conscience. "Oh yes, I see what you mean — you've been very nice about that; but why drag it in so often?" She had been perfectly urbane with him ever since the rough scene of explanation in his room the morning he made her accept *his* "terms" — the necessity of his making his case known to Morgan. She had felt no resentment after seeing there was no danger Morgan would take the matter up with her. Indeed, attributing this immunity to the good taste of his influence with the boy, she had once said to Pemberton "My dear fellow, it's an immense comfort you're a gentleman." She repeated this in substance now. "Of course you're a gentleman — that's a bother the less!" Pemberton reminded her that he had not "dragged in" anything that wasn't already in as much as his foot was in his shoe; and she also repeated her prayer that, somewhere and somehow, he would find her sixty francs. He took the liberty of hinting that if he could find them it wouldn't be to lend them to *her* — as to which he consciously did himself injustice, knowing that if he had them he would certainly put them at her disposal. He accused himself, at bottom and not unveraciously, of a fantastic, a demoralised sympathy with her. If misery made strange bed-fellows it also made strange sympathies. It was moreover a part of the abasement of living with such people that one had to make vulgar retorts, quite out of one's own tradition of good manners. "Morgan, Morgan, to what pass have I come for you?" he groaned while Mrs. Moreen floated voluminously down the *sala* again to liberate the boy, wailing as she went that everything was too odious.

Before their young friend was liberated there came a thump at the door communicating with the staircase, followed by the apparition of a dripping youth who poked in his head. Pemberton recognised him as the bearer of a telegram and recognised the telegram as addressed to himself. Morgan came back as, after glancing at the signature — that of a relative in London — he was reading the words: "Found jolly job for you, engagement to coach opulent youth on own terms. Come at once." The answer happily was paid and the messenger waited. Morgan, who had drawn near, waited too and looked hard at Pemberton; and Pemberton, after a moment, having met his look, handed him the telegram. It was really by wise looks — they knew each other so well now — that, while the telegraph boy, in his waterproof cape, made a great puddle on the floor, the thing was settled between them. Pemberton wrote the answer with a pencil against the frescoed wall, and the messenger departed. When he had gone the young man explained himself.

"I'll make a tremendous charge; I'll earn a lot of money in a short time, and we'll live on it."

"Well, I hope the opulent youth will be a dismal dunce — he probably will," Morgan parenthesised — "and keep you a long time a-hammering of it in."

"Of course the longer he keeps me the more we shall have for our old age."

"But suppose *they* don't pay you!" Morgan awfully suggested.

"Oh there are not two such — !" But Pemberton pulled up; he had been on the point of using too invidious a term. Instead of this he said "Two such fatalities."

Morgan flushed — the tears came to his eyes. "*Dites toujours* two such rascally crews!" Then in a different tone he added: "Happy opulent youth!"

"Not if he's a dismal dunce."

"Oh they're happier then. But you can't have everything, can you?" the boy smiled.

Pemberton held him fast, hands on his shoulders — he had never loved him so. "What will become of *you*, what will you do?" He thought of Mrs. Moreen, desperate for sixty francs.

"I shall become an *homme fait*." And then as if he recognised all the bearings of Pemberton's allusion: "I shall get on with them better when you're not here."

"Ah don't say that — it sounds as if I set you against them!"

"You do — the sight of you. It's all right; you know what I mean. I shall be beautiful. I'll take their affairs in hand; I'll marry my sisters."

"You'll marry yourself!" joked Pemberton; as high, rather tense pleasantry would evidently be the right, or the safest, tone for their separation.

It was, however, not purely in this strain that Morgan suddenly asked: "But I say — how will you get to your jolly job? You'll have to telegraph to the opulent youth for money to come on."

Pemberton bethought himself. "They won't like that, will they?"

"Oh look out for them!"

Then Pemberton brought out his remedy. "I'll go to the American Consul; I'll borrow some money of him — just for the few days, on the strength of the telegram."

Morgan was hilarious. "Show him the telegram — then collar the money and stay!"

Pemberton entered into the joke sufficiently to reply that for Morgan he was really capable of that; but the boy, growing more serious, and to prove he hadn't meant what he said, not only hurried him off to the Consulate — since he was to start that evening, as he had wired to his friend — but made sure of their affair by going with him. They splashed through the tortuous perforations and over the humpbacked bridges, and they passed through the Piazza, where they saw Mr. Moreen and Ulick go into a jeweller's shop. The Consul proved accommodating — Pemberton said it wasn't the letter, but Morgan's grand air — and on their way back they went into Saint Mark's for a hushed ten minutes. Later they took up and kept up the fun of it to the very end; and it seemed to Pemberton a part of that fun that Mrs. Moreen, who was very angry when he had announced her his intention, should charge him, grotesquely and vulgarly and in reference to the loan she had vainly endeavoured to effect, with bolting lest they should "get something out" of him. On the other hand he had to do Mr. Moreen and Ulick the justice to recognise that when on coming in *they* heard the cruel news they took it like perfect men of the world.

VIII

WHEN HE GOT AT WORK with the opulent youth, who was to be taken in hand for Balliol, he found himself unable to say if this aspirant had really such poor parts or if the appearance were only begotten of his own long association with an intensely living little mind. From Morgan he heard half a dozen times: the boy wrote charming young letters, a patchwork of tongues, with indulgent postscripts in the family Volapuk and, in little squares and rounds and crannies of the text, the drollest illustrations — letters that he was divided between the impulse to show his present charge as a vain, a wasted incentive, and the sense of something in them that publicity would profane. The opulent youth went up in due course and failed to pass; but it seemed to

add to the presumption that brilliancy was not
expected of him all at once that his parents, con-
doning the lapse, which they good-naturedly
treated as little as possible as if it were Pemberton's, should have sounded the rally again,
begged the young coach to renew the siege.

The young coach was now in a position to
lend Mrs. Moreen three louis, and he sent her a
post-office order even for a larger amount. In
return for his favour he received a frantic scrib-
bled line from her: "Implore you to come back
instantly — Morgan dreadfully ill." They were
on the rebound, once more in Paris — often as
Pemberton had seen them depressed he had
never seen them crushed — and communication
was therefore rapid. He wrote to the boy to ascer-
tain the state of his health, but awaited the answer in vain. He accordingly, after three days,
took an abrupt leave of the opulent youth and,
crossing the Channel, alighted at the small hotel,
in the quarter of the Champs Élysées, of which
Mrs. Moreen had given him the address. A deep
if dumb dissatisfaction with this lady and her
companions bore him company: they couldn't
be vulgarly honest, but they could live at hotels,
in velvety *entresols,* amid a smell of burnt pas-
tilles, surrounded by the most expensive city in
Europe. When he had left them in Venice it was
with an irrepressible suspicion that something
was going to happen; but the only thing that
could have taken place was again their masterly
retreat. "How is he? where is he?" he asked of
Mrs. Moreen; but before she could speak these
questions were answered by the pressure round

his neck of a pair of arms, in shrunken sleeves, which were still perfectly capable of an effusive young foreign squeeze.

"Dreadfully ill — I don't see it!" the young man cried. And then to Morgan: "Why on earth didn't you relieve me? Why didn't you answer my letter?"

Mrs. Moreen declared that when she wrote he was very bad, and Pemberton learned at the same time from the boy that he had answered every letter he had received. This led to the clear inference that Pemberton's note had been kept from him so that the game to be practised should not be interfered with. Mrs. Moreen was prepared to see the fact exposed, as Pemberton saw the moment he faced her that she was prepared for a good many other things. She was prepared above all to maintain that she had acted from a sense of duty, that she was enchanted she had got him over, whatever they might say, and that it was useless of him to pretend he didn't know in all his bones that his place at such a time was with Morgan. He had taken the boy away from them and now had no right to abandon him. He had created for himself the gravest responsibilities and must at least abide by what he had done.

"Taken him away from you?" Pemberton exclaimed indignantly.

"Do it — do it for pity's sake; that's just what I want. I can't stand *this* — and such scenes. They're awful frauds — poor dears!" These words broke from Morgan, who had intermitted his embrace, in a key which made Pemberton turn quickly to him and see that he had suddenly

seated himself, was breathing in great pain and was very pale.

"*Now* do you say he's not in a state, my precious pet?" shouted his mother, dropping on her knees before him with clasped hands, but touching him no more than if he had been a gilded idol. "It will pass — it's only for an instant; but don't say such dreadful things!"

"I'm all right — all right," Morgan panted to Pemberton, whom he sat looking up at with a strange smile, his hands resting on either side on the sofa.

"Now do you pretend I've been dishonest, that I've deceived?" Mrs. Moreen flashed at Pemberton as she got up.

"It isn't *he* says it, it's I!" the boy returned, apparently easier but sinking back against the wall; while his restored friend, who had sat down beside him, took his hand and bent over him.

"Darling child, one does what one can; there are so many things to consider," urged Mrs. Moreen. "It's his *place* — his only place. You see *you* think it is now."

"Take me away — take me away," Morgan went on, smiling to Pemberton with his white face.

"Where shall I take you, and how — oh *how*, my boy?" the young man stammered, thinking of the rude way in which his friends in London held that, for his convenience, with no assurance of prompt return, he had thrown them over; of the just resentment with which they would already have called in a successor, and of the scant help to finding fresh employment that resided for him in the grossness of his having failed to pass his pupil.

"Oh we'll settle that. You used to talk about it," said Morgan. "If we can only go all the rest's a detail."

"Talk about it as much as you like, but don't think you can attempt it. Mr. Moreen would never consent — it would be so *very* hand-to-mouth," Pemberton's hostess beautifully explained to him. Then to Morgan she made it clearer: "It would destroy our peace, it would break our hearts. Now that he's back it will be all the same again. You'll have your life, your work and your freedom, and we'll all be happy as we used to be. You'll bloom and grow perfectly well, and we won't have any more silly experiments, will we? They're too absurd. It's Mr. Pemberton's place — every one in his place. You in yours, your papa in his, me in mine — *n'est-ce pas, chéri?* We'll all forget how foolish we've been and have lovely times."

She continued to talk and to surge vaguely about the little draped stuffy salon while Pemberton sat with the boy, whose colour gradually came back; and she mixed up her reasons, hinting that there were going to be changes, that the other children might scatter (who knew? — Paula had her ideas) and that then it might be fancied how much the poor old parent-birds would want the little nestling. Morgan looked at Pemberton, who wouldn't let him move; and Pemberton knew exactly how he felt at hearing himself called a little nestling. He admitted that he had had one or two bad days, but he protested afresh against the wrong of his mother's having made them the ground of an appeal to poor Pemberton. Poor Pemberton could laugh now, apart from the comicality of Mrs. Moreen's mustering so much philosophy for her defence — she seemed to shake it out of her agitated petticoats, which knocked over the light gilt chairs — so little did their young companion, *marked,* unmistakably marked at the best, strike him as qualified to repudiate any advantage.

He himself was in for it at any rate. He should have Morgan on his hands again indefinitely; though indeed he saw the lad had a private theory to produce which would be intended to smooth this down. He was obliged to him for it in advance; but the suggested amendment didn't keep his heart rather from sinking, any more than it prevented him from accepting the prospect on the spot, with some confidence moreover that he should do even better if he could have a little supper. Mrs. Moreen threw out more hints about the changes that were to be looked for, but she was such a mixture of smiles and shudders — she confessed she was very nervous — that he couldn't tell if she were in high feather or only in hysterics. If the family was really at last going to pieces why shouldn't she recognise the necessity of pitching Morgan into some sort of lifeboat? This presumption was fostered by the fact that they were established in luxurious quarters in the capital of pleasure; that was exactly where they naturally *would* be established in view of going to pieces. Moreover didn't she mention that Mr. Moreen and the others were enjoying themselves at the opera with Mr. Granger, and wasn't *that* also precisely where one would look for them on the eve of a smash? Pemberton gathered that Mr. Granger was a rich vacant American — a big bill with a flourishy heading and no items; so that one of Paula's "ideas" was probably that this time she hadn't missed fire — by which straight shot indeed she would have shattered the general cohesion. And if the cohesion was to crumble what would become of poor Pemberton? He felt quite enough bound up with them to figure to his alarm as a dislodged block in the edifice.

It was Morgan who eventually asked if no supper had been ordered for him; sitting with him below, later, at the dim delayed meal, in the presence of a great deal of corded green plush, a plate of ornamental biscuit and an aloofness marked on the part of the waiter. Mrs. Moreen had explained that they had been obliged to secure a room for the visitor out of the house; and Morgan's consolation — he offered it while Pemberton reflected on the nastiness of lukewarm sauces — proved to be, largely, that this circumstance would facilitate their escape. He talked of their escape — recurring to it often afterwards — as if they were making up a "boy's book" together. But he likewise expressed his sense that there was something in the air, that the Moreens couldn't keep it up much longer. In point of fact, as Pemberton was to see, they kept it up for five or six months. All the while, however, Morgan's contention was designed to cheer him. Mr. Moreen and Ulick, whom he had met the day after

his return, accepted that return like perfect men
of the world. If Paula and Amy treated it even
with less formality an allowance was to be made
for them, inasmuch as Mr. Granger hadn't come
to the opera after all. He had only placed his
box at their service, with a bouquet for each of
the party; there was even one apiece, embittering
the thought of his profusion, for Mr. Moreen
and Ulick. "They're all like that," was Morgan's
comment; "at the very last, just when we think
we've landed them they're back in the deep sea!"

Morgan's comments in these days were more
and more free; they even included a large recognition of the extraordinary tenderness with
which he had been treated while Pemberton was
away. Oh yes, they couldn't do enough to be nice
to him, to show him they had him on their mind
and make up for his loss. That was just what
made the whole thing so sad and caused him to
rejoice after all in Pemberton's return — he had
to keep thinking of their affection less, had less
sense of obligation. Pemberton laughed out at
this last reason, and Morgan blushed and said
"Well, dash it, you know what I mean." Pemberton knew perfectly what he meant; but there
were a good many things that — dash it too! —
it didn't make any clearer. This episode of his
second sojourn in Paris stretched itself out
wearily, with their resumed readings and wanderings and maunderings, their potterings on
the quays, their hauntings of the museums, their
occasional lingerings in the Palais Royal when
the first sharp weather came on and there was a
comfort in warm emanations, before Chevet's

wonderful succulent window. Morgan wanted to
hear all about the opulent youth — he took an
immense interest in him. Some of the details of
his opulence — Pemberton could spare him none
of them — evidently fed the boy's appreciation
of all his friend had given up to come back to
him; but in addition to the greater reciprocity
established by that heroism he had always his
little brooding theory, in which there was a friv-
olous gaiety too, that their long probation was
drawing to a close. Morgan's conviction that the
Moreens couldn't go on much longer kept pace
with the unexpended impetus with which, from
month to month, they did go on. Three weeks
after Pemberton had rejoined them they went
on to another hotel, a dingier one than the first;
but Morgan rejoiced that his tutor had at least
still not sacrificed the advantage of a room outside. He clung to the romantic utility of this
when the day, or rather the night, should arrive
for their escape.

For the first time, in this complicated connexion, our friend felt his collar gall him. It was,
as he had said to Mrs. Moreen in Venice, *trop
fort* — everything was *trop fort*. He could neither really throw off his blighting burden nor
find in it the benefit of a pacified conscience or
of a rewarded affection. He had spent all the
money accruing to him in England, and he saw
his youth going and that he was getting nothing
back for it. It was all very well of Morgan to
count it for reparation that he should now settle
on him permanently — there was an irritating
flaw in such a view. He saw what the boy had in

his mind; the conception that as his friend had had the generosity to come back he must show his gratitude by giving him his life. But the poor friend didn't desire the gift — what could he do with Morgan's dreadful little life? Of course at the same time that Pemberton was irritated he remembered the reason, which was very honourable to Morgan and which dwelt simply in his making one so forget that he was no more than a patched urchin. If one dealt with him on a different basis one's misadventures were one's own fault. So Pemberton waited in a queer confusion of yearning and alarm for the catastrophe which was held to hang over the house of Moreen, of which he certainly at moments felt the symptoms brush his cheek and as to which he wondered much in what form it would find its liveliest effect.

Perhaps it would take the form of sudden dispersal — a frightened *sauve qui peut,* a scuttling into selfish corners. Certainly they were less elastic than of yore; they were evidently looking for something they didn't find. The Dorringtons hadn't re-appeared, the princes had scattered; wasn't that the beginning of the end? Mrs. Moreen had lost her reckoning of the famous "days"; her social calendar was blurred — it had turned its face to the wall. Pemberton suspected that the great, the cruel discomfiture had been the unspeakable behaviour of Mr. Granger, who seemed not to know what he wanted, or, what was much worse, what *they* wanted. He kept sending flowers, as if to bestrew the path of his retreat, which was never the path of a return. Flowers were all very well, but — Pemberton could complete the proposition. It was now positively conspicuous that in the long run the Moreens were a social failure; so that the young man was almost grateful the run had not been short. Mr. Moreen indeed was still occasionally able to get away on business and, what was more surprising, was likewise able to get back. Ulick had no club, but you couldn't have discovered it from his appearance, which was as much as ever that of a person looking at life from the window of such an institution; therefore Pemberton was doubly surprised at an answer he once heard him make his mother in the desperate tone of a man familiar with the worst privations. Her question Pemberton had not quite caught; it appeared to be an appeal for a suggestion as to whom they might get to take Amy. "Let the Devil take her!" Ulick snapped; so that Pemberton could see that they had not only lost their amiability but had ceased to believe in themselves. He could also see that if Mrs. Moreen was trying to get people to take her children she might be regarded as closing the hatches for the storm. But Morgan would be the last she would part with.

One winter afternoon — it was a Sunday — he and the boy walked far together in the Bois de Boulogne. The evening was so splendid, the cold lemon-coloured sunset so clear, the stream of carriages and pedestrians so amusing and the fascination of Paris so great, that they stayed out later than usual and became aware that they should have to hurry home to arrive in time for dinner. They hurried accordingly, arm-in-arm, good-humoured and hungry, agreeing that there was nothing like Paris after all and that after everything too that had come and gone they were not yet sated with innocent pleasures. When they reached the hotel they found that, though scandalously late, they were in time for all the dinner they were likely to sit down to. Confusion reigned in the apartments of the Moreens — very shabby ones this time, but the best in the house — and before the interrupted service of the table, with objects displaced almost as if there had been a scuffle and a great wine-stain from an overturned bottle, Pemberton couldn't blink the fact that there had been a scene of the last proprietary firmness. The storm had come — they were all seeking refuge. The hatches were down, Paula and Amy were invisible — they had never tried the most casual art upon Pemberton, but he felt they had enough of an eye to him not to wish to meet him as young ladies whose frocks had been confiscated — and Ulick appeared to have jumped overboard. The host and his staff, in a word, had ceased to "go on" at the pace of their guests, and the air of embarrassed detention, thanks to a pile of gaping trunks in the passage, was strangely commingled with the air of indignant withdrawal.

When Morgan took all this in — and he took it in very quickly — he coloured to the roots of his hair. He had walked from his infancy among difficulties and dangers, but he had never seen a public exposure. Pemberton noticed in a second glance at him that the tears had rushed into his eyes and that they were tears of a new and untasted bitterness. He wondered an instant, for the boy's sake, whether he might successfully pretend not to understand. Not successfully, he felt, as Mr. and Mrs. Moreen, dinnerless by their extinguished hearth, rose before him in their little dishonoured salon, casting about with glassy eyes for the nearest port in such a storm. They were not prostrate but were horribly white, and Mrs. Moreen had evidently been crying. Pemberton quickly learned however that her grief was not for the loss of her dinner, much as she usually enjoyed it, but the fruit of a blow that struck even deeper, as she made all haste to explain. He would see for himself, so far as that went, how the great change had come, the dreadful bolt had fallen, and how they would now all have to turn themselves about. Therefore cruel as it was to them to part with their darling she must look to him to carry a little further the influence he had so fortunately acquired with the boy — to induce his young charge to follow him into some modest retreat. They depended on him — that was the fact — to take their delightful child temporarily under his protection: it would leave Mr. Moreen and herself so much more free to give the proper attention (too little, alas! had been given) to the readjustment of their affairs.

"We trust you — we feel we *can*," said Mrs. Moreen, slowly rubbing her plump white hands and looking with compunction hard at Morgan, whose chin, not to take liberties, her husband stroked with a tentative paternal forefinger.

"Oh yes — we feel that we *can*. We trust Mr.

Pemberton fully, Morgan," Mr. Moreen pursued.

Pemberton wondered again if he might pretend not to understand; but everything good gave way to the intensity of Morgan's understanding. "Do you mean he may take me to live with him for ever and ever?" cried the boy. "May take me away, away, anywhere he likes?"

"For ever and ever? *Comme vous-y-allez!*" Mr. Moreen laughed indulgently. "For as long as Mr. Pemberton may be so good."

"We've struggled, we've suffered," his wife went on; "but you've made him so your own that we've already been through the worst of the sacrifice."

Morgan had turned away from his father — he stood looking at Pemberton with a light in his face. His sense of shame for their common humiliated state had dropped; the case had another side — the thing was to clutch at *that*. He had a moment of boyish joy, scarcely mitigated by the reflexion that with this unexpected consecration of his hope — too sudden and too violent; the turn taken was away from a *good* boy's book — the "escape" was left on their hands. The boyish joy was there an instant, and Pemberton was almost scared at the rush of gratitude and affection that broke through his first abasement. When he stammered "My dear fellow, what do you say to that?" how could one not say something enthusiastic? But there was more need for courage at something else that immediately followed and that made the lad sit down quickly on the nearest chair. He had turned quite livid and had raised his hand to his left side. They were all three looking at him, but Mrs. Moreen suddenly bounded forward. "Ah his darling little heart!" she broke out; and this time, on her knees before him and without respect for the idol, she caught him ardently in her arms. "You walked him too far, you hurried him too fast!" she hurled over her shoulder at Pemberton. Her son made no protest, and the next instant, still holding him, she sprang up with her face convulsed and with the terrified cry "Help, help! he's going, he's gone!" Pemberton saw with equal horror, by Morgan's own stricken face, that he was beyond their wildest recall. He pulled him half out of his mother's hands, and for a moment, while they held him together, they looked all their dismay into each other's eyes. "He couldn't stand it with his weak organ," said Pemberton — "the shock, the whole scene, the violent emotion."

"But I thought he *wanted* to go to you!" wailed Mrs. Moreen.

"I *told* you he didn't, my dear," her husband made answer. Mr. Moreen was trembling all over and was in his way as deeply affected as his wife. But after the very first he took his bereavement as a man of the world.

THE TREE OF KNOWLEDGE

IT WAS ONE OF THE SECRET OPINIONS, such as we all have, of Peter Brench that his main success in life would have consisted in his never having committed himself about the work, as it was called, of his friend Morgan Mallow. This was a subject on which it was, to the best of his belief, impossible with veracity to quote him, and it was nowhere on record that he had, in the connexion, on any occasion and in any embarrassment, either lied or spoken the truth. Such a triumph had its honour even for a man of other triumphs — a man who had reached fifty, who had escaped marriage, who had lived within his means, who had been in love with Mrs. Mallow for years without breathing it, and who, last but not least, had judged himself once for all. He had so judged himself in fact that he felt an extreme and general humility to be his proper portion; yet there was nothing that made him think so well of his parts as the course he had steered so often through the shallows just mentioned. It became thus a real wonder that the friends in whom he had most confidence were just those with whom he had most reserves. He couldn't tell Mrs. Mallow — or at least he supposed, excellent man, he couldn't — that she was the one beautiful reason he had never married; any more than he could tell her husband that the sight of the multiplied marbles in that gentleman's studio was an affliction of which even time had never blunted the edge. His victory, however, as I have intimated, in regard to these productions, was not simply in his not having let it out that he deplored them; it was, remarkably, in his not having kept it in by anything else.

The whole situation, among these good people, was verily a marvel, and there was probably not such another for a long way from the spot that engages us — the point at which the soft declivity of Hampstead began at that time to confess in broken accents to Saint John's Wood. He despised Mallow's statues and adored Mallow's wife, and yet was distinctly fond of Mallow, to whom, in turn, he was equally dear. Mrs. Mallow rejoiced in the statues — though she preferred, when pressed, the busts; and if she was visibly attached to Peter Brench it was because of his affection for Morgan. Each loved the other moreover for the love borne in each case to Lancelot, whom the Mallows respectively cherished as their only child and whom the friend of their fireside identified as the third — but decidedly the handsomest — of his godsons. Already in the old years it had come to that — that no one, for such a relation, could possibly have occurred to any of them, even to the baby itself, but Peter. There was luckily a certain independence, of the pecuniary sort, all round: the Master could never otherwise have spent his solemn *Wanderjahre* in Florence and Rome, and continued by the Thames as well as by the Arno and the Tiber to add unpurchased group to group and model, for what was too apt to prove in the event mere love, fancy-heads of celebrities either too busy or too buried — too much of the age or too little of it — to sit. Neither could Peter, lounging in almost daily, have found time to keep the whole complicated tradition so alive by his presence. He was massive but mild, the depositary of these mysteries — large and loose and ruddy and curly, with deep tones, deep eyes, deep pockets, to say nothing of the habit of long pipes, soft hats and brownish greyish weatherfaded clothes, apparently always the same.

He had "written," it was known, but had never spoken, never spoken in particular of that; and he had the air (since, as was believed, he continued to write) of keeping it up in order to have something more — as if he hadn't at the worst enough — to be silent about. Whatever his air, at any rate, Peter's occasional unmentioned prose and verse were quite truly the result of an impulse to maintain the purity of his taste by establishing still more firmly the right relation of fame to feebleness. The little green door of his domain was in a garden-wall on which the discoloured stucco made patches, and in the small detached villa behind it everything was old, the furniture, the servants, the books, the prints, the immemorial habits and the new improvements. The Mallows, at Carrara Lodge, were within ten minutes, and the studio there was on their little land, to which they had added, in their happy faith, for building it. This was the good fortune, if it was not the ill, of her having brought him in marriage a portion that put them in a manner at their ease and enabled them thus, on their side, to keep it up. And they did keep it up — they always had — the infatuated sculptor and his wife, for whom nature had refined on the impossible by relieving them of the sense of the difficult. Morgan had at all events everything of the sculptor but the spirit of Phidias — the brown velvet, the becoming *beretto,* the "plastic" presence, the fine fingers, the beautiful accent in Italian and the old Italian factotum. He seemed to make up for everything when he addressed Egidio with the "tu" and waved him to turn one of the rotary pedestals of which the place was full. They were tremendous Italians at Carrara Lodge, and the secret of the part played by this fact in Peter's life was in a large degree that it gave him, sturdy Briton as he was, just the amount of "going abroad" he could bear. The Mallows were all his Italy, but it was in a measure for Italy he liked them. His one worry was that Lance — to which they had shortened his godson — was, in spite of a public school, perhaps a shade too Italian. Morgan meanwhile looked like somebody's flattering idea of somebody's own person as expressed in the great room provided at the Uffizi Museum for the general illustration of that idea by eminent hands. The

Master's sole regret that he hadn't been born rather to the brush than to the chisel sprang from his wish that he might have contributed to that collection.

It appeared with time at any rate to be to the brush that Lance had been born; for Mrs. Mallow, one day when the boy was turning twenty, broke it to their friend, who shared, to the last delicate morsel, their problems and pains, that it seemed as if nothing would really do but that he should embrace the career. It had been impossible longer to remain blind to the fact that he was gaining no glory at Cambridge, where Brench's own college had for a year tempered its tone to him as for Brench's own sake. Therefore why renew the vain form of preparing him for the impossible? The impossible — it had become clear — was that he should be anything but an artist.

"Oh dear, dear!" said poor Peter.

"Don't you believe in it?" asked Mrs. Mallow, who still, at more than forty, had her violet velvet eyes, her creamy satin skin and her silken chestnut hair.

"Believe in what?"

"Why in Lance's passion."

"I don't know what you mean by 'believing in it.' I've never been unaware, certainly, of his disposition, from his earliest time, to daub and draw; but I confess I've hoped it would burn out."

"But why should it," she sweetly smiled, "with his wonderful heredity? Passion is passion — though of course indeed *you*, dear Peter, know

226

nothing of that. Has the Master's ever burned out?"

Peter looked off a little and, in his familiar formless way, kept up for a moment, a sound between a smothered whistle and a subdued hum. "Do you think he's going to be another Master?"

She seemed scarce prepared to go that length, yet she had on the whole a marvellous trust. "I know what you mean by that. Will it be a career to incur the jealousies and provoke the machinations that have been at times almost too much for his father? Well — say it may be, since nothing but clap-trap, in these dreadful days, *can*, it would seem, make its way, and since, with the curse of refinement and distinction, one may easily find one's self begging one's bread. Put it at the worst — say he *has* the misfortune to wing his flight further than the vulgar taste of his stupid countrymen can follow. Think, all the same, of the happiness — the same the Master has had. He'll *know*."

Peter looked rueful. "Ah but *what* will he know?"

"Quiet joy!" cried Mrs. Mallow, quite impatient and turning away.

II

HE HAD OF COURSE before long to meet the boy himself on it and to hear that practically everything was settled. Lance was not to go up again, but to go instead to Paris where, since the die was cast, he would find the best advantages. Peter had always felt he must be taken as he was, but had never perhaps found him so much of that pattern as on this occasion. "You chuck Cambridge then altogether? Doesn't that seem rather a pity?"

Lance would have been like his father, to his friend's sense, had he had less humour, and like his mother had he had more beauty. Yet it was a good middle way for Peter that, in the modern manner, he was, to the eye, rather the young stockbroker than the young artist. The youth reasoned that it was a question of time — there was such a mill to go through, such an awful lot to learn. He had talked with fellows and had judged. "One has got, today," he said, "don't you see? to know."

His interlocutor, at this, gave a groan. "Oh hang it, *don't* know!"

Lance wondered. " 'Don't'? Then what's the use — ?"

"The use of what?"

"Why of anything. Don't you think I've talent?"

Peter smoked away for a little in silence; then went on: "It isn't knowledge, it's ignorance that — as we've been beautifully told — is bliss."

"Don't you think I've talent?" Lance repeated.

Peter, with his trick of queer kind demonstrations, passed his arm round his godson and held him a moment. "How do I know?"

"Oh," said the boy, "if it's your own ignorance you're defending — !"

Again, for a pause, on the sofa, his godfather smoked. "It isn't. I've the misfortune to be omniscient."

"Oh well," Lance laughed again, "if you know *too* much — !"

"That's what I do, and it's why I'm so wretched."

Lance's gaiety grew. "Wretched? Come, I say!"

"But I forgot," his companion went on — "you're not to know about that. It would indeed for you too make the too much. Only I'll tell you what I'll do." And Peter got up from the sofa. "If you'll go up again I'll pay your way at Cambridge."

Lance stared, a little rueful in spite of being still more amused. "Oh Peter! You disapprove so of Paris?"

"Well, I'm afraid of it."

"Ah I see!"

"No, you don't see — yet. But you will — that is you would. And you mustn't."

The young man thought more gravely. "But one's innocence, already — !"

"Is considerably damaged? Ah that won't matter," Peter persisted — "we'll patch it up here."

"Here? Then you want me to stay at home?"

Peter almost confessed to it. "Well, we're so right — we four together — just as we are. We're so safe. Come, don't spoil it."

The boy, who had turned to gravity, turned from this, on the real pressure in his friend's tone, to consternation. "Then what's a fellow to be?"

"My particular care. Come, old man" — and Peter now fairly pleaded — "*I'll* look out for you."

Lance, who had remained on the sofa with his legs out and his hands in his pockets, watched him with eyes that showed suspicion. Then he got up. "You think there's something the matter with me — that I can't make a success."

"Well, what do you call a success?"

Lance thought again. "Why the best sort, I suppose, is to please one's self. Isn't that the sort that, in spite of cabals and things, is — in his own peculiar line — the Master's?"

There were so much too many things in this question to be answered at once that they practically checked the discussion, which became particularly difficult in the light of such renewed proof that, though the young man's innocence might, in the course of his studies, as he contended, somewhat have shrunken, the finer essence of it still remained. That was indeed exactly what Peter had assumed and what above all he desired; yet perversely enough it gave him a chill. The boy believed in the cabals and things, believed in the peculiar line, believed, to be brief, in the Master. What happened a month or two later wasn't that he went up again at the expense of his godfather, but that a fortnight after he had got settled in Paris this personage sent him fifty pounds.

He had meanwhile at home, this personage, made up his mind to the worst; and what that might be had never yet grown quite so vivid to him as when, on his presenting himself one Sunday night, as he never failed to do, for supper, the mistress of Carrara Lodge met him with an appeal as to — of all things in the world — the wealth of the Canadians. She was earnest, she was even excited. "Are many of them *really* rich?"

He had to confess he knew nothing about

them, but he often thought afterwards of that evening. The room in which they sat was adorned with sundry specimens of the Master's genius, which had the merit of being, as Mrs. Mallow herself frequently suggested, of an unusually convenient size. They were indeed of dimensions not customary in the products of the chisel, and they had the singularity that, if the objects and features intended to be small looked too large, the objects and features intended to be large looked too small. The Master's idea, either in respect to this matter or to any other, had in almost any case, even after years, remained undiscoverable to Peter Brench. The creations that so failed to reveal it stood about on pedestals and brackets, on tables and shelves, a little staring white population, heroic, idyllic, allegoric, mythic, symbolic, in which "scale" had so strayed and lost itself that the public square and the chimney-piece seemed to have changed places, the monumental being all diminutive and the diminutive all monumental; branches at any rate, markedly, of a family in which stature was rather oddly irrespective of function, age and sex. They formed, like the Mallows themselves, poor Brench's own family — having at least to such a degree the note of familiarity. The occasion was one of those he had long ago learnt to know and to name — short flickers of the faint flame, soft gusts of a kinder air. Twice a year regularly the Master believed in his fortune, in addition to believing all the year round in his genius. This time it was to be made by a bereaved couple from Toronto, who had given him the handsomest order for a tomb to three lost children, each of whom they desired to see, in the composition, emblematically and characteristically represented.

Such was naturally the moral of Mrs. Mallow's question: if their wealth was to be assumed, it was clear, from the nature of their admiration, as well as from mysterious hints thrown out (they were a little odd!) as to other possibilities of the same mortuary sort, that their further patronage might be; and not less evident that should the Master become at all known in those climes nothing would be more inevitable than a run of Canadian custom. Peter had been present before at runs of custom, colonial and domestic — present at each of those of which the aggregation had left so few gaps in the marble company round him; but it was his habit never at these junctures to prick the bubble in advance. The fond illusion, while it lasted, eased the wound of elections never won, the long ache of medals and diplomas carried off, on every chance, by every one but the Master; it moreover lighted the lamp that would glimmer through the next eclipse. They lived, however, after all — as it was always beautiful to see — at a height scarce susceptible of ups and downs. They strained a point at times charmingly, strained it to admit that the public was here and there not too bad to buy; but they would have been nowhere without their attitude that the Master was always too good to sell. They were at all events deliciously formed, Peter often said to himself, for their fate; the Master had a vanity, his wife had a loyalty, of which success, depriving these things of innocence, would have diminished the merit and the grace. Any one could be charming under a charm, and as he looked about him at a world of prosperity more void of proportion even than the Master's museum he wondered if he knew another pair that so completely escaped vulgarity.

"What a pity Lance isn't with us to rejoice!" Mrs. Mallow on this occasion sighed at supper.

"We'll drink to the health of the absent," her husband replied, filling his friend's glass and his own and giving a drop to their companion; "but we must hope he's preparing himself for a happiness much less like this of ours this evening — excusable as I grant it to be! — than like the comfort we have always (whatever has happened or has not happened) been able to trust ourselves to enjoy. The comfort," the Master explained, leaning back in the pleasant lamplight and firelight, holding up his glass and looking round at his marble family, quartered more or less, a monstrous brood, in every room — "the comfort of art in itself!"

Peter looked a little shyly at his wine. "Well — I don't care what you may call it when a fellow doesn't — but Lance must learn to *sell,* you know. I drink to his acquisition of the secret of a base popularity!"

"Oh yes, *he* must sell," the boy's mother, who was still more, however, this seemed to give out, the Master's wife, rather artlessly allowed.

"Ah," the sculptor after a moment confidently pronounced, "Lance *will.* Don't be afraid. He'll have learnt."

"Which is exactly what Peter," Mrs. Mallow gaily returned — "why in the world were you so perverse, Peter? — wouldn't when he told him hear of."

Peter, when this lady looked at him with accusatory affection — a grace on her part not infrequent — could never find a word; but the Master, who was always all amenity and tact, helped him out now as he had often helped him before. "That's his old idea, you know — on which we've so often differed: his theory that the artist should be all impulse and instinct. *I* go in of course for a certain amount of school. Not too much — but a due proportion. There's where his protest came in," he continued to explain to his wife, "as against what *might*, don't you see? be in question for Lance."

"Ah well" — and Mrs. Mallow turned the violet eyes across the table at the subject of this discourse — "he's sure to have meant of course nothing but good. Only that wouldn't have prevented him, if Lance *had* taken his advice, from being in effect horribly cruel."

They had a sociable way of talking of him to his face as if he had been in the clay or — at most — in the plaster, and the Master was unfailingly generous. He might have been waving Egidio to make him revolve. "Ah but poor Peter wasn't so wrong as to what it may after all come to that he *will* learn."

"Oh but nothing artistically bad," she urged — still, for poor Peter, arch and dewy.

"Why just the little French tricks," said the Master: on which their friend had to pretend to admit, when pressed by Mrs. Mallow, that these aesthetic vices had been the objects of his dread.

234

III

"I KNOW NOW," Lance said to him the next year, "why you were so much against it." He had come back supposedly for a mere interval and was looking about him at Carrara Lodge, where indeed he had already on two or three occasions since his expatriation briefly reappeared. This had the air of a longer holiday. "Something rather awful has happened to me. It *isn't* so very good to know."

"I'm bound to say high spirits don't show in your face," Peter was rather ruefully forced to confess. "Still, are you very sure you do know?"

"Well, I at least know about as much as I can bear." These remarks were exchanged in Peter's den, and the young man, smoking cigarettes, stood before the fire with his back against the mantel. Something of his bloom seemed really to have left him.

Poor Peter wondered. "You're clear then as to what in particular I wanted you not to go for?"

"In particular?" Lance thought. "It seems to me that in particular there can have been only one thing."

They stood for a little sounding each other. "Are you quite sure?"

"Quite sure I'm a beastly duffer? Quite — by this time."

"Oh!" — and Peter turned away as if almost with relief.

"It's *that* that isn't pleasant to find out."

235

"Oh I don't care for 'that,' " said Peter, presently coming round again. "I mean I personally don't."

"Yet I hope you can understand a little that I myself should!"

"Well, what do you mean by it?" Peter sceptically asked.

And on this Lance had to explain — how the upshot of his studies in Paris had inexorably proved a mere deep doubt of his means. These studies had so waked him up that a new light was in his eyes; but what the new light did was really to show him too much. "Do you know what's the matter with me? I'm too horribly intelligent. Paris was really the last place for me. I've learnt what I can't do."

Poor Peter stared — it was a staggerer; but even after they had had, on the subject, a longish talk in which the boy brought out to the full the hard truth of his lesson, his friend betrayed less pleasure than usually breaks into a face to the happy tune of "I told you so!" Poor Peter himself made now indeed so little a point of having told him so that Lance broke ground in a different place a day or two after. "What was it then that — before I went — you were afraid I should find out?" This, however, Peter refused to tell him — on the ground that if he hadn't yet guessed perhaps he never would, and that in any case nothing at all for either of them was to be gained by giving the thing a name. Lance eyed him on this an instant with the bold curiosity of youth — with the air indeed of having in his mind two or three names, of which one or other would be right. Peter nevertheless, turning his back again, offered no encouragement, and when they parted afresh it was with some show of impatience on the side of the boy. Accordingly on their next encounter Peter saw at a glance that he had now, in the interval, divined and that, to sound his note, he was only waiting till they should find themselves alone. This he had soon arranged and he then broke straight out. "Do you know your conundrum has been keeping me awake? But in the watches of the night the answer came over me — so that, upon my honour, I quite laughed out. Had you been supposing I had to go to Paris to learn *that?*" Even now, to see him still so sublimely on his guard, Peter's young friend had to laugh afresh. "You won't give a sign till you're sure? Beautiful old Peter!" But Lance at last produced it. "Why, hang it, the truth about the Master."

It made between them for some minutes a lively passage, full of wonder for each at the wonder of the other. "Then how long have you understood — "

"The true value of his work? I understood it," Lance recalled, "as soon as I began to understand anything. But I didn't begin fully to do that, I admit, till I got *là-bas.*"

"Dear, dear!" — Peter gasped with retrospective dread.

"But for what have you taken me? I'm a hopeless muff — that I *had* to have rubbed in. But I'm not such a muff as the Master!" Lance declared.

"Then why did you never tell me — ?"

"That I hadn't, after all" — the boy took him up — "remained such an idiot? Just because I

237

never dreamed *you* knew. But I beg your pardon. I only wanted to spare you. And what I don't now understand is how the deuce then for so long you've managed to keep bottled."

Peter produced his explanation, but only after some delay and with a gravity not void of embarrassment. "It was for your mother."

"Oh!" said Lance.

"And that's the great thing now — since the murder *is* out. I want a promise from you. I mean" — and Peter almost feverishly followed it up — "a vow from you, solemn and such as you owe me here on the spot, that you'll sacrifice anything rather than let her ever guess — "

"That *I've* guessed?" — Lance took it in. "I see." He evidently after a moment had taken in much. "But what is it you've in mind that I may have a chance to sacrifice?"

"Oh one has always something."

Lance looked at him hard. "Do you mean that *you've* had — ?" The look he received back, however, so put the question by that he found soon enough another. "Are you really sure my mother doesn't know?"

Peter, after renewed reflexion, was really sure. "If she does she's too wonderful."

"But aren't we all too wonderful?"

"Yes," Peter granted — "but in different ways. The thing's so desperately important because your father's little public consists only, as you know then," Peter developed — "well, of how many?"

"First of all," the Master's son risked, "of himself. And last of all too. I don't quite see of whom else."

Peter had an approach to impatience. "Of your mother, I say — *always*."

Lance cast it all up. "You absolutely feel that?"

"Absolutely."

"Well then with yourself that makes three."

"Oh *me!*" — and Peter, with a wag of his kind old head, modestly excused himself. "The number's at any rate small enough for any individual dropping out to be too dreadfully missed. Therefore, to put it in a nutshell, take care, my boy — that's all — that *you're* not!"

"I've got to keep on humbugging?" Lance wailed.

"It's just to warn you of the danger of your failing of that that I've seized this opportunity."

"And what do you regard in particular," the young man asked, "as the danger?"

"Why this certainty: that the moment your mother, who feels so strongly, should suspect your secret — well," said Peter desperately, "the fat would be on the fire."

Lance for a moment seemed to stare at the blaze. "She'd throw me over?"

"She'd throw *him* over."

"And come round to us?"

Peter, before he answered, turned away. "Come round to *you*." But he had said enough to indicate — and, as he evidently trusted, to avert — the horrid contingency.

IV

WITHIN SIX MONTHS AGAIN, none the less, his fear was on more occasions than one all before him. Lance had returned to Paris for another trial; then had reappeared at home and had had, with his father, for the first time in his life, one of the scenes that strike sparks. He described it with much expression to Peter, touching whom (since they had never done so before) it was the sign of a new reserve on the part of the pair at Carrara Lodge that they at present failed, on a matter of intimate interest, to open themselves — if not in joy then in sorrow — to their good friend. This produced perhaps practically between the parties a shade of alienation and a slight intermission of commerce — marked mainly indeed by the fact that to talk at his ease with his old playmate Lance had in general to come to see him. The closest if not quite the gayest relation they had yet known together was thus ushered in. The difficulty for poor Lance was a tension at home — begotten by the fact that his father wished him to be at least the sort of success he himself had been. He hadn't "chucked" Paris — though nothing appeared more vivid to him than that Paris had chucked him: he would go back again because of the fascination in trying, in seeing, in sounding the depths — in learning one's lesson, briefly, even if the lesson were simply that of one's impotence in the presence of one's larger vision. But what did the Master, all aloft in his senseless fluency, know of impotence, and what vision — to be called such — had he in all his blind life ever had? Lance, heated and indignant, frankly appealed to his godparent on this score.

His father, it appeared, had come down on him for having, after so long, nothing to show, and hoped that on his next return this deficiency would be repaired. *The* thing, the Master complacently set forth was — for any artist, however inferior to himself — at least to "do" something. "What can you do? That's all I ask!" *He* had certainly done enough, and there was no mistake about what he had to show. Lance had tears in his eyes when it came thus to letting his old friend know how great the strain might be on the "sacrifice" asked of him. It wasn't so easy to continue humbugging — as from son to parent — after feeling one's self despised for not grovelling in mediocrity. Yet a noble duplicity was what, as they intimately faced the situation, Peter went on requiring; and it was still for a time what his young friend, bitter and sore, managed loyally to comfort him with. Fifty pounds more than once again, it was true, rewarded both in London and in Paris the young friend's loyalty; none the less sensibly, doubtless, at the moment, that the money was a direct advance on a decent sum for which Peter had long since privately prearranged an ultimate function. Whether by these arts or others, at all events, Lance's just resentment was kept for a season — but only for a season — at bay. The day arrived when he warned his companion that he could hold out — or hold in — no longer. Carrara Lodge had had to listen to another lecture delivered from a great height — an infliction really heavier at last than, without striking back or in some way letting the Master have the truth, flesh and blood could bear.

"And what I don't see is," Lance observed with a certain irritated eye for what was after all, if it came to that, owing to himself too; "what I don't see is, upon my honour, how *you*, as things are going, can keep the game up."

"Oh the game for me is only to hold my tongue," said placid Peter. "And I have my reason."

"Still my mother?"

Peter showed a queer face as he had often shown it before — that is by turning it straight away. "What will you have? I haven't ceased to like her."

"She's beautiful — she's a dear of course," Lance allowed; "but what is she to you, after all, and what is it to you that, as to anything whatever, she should or she shouldn't?"

Peter, who had turned red, hung fire a little. "Well — it's all simply what I make of it."

There was now, however, in his young friend a strange, an adopted insistence. "What are you after all to *her*?"

"Oh nothing. But that's another matter."

"She cares only for my father," said Lance the Parisian.

"Naturally — and that's just why."

"Why you've wished to spare her?"

"Because she cares so tremendously much."

Lance took a turn about the room, but with his eyes still on his host. "How awfully — always — you must have liked her!"

"Awfully. Always," said Peter Brench.

The young man continued for a moment to muse — then stopped again in front of him. "Do you know how much she cares?" Their eyes met on it, but Peter, as if his own found something new in Lance's, appeared to hesitate, for the first time in an age, to say he did know. "*I've* only just found out," said Lance. "She came to my room last night, after being present, in silence and only with her eyes on me, at what I had had to take from him; she came — and she was with me an extraordinary hour."

He had paused again and they had again for a while sounded each other. Then something — and it made him suddenly turn pale — came to Peter. "She *does* know?"

"She does know. She let it all out to me — so as to demand of me no more than 'that,' as she said, of which she herself had been capable. She has always, always known," said Lance without pity.

Peter was silent a long time; during which his companion might have heard him gently breathe, and on touching him might have felt within him the vibration of a long low sound suppressed. By the time he spoke at last he had taken everything in. "Then I do see how tremendously much."

"Isn't it wonderful?" Lance asked.

"Wonderful," Peter mused.

"So that if your original effort to keep me from Paris was to keep me from knowledge — !" Lance exclaimed as if with a sufficient indication of this futility.

It might have been at the futility Peter appeared for a little to gaze. "I think it must have been — without my quite at the time knowing it — to keep *me*!" he replied at last as he turned away.

THE FIGURE IN THE CARPET

I HAD DONE A FEW THINGS and earned a few pence — I had perhaps even had time to begin to think I was finer than was perceived by the patronising; but when I take the little measure of my course (a fidgety habit, for it's none of the longest yet) I count my real start from the evening George Corvick, breathless and worried, came in to ask me a service. He had done more things than I, and earned more pence, though there were chances for cleverness I thought he sometimes missed. I could only, however, that evening declare to him that he never missed one for kindness. There was almost rapture in hearing it proposed to me to prepare for *The Middle*, the organ of our lucubrations, so called from the position in the week of its day of appearance, an article for which he had made himself responsible and of which, tied up with a stout string, he laid on my table the subject. I pounced upon my opportunity — that is on the first volume of it — and paid scant attention to my friend's explanation of his appeal. What explanation could be more to the point than my obvious fitness for the task? I had written on Hugh Vereker, but never a word in *The Middle*, where my dealings were mainly with the ladies and the minor poets. This was his new novel, an advance copy, and whatever much or little it should do for his reputation I was clear on the spot as to what it should do for mine. Moreover if I always read him soon as I could get hold of him I had a particular reason for wishing to read him now: I had accepted an invitation to Bridges for the following Sunday, and it had been mentioned in Lady Jane's note that Mr. Vereker was to be there. I was young enough for a flutter at meeting a man of his renown, and innocent enough to believe the occasion would demand the display of an acquaintance with his "last."

Corvick, who had promised a review of it, had not even had time to read it; he had gone to pieces in consequence of news requiring — as on precipitate reflexion he judged — that he should catch the night-mail to Paris. He had had a telegram from Gwendolen Erme in answer to his letter offering to fly to her aid. I knew already about Gwendolen Erme; I had never seen her, but I had my ideas, which were mainly to the effect that Corvick would marry her if her mother would only die. That lady seemed now in a fair way to oblige him; after some dreadful mistake about a climate or a "cure" she had suddenly collapsed on the return from abroad. Her daughter, unsupported and alarmed, desiring to make a rush for home but hesitating at the risk, had accepted our friend's assistance, and it was my secret belief that at sight of him Mrs. Erme would pull around. His own belief was scarcely to be called secret; it discernibly at any rate differed from mine. He had showed me Gwendolen's photograph with the remark that she wasn't pretty but was awfully interesting; she had published at the age of nineteen a novel in three volumes, "Deep Down," about which, in *The Middle,* he had been really splendid. He appreciated my present eagerness and undertook that the periodical in question should do no less; then at the last, with his hand on the door, he said to me: "Of course you'll be all right, you know." Seeing I was a trifle vague he added: "I mean you won't be silly."

"Silly — about Vereker! Why what do I ever find him but awfully clever?"

"Well, what's that but silly? What on earth does 'awfully clever' mean? For God's sake try to get *at* him. Don't let him suffer by our arrangement. Speak of him, you know, if you can, as *I* should have spoken of him."

I wondered an instant. "You mean as far and away the biggest of the lot — that sort of thing?"

Corvick almost groaned. "Oh you know, I don't put them back to back that way; it's the infancy of art! But he gives me a pleasure so rare; the sense of" — he mused a little — "something or other."

I wondered again. "The sense, pray, of what?"

"My dear man, that's just what I want *you* to say!"

Even before he had banged the door I had begun, book in hand, to prepare myself to say it. I sat up with Vereker half the night; Corvick couldn't have done more than that. He was awfully clever — I stuck to that, but he wasn't a bit the biggest of the lot. I didn't allude to the lot, however; I flattered myself that I emerged on this occasion from the infancy of art. "It's all right," they declared vividly at the office; and when the number appeared I felt there was a basis on which I could meet the great man. It gave me confidence for a day or two — then that confidence dropped. I had fancied him reading it with relish, but if Corvick wasn't satisfied how could Vereker himself be? I reflected indeed that the heat of the admirer was sometimes grosser even than the appetite of the scribe. Corvick at all events wrote me from Paris a little ill-humouredly. Mrs. Erme was pulling round, and I hadn't at all said what Vereker gave him the sense of.

II

THE EFFECT OF MY VISIT to Bridges was to turn me out for more profundity. Hugh Vereker, as I saw him there, was of a contact so void of angles that I blushed for the poverty of imagination involved in my small precautions. If he was in spirits it wasn't because he had read my review; in fact on the Sunday morning I felt sure he hadn't read it, though *The Middle* had been out three days and bloomed, I assured myself, in the stiff garden of periodicals which gave one of the ormolu tables the air of a stand at a station. The impression he made on me personally was such that I wished him to read it, and I corrected to this end with a surreptitious hand what might be wanting in the careless conspicuity of the sheet. I'm afraid I even watched the result of my manœuvre, but up to luncheon I watched in vain.

When afterwards, in the course of our gregarious walk, I found myself for half an hour, not perhaps without another manœuvre, at the great man's side, the result of his affability was a still livelier desire that he shouldn't remain in ignorance of the peculiar justice I had done him. It wasn't that he seemed to thirst for justice; on the contrary I hadn't yet caught in his talk the faintest grunt of a grudge — a note for which my young experience had already given me an ear. Of late he had had more recognition, and it was pleasant, as we used to say in *The Middle,* to see how it drew him out. He wasn't of course popular, but I judged one of the sources of his good humour to be precisely that his success was independent of that. He had none the less become in a manner the fashion; the critics at least had put on a spurt and caught up with him. We had found out at last how clever he was, and he had had to make the best of the loss of his mystery. I was strongly tempted, as I walked beside him, to let him know how much of that unveiling was my act; and there was a moment when I probably should have done so had not one of the ladies of our party, snatching a place at his other elbow, just then appealed to him in a spirit comparatively selfish. It was very discouraging: I almost felt the liberty had been taken with myself.

I had had on my tongue's end, for my own part, a phrase or two about the right word at the right time; but later on I was glad not to have spoken, for when on our return we clustered at tea I perceived Lady Jane, who had not been out with us, brandishing *The Middle* with her longest arm. She had taken it up at her leisure; she was delighted with what she had found, and I saw that, as a mistake in a man may often be a felicity in a woman, she would practically do for me what I hadn't been able to do for myself. "Some sweet little truths that needed to be spoken," I heard her declare, thrusting the paper at rather a bewildered couple by the fireplace. She grabbed it away from them again on the reappearance of Hugh Vereker, who after our walk had been upstairs to change something. "I know you don't in general look at this kind of thing, but it's an occasion really for doing so. You *haven't* seen it? Then you must. The man has actually got *at* you, at what *I* always feel, you know." Lady Jane threw into her eyes a look evidently intended to give an idea of what she always felt; but she added that she couldn't have expressed it. The man in the paper expressed it in a striking manner. "Just see there, and there, where I've dashed it, how he brings it out." She had literally marked for him the brightest patches of my prose, and if I was a little amused Vereker himself may well have been. He showed how much he was when before us all Lady Jane wanted to read something aloud. I liked at any rate the way he defeated her purpose by jerking the paper affectionately out of her clutch. He'd take it upstairs with him and look at it on going to dress. He did this half an hour later — I saw it in his hand when he repaired to his room. That was the moment at which, thinking to give her pleasure, I mentioned to Lady Jane that I was the author of the review. I did give her pleasure, I judged, but perhaps not quite so much as I had expected. If the author was "only me" the thing didn't seem quite so remarkable. Hadn't I had the effect rather of diminishing the lustre of the article than of adding to my own? Her ladyship was subject to the most extraordinary drops. It didn't matter; the only effect I cared about was the one it would have on Vereker up there by his bedroom fire.

At dinner I watched for the signs of this impression, tried to fancy some happier light in his eyes; but to my disappointment Lady Jane gave me no chance to make sure. I had hoped she'd call triumphantly down the table, publicly demand if she hadn't been right. The party was large — there were people from outside as well, but I had never seen a table long enough to deprive Lady Jane of a triumph. I was just reflecting in truth that this interminable board would deprive *me* of one when the guest next to me, dear woman — she was Miss Poyle, the vicar's sister, a robust unmodulated person — had the happy inspiration and the unusual courage to address herself across it to Vereker, who was opposite, but not directly, so that when he replied they were both leaning forward. She inquired, artless body, what he thought of Lady Jane's "panegyric," which she had read — not connecting it however with her right-hand neighbour; and while I strained my ear for his reply I heard him, to my stupefaction, call back gaily, his mouth full of bread: "Oh it's all right — the usual twaddle!"

I had caught Vereker's glance as he spoke, but Miss Poyle's surprise was a fortunate cover for my own. "You mean he doesn't do you justice?" said the excellent woman.

Vereker laughed out, and I was happy to be able to do the same. "It's a charming article," he tossed us.

Miss Poyle thrust her chin half across the cloth. "Oh you're so deep!" she drove home.

"As deep as the ocean! All I pretend is that the author doesn't see — " But a dish was at this point passed over his shoulder, and we had to wait while he helped himself.

"Doesn't see what?" my neighbour continued.

"Doesn't see anything."

"Dear me — how very stupid!"

"Not a bit," Vereker laughed again. "Nobody does."

The lady on his further side appealed to him and Miss Poyle sank back to myself. "Nobody sees anything!" she cheerfully announced; to which I replied that I had often thought so too, but had somehow taken the thought for a proof on my own part of a tremendous eye. I didn't tell her the article was mine; and I observed that Lady Jane, occupied at the end of the table, had not caught Vereker's words.

I rather avoided him after dinner, for I confess he struck me as cruelly conceited, and the revelation was a pain. "The usual twaddle" — my acute little study! That one's admiration should have had a reserve or two could gall him to that point? I had thought him placid, and he was placid enough; such a surface was the hard polished glass that encased the bauble of his vanity. I was really ruffled, and the only comfort was that if nobody saw anything George Corvick was quite as much out of it as I. This comfort however was not sufficient, after the ladies had dispersed, to carry me in the proper manner — I mean in a spotted jacket and humming an air — into the smoking-room. I took my way in some dejection to bed; but in the passage I encountered Mr. Vereker, who had been up once more to change, coming out of his room. *He* was humming an air and had on a spotted jacket, and as soon as he saw me his gaiety gave a start.

"My dear young man," he exclaimed, "I'm so glad to lay hands on you! I'm afraid I most unwittingly wounded you by those words of mine at dinner to Miss Poyle. I learned but half an hour ago from Lady Jane that you're the author of the little notice in *The Middle*."

I protested that no bones were broken; but he moved with me to my own door, his hand, on my shoulder, kindly feeling for a fracture; and on hearing that I had come up to bed he asked leave to cross my threshold and just tell me in three words what his qualification of my remarks had represented. It was plain he really feared I was hurt, and the sense of his solicitude suddenly made all the difference to me. My cheap review fluttered off into space, and the best things I had said in it became flat enough beside the brilliancy of his being there. I can see him there still, on my rug, in the firelight and his spotted jacket, his fine clear face all bright with the desire to be tender to my youth. I don't know what he had at first meant to say, but I think the sight of my relief touched him, excited him, brought up words to his lips from far within. It was so these words presently conveyed to me something that, as I afterwards knew, he had never uttered to any one. I've always done justice to the generous impulse that made him speak; it was simply compunction for a snub unconsciously administered to a man of letters in a position inferior to his own, a man of letters moreover in the very act of praising him. To make the thing right he talked to me exactly as an equal and on the ground of what we both loved best. The hour, the place, the unexpectedness deepened the impression: he couldn't have done anything more intensely effective.

III

"I DON'T QUITE KNOW HOW to explain it to you," he said, "but it was the very fact that your notice of my book had a spice of intelligence, it was just your exceptional sharpness, that produced the feeling — a very old story with me, I beg you to believe — under the momentary influence of which I used in speaking to that good lady the words you so naturally resent. I don't read the things in the newspapers unless they're thrust upon me as that one was — it's always one's best friend who does it! But I used to read

them sometimes — ten years ago. I dare say they
were in general rather stupider then; at any rate
it always struck me they missed my little point
with a perfection exactly as admirable when they
patted me on the back as when they kicked me
in the shins. Whenever since I've happened to
have a glimpse of them they were still blazing
away — still missing it, I mean, deliciously. *You*
miss it, my dear fellow, with inimitable assurance;
the fact of your being awfully clever and your
article's being awfully nice doesn't make a hair's
breadth of difference. It's quite with you rising
young men," Vereker laughed, "that I feel most
what a failure I am!"

I listened with keen interest; it grew keener
as he talked. "You a failure — heavens! What
then may your 'little point' happen to be?"

"Have I got to *tell* you, after all these years
and labours?" There was something in the
friendly reproach of this — jocosely exaggerated
— that made me, as an ardent young seeker for
truth, blush to the roots of my hair. I'm as
much in the dark as ever, though I've grown
used in a sense to my obtuseness; at that moment,
however, Vereker's happy accent made me appear to myself, and probably to him, a rare dunce.
I was on the point of exclaiming "Ah yes, don't
tell me: for my honour, for that of the craft,
don't!" when he went on in a manner that
showed he had read my thought and had his
own idea of the probability of our some day re-
deeming ourselves. "By my little point I mean
— what shall I call it? — the particular thing I've
written my books most *for*. Isn't there for every
writer a particular thing of that sort, the thing

that most makes him apply himself, the thing without the effort to achieve which he wouldn't write at all, the very passion of his passion, the part of the business in which, for him, the flame of art burns most intensely? Well, it's *that!*"

I considered a moment — that is I followed at a respectful distance, rather gasping. I was fascinated — easily, you'll say; but I wasn't going after all to be put off my guard. "Your description's certainly beautiful, but it doesn't make what you describe very distinct."

"I promise you it would be distinct if it should dawn on you at all." I saw that the charm of our topic overflowed for my companion into an emotion as lively as my own. "At any rate," he went on, "I can speak for myself: there's an idea in my work without which I wouldn't have given a straw for the whole job. It's the finest fullest intention of the lot, and the application of it has been, I think, a triumph of patience, of ingenuity. I ought to leave that to somebody else to say; but that nobody does say it is precisely what we're talking about. It stretches, this little trick of mine, from book to book, and everything else, comparatively, plays over the surface of it. The order, the form, the texture of my books will perhaps someday constitute for the initiated a complete representation of it. So it's naturally the thing for the critic to look for. It strikes me," my visitor added, smiling, "even as the thing for the critic to find."

This seemed a responsibility indeed. "You call it a little trick?"

"That's only my little modesty. It's really an exquisite scheme."

"And you hold that you've carried the scheme out?"

"The way I've carried it out is the thing in life I think a bit well of myself for."

I had a pause. "Don't you think you ought — just a trifle — to assist the critic?"

"Assist him? What else have I done with every stroke of my pen? I've shouted my intention in his great blank face!" At this, laughing out again, Vereker laid his hand on my shoulder to show the allusion wasn't to my personal appearance.

"But you talk about the initiated. There must therefore, you see, *be* initiation."

"What else in heaven's name is criticism supposed to be?" I'm afraid I coloured at this too; but I took refuge in repeating that his account of his silver lining was poor in something or other that a plain man knows things by. "That's only because you've never had a glimpse of it," he returned. "If you had had one the element in question would soon have become practically all you'd see. To me it's exactly as palpable as the marble of this chimney. Besides, the critic just *isn't* a plain man: if he were, pray, what would he be doing in his neighbour's garden? You're anything but a plain man yourself, and the very *raison d'être* of you all is that you're little demons of subtlety. If my great affair's a secret, that's only because it's a secret in spite of itself — the amazing event has made it one. I not only never took the smallest precaution to keep it so, but never dreamed of any such accident. If I had I shouldn't in advance have had the heart to go on. As it was, I only became aware little by little, and meanwhile I had done my work."

"And now you quite like it?" I risked.

"My work?"

"Your secret. It's the same thing."

"Your guessing that," Vereker replied, "is a proof that you're as clever as I say!" I was encouraged by this to remark that he would clearly be pained to part with it, and he confessed that it was indeed with him now the great amusement of life. "I live almost to see if it will ever be detected." He looked at me for a jesting challenge; something far within his eyes seemed to peep out. "But I needn't worry — it won't!"

"You fire me as I've never been fired," I declared; "you make me determined to do or die." Then I asked: "Is it a kind of esoteric message?"

His countenance fell at this — he put out his hand as if to bid me good-night. "Ah my dear fellow, it can't be described in cheap journalese!"

I knew of course he'd be awfully fastidious, but our talk had made me feel how much his nerves were exposed. I was unsatisfied — I kept hold of his hand. "I won't make use of the expression then," I said, "in the article in which I shall eventually announce my discovery, though I dare say I shall have hard work to do without it. But meanwhile, just to hasten that difficult birth, can't you give a fellow a clue?" I felt much more at my ease.

"My whole lucid effort gives him the clue — every page and line and letter. The thing's as concrete there as a bird in a cage, a bait on a hook, a piece of cheese in a mouse-trap. It's stuck into every volume as your foot is stuck into your shoe. It governs every line, it chooses every word, it dots every i, it places every comma."

I scratched my head. "Is it something in the style or something in the thought? An element of form or an element of feeling?"

He indulgently shook my hand again, and I felt my questions to be crude and my distinctions pitiful. "Good-night, my dear boy — don't bother about it. After all, you do like a fellow."

"And a little intelligence might spoil it?" I still detained him.

He hesitated. "Well, you've got a heart in your body. Is that an element of form or an element of feeling? What I contend that nobody has ever mentioned in my work is the organ of life."

"I see — it's some idea *about* life, some sort of philosophy. Unless it be," I added with the eagerness of a thought perhaps still happier, "some kind of game you're up to with your style, something you're after in the language. Perhaps it's a preference for the letter P!" I ventured profanely to break out. "Papa, potatoes, prunes — that sort of thing?" He was suitably indulgent: he only said I hadn't got the right letter. But his amusement was over; I could see he was bored. There was nevertheless something else I had absolutely to learn. "Should you be able, pen in hand, to state it clearly yourself — to name it, phrase it, formulate it?"

"Oh," he almost passionately sighed, "if I were only, pen in hand, one of *you* chaps!"

"That would be a great chance for you of course. But why should you despise us chaps for not doing what you can't do yourself?"

"Can't do?" He opened his eyes. "Haven't I done it in twenty volumes? I do it in my way," he continued. "Go *you* and do it in yours."

"Ours is so devilish difficult," I weakly observed.

"So's mine! We each choose our own. There's no compulsion. You won't come down and smoke?"

"No. I want to think this thing out."

"You'll tell me then in the morning that you've laid me bare?"

"I'll see what I can do; I'll sleep on it. But just one word more," I added. We had left the room — I walked again with him a few steps along the passage. "This extraordinary 'general intention,' as you call it — for that's the most vivid description I can induce you to make of it — is then, generally, a sort of buried treasure?"

His face lighted. "Yes, call it that, though it's perhaps not for me to do so."

"Nonsense!" I laughed. "You know you're hugely proud of it."

"Well, I didn't propose to tell you so; but it *is* the joy of my soul!"

"You mean it's a beauty so rare, so great?"

He waited a little again. "The loveliest thing in the world!" We had stopped, and on these words he left me; but at the end of the corridor, while I looked after him rather yearningly, he turned and caught sight of my puzzled face. It made him earnestly, indeed I thought quite anxiously, shake his head and wave his finger. "Give it up — give it up!"

This wasn't a challenge — it was fatherly advice. If I had had one of his books at hand I'd have repeated my recent act of faith — I'd have spent half the night with him. At three o'clock in the morning, not sleeping, remembering moreover how indispensable he was to Lady Jane, I stole down to the library with a candle. There wasn't, so far as I could discover, a line of his writing in the house.

IV

RETURNING TO TOWN I feverishly collected them all; I picked out each in its order and held it up to the light. This gave me a maddening month, in the course of which several things took place. One of these, the last, I may as well immediately mention, was that I acted on Vereker's advice: I renounced my ridiculous attempt. I could really make nothing of the business; it proved a dead loss. After all I had always, as he had himself noted, liked him; and what now occurred was simply that my new intelligence and vain preoccupation damaged my liking. I not only failed to run a general intention to earth, I found myself missing the subordinate intentions I had formerly enjoyed. His books didn't even remain the charming things they had been for me; the exasperation of my search put me out of conceit of them. Instead of being a pleasure the more they became a resource the less; for from the moment I was unable to follow up the author's hint I of course felt it a point of honour not to make use professionally of my knowledge of them. I *had* no knowledge — nobody had any. It was humiliating, but I could bear it — they only annoyed me now. At last they even bored me, and I accounted for my confusion — perversely, I allow — by the idea that Vereker had made a fool of me. The buried treasure was a bad joke, the general intention a monstrous *pose*.

The great point of it all is, however, that I told George Corvick what had befallen me and that my information had an immense effect on him. He had at last come back, but so, unfortunately, had Mrs. Erme, and there was as yet, I could see, no question of his nuptials. He was immensely stirred up by the anecdote I had brought from Bridges; it fell in so completely with the sense he had had from the first that there was more in Vereker than met the eye. When I remarked that the eye seemed what the printed page had been expressly invented to meet he immediately accused me of being spiteful because I had been foiled. Our commerce had always that pleasant latitude. The thing Vereker had mentioned to me was exactly the thing he, Corvick, had wanted me to speak of in my review. On my suggesting at last that with the assistance I had now given him he would doubtless be prepared to speak of it himself he admitted freely that before doing this there was more he must understand. What he would have said, had he reviewed the new book, was that there was evidently in the writer's inmost art something to *be* understood. I hadn't so much as hinted at that: no wonder the writer hadn't been flattered! I asked Corvick what he really considered he meant by his own supersubtlety, and, unmistakably kindled, he replied: "It isn't for the vulgar — it isn't for the vulgar!" He had hold of the tail of something: he would pull hard, pull it right out. He pumped me dry on Vereker's strange confidence and, pronouncing me the luckiest of mortals, mentioned half-a-dozen questions he wished to goodness I had had the gumption to put. Yet on the other hand he didn't want to be told too much — it would spoil the fun of seeing what would come. The failure of *my* fun was at the moment of our meeting not complete, but I saw it ahead, and Corvick saw that I saw it. I, on my side, saw likewise that one of the first things he would do would be to rush off with my story to Gwendolen.

On the very day after my talk with him I was surprised by the receipt of a note from Hugh Vereker, to whom our encounter at Bridges had been recalled, as he mentioned, by his falling, in a magazine, on some article to which my signature was attached. "I read it with great pleasure," he wrote, "and remembered under its influence our lively conversation by your bedroom fire. The consequence of this has been that I begin to measure the temerity of my having saddled you with a knowledge that you may find something of a burden. Now that the fit's over I can't imagine how I came to be moved so much beyond my wont. I had never before mentioned, no matter in what state of expansion, the fact of my little secret, and I shall never speak of that mystery again. I was accidentally so much more explicit with you than it had ever entered into my game to be, that I find this game — I mean the pleasure of playing it — suffers considerably. In short, if you can understand it, I've rather spoiled my sport. I really don't want to give anybody what I believe you clever young men call the tip. That's of course a selfish solicitude, and I name it to you for what it may be worth to you. If you're disposed to humour me don't repeat my revelation. Think me demented — it's your right; but don't tell anybody why."

The sequel to this communication was that as early on the morrow as I dared I drove straight to Mr. Vereker's door. He occupied in those years one of the honest old houses in Kensington Square. He received me immediately, and as soon as I came in I saw I hadn't lost my power to minister to his mirth. He laughed out at sight of my face, which doubtless expressed my perturbation. I had been indiscreet — my compunction was great. "I *have* told somebody," I panted, "and I'm sure that person will by this time have told somebody else! It's a woman, into the bargain."

"The person you've told?"

"No, the other person. I'm quite sure he must have told her."

"For all the good it will do her — or do *me!* A woman will never find out."

"No, but she'll talk all over the place: she'll do just what you don't want."

Vereker thought a moment, but wasn't so disconcerted as I had feared: he felt that if the harm was done it only served him right. "It doesn't matter — don't worry."

"I'll do my best, I promise you, that your talk with me shall go no further."

"Very good; do what you can."

"In the meantime," I pursued, "George Corvick's possession of the tip may, on his part, really lead to something."

"That will be a brave day."

I told him about Corvick's cleverness, his admiration, the intensity of his interest in my anecdote; and without making too much of the divergence of our respective estimates mentioned that my friend was already of opinion that he saw much further into a certain affair than most people. He was quite as fired as I had been at Bridges. He was moreover in love with the young lady: perhaps the two together would puzzle something out.

Vereker seemed struck with this. "Do you mean they're to be married?"

"I dare say that's what it will come to."

"That may help them," he conceded, "but we must give them time!"

I spoke of my own renewed assault and confessed my difficulties; whereupon he repeated his former advice: "Give it up, give it up!" He evidently didn't think me intellectually equipped for the adventure. I stayed half an hour, and he was most good-natured, but I couldn't help pronouncing him a man of unstable moods. He had been free with me in a mood, he had repented in a mood, and now in a mood he had turned indifferent. This general levity helped me to believe that, so far as the subject of the tip went, there wasn't much in it. I contrived however to make him answer a few more questions about it, though he did so with visible impatience. For himself, beyond doubt, the thing we were all so blank about was vividly there. It was something, I guessed, in the primal plan; something like a complex figure in a Persian carpet. He highly approved of this image when I used it, and he used another himself. "It's the very string," he said, "that my pearls are strung on!" The reason of his note to me had been that he really didn't want to give us a grain of succour — our density was a thing too perfect in its way to touch. He had formed the habit of depending on it, and if the spell was to break it must break by some force of its own. He comes back to me from that last occasion — for I was never to speak to him again — as a man with some safe preserve for sport. I wondered as I walked away where he had got *his* tip.

V

WHEN I SPOKE TO GEORGE CORVICK of the caution I had received he made me feel that any doubt of his delicacy would be almost an insult. He had instantly told Gwendolen, but Gwendolen's ardent response was in itself a pledge of discretion. The question would now absorb them and would offer them a pastime too precious to be shared with the crowd. They appeared to have caught instinctively at Vereker's high idea of enjoyment. Their intellectual pride, however, was not such as to make them indifferent to any further light I might throw on the affair they had in hand. They were indeed of the "artistic temperament," and I was freshly struck with my colleague's power to excite himself over a question of art. He'd call it letters, he'd call it life, but it was all one thing. In what he said I now seemed to understand that he spoke equally for Gwendolen, to whom, as soon as Mrs. Erme was sufficiently better to allow her a little leisure, he made a point of introducing me. I remember our going together one Sunday in August to a huddled house in Chelsea, and my renewed envy

of Corvick's possession of a friend who had some
light to mingle with his own. He could say
things to her that I could never say to him. She
had indeed no sense of humour and, with her
pretty way of holding her head on one side, was
one of those persons whom you want, as the
phrase is, to shake, but who have learnt Hungarian by themselves. She conversed perhaps in
Hungarian with Corvick; she had remarkably little English for his friend. Corvick afterwards told
me that I had chilled her by my apparent in-
disposition to oblige them with the detail of
what Vereker had said to me. I allowed that I
felt I had given thought enough to that indication: hadn't I even made up my mind that it was
vain and would lead nowhere? The importance
they attached to it was irritating and quite en-
venomed my doubts.

That statement looks unamiable, and what
probably happened was that I felt humiliated at
seeing other persons deeply beguiled by an experiment that had brought me only chagrin. I
was out in the cold while, by the evening fire,
under the lamp, they followed the chase for
which I myself had sounded the horn. They did
as I had done, only more deliberately and socia-
bly — they went over their author from the beginning. There was no hurry, Corvick said —
the future was before them and the fascination
could only grow; they would take him page by
page, as they would take one of the classics, in
hale him in slow draughts and let him sink all
the way in. They would scarce have got so wound
up, I think, if they hadn't been in love· poor
Vereker's inner meaning gave them endless oc-

casion to put and to keep their young heads together. None the less it represented the kind of problem for which Corvick had a special aptitude, drew out the particular pointed patience of which, had he lived, he would have given more striking and, it is to be hoped, more fruitful examples. He at least was, in Vereker's words, a little demon of subtlety. We had begun by disputing, but I soon saw that without my stirring a finger his infatuation would have its bad hours. He would bound off on false scents as I had done — he would clap his hands over new lights and see them blown out by the wind of the turned page. He was like nothing, I told him, but the maniacs who embrace some bedlamitical theory of the cryptic character of Shakespeare. To this he replied that if we had had Shakespeare's own word for his being cryptic he would at once have accepted it. The case there was altogether different — we had nothing but the word of Mr. Snooks. I returned that I was stupefied to see him attach such importance even to the word of Mr. Vereker. He wanted thereupon to know if I treated Mr. Vereker's word as a lie. I wasn't perhaps prepared, in my unhappy rebound, to go so far as that, but I insisted that till the contrary was proved I should view it as too fond an imagination. I didn't, I confess, say — I didn't at that time quite know — all I felt. Deep down, as Miss Erme would have said, I was uneasy, I was expectant. At the core of my disconcerted state — for my wonted curiosity lived in its ashes — was the sharpness of a sense that Corvick would at last probably come out somewhere. He made, in defence of his credulity, a great point of the fact that from of old, in his study of this genius, he had caught whiffs and hints of he didn't know what, faint wandering notes of a hidden music. That was just the rarity, that was the charm: it fitted so perfectly into what I reported.

If I returned on several occasions to the little house in Chelsea I dare say it was as much for news of Vereker as for news of Miss Erme's ailing parent. The hours spent there by Corvick were present to my fancy as those of a chessplayer bent with a silent scowl, all the lamplit winter, over his board and his moves. As my imagination filled it out the picture held me fast. On the other side of the table was a ghostlier form, the faint figure of an antagonist good-humouredly but a little wearily secure — an antagonist who leaned back in his chair with his hands in his pockets and a smile on his fine clear face. Close to Corvick, behind him, was a girl who had begun to strike me as pale and wasted and even, on more familiar view, as rather handsome, and who rested on his shoulder and hung on his moves. He would take up a chessman and hold it poised a while over one of the little squares, and then would put it back in its place with a long sigh of disappointment. The young lady, at this, would slightly but uneasily shift her position and look across, very hard, very long, very strangely, at their dim participant. I had asked them at an early stage of the business if it mightn't contribute to their success to have some closer communication with him. The special circumstances would surely be held to have given me a right to introduce them. Corvick immediately replied that he had no wish to approach the altar before he had prepared the sacrifice. He quite agreed with our friend both as to the delight and as to the honour of the chase — he would bring down the animal with his own rifle. When I asked him if Miss Erme were as keen a shot he said after thinking: "No, I'm ashamed to say she wants to set a trap. She'd give anything to see him; she says she requires another tip. She's really quite morbid about it. But she must play fair — she *shan't* see him!" he emphatically added. I wondered if they hadn't even quarrelled a little on the subject — a suspicion not corrected by the way he more than once exclaimed to me: "She's quite incredibly literary, you know — quite fantastically!" I remember his saying of her that she felt in italics and thought in capitals. "Oh when I've run him to earth," he also said, "then, you know, I shall knock at his door. Rather — I beg you to believe. I'll have it from his own lips: 'Right you are, my boy; you've done it this time!' He shall crown me victor — with the critical laurel."

Meanwhile he really avoided the chances London life might have given him of meeting the distinguished novelist; a danger, however, that disappeared with Vereker's leaving England for an indefinite absence as the newspapers announced — going to the south for motives connected with the health of his wife, which had long kept her in retirement. A year — more than a year — had elapsed since the incident at Bridges, but I had had no further sight of him. I think I was at the bottom rather ashamed — I hated to remind him that, though I had irremediably missed his point, a reputation for acuteness was rapidly overtaking me. This scruple led me a dance; kept me out of Lady Jane's house, made me even decline, when in spite of my bad manners she was a second time so good as to make me a sign, an invitation to her beautiful seat. I once became aware of her under Vereker's escort at a concert, and was sure I was seen by them, but I slipped out without being caught. I felt, as on that occasion I splashed along in the rain, that I couldn't have done anything else; and yet I remember saying to myself that it was hard, was even cruel. Not only had I lost the books, but I had lost the man himself: they and their author had been alike spoiled for me. I knew too which was the loss I most regretted. I had taken to the man still more than I had ever taken to the books.

VI

SIX MONTHS AFTER our friend had left England George Corvick, who made his living by his pen, contracted for a piece of work which imposed on him an absence of some length and a journey of some difficulty, and his undertaking of which was much of a surprise to me. His brother-in-law had become editor of a great provincial paper, and the great provincial paper, in a fine flight of fancy, had conceived the idea of sending a "special commissioner" to India. Special commissioners had begun, in the "metropolitan press," to be the fashion, and the journal in question must have felt it had passed too long for a mere country cousin. Corvick had no hand, I knew, for the big brush of the correspondent, but that was his brother-in-law's affair, and the fact that a particular task was not in his line was apt to be with himself exactly a reason for accepting it. He was prepared to out-Herod the metropolitan press; he took solemn precautions against priggishness, he exquisitely outraged taste. Nobody ever knew it — that offended principle was all his own. In addition to his expenses he was to be conveniently paid, and I found myself able to help him, for the usual fat book, to a plausible arrangement with the usual fat publisher. I naturally inferred that his obvious desire to make a little money was not unconnected with the prospect of a union with Gwendolen Erme. I was aware that her mother's opposition was largely addressed to his want of means and of lucrative abilities, but it so happened that, on my saying the last time I saw him something that bore on the question of his separation from our young lady, he brought out with an emphasis that startled me: "Ah I'm not a bit engaged to her, you know!"

"Not overtly," I answered, "because her mother doesn't like you. But I've always taken for granted a private understanding."

"Well, there *was* one. But there isn't now." That was all he said save something about Mrs. Erme's having got on her feet again in the most extraordinary way — a remark pointing, as I supposed, the moral that private understandings were of little use when the doctor didn't share them. What I took the liberty of more closely inferring was that the girl might in some way have estranged him. Well, if he had taken the turn of jealousy, for instance, it could scarcely

271

be jealousy of me. In that case — over and above the absurdity of it — he wouldn't have gone away just to leave us together. For some time before his going we had indulged in no allusion to the buried treasure, and from his silence, which my reserve simply emulated, I had drawn a sharp conclusion. His courage had dropped, his ardour had gone the way of mine — this appearance at least he left me to scan. More than that he couldn't do; he couldn't face the triumph with which I might have greeted an explicit admission. He needn't have been afraid, poor dear, for I had by this time lost all need to triumph. In fact I considered I showed magnanimity in not reproaching him with his collapse, for the sense of his having thrown up the game made me feel more than ever how much I at last depended on him. If Corvick had broken down I should never know; no one would be of any use if *he* wasn't. It wasn't a bit true I had ceased to care for knowledge; little by little my curiosity not only had begun to ache again, but had become the familiar torment of my days and my nights. There are doubtless people to whom torments of such an order appear hardly more natural than the contortions of disease; but I don't after all know why I should in this connexion so much as mention them. For the few persons, at any rate, abnormal or not, with whom my anecdote is concerned, literature was a game of skill, and skill meant courage, and courage meant honour, and honour meant passion, meant life. The stake on the table was a special substance and our roulette the revolving mind, but we sat round the green board as intently as the grim gamblers at Monte Carlo. Gwendolen Erme, for that matter, with her white face and her fixed eyes, was of the very type of the lean ladies one had met in the temples of chance. I recognised in Corvick's absence that she made this analogy vivid. It was extravagant, I admit, the way she lived for the art of the pen. Her passion visibly preyed on her, and in her presence I felt almost tepid. I got hold of "Deep Down" again: it was a desert in which she had lost herself, but in which too she had dug a wonderful hole in the sand — a cavity out of which Corvick had still more remarkably pulled her.

Early in March I had a telegram from her, in consequence of which I repaired immediately to Chelsea, where the first thing she said to me was: "He has got it, he has got it!"

She was moved, as I could see, to such depths that she must mean the great thing. "Vereker's idea?"

"His general intention. George has cabled from Bombay."

She had the missive open there; it was emphatic though concise. "Eureka. Immense." That was all — he had saved the cost of the signature. I shared her emotion, but I was disappointed. "He doesn't say what it is."

"How could he — in a telegram? He'll write it."

"But how does he know?"

"Know it's the real thing? Oh I'm sure that when you see it you do know. *Vera incessu patuit dea!*"

"It's you, Miss Erme, who are a 'dear' for bringing me such news!" — I went all lengths in my high spirits. "But fancy finding our goddess in the temple of Vishnu! How strange of George to have been able to go into the thing again in the midst of such different and such powerful solicitations!"

"He hasn't gone into it, I know; it's the thing itself, let severely alone for six months, that has simply sprung out at him like a tigress out of the jungle. He didn't take a book with him — on purpose; indeed he wouldn't have needed to — he knows every page, as I do, by heart. They all worked in him together, and some day somewhere, when he wasn't thinking, they fell, in all their superb intricacy, into the one right combination. The figure in the carpet came out. That's the way he knew it would come and the real reason — you didn't in the least understand, but I suppose I may tell you now — why he went and why I consented to his going. We knew the change would do it — that the difference of thought, of scene, would give the needed touch, the magic shake. We had perfectly, we had admirably calculated. The elements were all in his mind, and in the *secousse* of a new and intense experience they just struck light." She positively struck light herself — she was literally, facially luminous. I stammered something about unconscious cerebration, and she continued: "He'll come right home — this will bring him."

"To see Vereker, you mean?"

"To see Vereker — and to see *me*. Think what he'll have to tell me!"

I hesitated, "About India?"

"About fiddlesticks! About Vereker — about the figure in the carpet."

"But, as you say, we shall surely have that in a letter."

She thought like one inspired, and I remembered how Corvick had told me long before that her face was interesting. "Perhaps it can't be got into a letter if it's 'immense.'"

"Perhaps not if it's immense bosh. If he has hold of something that can't be got into a letter he hasn't hold of *the* thing. Vereker's own statement to me was exactly that the 'figure' *would* fit into a letter."

"Well, I cabled to George an hour ago — two words," said Gwendolen.

"Is it indiscreet of me to ask what they were?"

She hung fire, but at last brought them out. "'Angel, write.'"

"Good!" I cried. "I'll make it sure — I'll send him the same."

VII

MY WORDS HOWEVER were not absolutely the same — I put something instead of "angel"; and in the sequel my epithet seemed the more apt, for when eventually we heard from our traveller it was merely, it was thoroughly to be tantalised. He was magnificent in his triumph, he described his discovery as stupendous; but his ecstasy only obscured it — there were to be no particulars till he should have submitted his conception to the supreme authority. He had thrown up his commission, he had thrown up his book, he had thrown up everything but the instant need to hurry to Rapallo, on the Genoese shore, where Vereker was making a stay. I wrote

275

him a letter which was to await him at Aden —
I besought him to relieve my suspense. That he
had found my letter was indicated by a telegram
which, reaching me after weary days and in the
absence of any answer to my laconic dispatch to
him at Bombay, was evidently intended as a reply to both communications. Those few words
were in familiar French, the French of the day,
which Corvick often made use of to show he
wasn't a prig. It had for some persons the opposite effect, but his message may fairly be para-
phrased. "Have patience; I want to see, as it
breaks on you, the face you'll make!" *"Tellement
envie de voir ta tête!"* — that was what I had to
sit down with. I can certainly not be said to have
sat down, for I seem to remember myself at this
time as rattling constantly between the little
house in Chelsea and my own. Our impatience,
Gwendolen's and mine, was equal, but I kept
hoping her light would be greater. We all spent
during this episode, for people of our means, a
great deal of money in telegrams and cabs, and I
counted on the receipt of news from Rapallo
immediately after the junction of the discoverer
with the discovered. The interval seemed an
age, but late one day I heard a hansom precipitated to my door with the crash engendered by
a hint of liberality. I lived with my heart in my
mouth and accordingly bounded to the window
— a movement which gave me a view of a young
lady erect on the footboard of the vehicle and
eagerly looking up at my house. At sight of me
she flourished a paper with a movement that
brought me straight down, the movement with
which, in melodramas, handkerchiefs and re-

prieves are flourished at the foot of the scaffold.

"Just seen Vereker — not a note wrong. Pressed me to bosom — keeps me a month." So much I read on her paper while the cabby dropped a grin from his perch. In my excitement I paid him profusely and in hers she suffered it; then as he drove away we started to walk about and talk. We had talked, heaven knows, enough before, but this was a wondrous lift. We pictured the whole scene at Rapallo, where he would have written, mentioning my name, for permission to call; that is *I* pictured it, having more material than my companion, whom I felt hang on my lips as we stopped on purpose before shop-windows we didn't look into. About one thing we were clear: if he was staying on for fuller communication we should at least have a letter from him that would help us through the dregs of delay. We understood his staying on, and yet each of us saw, I think, that the other hated it. The letter we were clear about arrived; it was for Gwendolen, and I called on her in time to save her the trouble of bringing it to me. She didn't read it out, as was natural enough; but she repeated to me what it chiefly embodied. This consisted of the remarkable statement that he'd tell her after they were married exactly what she wanted to know.

"Only *then*, when I'm his wife — not before," she explained. "It's tantamount to saying — isn't it? — that I must marry him straight off!" She smiled at me while I flushed with disappointment, a vision of fresh delay that made me at first unconscious of my surprise. It seemed more than a hint that on me as well he would impose some tiresome condition. Suddenly, while she reported several more things from his letter, I remembered what he had told me before going away. He had found Mr. Vereker deliriously interesting and his own possession of the secret a real intoxication. The buried treasure was all gold and gems. Now that it was there it seemed to grow and grow before him; it would have been, through all time and taking all tongues, one of the most wonderful flowers of literary art. Nothing, in especial, once you were face to face with it, could show for more consummately *done*. When once it came out it came out, was there with a splendour that made you ashamed; and there hadn't been, save in the bottomless vulgarity of the age, with every one tasteless and tainted, every sense stopped, the smallest reason why it should have been overlooked. It was great, yet so simple, was simple, yet so great, and the final knowledge of it was an experience quite apart. He intimated that the charm of such an experience, the desire to drain it, in its freshness, to the last drop, was what kept him there close to the source. Gwendolen, frankly radiant as she tossed me these fragments, showed the elation of a prospect more assured than my own. That brought me back to the question of her marriage, prompted me to ask if what she meant by what she had just surprised me with was that she was under an engagement.

"Of course I am!" she answered. "Didn't you know it?" She seemed astonished, but I was still more so, for Corvick had told me the exact contrary. I didn't mention this, however; I only reminded her how little I had been on that score in her confidence, or even in Corvick's, and that moreover I wasn't in ignorance of her mother's interdict. At bottom I was troubled by the disparity of the two accounts; but after a little I felt Corvick's to be the one I least doubted. This simply reduced me to asking myself if the girl had on the spot improvised an engagement — vamped up an old one or dashed off a new — in order to arrive at the satisfaction she desired. She must have had resources of which I was destitute, but she made her case slightly more intelligible by returning presently: "What the state of things has been is that we felt of course bound to do nothing in mamma's lifetime."

"But now you think you'll just dispense with mamma's consent?"

"Ah it mayn't come to that!" I wondered what it might come to, and she went on: "Poor dear, she may swallow the dose. In fact, you know," she added with a laugh, "she really *must!*" — a proposition of which, on behalf of everyone concerned, I fully acknowledged the force.

VIII

NOTHING MORE VEXATIOUS had ever happened to me than to become aware before Corvick's arrival in England that I shouldn't be there to put him through. I found myself abruptly called to Germany by the alarming illness of my younger brother, who, against my advice, had gone to Munich to study, at the feet indeed of a great master, the art of portraiture in oils. The near relative who made him an allowance had threatened to withdraw it if he should, under specious pretexts, turn for superior truth to Paris — Paris being somehow, for a Cheltenham aunt, the school of evil, the abyss. I deplored this prejudice at the time, and the deep injury of it was now visible — first in the fact that it hadn't saved the poor boy, who was clever, frail and foolish, from congestion of the lungs, and second in the greater break with London to which the event condemned me. I'm afraid that what was uppermost in my mind during several anxious weeks was the sense that if we had only been in Paris I might have run over to see Corvick. This was actually out of the question from every point of view: my brother, whose recovery gave us both plenty to do, was ill for three months, during which I never left him and at the end of which we had to face the absolute prohibition of a return to England. The consideration of climate imposed itself, and he was in no state to meet it alone. I took him to Meran and there spent the summer with him, trying to show him by example how to get back to work and nursing a rage of another sort that I tried *not* to show him.

The whole business proved the first of a series of phenomena so strangely interlaced that, taken all together — which was how I had to take them — they form as good an illustration as I can recall of the manner in which, for the good of his soul doubtless, fate sometimes deals with a man's avidity. These incidents certainly had larger bearings than the comparatively meagre consequence we are here concerned with — though I feel that consequence also a thing to speak of with some respect. It's mainly in such a light, I must confess, at any rate, that the ugly fruit of my exile is at this hour present to me. Even at first indeed the spirit in which my avidity, as I have called it, made me regard that term owed no element of ease to the fact that before coming back from Rapallo George Corvick addressed me in a way I objected to. His letter had none of the sedative action I must to-day profess myself sure he had wished to give it, and the march of occurrences was not so ordered as to make up for what it lacked. He had begun on the spot, for one of the quarterlies, a great last word on Vereker's writings, and this exhaustive study, the only one that would have counted, have existed, was to turn on the new light, to utter — oh so quietly! — the unimagined truth. It was in other words to trace the figure in the carpet through every convolution, to reproduce it in every tint. The result, according to my friend, would be the greatest literary portrait ever painted, and what he asked of me was just to be so good as not to trouble him with questions till he should hang up his masterpiece before me. He did me the honour to declare that, putting aside the great sitter himself, all aloft in his indifference, I was individually the connoisseur he was most working for. I was therefore to be a good boy and not try to peep under the curtain before the show was ready: I should enjoy it all the more if I sat very still.

I did my best to sit very still, but I couldn't help giving a jump on seeing *The Times*, after I had been a week or two in Munich and before, as I knew, Corvick had reached London, the announcement of the sudden death of poor Mrs. Erme. I instantly, by letter, appealed to

Gwendolen for particulars, and she wrote me that her mother had yielded to long-threatened failure of the heart. She didn't say, but I took the liberty of reading into her words, that from the point of view of her marriage and also of her eagerness, which was quite a match for mine, this was a solution more prompt than could have been expected and more radical than waiting for the old lady to swallow the dose. I candidly admit indeed that at the time — for I heard from her repeatedly — I read some singular things into Gwendolen's words and some still more extraordinary ones into her silences. Pen in hand, this way, I live the time over, and it brings back the oddest sense of my having been, both for months and in spite of myself, a kind of coerced spectator. All my life had taken refuge in my eyes, which the procession of events appeared to have committed itself to keep astare. There were days when I thought of writing to Hugh Vereker and simply throwing myself on his charity. But I felt more deeply that I hadn't fallen quite so low—besides which, quite properly, he would send me about my business. Mrs. Erme's death brought Corvick straight home, and within the month he was united "very quietly" — as quietly, I seemed to make out, as he meant in his article to bring out his *trouvaille* — to the young lady he had loved and quitted. I use this last term, I may parenthetically say, because I subsequently grew sure that at the time he went to India, at the time of his great news from Bombay, there had been no positive pledge between them whatever. There had been none at the moment she was affirming to me the very opposite. On the

282

other hand he had certainly become engaged the day he returned. The happy pair went down to Torquay for their honeymoon, and there, in a reckless hour, it occurred to poor Corvick to take his young bride for a drive. He had no command of that business: this had been brought home to me of old in a little tour we had once made together in a dogcart. In a dogcart he perched his companion for a rattle over Devonshire hills, on one of the likeliest of which he brought his horse, who, it was true, had bolted, down with such violence that the occupants of the cart were hurled forward and that he fell horribly on his head. He was killed on the spot; Gwendolen escaped unhurt.

I pass rapidly over the question of this unmitigated tragedy, of what the loss of my best friend meant for me, and I complete my little history of my patience and my pain by the frank statement of my having, in a postscript to my very first letter to her after the receipt of the hideous news, asked Mrs. Corvick whether her husband mightn't at least have finished the great article on Vereker. Her answer was as prompt as my question: the article, which had been barely begun, was a mere heartbreaking scrap. She explained that our friend, abroad, had just settled down to it when interrupted by her mother's death, and that then, on his return, he had been kept from work by the engrossments into which that calamity was to plunge them. The opening pages were all that existed; they were striking, they were promising, but they didn't unveil the idol. That great intellectual feat was obviously to have formed his climax. She said nothing more, nothing to enlighten me as to the state of her own knowledge — the knowledge for the acquisition of which I had fancied her prodigiously acting. This was above all what I wanted to know: had *she* seen the idol unveiled? Had there been a private ceremony for a palpitating audience of one? For what else but that ceremony had the nuptials taken place? I didn't like as yet to press her, though when I thought of what had passed between us on the subject in Corvick's absence her reticence surprised me. It was therefore not till much later, from Meran, that I risked another appeal, risked it in some trepidation, for she continued to tell me nothing. "Did you hear in those few days of your blighted bliss," I wrote, "what we desired so to hear?" I said "we" as a little hint; and she showed me she could take a little hint. "I heard everything," she replied, "and I mean to keep it to myself!"

IX

IT WAS IMPOSSIBLE not to be moved with the strongest sympathy for her, and on my return to England I showed her every kindness in my power. Her mother's death had made her means sufficient, and she had gone to live in a more convenient quarter. But her loss had been great and her visitation cruel; it never would have occurred to me, moreover, to suppose she could come to feel the possession of a technical tip, of a piece of literary experience, a counterpoise to her grief. Strange to say, none the less, I couldn't help believing after I had seen her a few times that I caught a glimpse of some such oddity. I hasten to add that there had been other things I couldn't help believing, or at least imagining; and as I never felt I was really clear about these, so, as to the point I here touch on, I give her memory the benefit of the doubt. Stricken and solitary, highly accomplished and now, in her deep mourning, her maturer grace and her uncomplaining sorrow, incontestably handsome, she presented herself as leading a life of singular dignity and beauty. I had at first found a way to persuade myself that I should soon get the better of the reserve formulated, the week after the catastrophe, in her reply to an appeal as to which I was not unconscious that it might strike her as mistimed. Certainly that reserve was something of a shock to me — certainly it puzzled me the more I thought of it and even though I tried to explain it (with moments of success) by an imputation of exalted sentiments, of superstitious scruples, of a refinement of loyalty. Certainly it added at the same time hugely to the price of Vereker's secret, precious as this mystery already appeared, I may as well confess abjectly that Mrs. Corvick's unexpected attitude was the final tap on the nail that was to fix fast my luckless idea, convert it into the obsession of which I'm for ever conscious.

But this only helped me the more to be artful, to be adroit, to allow time to elapse before renewing my suit. There were plenty of speculations for the interval, and one of them was deeply absorbing. Corvick had kept his information from his young friend till after the removal of the last barrier to their intimacy — then only had he let the cat out of the bag. Was it Gwendolen's idea, taking a hint from him, to liberate this animal only on the basis of the renewal of such a relation? Was the figure in the carpet traceable or describable only for husbands and wives — for lovers supremely united? It came back to me in a mystifying manner that in Kensington Square, when I mentioned that Corvick would have told the girl he loved, some word had dropped from Vereker that gave colour to this possibility. There might be little in it, but there was enough to make me wonder if I should have to marry Mrs. Corvick to get what I wanted. Was I prepared to offer her this price for the blessing of her knowledge? Ah that way madness lay! — so I at least said to myself in bewildered hours. I could see meanwhile the torch she refused to pass on flame away in her chamber of memory — pour through her eyes a light that shone in her lonely house. At the end of six months I was fully sure of what this warm presence made up to her for. We had talked again and again of the man who had brought us together — of his talent, his character, his personal charm, his certain career, his dreadful doom, and even of his clear purpose in that great study which was to have been a supreme literary portrait, a kind of critical Vandyke or Velasquez. She had conveyed to me in abundance that she was tongue-tied by her perversity, by her piety, that she would never break the silence it had not been given to the "right person," as she said, to break. The hour, however, finally arrived. One evening when I had been sitting with her longer than usual I laid my hand firmly on her arm. "Now at last what *is* it?"

She had been expecting me and was ready. She gave a long slow soundless headshake, merciful only in being inarticulate. This mercy didn't prevent its hurling at me the largest finest coldest "Never!" I had yet, in the course of a life that had known denials, had to take full in the face. I took it and was aware that with the hard blow the tears had come into my eyes. So for a while we sat and looked at each other; after which I slowly rose. I was wondering if some day she would accept me; but this was not what I brought out. I said as I smoothed down my hat: "I know what to think then. It's nothing!"

A remote disdainful pity for me gathered in her dim smile; then she spoke in a voice that I hear at this hour. "It's my *life!*" As I stood at the door she added: "You've insulted him!"

"Do you mean Vereker?"

"I mean the Dead!"

I recognised when I reached the street the justice of her charge. Yes, it was her life — I recognised that too; but her life none the less made room with the lapse of time for another interest. A year and a half after Corvick's death she published in a single volume her second novel, "Overmastered," which I pounced on in the hope of finding in it some tell-tale echo or some peeping face. All I found was a much better book than her younger performance, showing I thought the better company she had kept. As a tissue tolerably intricate it was a carpet with a figure of its own; but the figure was not the figure I was looking for. On sending a review of it to *The Middle* I was surprised to learn from the office that a notice was already in type. When the paper came out I had no hesitation in attributing this article, which I thought rather vulgarly overdone, to Drayton Deane, who in the old days had been something of a friend of Corvick's, yet had only within a few weeks made the acquaintance of his widow. I had had an early copy of the book, but Deane had evidently had an earlier. He lacked all the same the light hand with which Corvick had gilded the gingerbread — he laid on the tinsel in splotches.

X

SIX MONTHS LATER appeared "The Right of Way," the last chance, though we didn't know it, that we were to have to redeem ourselves. Written wholly during Vereker's sojourn abroad, the book had been heralded, in a hundred paragraphs, by the usual ineptitudes. I carried it, as early a copy as any, I this time flattered myself, straightway to Mrs. Corvick. This was the only use I had for it; I left the inevitable tribute of *The Middle* to some more ingenious mind and some less irritated temper. "But I already have it," Gwendolen said. "Drayton Deane was so good as to bring it to me yesterday, and I've just finished it."

"Yesterday? How did he get it so soon?"

"He gets everything so soon! He's to review it in *The Middle*."

"He — Drayton Deane — review Vereker?" I couldn't believe my ears.

"Why not? One fine ignorance is as good as another."

I winced but I presently said: "You ought to review him yourself!"

"I don't 'review,'" she laughed. "I'm reviewed!"

Just then the door was thrown open. "Ah yes, here's your reviewer!" Drayton Deane was there with his long legs and his tall forehead: he had come to see what she thought of "The Right of Way," and to bring news that was singularly relevant. The evening papers were just out with a telegram on the author of that work, who, in Rome, had been ill for some days with an attack of malarial fever. It had at first not been thought grave, but had taken, in consequence of complications, a turn that might give rise to anxiety. Anxiety had indeed at the latest hour begun to be felt.

I was struck in the presence of these tidings with the fundamental detachment that Mrs. Corvick's overt concern quite failed to hide: it gave me the measure of her consummate independence. That independence rested on her knowledge, the knowledge which nothing now could destroy and which nothing could make different. The figure in the carpet might take on another twist or two, but the sentence had virtually been written. The writer might go down to his grave: she was the person in the world to whom — as if she had been his favoured heir — his continued existence was least of a need. This reminded me how I had observed at a particular moment — after Corvick's death — the drop of her desire to see him face to face. She had got what she wanted without that. I had been sure

289

that if she hadn't got it she wouldn't have been restrained from the endeavour to sound him personally by those superior reflexions, more conceivable on a man's part than on a woman's, which in my case had served as a deterrent. It wasn't however, I hasten to add, that my case, in spite of this invidious comparison, wasn't ambiguous enough. At the thought that Vereker was perhaps at that moment dying there rolled over me a wave of anguish — a poignant sense of how inconsistently I still depended on him. A delicacy that it was my one compensation to suffer to rule me had left the Alps and the Apennines between us, but the sense of the waning occasion suggested that I might in my despair at last have gone to him. Of course I should really have done nothing of the sort. I remained five minutes, while my companions talked of the new book, and when Drayton Deane appealed to me for my opinion of it I made answer, getting up, that I detested Hugh Vereker and simply couldn't read him. I departed with the moral certainty that as the door closed behind me Deane would brand me for awfully superficial. His hostess wouldn't contradict *that* at least.

I continue to trace with a briefer touch our intensely odd successions. Three weeks after this came Vereker's death, and before the year was out the death of his wife. That poor lady I had never seen, but I had had a futile theory that, should she survive him long enough to be decorously accessible, I might approach her with the feeble flicker of my plea. Did she know and if she knew would she speak? It was much to be presumed that for more reasons than one she would have nothing to say; but when she passed out of all reach I felt renouncement indeed my appointed lot. I was shut up in my obsession for ever — my gaolers had gone off with the key. I find myself quite as vague as a captive in a dungeon about the time that further elapsed before Mrs. Corvick became the wife of Drayton Deane. I had foreseen, through my bars, this end of the business, though there was no indecent haste and our friendship had rather fallen off. They were both so "awfully intellectual" that it struck people as a suitable match, but I had measured better than any one the wealth of understanding the bride would contribute to the union. Never, for a marriage in literary circles — so the newspapers described the alliance — had a lady been so bravely dowered. I began with due promptness to look for the fruit of the affair — that fruit, I mean, of which the premonitory symptoms would be peculiarly visible in the husband. Taking for granted the splendour of the other party's nuptial gift, I expected to see him make a show commensurate with his increase of means. I knew what his means had been — his article on "The Right of Way" had distinctly given one the figure. As he was now exactly in the position in which still more exactly I was not I watched from month to month, in the likely periodicals, for the heavy message poor Corvick had been unable to deliver and the responsibility of which would have fallen on his successor. The widow and wife would have broken by the rekindled hearth the silence that only a widow and wife might break, and Deane would be as aflame with the knowledge as Corvick in his own hour, as Gwendolen in hers, had been. Well, he was aflame doubtless, but the fire was apparently not to become a public blaze. I scanned the periodicals in vain: Drayton Deane filled them with exuberant pages, but he withheld the page I most feverishly sought. He wrote on a thousand subjects, but never on the subject of Vereker. His special line was to tell truths that other people either "funked," as he said, or overlooked, but he never told the only truth that seemed to me in these days to signify. I met the couple in those literary circles referred to in the papers: I have sufficiently intimated that it was only in such circles we were all constructed to revolve. Gwendolen was more than ever committed to them by the publication of her third novel, and I myself definitely classed by holding the opinion that this work was inferior to its immediate predecessor. Was it worse because she had been keeping worse company? If her secret was, as she had told me, her life — a fact discernible in her increasing bloom, an air of conscious privilege that, cleverly corrected by pretty charities, gave distinction to her appearance — it had yet not a direct influence on her work. That only made one — everything only made one — yearn the more for it; only rounded it off with a mystery finer and subtler.

XI

IT WAS THEREFORE from her husband I could never remove my eyes: I beset him in a manner that might have made him uneasy. I went even so far as to engage him in conversation.

Didn't he know, hadn't he come into it as a matter of course? — that question hummed in my brain. Of course he knew; otherwise he wouldn't return my stare so queerly. His wife had told him what I wanted and he was amiably amused at my impotence. He didn't laugh — he wasn't a laugher: his system was to present to my irritation, so that I should crudely expose myself, a conversational blank as vast as his big bare brow. It always happened that I turned away with a settled conviction from these unpeopled expanses, which seemed to complete each other geographically and to symbolise together Drayton Deane's want of voice, want of form. He simply hadn't the art to use what he knew; he literally was incompetent to take up the duty where Corvick had left it. I went still further — it was the only glimpse of happiness I had. I made up my mind that the duty didn't appeal to him. He wasn't interested, he didn't care. Yes, it quite comforted me to believe him too stupid to have joy of the thing I lacked. He was as stupid after as he had been before, and that deepened for me the golden glory in which the mystery was wrapped. I had of course none the less to recollect that his wife might have imposed her conditions and exactions. I had above all to remind myself that with Vereker's death the major incentive dropped. He was still there to be honoured by what might be done — he was no longer there to give it his sanction. Who alas but he had the authority?

Two children were born to the pair, but the second cost the mother her life. After this stroke I seemed to see another ghost of a chance. I jumped at it in thought, but I waited a certain time for manners, and at last my opportunity arrived in a remunerative way. His wife had been dead a year when I met Drayton Deane in the smoking-room of a small club of which we both were members, but where for months — perhaps because I rarely entered it — I hadn't seen him. The room was empty and the occasion propitious. I deliberately offered him, to have done with the matter for ever, that advantage for which I felt he had long been looking.

"As an older acquaintance of your late wife's than even you were," I began, "you must let me say to you something I have on my mind. I shall be glad to make any terms with you that you see fit to name for the information she must have had from George Corvick — the information, you know, that had come to *him,* poor chap, in one of the happiest hours of his life, straight from Hugh Vereker."

He looked at me like a dim phrenological bust. "The information — ?"

"Vereker's secret, my dear man — the general intention of his books: the string the pearls were strung on, the buried treasure, the figure in the carpet."

He began to flush — the numbers on his bumps to come out. "Vereker's books had a general intention?"

I stared in my turn. "You don't mean to say you don't know it?" I thought for a moment he was playing with me. "Mrs. Deane knew it; she had it, as I say, straight from Corvick, who had, after infinite search and to Vereker's own delight, found the very mouth of the cave. Where *is* the mouth? He told after their marriage — and told alone — the person who, when the circumstances were reproduced, must have told *you*. Have I been wrong in taking for granted that she admitted you, as one of the highest privileges of the relation in which you stood to her, to the knowledge of which she was after Corvick's death the sole depository? All *I* know is that that knowledge is infinitely precious, and what I want you to understand is that if you'll in your turn admit me to it you'll do me a kindness for which I shall be lastingly grateful."

He had turned at last very red; I dare say he had begun by thinking I had lost my wits. Little by little he followed me; on my own side I stared with a livelier surprise. Then he spoke. "I don't know what you're talking about."

He wasn't acting — it was the absurd truth. "She *didn't* tell you — ?"

"Nothing about Hugh Vereker."

I was stupefied; the room went round. It had been too good even for that! "Upon your honour?"

"Upon my honour. What the devil's the matter with you?" he growled.

"I'm astounded — I'm disappointed. I wanted to get it out of you."

"It isn't *in* me!" he awkwardly laughed. "And even if it were — "

"If it were you'd let me have it — oh yes, in common humanity. But I believe you. I see — I see!" I went on, conscious, with the full turn of the wheel, of my great delusion, my false view of the poor man's attitude. What I saw, though I couldn't say it, was that his wife hadn't thought him worth enlightening. This struck me as strange for a woman who had thought him worth marrying. At last I explained it by the reflexion that she couldn't possibly have married him for his understanding. She had married him for something else.

He was to some extent enlightened now, but he was even more astonished, more disconcerted: he took a moment to compare my story with his quickened memories. The result of his meditation was his presently saying with a good deal of rather feeble form: "This is the first I hear of what you allude to. I think you must be mistaken as to Mrs. Drayton Deane's having had any unmentioned, and still less any unmentionable, knowledge of Hugh Vereker. She'd certainly have wished it — should it have borne on his literary character — to be used."

"It *was* used. She used it herself. She told me with her own lips that she 'lived' on it."

I had no sooner spoken than I repented of my words; he grew so pale that I felt as if I had struck him. "Ah 'lived' — !" he murmured, turning short away from me.

My compunction was real; I laid my hand on his shoulder. "I beg you to forgive me — I've made a mistake. You *don't* know what I thought you knew. You could, if I had been right, have rendered me a service; and I had my reasons for assuming that you'd be in a position to meet me."

"Your reasons?" he echoed. "What were your reasons?"

I looked at him well; I hesitated; I considered. "Come and sit down with me here and I'll tell

296

you." I drew him to a sofa, I lighted another cigar and, beginning with the anecdote of Vereker's one descent from the clouds, I recited to him the extraordinary chain of accidents that had, in spite of the original gleam, kept me till that hour in the dark. I told him in a word just what I've written out here. He listened with deepening attention, and I became aware, to my surprise, by his ejaculations, by his questions, that he would have been after all not unworthy to be trusted by his wife. So abrupt an experience of her want of trust had now a disturbing effect on him; but I saw the immediate shock throb away little by little and then gather again into waves of wonder and curiosity — waves that promised, I could perfectly judge, to break in the end with the fury of my own highest tides. I may say that to-day as victims of unappeased desire there isn't a pin to choose between us. The poor man's state is almost my consolation; there are really moments when I feel it to be quite my revenge.

✦ To the Reader

HUMORIST JAMES THURBER, who deeply admired Henry James, once described James's narrative technique this way: "Instead of simply telling what occurred when two persons came together, he would have presented it through the consciousness of a Worcester, Massachusetts, lawyer who got it from the proprietor of a café who had overheard two people at a table piecing together a story they had listened in on at a large and crowded party." Thurber was right in suggesting that James's technique can amuse or baffle his readers. But it has a serious purpose.

Most important in reading and understanding Henry James is the recognition that his way of telling a story depends upon the kind of human experience he is trying to represent. In thinking about poetry, we are used to the idea of relating form to the quality of an experience, but a story usually interests us through what is actually said and done in it. James's tales, however, are not simple, journalistic reports of life. Nor does he use unlikely coincidences or twists of circumstance to concoct a satisfying moral lesson for the reader. He believed that the value of a novel lay in "the amount of felt life concerned in producing it," not in a clear "message" about good and evil. By this he meant not life simply as we observe it, but as it is perceived by the author and, ultimately, by his characters. James insisted that a writer's greatest task was to convey what men and women felt and thought, mainly about each other. In this sense James's best tales are passionately accurate reports: what his characters find it in themselves to say, and how they affect one another, are the object of fine, slow observation in James's world. Our peculiar excitement in reading these stories, then, arises from an essential vision of human experience.

Because James sought to represent the greatest amount of felt, imagined life, his stories had to be told by a feeling person, a central conscience or consciousness. So the "I" who relates "The Turn of the Screw" or "The Figure in the Carpet" provides first a portrait of himself, and only indirectly a story of events. Even when James's narrative is in the third person, as is "The Tree of Knowledge," it filters through the consciousness of a particular character, Peter Brench. The crux of James's storytelling, and its beauty, is that he combines artistic necessity and psychological truth. A story told by an omniscient reporter, and filled with the author's sentiments as well as the chararters', would be clumsy and essentially undramatic; at the same time it would give the reader a false vision of life. The problems that concern James deeply, those of conscience and motive, are clear and forceful only when perceived from a single person's point of view. Otherwise they are abstract, and unlike life.

And so, peculiar and overcareful as it may sometimes be, James's technique is at the heart of what makes his stories worth reading. Their ambiguity is their truth. Often enough, we want to urge a character to stop for a moment and tell us plainly his own *raison d'être,* or the meaning of his predicament. None of them ever does so. They never step out and sum up James's, or even their own philosophy.

D. H. Lawrence's characters can do this, and sometimes Faulkner's, but not James's. Their conversation seems perpetually to miss the point, consisting of hints and guesses and circumlocutions. We may be baffled by such inconclusiveness, until we realize that James's perfect tact — his artistic conscience — has given us no more than life itself, though more fully than we could have imagined it for ourselves. James's vision is fastidiously aesthetic, but it comprehends our common experience, which seldom yields immediate, obvious solutions. Finally, the author's principle is clear, and it is both generous and demanding: the reader's own imaginative response is the only vital interpretation of the work of fiction.

Our responses may leap ahead of the story, but James asks for patience. If the governess and Mrs. Grose are slow to understand each other, in "The Turn of the Screw," and if her children deeply puzzle the governess, this tentativeness belongs to James's storytelling method as well as to his liking for suspense and intrigue. And the dark progress of that story brings out a recurrent Jamesian theme: the failure of communication between generations and, more important, between different temperaments. Similarly, in the dissolving of pretense in "The Tree of Knowledge," the distance between Morgan and his family in "The Pupil," and the gradual frustration of the critic in "The Figure in the Carpet," this characteristic estrangement appears as it must, in the slow discoveries of a central consciousness — governess, friend of the family, tutor, critic.

One may well ask, especially of so brief a story as "The Tree of Knowledge," whether so much discovery of motive and attitude can be encompassed in a few pages. Economy is a virtue in a short story, but if the background, incidents and characters are too abbreviated, economy is self-defeating. Typically, James welcomed the formal difficulty. "I mean never to write another novel," he wrote to Robert Louis Stevenson in 1891. "I have solemnly dedicated myself to a masterly brevity." This is a strange announcement, coming from a man who was still to write what many critics consider the finest novels of this century — *The Wings of the Dove, The Ambassadors, The Golden Bowl.* Yet during the next ten years, James did write over forty tales, including all those in this collection. And though his novels ordinarily ran to four or five hundred pages, the writing of an anecdote — as James once described "The Tree of Knowledge" — was not a relaxation from sustained effort, not an excuse for dim sketching instead of deep development.

James's economy comes from a precise control of what we know and don't know. For the sake of brevity, he will summarize twenty years of personal history in a paragraph. For the same reason, curiously enough, he will use a momentary conversation to reveal the fullest emotional state of two characters — their accumulated memories, desires, conflicts, fears, misunderstandings — by spending an entire paragraph of speculation on each gesture and expression. What is more, we seldom find out the customary things about his characters: what they look like and how they dress, when they get angry or make love, how they feel about war or religion, where their money comes from. James's people are usually at home, and seem to have no particular career in the world. They are husband, wife, child, tutor, governess, pupil, fiancé and friend, rather than sea captain, executive or enemy of the state. They have infinite leisure for paying calls, and never meet anyone who is impatient or contemptuous of them. We find them in their ordinary relations, thinking about one another and communicating as best they can.

Such writers as Conrad, Hemingway and Kerouac lead us to assume that the ultimate meaning of experience is yielded only to extraordinary men in extreme or perilous situations. If this is so, what of James's men and women? Certainly they don't seem, in Conrad's phrase, to have immersed themselves in the destructive element of life. What hard-bought truths can we expect from them? And again, if we value the radical quester, Henry James's odd, sheltered children will be unrevealing characters. Admittedly, they are precocious. Miles and Flora astonish their governess at every turn, and Morgan Moreen is cleverer than his tutor. But the experience of these children is strictly limited; so is that of Lance Mallow and the critic, in the other tales. Why did James choose them as subjects if he sought to bring the fullest view of life into his work?

This question brings us to James's central preoccupation — that is, the exposure of innocence, and the precarious movement of mind from ignorance to knowledge. All four tales explore the theme, and always through the filter of a questionable but highly sensitive consciousness. Thus, Lance's knowledge of his father's pathetic incompetence is less important than his mother's knowledge; and her knowledge, in turn, is what Peter Brench must come to understand. Whether or not Corvick really sees the figure in the carpet is only an element in the narrator's own search for insight. Both Morgan and Pemberton see through the parents' futile pretense, but Morgan also understands that there is no rescue from futility. And we learn what Miles and Flora know of the ghosts only through their governess's craving to know as well.

With knowledge, the tree brings dismay and pain — or worse, as James emphasizes in having Miles and Morgan perish near the verge of adolescence. Even Corvick and his wife die, after learning what they had to. Despite James's great delicacy and kindness in creating a social world, there is in his work an awareness of horror and death that must qualify what has been said about the ordinary serenity of his people. James wrote over a dozen ghostly tales in the decade before "The Turn of the Screw," and confessed a strong personal sense of the supernatural impinging on everyday life. Besides what he called the "dear old sacred terror" of a well-told thriller, one senses in those tales that the supernatural has real moral authority for certain persons, just as the subtle creatures in James's later novels observe scruples that are invisible to us. Whether imagined or "real," the ghosts affect Miles and Flora through the narrator's persuasion. And probably the boy's taut, intuitive sensibility, which kills him in the confrontation with Quint's ghost, is also the virtue by which he was potentially a finer, richer person than the governess. Yet the children's bright purity, too, must be partly her invention.

Such speculation, however, is better left to the reader, who would do, James hoped, "quite half the labor" of imagining ghosts and creating meaning in the stories. In this respect, "The Figure in the Carpet" serves us as a parable. Its narrator's earnest account of the search for meaning in Hugh Vereker's novels is full of irony — as if a critic should take himself so seriously! But at least a few readers of Vereker give him what a writer deserves: they read him as if their lives depended on it, with total attention. The irony of James appears also in "The Tree of Knowledge," in Brench's pride at not showing his disrespect for the master sculptor. But "The Figure in the Carpet" has the urgent undertone of a committed writer hoping for full critical response. What is the crux of his writing? the critic asks Vereker. "Is it something in the style or something in the thought? An element of form or an element of feeling?" Vereker answers for James, as few characters do in the fifty years of novels and tales. And his answer, another question, brings us back to the only beginning of a serious reading of Henry James.

JOHN FELSTINER

❦ Notes on the Stories

The Turn of the Screw

IN A PREFACE to "The Turn of the Screw," James called his tale an "irresponsible little fiction . . . a fairy-tale pure and simple," a trifle "to catch those not easily caught." He caught many — witness the "Casebook" on James's story, a collection of critical reading from half a century, gathered as if "The Turn of the Screw" were a famous unsolved crime. The central issue is necessarily dubious; Peter Quint and Miss Jessel could be either ghosts or hallucinations of the governess. Freudian readings such as Edmund Wilson's rest on the second possibility, taking the governess as "a neurotic case," and her hallucinations as expressions of inhibited desire. After all, she was only "a fluttered, anxious girl out of a Hampshire vicarage."

Fortunately, James's preface is also highly suggestive. He wrote that objectively real ghosts, those recorded and attested by a psychical research society, were of no use to him. To have dramatic value, an evil apparition, like any human experience, must be felt vividly by character or reader. James also said: "Make him *think* the evil, make him think it for himself, and you are released from weak specifications."

"The Turn of the Screw" reveals the nature of the young woman, but not because she talks about herself. Again James's notebook entry on the story is significant, for it barely mentions the governess. And the notebook states definitely everything that she, in the story, finds doubtful: that depraved servants actually corrupted the children, and that the children were later haunted by apparitions. James's note ends simply: "The story to be told — tolerably obviously — an outside spectator." In fact, the governess tells her story neither obviously nor from outside. This change from the notebook indicates James's desire to thicken his subject by presenting it through another human consciousness than his own. Thus he shows the governess trying to resist inhuman ghosts with what she calls "only another turn of the screw of ordinary human virtue."

James may also have taken his title from Douglas's remark at the beginning, that the involvement of children in a supernatural occurrence "gives the effect another turn of the screw." James was horrified that childhood could be exposed to evil — or to deception, as in "The Pupil."

"As to understanding it," James wrote to a friend about his ghostly tale, "it is just gleams and glooms." The menace in "The Turn of the Screw" is inarticulate, and James asks us for the utmost attention and creative response. Like the horror of Kurtz in Conrad's *Heart of Darkness*, the menace is that of life itself, unspeakable.

The Pupil

THOUGH THE EDUCATION of Henry James had come mostly in wandering through Europe with his family and tutors, the shabby, irresponsible Moreens are not autobiographical. James was fascinated by them because they came from a "golden age" he remembered: Europe in 1850, when Americans were only beginning to be at home in Paris, Nice, Venice, and Florence, when St. Mark's and the Bois de Boulogne were still a romantic adventure.

James called them the poor, dear Moreens, but the *Atlantic Monthly* found this American family too deceitful and turned down the story, though they regularly published James. In a later preface, James emphasized the real intention of "The Pupil" by this comment about the Moreens: "All I have given is little Morgan's troubled vision of them as reflected in the vision, also troubled enough, of his devoted friend."

While it is Pemberton's story, "The Pupil" is not so much an account of his experience or a condemnation of the parents, as a tribute to Morgan. The boy's "intelligent innocent eyes" are wiser than his tutor's, sometimes impossibly wise. There is humor and pain in the friendship, and finally a deeper irony in Pemberton's casual comment — "My dear fellow, you're too clever to live."

The Tree of Knowledge

JAMES CALLED "THE TREE OF KNOWLEDGE" an intensely compressed novel. He was particularly fond of it because it had cost him such effort to compress, so many "full revolutions of the merciless screw." But no magazine accepted the story. We might ask whether it ought to be so short, and whether the emotions of Peter Brench and the Mallows appear too abruptly.

The themes of the story are potentially expansive: failure in art; the nature of the artist; married love and family loyalty; unrequited love. And the characters' shifting states of mind-innocence and knowl-

307

edge — are fundamental enough to demand leisurely presentation. But James limits us to Brench's point of view, as the first paragraph makes fully clear. That must be the source of the story's economy and of its truth to experience.

Significantly, the germ of "The Tree of Knowledge" in James's notebook — a story told him by a friend — contains only the sculptor's family, nothing of Brench. James's creation of "placid Peter" added pathos and humor to the situation — as, for example, the careful irony in Brench's remark to Mrs. Mallow, "Do you think he's going to be another Master?" Such irony is a symptom of James's nearly tragic vision, for it is based on a fatal mixture of qualities in Brench: his skepticism about the work of the Master, and his love for the woman who loves the Master.

The Figure in the Carpet

JUST BEFORE he wrote "The Figure in the Carpet," James had been mortified by the public derision of a play of his, and he was deeply aware how small a public his novels had. That he could write a fable for critics with so much humor testifies to his resilience.

James's preface to this and other stories about the divorce of the artist from society did not apologize for such exclusive, "supersubtle" creatures as Hugh Vereker. "If the life about us for the last thirty years refuses warrant for these examples," wrote James, "then so much the worse for that life." And he added that for the narrator and for Corvick, "literature was a game of skill, and skill meant courage, and courage meant honor, and honor meant passion, meant life." If the fable implies a satire on critics, then, it still has behind it moral urgency.

308

The first-person narration of this story, like that of "The Turn of the Screw," adds interest and dimension. Here the critic-narrator's earnestness intensifies the humor of his futile search. His tact about the secret, his endless scrupling with himself, are funny and pathetic. However, James's irony also plays over Vereker, who remains so austere and uncompromising with regard to the numbness of critical sensibility. In the preface James called him "my hapless friend."

James Thurber wrote a brilliant parody of "The Figure in the Carpet," called "A Final Note on Chanda Bell," in which a critic similarly sacrifices his life to get at the secret of a writer's work. Thurber as critic-narrator is bewildered by Chanda Bell's use of the triple negative, in such expressions as "not unmeaningless"; he searches for "esoteric anagrams. . . . I scrutinized, investigated, explored, took apart, and put back together again the entire fibre and fabric, uncertain of what shape and texture I was looking for. I read the thing backward, and I even tried to read it upside down and in the mirror of my bureau." He is frustrated even when he seems to triumph: "You have found the figure, Thurber,' she told me one afternoon, 'but have you found the carpet?' " *

Chanda Bell dies, and finally Thurber, like the narrator in James's story, goes back again to read with wonder and curiosity, as we all must — "I have hit on a new approach to the works of Chanda Bell. I am trying to read them sideways."

---

* Copyright © 1953 James Thurber. From *Thurber Country*, published by Simon and Schuster.

❧ Henry James
A Biographical Sketch

THE SALIENT EVENTS are few in Henry James's life. He was born in New York City on April 15, 1843, and lived mostly in Cambridge and Boston during the Civil War. Owing to a severe back injury, he could not fight. He studied painting and then law, but gave them up for literature at the age of twenty-one. In 1875, after five extended trips to Europe, he left America to live abroad permanently — in England, and in France and Italy. He did not marry, and left religion alone. James became a British subject in 1915, when the United States was still neutral in World War I, to affirm his faith in the Allies. He was given the British Order of Merit on his deathbed, and died on February 28, 1916, having lived comfortably all his life and worked at nothing but the craft of writing.

James's life suggests that biography is sometimes the last thing we need to know about a writer. The more devoted he is to his art, and the more in control of it, the less personal probing he invites. Yet James was as insatiable as Dylan Thomas in his openness to the turmoil of life. He claimed to have "lived and loved and cursed and floundered and enjoyed and suffered." The difference is that for James the turmoil was all in the emotions, all in the felt life — it began and ended with him. Writing grew out of his sensibility and at the same time nourished it. "It is art that *makes* life, makes interest, makes importance . . . ,"he wrote to H. G. Wells, "and I know of no substitute whatever for the force and beauty of its process." To find the central vision of James's novels and tales, then, is to approach the source of his life.

James's father, an informal philosopher and theologian, and friend of Emerson and Carlyle, wanted his sons to have something like a universal education. Before Henry was one year old, he was taken to Europe with his brother William (psychologist, philosopher, and author of *The Varieties of Religious Experience*) and years later still had a visual memory of Paris from the age of sixteen months. At seventy, when World War I broke out, James's shock and despair were rooted in the ideal he had had of European civilization, embodied chiefly in France.

The fact of James's early travel and decision to live abroad certainly underlies much of his work, especially the novels, where the "international theme" is more evident than in the tales selected here.

James was an exile, but not merely because America was uncongenial for the artist; like T. S. Eliot, he considered the European tradition his own. He loved the art of Italy and France, and was at home in palaces, cathedrals, and country houses of England and the Continent. Despite his many friends, James's audience was not large, and this he realized with some bitterness midway in his career. He called the reading public "absolutely idiotic," and wrote to William Dean Howells in 1888: "I am still staggering a good deal under the mysterious and (to me) inexplicable injury wrought — apparently — upon my situation by my last two novels, *The Bostonians* and *The Princess,*

311

from which I expected so much and derived so little. They have reduced the desire, and the demand, for my productions to zero." Yet James continued to write, confident that his finest work was to come.

During the nineties James gave himself over to short stories and the theatre, hoping to regain the fame which *Daisy Miller* (1879) and *The Portrait of a Lady* (1881) had brought him, and to earn money. Essentially, he was intrigued by problems of dramatic presentation, but could not translate his fictional powers to the stage. The failure of his play *Guy Domville* in 1895 was for James a dismal sign that he was utterly out of touch with the public. Again he responded with a determination to write. A week after the terrible night, he sketched in his notebook the outlines of a ghost story the Archbishop of Canterbury had just told him at dinner, and which ultimately became "The Turn of the Screw." And in the notebook, where he spoke to himself with an accent of passion and nobility that occurs nowhere else, he wrote a few days later:

I take up my *own* old pen again — the pen of all my old unforgettable efforts and sacred struggles. . . . Large and full and high the future still opens. It is now indeed that I may do the work of my life. And I will. I have only to *face* my problems. But all that is of the ineffable — too deep and pure for any utterance. Shrouded in sacred silence let it rest.

From 1897 until his death James lived in a quiet house in Sussex. He had relinquished any hope of widespread popularity, but nonetheless produced in three years three great novels — *The Wings of the Dove, The Ambassadors, The Golden Bowl.* A ten-month visit to America followed, in which James, happy but homesick for England, toured from New

England to California. Then for three years he labored to revise all his major works, deepening them with the tone of his complex "later manner," as his matured style came to be known. More important, he wrote for the collected edition of his works a series of eighteen prefaces, an eloquent revelation of the art of fiction and its first full criticism.

He was alive to historical and social change, throughout this period but only the remote effects of it came into his work. His anguish in 1914, however, reflects how closely James's artistic ideal was bound in with the state of the world.

The plunge of civilization into this abyss of blood and darkness by the wanton feat of those two infamous autocrats is a thing that so gives away the whole long age during which we have supposed the world to be, with whatever abatement, gradually bettering, that to have to take it all now for what the treacherous years were all the while really making for and *meaning* is too tragic for any words.

Joseph Conrad praised him as a "historian of fine consciences," but others carped at James for being only that. H. G. Wells turned on him, saying, "I had rather be called a journalist than an artist," and published an annoyed satire on the lack of humanity in James's view of life — the lack of opinion, lust, war, sweat, dreams. Henry James answered that art *makes* life, and that was as much as he knew.

Still the self behind the writings troubles us. James's books plead so urgently for life and more life; his great story, "The Beast in the Jungle," is the tragedy of a man who realized too late that his life was void. And yet to make this plea for more and more conscious life, James sacrificed his own life to art. A discovery of the author through his fiction can carry us so far, and then we return to the work. There we find a record of emotions so pervaded by fine, deep observation — the writer, James said, should be one "on whom nothing is lost" — that the art of presenting human consciousness becomes, for a confused and senseless age, the creation of a conscience.